DOORWAYS FOR THE DISPOSSESSED

DOORWAYS FOR THE DISPOSSESSED

PAUL HAINES

PRIME BOOKS

ACKNOWLEDGMENTS: Big thanks to: SuperNOVA, the Melbourne-based, SF writers' group, who have helped shape each and every one of these stories; the Clarion South 2004 family for making me believe; James Wigney for copy-editing between new-born wails; Lucy Gardner for what we didn't see; Anna Tambour for advice and encouragement; Lee Battersby for giving me the nod to The Man; and Geoff Maloney—The Man!—without whom this just wouldn't have happened.

Prime Books
www.prime-books.com

Jealousy

'You built this in seven?'

'Yes,' she said. The word dripped with pride.

He examined it, hating her as he did so. 'It's flawed to hell.'

'You can do better?'

'Sure,' he lied. 'I can build this faster, bigger and better.'

'Can't be done. You'll only fuck it up.'

'Nah, it'll be *perfect*!'

'Right, little brother.' She smiled smugly.

Wiping his palms, he stepped forth. 'Let there be light . . . '

TABLE OF CONTENTS

DANGER: FERAL AUTHOR

Jack Dann

I always seem to be doing introductions to short story collections when I'm 35,000 feet above a black, dream-deep ocean, sitting in the crowded, blinking darkness of a Boeing 747 as tiny CRT screens embedded into the backs of headrests silently arrange billions of photons into the dizzy-gauzy patterns of movies and sitcoms. Bathroom doors click shut. Overhead storage compartments creak. A rumpled woman with two children stumbles through the aisle, followed by an ever-patient "hostie passing out plastic cups of ice water." (This is Qantas, an Australian airline, after all, and in Australia, we use *ie* as a contraction; thus, football becomes footie, wharf workers become wharfies, and . . . you get the idea.) Someone snores. Someone coughs. Someone belches.

I write.

Computer on the collapsible food tray.

The ever-present white noise of the jet engines.

The dreaming darkness . . .

The last time I did this, typing in the floating darkness, I was writing an introduction to Terry Dowling's brilliant collection *Antique Futures*. If the name Terry Dowling doesn't ring a bell, I strongly suggest you go out and buy one of his titles . . . but only after you finish *this* book.

I was—and am—angry and disappointed because many readers don't recognize the name Terry Dowling, just as they don't recognize Howard Waldrop or Harvey Jacobs, important, vital writers, writers writing for the generations. But lest you think I'm embarking on another one of my famous rants, let me forestall. This isn't a rant; it's a celebration, a dance complete with boogie-woogie theme music and heavy breathing, for it's my great pleasure to introduce you to a brand new writer, strong in body and mind, steady-eyed and focused, a writer whom you probably *haven't* heard of . . . *yet.*

His name is Paul Haines, and he's a writer who can "do the dance" . . . who will amaze and astonish you. And you, oh, kind, patient, perceptive, perspicacious reader, have gotten in on the ground floor, for this is Paul's first collection. His debut. Here shines his numinous light. Here be shuddery-shivery dangers and earthly and unearthly delights for your delectation.

If you surf around on the web, you won't find much about Paul. There is a website, which he refers to as "crappy". The short bio tells you that he was "raised in the '70s, in the wrong part of Auckland, New Zealand. After completing a degree in the frozen, drunken depths of Otago he wound up working in computers and was eventually lured by sex and money to Australia in the '90s. Vowing to never call it home, he now lives in Melbourne with his wife, a loving mortgage, and a violent stray cat called Mr. Pussy."

The usual stuff.

What isn't usual is that he's already won an Aurealis Award and two Ditmar Awards. Not bad for someone just starting out. The *real* Paul Haines lives in the pages of the book you're holding; and once you begin reading the stories that follow, you should forget what I said and listen to *him.* He'll be talking to you through his characters, which are varied and myriad. His stories range from psychological horror to fantasy and science fiction. His characters are real, bone and blood.

I feel somewhat responsible for one of the stories in this collection . . . proudly so, I might add. The story is "Warchalking," written in collaboration with Claire McKenna. Both Paul and Claire are Clarion

South workshop survivors. I was a tutor at the first Clarion South, held in Brisbane, Australia. That's where I met them. All of them.

The ferals.

The Clarion Class of 2004.

Well, I should probably equivocate and say that they were ferals when I met them in February. The weather was stinking-hot, humid as Miami in summer. Because I was a tutor—and thus given special treatment—I worked and rested in an air-conditioned Travelodge motel and was chauffeured back and forth to the Griffith University campus to workshop stories and teach in an air-conditioned classroom. The poor, disenfranchised Clarion students had a few hours with me in said air-conditioned classroom; the rest of the time they ate, slept, and wrote their obligatory story a week in the non-air-conditioned, oven-hot campus dorms. The thermometers were pushing 100 degrees Fahrenheit during those halcyon days.

Every week a different tutor—a well known genre writer or editor—arrived to work with them. (One of those tutors, incidentally, was the aforementioned Terry Dowling.) The constant, grueling pressure to produce copy, which would then immediately be read and workshopped, was enormous.

Upon my arrival, the students were exhausted, ill, frustrated, blocked (as in writer's block), and angry . . . angry that some smiling gray-haired schmuck, a stranger with a rep and an American accent, was sitting on the opposite side of a long table with the sole, relentless purpose of pressing them through more literary rigors and agonies.

They were not happy.

I, on the other hand, had had a lot of experience as a corporate troubleshooter and was used to working with salespeople, who, like writers and werewolves, could turn feral in an instant. I was cheered. Although the surroundings were new, the atmosphere was familiar.

It was the tribe, the pack versus . . . me.

These fledging writers had worked so hard—literally sweating it out together, writing under more pressure than most professionals with drop-dead deadlines ever experience—that they had bonded together. They had become family.

Frankly, they will always be family.

That's one of the benefits of surviving Clarion.

I said "Hello," smiled at them, threw them a sop by telling them I understood what they were going through (which I did!), and suggested that although they were completely burned-out, what they *really* needed was something entirely new. They needed ideas, they needed to get juiced up, they needed to work together to focus their strengths and overcome their weaknesses.

They needed to collaborate on stories.

That was my initial suggestion, but the glaring, baleful gazes that were focused upon me forced me to question my very self, right down to the depths of my ontological beingness. Nevertheless, I stood my ground while they pissed-and-moaned and made it very clear that they considered this new tutor not only an outsider, but not a very bright outsider.

I spent the rest of the day workshopping two stories with them. They workshopped well; after all, they'd been doing it night and day for a month. And almost all of the "students" were published writers. They were polite, professional, and somehow I managed to get through that first day . . . alive.

After a few days, magically, I began to bond with this tight-knit in-group. Perhaps it was after some of those who had groaned the loudest at my suggestion of collaboration . . . started collaborating like mad fiends intent on global destruction. Stylists began working with action, plot oriented writers. Excitement replaced, or perhaps limned everyone's exhaustion. By the end of the week, we were all sweaty, all working. Clarion will kill you or cure you . . . or turn you into a writer.

But these writers were *already* writers.

They'd become a family of writers.

And standing tall among them was Paul Haines, already experienced and world-weary, yet interested in everything, wanting to swallow the world in one gulp, the proverbial Young Turk. I have a photo of the feral gang; all standing or sitting together, and on the edge, hands in his pockets, bearded, quintessentially cool, stands Paul Haines.

The outsider-insider.

And here laid out before you are his stories, his roadmaps to worlds only he can share with you. He's only beginning. Best to keep an eye on him. He's on an astounding journey, and he'll shock the hell right out of you.

Windhover Farm,
Foster, Victoria, Australia
23 September 2005

THE LAST DAYS OF KALI YUGA

The sun sets early in Kathmandu's spring, dipping behind the Himalayas, its last rays failing to penetrate the pollution choking this city. Darkness will descend quickly. It's easy to get lost here, in this place, at the end of the world.

'You know what I love about travelling?' Gabe drawls the words in his lazy Mississippi accent. He leans out the hotel window in the tourist heart of the city, watching the busy streets of Thamel. From the bed, I hear the shouting as the police use batons to enforce curfew.

I lie on my bed staring at the ceiling. Cracks spider outwards where the slow, rotating ceiling fan is attached to the plaster. The air is cool this time of year, comforting.

'What?'

'Moving from country to country.' Gabe turns toward me, his face shadowed, his body blocking the last of the sun. 'It becomes too easy.'

'Yes.' I'm not sure what he means but the response feels true.

It *has* become too easy. Degradation slides into the soul, festering in its malevolence, ready to burst free. I can still see her now, her smooth adolescent skin, my fingers curled in her soft black hair, moving it away from her face to see the pain in her eyes. She sucks busily, this cheap Bangkok whore, the kind from Soi Cowboy where the beer is cheap, the neon bright and the women fuck too much, dripping poison from the slit between their thighs. And I force *my* poison into her mouth—it only takes a little more

15

worthless coin for skin on skin. I need to punish someone, anyone, and she'll do. She can swallow all my guilt, resolve me of the blame. Afterwards, as I watch Gabe fucking another whore on the table, I hear mine vomiting in the hotel bathroom. With my seed spilt, I feel nothing. And I bury myself in it. Bangkok to Kathmandu has been a blur.

An insect crawls from the cracks in the ceiling and scuttles to the window frame. Gabe pulls on a loose cotton shirt and sprays cologne onto his tanned face.

It has taken time but I finally realise who I hate. Me.

And from there where can you go?

'Come on,' says Gabe. 'There must be a bar somewhere in this shit-hole not under curfew. Let's go get pissed.'

If it weren't for Gabe I'd already be dead. Somehow he keeps me going. So I rise from the hard bed with the stained sheets and follow him down into the light and the living.

☉

'You girls want another drink?' Gabe places his empty San Miguel down on the upturned barrel.

'Sure,' Carly replies. She's young, maybe eighteen, and wears colourful hippie clothing that looks brand new.

'Love one.' Luna runs a hand through her recently braided hair. Costs less than a pound for an hour's braiding, she'd told us. Her fingernails are clean, long and unchipped.

'Your round, Saul.' Gabe gives me a nod. He's drinking fast. I'm only halfway through my beer.

I leave him impressing their minds with journeys of wonder and tales of bullshit. At the bar there's a plastic cactus near swinging doors beneath purple, flashing neon *Mano's Mexican Canteena*. Peanut shells are scattered on the floor. The real Himalayan experience, right here, in all its Western glory. The Nepalese barman dressed as a Mexican clasps his hands forward in prayer, bowing his head and shoulders slightly.

'*Namaste,*' he says with a grin. He pronounces it *numma-stay*. 'You want more beer? Four San Miguel, yes?'

'What's cheapest?'

'Not the bottles.' He indicates the clattering cooler half-full of imported beers. 'Maybe you want pitcher of *chang*. Is Nepalese beer. Cheap.'

'Yeah, whatever.'

A smattering of tourists dot the barrels around the bar. The atmosphere is subdued, the conversation hushed. Pink Floyd's *Dark Side of the Moon* drones from speakers hidden in the ceiling in an attempt to recreate the rush of the long-dead hippy days. The Maoist rebels are doing their best to kill Kathmandu; kill its spirit and people; kill off its thousands of gods in one mighty red-devil swoop. The rebels have been doing it for over a decade now. And overdeveloped tourism killed Thamel years before that. I don't know why tourists come here at all. I can't fathom Gabe's reasons for being here and he doesn't know mine. I'm not going back to the West and what it holds for me. I'm here to stay. And in this current political climate, it won't be for long. Perhaps a bullet from a machinegun or the cold steel of the *khukuri* will release me before I reach the next stage of infection. I don't care anymore.

☉

Gabe has the girls laughing. His hand rests on Carly's thigh as he traces a finger over Luna's upturned palm.

I slip three hundred dirty Nepalese rupees, roughly nine dollars, across the bar in exchange for the pitcher of *chang*. Brown froth slops from the brim as I set it down on our barrel. They briefly break from their laughter to thank me and fill their glasses. Luna smiles, trying to engage. I nod and look away. In the doorway, a figure ducks back into the shadows. Someone small and dark. I stare at the door, waiting for the spy to slink back in, but no one comes. So I sip and wait.

Gabe hits me on the arm. 'What's up with you?'

'What? Where have the girls gone?'

'Toilets. I got two girls here keen for it. What the hell are you playing at?'

'Gabe . . .'

'Don't fucking *Gabe* me. You've been a depressed son of a bitch ever since we got off the train.'

'Have yourself a threesome. I don't . . . '

'They're not up for one. I want you to show a bit of interest in Luna. Help me out. She's pretty sexy, Saul. I know you've fucked a lot worse, man.'

'Look, I dunno. I'm just not . . . feeling . . . you know . . . '

Gabe flicks a fat joint across the barrel top. 'You need to chill out.'

'Jesus Christ.' I pocket the joint, making sure no one sees it. 'This place isn't licenced.'

Gabe fills my glass. 'It's not illegal either. There's a balcony over there. Don't fuck this evening up. Go, before the girls come back.'

The balcony is refreshing, both in its lack of draped neon and the coolness of the night. Fires sprinkle the mountain walls of the Kathmandu valley, the only stars you can see in the evening. The pollution is relentless in its vigilance over the city, day and night.

I drag deeply on the marijuana, letting it settle in my lungs, counting down the seconds as it is absorbed into my bloodstream before exhaling, watching the cloud of smoke dissipate, whirling away with my thoughts. I drag again and it hits quickly, a buzzing numbness spreading behind the eyes, across my temples and over the skin's surface. Gabe always has good ganja. I close my eyes and just as my eyelids shut I realise there is someone down on the street looking up at me. Someone small and dark. Before I focus, the person slips away.

'Mind if I have some?' Luna startles me.

Her fingers brush lightly against mine as she takes the joint. She leans over the balcony rail, exposing the cleft of her breasts. Her skin goosebumps and I want to run my finger over it to feel the fleeing warmth. Gabe is right: Luna is sexy. Her skin is clear, lightly tanned and looks soft. Her body is curvaceous yet firm with youth.

'Kathmandu's supposed to be shaped like the sword of Manjushri, the bodhisattva of wisdom.' She takes another puff. 'I think that's bullshit; the streets are a maze. Carly and I got lost yesterday. Best way to see the city. It amazes me that the Maoists think they can take this city. This place teems with religion and superstition. Gods look down on you at every corner. Do they really think they can kill the heart of this culture?'

I know little about Kathmandu, except that the hippies came in droves to drop out over half a century ago.

Smoke coils from her lips. 'Wow, this is good.' Luna giggles and looks at me from the corner of her eye. 'You know something? Good grass makes me really horny.'

The beast within betrays me. They're only words, yet they stir. The blood pulses, giving life to the monster who delivers poison. I sip my beer.

'You don't say much, do you?' Luna straightens and hands back the joint.

Her nipples stand erect beneath her cotton blouse. She catches my darting eyes and smiles.

'It's cold out here,' she says.

'Do you want to go back in?'

'No.' She snuggles in against me, her back to my chest and pulls my arms around her. 'We don't have to do anything. Just hold me in this moment.'

We stand, warm against each other, watching the fires flare and fade up in the mountains. Music drifts from other bars through the empty street, lonely and lost, and as the dope takes hold . . .

I move my hand over my wife Laura's swelling belly, over the bulge that is our unborn daughter. Laura clasps her hands tight over mine and whispers, 'I love you.' The world feels safe. I breathe in her scent and kiss her neck.

. . . and Luna wriggles free of my arms.

'Why did you stop?' She wipes the tears from my cheeks. 'What's wrong?'

I almost tell her everything, this girl who is innocent to the world, yet knows more of its past than I. This woman who shows me warmth and reminds me of a time when . . . 'Nothing. I lost myself for a second.'

Luna kisses me where the salt has not yet dried. 'Do you want to talk about it? No? Shall we go back in?'

As Luna leads me inside, I see clearly a man on the street. A Nepalese midget standing crookedly, staring up at me. He points toward the end of the street, beckoning me to follow. An enormous white horse canters in the distance, shining in the streetlight. The midget scurries in the direction of the horse, stopping to beckon once more.

Luna takes me by the hand, pulling me into the warm banality of *Mano's Mexican Canteena* for more beer and peanuts.

'Did you see that?' I ask her as we walk to the table where Gabe and Carly are kissing.

'Yeah. That's why I came out to find you. They were already into each other.'

'No, I mean the horse and the midget.'

Luna laughs. 'What are you talking about?'

And though her laughter is not unkind, it stings and I withdraw. I don't know anything about this girl. Why should I explain?

'Up for another beer?' Gabe grins sharkly, his lips wet with Carly's saliva. She's staring at him, her cheeks flushed with blood. 'Your round, Saul,' says Gabe.

'I'll get this one.' Luna rests a hand on my arm. 'You got the last one.'

Gabe winks and Carly pulls his mouth to hers again. He stares at me as they kiss. For a man embraced in passion, his eyes are cold.

☙

Sweat shines on Gabe's back, and Carly's hands slide down to his buttocks, grasping on the hard muscle and pulling him deeper inside. She arches her back and lifts her legs higher, moaning loudly with each thrust. Gabe is moving faster now, his balls slap, slap, slap against her vagina as he increases his momentum. The bed creaks and groans under their weight.

'I'm going to cum, I'm going to cum,' Carly whispers between breaths.

Gabe throws her lean legs over his shoulders and thrusts deeper. Carly moans, her eyes closed. Her hand scrunches the sheets as she heaves, her body wracking with orgasm.

As she cums, Gabe turns his head toward me, his grin now a leer. His eyes burn in the candlelight of the room, shadows casting demonic distortions upon his face. He snarls, and his buttocks shudder, the muscles flinching, spasming as he finally cums.

Carly kisses his chest, his arms, tries for his lips and settles for his hand. 'I love you I love you I love you . . . ' Her eyes roll in her head, unable to focus on anything but the sensations rocking her body.

He slides out of her and reaches over to extinguish the candles on his bedside table. Gabe winks at me and nods. Before the darkness takes back the room, I see the condom he'd donned before having sex is missing from his shining penis.

Luna murmurs something in her sleep, her head on my chest. We're still fully dressed, unlike the two in the bed on the far side of the room. I hope she's not disappointed I didn't try to kiss her or touch her. I run my fingers through her braids, the hair still soft and silky, careful not to blow the smoke near her face. The glow from the end of the joint looks like one of the fires burning on the mountainside. It fades quickly.

◉

Laura's image slips into my dreams, her face shifting between anger and hatred, sorrow and fear. She weeps blood. Her skin is translucent, the virus shifting beneath, calling out, accusing me, building the broken body of our daughter curled in her stomach. The baby slips from between her thighs, slopping onto the floor in a splatter of fluid, and tries to stand, its torso twisted and scrunched. A brown arm streaked in blood points behind me as the baby staggers forward. *How can her skin be brown? Had Laura slept around too?*

A white horse rears up inches from my face, its hooves threatening to crush my skull. I stagger back but the hooves crash down on my chest, slapping away with painted hands I need skin on skin must have skin it will cost you she says it will cost you her nipples brown and erect the company can pay the company always pays for skin pussy shaved and pierced fuckie-fuckie I can pay and pay and pay . . .

'Find the white horse,' our baby whispers, pinching the whore's nipples between his midget fingers. His face is hairy and smeared with blood and he perches atop my chest.

'I don't want to pay anymore!' The umbilical cord around my throat is strangling me.

'Find the horse,' the midget whispers and the world suddenly rips apart . . .

◉

The light in the room is on and Gabe is pulling on his trousers. It's still dark outside.

'Did you hear that?' he asks.

Luna leans out of the window. 'I can't see anything from here.'

'It sounded like an explosion. A big one.'

Another thunderous roar splits the night, its force sending tremors through the hotel. The bed shakes, rattling against the wall and each rattle reverberates in my bones. The light flickers and sparks. Flakes of plaster drift from the ceiling.

Carly screams and pulls the blanket over her head. Voices can be heard in the streets, then the warble of rising sirens.

'We can see most of the city from the roof,' says Luna.

I chase them up the stairwell, past opening doors and confused, frightened faces thick with sleep. Gabe leaps steps two, three at a time, already a flight ahead of Luna and me. We hear him laughing before we reach the rooftop, a coarse sound devoid of humour.

Gabe dances near the edge of the balcony, his body framed by flames in the distance, his arms raised. Fire shoots into the sky as another explosion rocks the city, then another, and yet another.

'The airport!' Gabe cackles as he twists in his dance. 'The rebels took the airport!'

'Oh, no,' says Luna. 'I've got to get Carly.' Her eyes brim with fear, teeming with innocence. She rushes to the door and down, past other travellers venturing to the rooftop view.

And Gabe dances and sings, the firelight alive on his skin. Dancing, chanting . . .

. . . as the sleeping city wakes prematurely and wails.

◉

Our room is empty; the girls have returned to their own.

I lie in my bed in a darkness full of noise. Perhaps that bullet, that *khukuri* blade, that last lover, death, is closer than I thought.

'This can only be good for us,' says Gabe. 'This chaos.'

'I don't know what you're talking about.'

He rustles in his sheets. 'You and me, Saul. You know what I mean.'

But I don't. I hardly know this man—this woman-fucking machine—I know him on a superficial level. A level of skin and bone, where manhood is measured in the pussy you've had, the amount of booze and drugs you consume; where less than the surface of really being human is revealed. And it is all I need to know. It's all any of us need to know, to live from day to day. Any more and we'd run screaming. I know he hates—I've seen it on his face—but what he hates remains a mystery. I've seen it in the disrespect and disregard he shows for everyone, for anything. I know this much.

I see it in the mirror. Every time I look.

He's right. We are the same. No. We *were* the same. I know who I hate now. Me and only me.

'Have you ever wanted to kill anyone?' The confession needs to slip from my tongue, it needs to fall upon sympathetic ears. And as soon as the words are gone I want to bite them back, swallow them down. Bury them.

An intake of breath and a second's silence that lasts an eternity before Gabe replies, the answer lingering on his lips. And it slides like velvet through the room and blankets me.

'Yes.'

'I think I have killed someone, Gabe. Maybe more than one.'

Silence.

'Gabe?'

Only silence, then his voice of caramel. 'I thought that was what we were doing, man. You in your way and me in mine. You should try mine. It's so much more intense.'

And like a blanket over the face, his words start to suffocate. I choke in the dark stillness of our room, unable to speak, until all I hear is breathing, deep and heavy, from the other side of the room.

Sleep is a long time coming.

❥

Durbar Square continues as it has for centuries, the beating heart of Kathmandu pulsing with life and seemingly oblivious to the chaos of last night. Snake charmers coax hooded heads from cane baskets; bearded *sadhus* clad in bright robes and beads meditate, soothe and hassle passers-by; touts and rickshaws brim between temples and palaces, while pigeons scurry and peck and shit. There are fewer tourists now, and the streets are heavily patrolled by soldiers—the only obvious signs the city is unwell.

'She looks like a goddamn mean bitch,' Gabe says to Luna.

A massive black wooden statue snarls silently at us. Arms snake from the torso; one clutches a sword, another the severed head of a demon, others beckon and twirl. Her belly and breasts are smeared with blood, around which a girdle of dead men's hands is carved. A red tongue droops from a fanged mouth.

'Do you know much about Hinduism?' Luna asks.

'Nope,' I say.

'This is Kali, the Black Goddess,' says Luna. 'The mother goddess, the destroyer. The bloodied sword and severed head symbolise the destruction of ignorance and the dawning of knowledge.'

'They still believe in this shit?' asks Gabe.

'At least twice a week, on Tuesdays and Saturdays. It's a little like a Catholic confession, but instead of confessing to a priest, you offer a sacrifice at Kali's altar to rebalance your karma. The bigger the guilt the bigger the sacrifice.'

'There's one this Saturday,' says Carly. 'It's up in the valley about an hour from here. Do you guys want to come with us?'

'Sure.' Gabe laughs and stares at me. His smile fades. 'Who knows? Maybe I need a little karma rebalancing of my own.'

'Hey, can you take a photo of us, Saul?' Carly hands me her camera. 'It's automatic: just press the button.'

The girls smile and hug each other, striking would-be model poses, and behind them the statue of Kali leers. I press the button and before the shutter snaps, the camera focuses on a wooden garnet of human heads dangling around Kali's neck.

And on we move, past statues of lower deities, ornately carved buildings, sweeping curved roofs, the girls pointing and smiling, camera clicking, Gabe laughing and touching, and me, aimlessly following, lost amongst the noise of foreign tongues and the heady scent of spice and incense.

Luna stops before two large wooden doors, admiring the skulls carved into the door's lintels.

'This is where she lives, Carly,' says Luna.

'Kumari? This is Kumari's *Bahal*?' Carly steps back and takes a photo of the intricately carved wooden building.

'Who is Kumari?' asks Gabe.

Suddenly a pack of Nepalese boys swarm around us, tongues jabbering, hands waving. None of them attempt to engage me, instead clamouring for attention from the others.

'No tour guides,' yells Gabe. He swats at them like flies.

'It's okay.' Carly hands the eldest boy several rupees. The others slip back into the crowds searching for other trade. 'What better way to learn about the Living Goddess than from the locals?'

'Yes,' says the boy. 'Kumari is the Living Goddess, the virgin goddess.'

'Really?' Gabe's eyes widen. 'A Living Goddess . . . '

Carly produces a Dictaphone from her bumbag and starts recording as the guide speaks. Luna scribbles down notes in her journal. 'We're researching this at university,' she says.

'Kumari is an incarnation of Shiva's *shakti Parvati*—how you would say his wife. She is chosen at four years of age to come and live in this house and will remain here until she first loses blood when she reaches, what is the word? Puberty! Or through injury.'

'A goddess,' murmurs Gabe. His eyes scan the upper floors of the building. Three shuttered windows present themselves to the square. The middle one is open.

'If you are lucky, you might see her.' The guide notices Gabe's gaze. 'She appears once a day in the window for only a few seconds. She has not yet appeared today so there is still a chance. Legend has it . . . '

The guide's voice drones on. My shoulders prickle and the skin on my spine creeps. Someone is watching me. I turn, scanning the crowds in Durbar Square. Dozens of eyes in brown faces stare, but I pass them by. Their interest is purely tourist fascination or the chance to make a buck. I sweep past statues and temples until I'm drawn to the pyramidal-blocked steps forming the base of a large, stone temple rising from the middle of the square. Rickshaw drivers rest at its base, waving when I catch their eye, but it is not their gaze I feel lingering on me, pressing down inside and peering into my secrets.

I spy him on the topmost step of the temple, sitting amongst several tourists. Short and hunched, clad in brown cloth. From here I can't make out his features but I know he is the one. The midget. My stomach flutters and I'm pushing through the crowd to the bottom of the temple. Without taking my eyes from his face, lest he disappear, I stumble up the cracked stone steps toward him.

'*Namaste*,' he says. Nature did not bless this brown-skinned man. His nose is squat and his lip cleft. A wispy rust-coloured beard clings to his cheeks. His eyes, though, are intense and draw me into deep green, flecked with orange.

'Who are you? Why are you following me?' Sweat bursts from my brow, my chest heaves from the climb. The tourists edge away from us and I realise I'm shouting.

He sits motionless, calm. The voice that slides from between those cleft lips is rich and soothing, the accent unplaceable. 'You seem troubled, friend. Please, sit.'

'Who are you?' I take a seat. 'What do you want?'

'I'm not the one who is lost. I'm not the one who is wanting. I am not wandering blind through this world.'

I grab him by the collar of his shirt. 'Don't give me any of this mystical shit, pal. I don't believe in that crap.' I shake him hard; his body is surprisingly light, almost weightless. 'Don't fuck with me!'

'Don't fuck with me?' His hand closes gently around my wrist and suddenly all my strength is gone. 'The only person fucking with you is you.' He points down into the crowd near the *Bahal*, indicating Gabe. 'And him.'

'I . . . I . . . don't understand.' Laura is swelling somewhere deep inside, trying to break out, to engulf me. And the others, all the others I have slept with since. He releases my wrist.

'Some call me Anjaneya. Anje for short. It is as good a name as any, and many are given. You are named after a man made blind.'

'How can you know this?'

'Kathmandu is an ancient city, Saul, but it is a small city. One where tongue touches tongue to fill the street with the sound of the living. There are few tourists here these days. Why are you here?'

Everything is unravelling, too noisy, too bright. Heat rises from the earth, curling up the temple steps, distorting the square below me. I've felt this before, back when I first tested positive. Again when Laura killed herself. The world collapses, and it is all I can do to simply be. I can't talk. Nothing works.

'We are living in the last days of Kali Yuga,' Anje continues. 'The last Yuga. The last stage before the world begins anew. Everyone has a chance to be on the right side of the sword when the white horse comes, Saul.'

'White horse?'

'Seek Kali and you shall find the horse.'

'What do you mean?'

'Look there at the window!' Anje's face splits into an open-mouthed grin. There's a moon tattooed on his tongue. 'The Goddess awakes.' He rests his hand on my shoulder and the heat dissipates.

A small head peers around the corner of the middle shutter of the *Bahal*. Her face is powder white and the eyes mascara heavy. Even at this distance I see how wide her eyes are as she looks down on the square. A great cheer rises from the crowd and a childish smile plays upon her lips before she ducks out of sight. She looks about six years old, a child playing dress-up. The same age my never-born daughter would be.

'Do you believe she is a goddess, Anje?'

I'm sitting alone. I can barely focus on the people at the foot of the temple, let alone the shutters on the *Bahal*. I can't see the midget anywhere.

❀

A colour photo the size of a single bed sheet covers the back wall of the shop. The buff, a small buffalo-like animal, still stands as blood fountains from the stump of its neck. Its head is spinning through the air, yet to hit the ground. A man laughs as he holds the tail of the buff so it can't run. The other man, the one with the *khukuri*, is bent over double, still in the downward arc of the decapitating swing.

I don't remember coming in. I don't remember coming here. I don't remember.

'It is our most effective advertisement.' The shopkeeper indicates his wares under the glass cabinet. Large knives, thick in the middle, with ends tapering to the point and the hilt. 'The point of the *khukuri* is as sharp as a needle, so it answers equally for cutting or stabbing. In consequence of the great thickness of the metal, the blade is exceedingly heavy. A blow from such a weapon as this is a terrible one. The very weight of the blade will drive it half through a man's arm if it falls from even a little height. The *khukuri* also comes with these two small knives, much like the knives that come with the Highlander's dirk. Makes a complete set.'

'How much?'

The weight of the weapon is comforting. I remember leaving.

❀

Gabe meditates naked on the floor of our room. It's something he's practised for years, he tells me, not like this new-age crap that's insinuated itself into our Western lives. I don't know what he does or how he does it, and I don't care. All it means is I'll be spending the night alone; he tends to disappear for the evening after meditating.

There's a knock at the door. 'You guys in?' It's Carly.

'Tell her to fuck off,' whispers Gabe, emerging briefly from his trance.

I open the door a crack and block her view with my body. 'He's not here.'

'That's cool,' Carly says. The way her eyes dart around in her head tells me otherwise. 'There's this Tibetan restaurant near Durbar Square. We're thinking of going there a little later, if you guys want to come. One of the hotel guards will escort us, so there'll be no trouble with the curfew. It's called *Momo's*, you know, if you're keen.'

She tries to peek past me and I raise my hand to block her.

'Jesus!' Carly jumps back, her eyes wide. 'Where did you get that?'

I realise too late I'm holding the *khukuri*, brandishing it in front of her face. 'It's Nepalese,' I mutter. 'Traditional. I . . . uh . . . look, yeah. I'll let you know when Gabe gets back.' I shut the door on her confused face.

'Where'd you get this?' Gabe has risen from his trance. He takes the knife from my hand, slapping its weight in his palm. He runs a finger down the blade. 'Good quality.' He licks the thin welt of blood from his finger. 'I didn't think you took our conversation last night so seriously.' He passes the hilt of the knife back with a grin. 'But I must say I'm pleased you did.'

'I don't know why I bought it.' The handle is contoured to my hand; it feels made for me.

The hot water pipes shudder into action and the spatter of water on tiles follows.

'Make sure you swing upwards when you use it,' Gabe calls from the shower. 'You wouldn't want the blade swinging back into your knee, would you?'

I sheath the *khukuri*, reluctant to relinquish it, and put it into my backpack. 'I don't suppose you want to go to this restaurant tonight?'

'Carly said it was near Durbar Square. That suits me fine.'

The pipes shudder again and the splattering water stops. Gabe emerges from the shower with a towel wrapped around his waist. His eyes shine almost as bright as his skin.

'Did you see the Living Goddess?' he asks. 'Can you imagine it, Saul? What it would feel like? A goddess!'

His cock swells beneath the towel.

❧

Momo's is almost empty, aside from a few tourists sitting at another table in the gloom. I stab at one of the many *momos* in the middle of our table. I bite into the steamed dumpling, surprised this one contains a mild spiced meat, probably the legal form of beef, called buff. Most of the namesakes I've eaten tonight were vegetarian.

'Do you think Gabe's all right?' Carly asks. 'He's been in there a while now.'

'He's probably got the shits from eating these.' Luna laughs. Food is stuck between her teeth, and after her mouth closes, the lump her tongue makes beneath her lips works away at the food.

'He's been almost quarter of an hour,' says Carly.

'I once shat for twenty-seven minutes straight,' I say. 'He's hardly been gone.'

We eat in silence for the next few minutes, listening to each other chewing. A gunshot echoing from the mountains is the only other sound to penetrate the restaurant's walls.

'You girls know a lot about Hinduism, don't you?' I ask.

'We *are* studying it,' Carly says.

'What do you want to know?' There is a kindness in Luna's voice that is lacking in Carly's.

'I met a man today. He told me about someone called Kali Yuga. Do you know who she is?'

'Kali Yuga is not a person. A Yuga is a time period, and the Hindus have four of them. Kali Yuga is the last Yuga; the one we now live in. It's supposed to last for about 400,000 years,' says Luna.

Carly leans forward so the shadows from the candle flicker over her face. 'It's the age of vice, violence, ignorance and greed. Where the powers of the gods wane and evil walks the earth.'

She leans back and laughs, the sound strained in her throat. She glances back at the door leading to the toilets. Waiting for Gabe. Desperate for Gabe, the fuck of her lifetime. Waiting for the man who poured every drop of his hate into her while she mistook it for passion. I want to tell her she's wasting her time, her youth, on such a cold creature. To shake them both and yell at them to stay away from him, from us, before any hearts are broken. Or worse.

Luna saves me from having to act on my thoughts. 'Remember that bloodied black statue in the square today? The one with all the arms? When the world finally turns to shit, she's supposed to appear and start chopping her way through the evil hordes so Shiva can come riding in on his huge white stallion and smite all and sundry. Like when Christ comes back and takes the believers to heaven while he damns the rest of the world. And then the cycle begins anew, back to the pure and holy first Yuga.'

'I hope Gabe's okay.' Carly stares at the door. She's switched off our conversation already.

'That's weird. This guy told me to look for Kali and a white horse.'

'Did he want money? Maybe he was having you on.'

I'd think it was all bullshit, some tourist scam, if not for the other night on the balcony with Luna. But now I don't know what to think. I don't know what to say. For a second I almost tell her about the white horse rearing at the end of the street that night, huge even in the distance. And that sounds crazy, even to me.

'I've seen him around,' I say. 'Said his name was Angie-nayer or something. He's a midget.'

'That name sounds familiar,' Luna says.

'Can you check on Gabe, please, Saul? I'm worried.'

'He's okay, Carly. Jesus. Give him some space.'

'I'll check.' Luna rises from her chair.

'Nah, look, I'll go.' I avoid their eye contact and walk to the door leading to the toilets. It opens into a narrow, dark alleyway lined with crooked wooden walls. A dim bulb flickers at the end. The smell of shit and urine thickens in the air around me. I tread gingerly, my sandals sucking at waste leaked into the mud around the toilet doors. I wish I'd taken a deep breath several steps ago. I wish I'd worn my boots.

'Gabe? You okay?'

Silence.

'The girls are getting worried. Gabe?'

The toilet door is ajar, hanging lopsided on broken hinges. I pull my shirt up over my nose and push the door gently. It swings inwards, the hinges grinding in protest.

'Gabe?'

The stench crashes over me, permeating my shirt. I gag and stagger back, but not before realising the toilet is empty.

'He's not in there,' I say, back at the table.

'What?' Carly leaps from her seat and runs to the door. 'He must be. He hasn't come out.'

'He's not there!' My shout attracts the waiter who scurries over.

'Something is wrong?' Hands clasped, leaning forward, subservient.

'My mate went off to have a shit in your toilets and he's not in there.'

The waiter smiles and half bows. 'He has left then.'

'He hasn't come out the door.'

Carly appears in the doorway. 'He's not in there!' Her voice is too high, the seeds of panic settling in her throat.

'If your friend not in there,' says the waiter, the patience practised, 'then he must have come out. Unless,' and the waiter laughs, 'he climb the walls and run over roof.'

'He's not there!' Carly's voice is getting higher. Soon it will crack.

Luna sits there, watching, saying nothing. Carly rushes from the restaurant.

'Your friend is an arsehole.' Luna rises from the table. 'I don't know what he's done to Carly, but she's been acting weird ever since the other night.'

'Well, you better go chase her then. You never know what our escort from the hotel will do to your hysterical slut mate out there in the dark.'

She glares at me and leaves.

I don't need this shit; I don't need them; I don't need anything. I think it's time Gabe and I went our separate ways. If he's done his usual disappearing trick, he might not be back for a day or two then he'll want to leave.

And I have a confessional to attend this Saturday.

❧

My stomach churns by the time I get back to the hotel. Something twists in my bowels sending spasms through my gut. *Those fucking buff momos.* I stagger into the bathroom, tear down my pants, and collapse onto the stained toilet seat. The seat is icy against the heat of my skin. Sweat oozes from my body and the room slides at the edge of vision. The shit pours and pours from me, splattering against the bowl, the water and back onto my skin. I have to hold my head in my hands as another bout streams into the bowl. I move slightly, the seat sticky now from the sweat slicking my body. The stench of disease screams up at me. I throw up into my lap, vomit stinging the inside of my nostrils, throat burning and arse on fire. The room no longer slides, instead it lurches up at me. My face connects with the tiles. *Is this the beginning of the last stage of my condition? Am I now fully blown?* Vomit fills the grout between each tile, easing into dark and black and nothing . . .

. . . and chittering, chattering, chanting.

'. . . umanhanumanha . . . '

Hundreds of tiny white monkeys, each the size of a fist, scampering over my body. They stop to beat matchstick fists against my flesh, lips peeled back from fanged mouths.

'. . . manhanumanhan . . . '

Scrambling into my ears, down my throat, filling me from within, and still more scuttle into the room. I'm glued to the floor in bodily fluid. Can't move; can't breathe. Filling me to burst.

'. . . hanumanhanuman . . . '

A golden monkey turns my head in his hands. Its face hovers at the edge of my vision, blurred. It speaks to me, the voice rich in a texture of decayed dreams, of long-dead kings.

'Her boon is freedom. The freedom of the child to revel in the moment.'

I try to speak but the monkeys clog my lungs, stopping air needed to sound the words.

'Yes,' he continues. 'You seek freedom yet still you run. Accept death. Confront it. Do not provoke the laughter of Kali.'

He leans forward so I can see his face. 'To accept one's mortality is to let go.'

The monkeys scream as one. 'Hanuman!'

The golden monkey wears the twisted face of Anje the midget. 'Give Kali the angel to awake the avatar. Let Shiva ride the white horse again.' He grins an ivory snarl and flicks a moon-tattooed tongue at me before he is away, the army of monkeys swarming after him.

' . . . umaaaaaaannnnn . . . '

Fading, burning . . .

A baby crawls towards me, the bloody umbilical trailing through my filth. She grows Laura's thick black hair; her tiny mouth works soundlessly. She wears bright red lipstick, thick on baby lips. Her body snuggles in close, warm against my freezing flesh, the mouth searching for sustenance from nipples that can never work. She suckles my chest, sucking emptily, moving down and down until she finds my cock.

'Love you long time,' she coos before her mouth closes around me. Teeth sprout through the gums, biting, digging . . .

Screaming . . .

❧

'Jesus Christ.'

A tanned white foot leading to a well muscled calf next to my head. Hot water sprays down onto me, washing away my grime. Blood trickles amongst rivulets on the floor. I didn't know I was bleeding too. My body shudders sporadically.

'Good food, was it?' a man says.

I know the voice. *Is it mine?* Somehow I manage to turn onto my back. The water on my face feels like heaven. The man towers over me, his muscular thighs and chest tapering up and away to a haloed head. So far away. Something shines sharply in one of his hands.

'Glad I didn't stay,' he says.

A *haloed* head.

'Are you the angel?' I manage to croak.

He laughs. 'The archangel, Gabriel. Though tonight I am almost a god.'

In a moment of clarity the room sharpens. Gabe stands naked above me washing himself. It's not my blood running across the tiles into a drain clogged with semi-digested *momos*. It's Gabe's.

And he's cleaning my knife, *my khukuri*, washing blood from the blade. Steam billows up, making a golden mist with the light-bulb that had haloed Gabe's head, and in that moment he looks serenely beautiful. A man content with himself; a man revelling in the moment of his freedom.

As the blood washes from his body I see there are no wounds. He is an angel and with the Himalayan waters he has healed his wounds. Gabe. Gabriel. My saviour. My confidant.

'*I think I have killed someone, Gabe. Maybe more than one.*'

His voice of caramel. 'I thought that was what we were doing, Saul. You in your way and me in mine. You should try mine. It's so much more intense.'

And I realise it's not his blood at all.

❧

Wailing in the streets wakes me to a room warm with sunshine. I'm wrapped up in my bed, though I'm cold for the sheets are damp with sweat. Bells toll and the wailing rises and falls between each strike. Voices chant in prayer beneath the cries, accompanied by the melodic stamp of feet. It sounds like the streets teem with people. Gabe sits by the open window.

'Gabe?' It feels like sand has scoured the inside of my throat. 'What's happening?'

He turns slowly from the window, the last ghost of a smile on his face. 'It's a funeral. And you're alive again. How do you feel?'

I try to sit up and blood rushes to my head. The world spins and Luna is holding a glass of water to my lips. Gabe still sits staring out the window, lost to our presence.

'Carly was sick as well, though nowhere near as bad as you. We're trying for the Indian border tomorrow morning.'

'You're leaving?'

'It's too dangerous here now the Kumari has been murdered. We've met a guy who says he'll smuggle us past the roadblocks out of town.'

'Who's been murdered?'

'The Kumari. The Living Goddess. You remember the little girl from the square? The police are blaming the Maoist rebels, though that's hard to believe. Why would the rebels do something so stupid? The Hindu gods in Kathmandu are far from dead yet. The city is on the edge of civil war now. You better get out as soon as you can.'

In the window's reflection Gabe is smiling. *So much more intense.* Gabriel the angel. Of death.

'Anyway, Saul. It's been interesting. Take care.' For a brief moment Luna stares into my eyes, searching for something. She pats my hand, stands to leave and leans forward to kiss my cheek. 'You need to lose him,' she whispers.

'What is Hanuman?' I ask before she pulls away.

'This time the *what* is a *who*,' Luna says. 'Hanuman is the monkey god, the embodiment of devotion. He helped the hero of the *Ramayana* to conquer the demon king. He's also a shape-shifter, grants visions, helps us mere mortals out now and then.' Luna slaps the side of her head. 'That's it! I knew it would come to me.'

'What?'

'Anjaneya. The name of the man who told you about Kali Yuga. It's another name for Hanuman.'

'Does he have any tattoos?'

'A moon on his tongue. I didn't think you'd be the sort to get into studying this stuff. Why do you want to know about him?'

'Just heard the name, that's all.'

Gabe's no longer staring out the window. He's still smiling but he's staring *intensely* at me.

The local bus stop just outside the city centre is a massive intersection with roads radiating like spokes. Buses and trucks heave under the weight of clinging passengers as they weave haphazardly between and around other vehicles stopped to pick up people, horns blaring. Dust swirls in the exhaust fumes making it hard to breathe.

'Which bus are we supposed to take to get to this fucking thing?' Gabe has wrapped a muslin scarf around his face to keep out the grit.

'I'll know when I see it,' I lie.

It's Saturday morning and the sun that should beat down in the thin atmosphere finally cracks the layer of pollution and does. It will be our last morning together. Tomorrow Gabe has found passage to Tibet. I won't be going with him.

A bus pulls up, billowing dust into a thick cloud, its numbered destination on its side. If only I knew what they meant. Anje stares down at me through one of the windows. He beckons with stubby fingers.

'This is the one!'

We clamber on board and push our way into the crowded aisle as dark faces stare at us. I try to make my way to where I'd seen Anje but I can't find him.

The smell of chicken shit is strong and the sound of squawking is almost drowned out by the roar of the diesel engine. Someone has a small cow, most likely a buff, near the other end of the aisle. The buff has urinated on the floor but people don't seem to care as the urine spreads with the tilt of the bus.

The road winds up into the mountains and half an hour later we're above the pollution. Up here the soot and carbon monoxide hangs like a thick dirty blanket over Kathmandu. The organism has turned on itself; the city is indeed dying under its own waste.

The bus lurches to a halt in a grind of gears and engine roar, spilling its passengers from the mouth of its rusting doors. Processions of people, clad in rainbow-hued saris or drab colourless menswear, make their way up a narrow dirt road toward the summit of a small peak. They carry chickens and children; they lead buff and lamb and pigs, faces intent and conversation minimal. The noisy Nepal street is gone, for Saturday is Dhukankali. We walk with them in silence, the sun burning now in the high altitude. Gabe pulls away from me, his stride lengthening. I'm still weak from the food poisoning. His shirt already sticks to his back.

'I hoped to see you here,' a voice says behind me.

Anje struggles to keep up, his legs skip every third step to keep abreast. His rusty beard is golden in the sunlight. Like the monkey king. I wait for him to reach me then continue walking, this time slower.

'Who *are* you?' I ask.

'You know who I am. I have told you.'

'I know your name means *Hanuman*.' I'm scared too look at him. Just in case he's real.

Anje laughs bitterly. 'A cruel joke placed upon me for being a burden upon my family. I was set out to beg at an early age. The little monkey.'

I sneak a glance. His head is downcast and he struggles still to match my pace. His scalp is shiny with sweat and his breathing laboured. I'm feeling stronger. What the hell was I thinking? That this guy is a Hindu god?

Gabe stops and turns fifty metres ahead of me. 'Hurry up will you! We don't want to get separated.'

'We must catch him,' pants Anje. 'I need to show you two something near the altars. I'm afraid my health is poor. Perhaps you can carry me?'

I don't remember stopping, I don't recall lifting him onto my back, but his arms grip my shoulders. I hardly feel his weight at all. He's whispering things into my head, telling me my secrets, drawing out my poison. Suddenly he doesn't feel human anymore.

'Confront death, Saul. Accept it. Here you can buy positive karma with the price of blood.' He indicates those around me carrying chickens. He points to the lamb. 'The greater the guilt, the higher the price. Kali accepts all denominations.' Anje laughs, the sound sharp and acidic in my ear. 'All major credit cards, American Express included,' he hisses. 'What can you offer the goddess?'

Gabe has reached the summit and stands amongst the worshippers, the faithful and the guilty. A queue of patient humans and nervous animals has formed here.

'You gotta see this, man,' Gabe calls. 'It's incredible!'

'Offer the goddess!' Anje's voice ricochets inside my skull, bouncing on the brain. Then he's off and into the crowd, weaving through the saris and robes, feathers and hide. Sweat bursts on my skin. The air is suddenly thick and bubbly, hard to breathe. It flows into my lungs like a siren syrup, drawing an insect to its death. I almost collapse at Gabe's feet. My knees tremble and his strong arm pulls me up.

'What the fuck happened to you?' The look on his face doesn't speak concern, simply annoyance that I'm holding him back. 'I said you'd be too sick to do this. Before you pass out, Saul, check out the view.'

His arm sweeps along the queues lining a narrow path, winding its way around the edge of the hills down into a deep hollow. Thousands of Hindus, shuffling slowly forward; children clutching chickens to their chests; ash-eyed babies slung over shoulders while their mothers lead lambs; men herding buff and pigs; chickens, hundreds of chickens. Down and down they shuffle, into the heart of a massive stone pit flanked by ancient statues worn smooth by the centuries.

Gabe is almost running as he pushes his way through the crowd. His face is alive and yearning. 'Look at this! Look at all of this!' If I didn't know before, I do now. Blood excites Gabe like nothing else. I stumble along in his wake, my head feeling light. Sparkles dance before my eyes and sweat soaks my clothes. The crooked trees leaning from the banks of the hills teem with caterwauling monkeys. The copper stink of blood rises to greet us as we near the bottom. A hastily painted sign hangs over the entrance to the steps leading down into the pit. On it scrawled in faded black: 'Hindu only. No tourist.'

A buff is dragged shrieking to one of the sacrificial altars lining the pit. Gabe leans precariously over the edge of the pit, his grin as wide as the fear in the buff's eyes.

'This was used for humans once,' he says.

A priest forces the buff's neck onto the bloodied stone and the *khukuri* sweeps down, once, twice—the blade has been dulled on bone—until the head is severed from the still kicking body. The guilty one clasps his hands in prayer as the priest dots his forehead with blood fresh from the stone. He rises and the innocence is clear on his face. It drips down the bridge of his nose.

The altar to Kali the Black swarms with priests and followers. All chant over the screams of the animals, standing ankle-deep in the blood for a goddess. Long wicked blades flash in the light of the sun. Blood arcs through the air splattering the stone gods and flesh puppets; blessings are smeared and the slaughter is dragged away to where butchers prepare a pyre of carcasses.

I'm back on the shower floor covered in shit and puke. Blood washes down the muscled leg standing next to my head. Blood for a goddess. Blood of a goddess. The blood of my wife; my baby; the sluts, the whores I have since punished for their sins. My sins. The sins of my blood.

Gabe spreads his arms wide and laughs up at the sky above the pit. Dust whorls bloom on the lip lining the hollow, swirling up as the crowds cower under the onslaught. And darkness descends on the valley as coagulated clouds smother the sky, forced on by the ferocity of the winds sweeping over the mountains.

A golden monkey scampers across a roof beam over the pit. It grins with Anje's face. 'You cannot deny death.' Its mouth doesn't move. The words resonate within. *In my veins.* 'Pain and sorrow are woven into the texture of a man's life. Accept death, Saul. Believe in it, revel in it.'

This is karma. This is balance. But I do not believe.

Do not . . .

Believe.

I'm reaching into the daypack strapped to my back. The handle of the *khukuri* worn to the shape of my palm glides in. The handle swings past my face. Blood has dried into the fabric binding the hilt. Monkeys, monkeys, thousands of monkeys howling in the trees. Thunder rips the sky. I step toward Gabe as he turns to me. I swing up as hard as I can. The blade slices easily up through his groin and catches in his pelvic bone.

He doesn't make a sound. Instead he stares at me. The blood is draining fast from his face. His eyes not hateful, but full of the wonder of the newly converted. Thunder roars again through the heavens and the rain begins to fall, fat and heavy. I yank the blade from his bone and blood gushes hot over my hands. The air whistles from Gabe's lungs. I grab his hair and ready the *khukuri* for the killing blow. And he plunges one of the small knives into my neck, dragging the blade downwards as he collapses. I stagger back, slipping in the bloody mud. Blood spurts between the fingers pressed to my neck. I slip again and tumble across the altar, sliding into the sacrificial area. Blood in my mouth, coppery and acrid, in my eyes, my lungs. People scream. Gabe laughs, high-pitched and cracking. I struggle to stand but my legs have stopped working and I collapse against the wall. It's so cold, so cold. Gabe's blood pours down the sacrificial altar, driven by the rain. It washes over me.

People and animals flee the pit. The monkeys howl as one, then fall silent. A golden skinned priest stands over me, bare-chested, watching. From here he seems a giant, his face kind. There are terrible raw scars over his chest.

'Shiva comes as Kalki, the final avatar. The last days of Kali Yuga are closing.' He points a long, lean arm to the sky. 'Open your eyes and you will see.'

I follow his finger to the heavens. There is nothing but roiling black clouds, thundering across the sky, disgorging the essence of life. Nothing but clouds. Gabe has fallen silent. And I feel nothing. Nothing.

Nothing.

Then . . .

Above me, high in the clouds, a massive hoof slices through the darkness, followed by another, then another. An enormous white horse crashes through the sky bearing the most beautiful person I have ever seen. He thrusts something forward but the sky is too bright now and I cannot see clearly. His hand? His sword?

I reach up to the light.

THE FEASTIVE SEASON

The aroma of roasting turkey lured the young girl from her dreams into the kitchen. Her mother stood slicing potatoes amongst dishes of vegetables and trays of meats. There were pots of spices and herbs, and bowls of dough and chocolate. It had been a lean winter and the smells made her ravenous.

'What are you doing, Mother?' the girl asked, her eyes wide. She could not remember seeing so much food in their house.

'It's Christmas Eve, Emily.' Mother layered the potato slices into a flat, clay dish.

'Is all this food for tonight?' asked Emily, dipping a finger into a chocolate-coated mixing bowl.

'Most is for Saint Niklaus. He gets very hungry this time of year.' Mother sprinkled cracked pepper over the potatoes before smothering them in a cheese sauce. 'Don't you remember last Christmas?'

'Not really.' Emily sucked her fingers. 'Did I get a present?'

'The joys of being only four years old,' said Mother.

'She's lucky,' said a surly voice from the kitchen door.

Emily, absorbed in the bowl of chocolate, missed the look that her mother gave her older sister, Rebekah. A look at first hard, and then forgiving. She did, however, notice Rebekah's pale face and red eyes.

'Have you been crying?' asked Emily.

'It's none of your business,' Rebekah snapped, glaring at her mother.

Heat blasted from the potbelly stove as Mother slipped the potatoes onto the upper tray. The door banged shut, making Emily jump.

'Don't speak to your sister like that,' Mother said as she wiped her hands on her apron.

Rebekah's bottom lip quivered and her eyes brimmed. 'It's not fair!'

Mother moved fast. She wrapped Rebekah in her arms. 'Hush, child. Sshhhh . . . '

'I don't want to! Mother, please don't make me!' Rebekah sobbed into her mother's shallow bosom.

'It comes early on some, my love. For this Christmas Eve, you are a woman,' Mother soothed, while her eyes scowled at Emily to leave.

Father swept into the kitchen, a weary bear, snow clinging to his cloak, an axe in his hand. 'What is it, Marthe?'

Rebekah wailed again and Mother pulled her closer. 'Take Emily,' Mother said. 'Women's talk. She fears the coming eve.'

Father's nostrils flared and a sheet of ice slipped behind his eyes. 'Of course.'

He carried Emily from the kitchen into the living area, and she felt his arms tremble. Father sat her in front of the fire and hung his coat next to the hearth. He rubbed his hands as he blew them from blue to pink, smiling and laughing all the while.

'Why is Rebekah sad, Father?' Emily asked.

Father stood silent for a second before crouching beside her. 'She has grown into a woman of late. She must wait up on Christmas Eve with us now.'

'I wish *I* was grown up. Then I too could wait up for Saint Niklaus.'

Father sighed softly, his eyes staring into nothing as he worked his calloused fingers through the curls on her head. 'I pray you never grow up.'

He pulled her close to his chest and asked what sort of presents she hoped Saint Niklaus would bring. They talked as Rebekah sobbed in the kitchen.

Emily sat on her bed, tracing her fingers through the breath on her window-pane. Outside, the grey sky blossomed with white petals. She imagined Saint Niklaus loading up his sleigh for the evening's journey, warm in his thick, red coat—ruddy cheeks shining and eyes a-twinkling. Unhappy with her rein-deer drawing, she blew on the window and created a fresh canvas. The door creaked open. Rebekah slipped into the room and sat on the bed.

'What are you doing?' Rebekah asked. Her eyes were still red.

'I'm drawing Christmas,' said Emily, outlining a sharp, pointy tree on the windowpane.

'I hate Christmas.'

'I don't. I love it. I can't wait until I wake up tomorrow and open all my presents. Especially the ones Saint Niklaus will bring.'

Rebekah picked at the quilt on the bed. 'There is no Saint Niklaus,' she said quietly.

Emily's finger froze, hard-pressed against the glass. 'What?'

'I said there is no Saint Niklaus!' Rebekah leant forward, her mouth inches from Emily's face. 'It's just a game they play for babies. Like you!'

Emily's body shook and her face darkened. 'How . . . how do you know?'

'Some of the older children at school told me.' Rebekah dug at the quilt's weave. 'There's no such thing as Saint Niklaus. He's been dead for hundreds of years.'

For a second the room filled with silence as Emily sucked in all the noise. Her chest expanded and her breath hitched. With a mighty wail, she burst into tears.

'Mama!'

Rebekah glanced toward the door, shot off the bed and clamped a hand over Emily's mouth. 'Sshhh! Be quiet. I didn't mean it, Emily. I just said it to hurt you. There really *is* a Saint Niklaus. Please, stop crying and don't call Mother.'

Emily wiped a tear from her cheek as Rebekah released her. 'You're mean. I'm going to tell on you.'

'Please don't,' pleaded Rebekah. 'I'll share my pudding with you.'

'I don't care about your pudding. We've got lots of food today. I had some chocolate.'

'No, silly. That's not for us. Most of that food is left out for Saint Niklaus.'

'Even the chocolate?'

'*Especially* the chocolate. It's got lots of energy in it.'

'Are we still going to be hungry tonight?' Emily's face screwed up.

'We won't be hungry, Emily, but we don't get to eat all the nice food.' She kissed Emily on the cheek. 'I'm sorry. Remember, if you don't tell, I'll share my pudding with you.'

Rebekah left the room, and Emily noticed she had started crying again. Her mother appeared in the doorway and asked what was wrong, but Emily thought of the pudding and said nothing. The sun had set, and this time, when her finger drew a line on the window, it left only blackness.

☻

Emily stared at the thin, sliver of turkey, the dollop of mashed potato and the sprinkling of peas on her plate. It seemed so meagre compared to the feast her mother had cooked. The other plates on the table were equally empty. *Even her father's.*

'Is this all we get?'

Her father scowled and her mother said quickly, 'Be grateful we can celebrate Christmas Eve, Emily. Some families have less.'

'But all the food—'

'That is for when Saint Niklaus comes.' Mother sliced her meat, forked in a mouthful, chewed and swallowed. 'You never know. If the night is kind, there may be leftovers in the morning.'

'He can't eat all that,' Emily said. 'Not in one night. Not in a whole *week.*'

They ate in silence for several minutes. The cold crept in through the shuttered windows and Father threw another log into the hearth.

'Eat up, Rebekah,' Mother said.

Rebekah sat sullenly, pushing her fork around the plate—directing peas and potato. 'I feel sick.'

'It's okay, honey. It's just nerves. It's not as bad as you think.' Mother paused, the hint of a smile on her lips. 'There is a certain amount of . . . pleasure . . . involved, and after a while you almost long for—'

'Marthe!' Father, his face stone, glared at Mother. He squeezed the knife in his burly hand, turning his knuckles bone-white.

'Pleasure?' asked Rebekah.

'That's enough!' Father thumped the table and the plates rattled. Emily jumped in her seat. Mother sat quietly, eyes downcast. Father glowered at each of them, stood and went into the kitchen. He returned with a chunk of raw meat and shaved off several slices.

'You must eat this,' he said.

'What is it?' Rebekah's hands shook as she reached for the meat.

'Liver. I don't want you with thin blood.'

She swallowed and grimaced.

'If you don't like the taste,' said Father, 'then swallow it with some of your dinner.'

He sliced some more and passed it to Mother. 'Just to be sure.'

'What about me?' asked Emily.

'You're not yet a woman,' her mother said softly.

'I am so!'

Father interrupted, his voice gravel. 'You are not staying up, Emily. Be thankful you do not need to eat it.'

Emily wanted to cry. Why was her father being so mean on Christmas Eve? When she found the courage to look back at him, she saw tears in his eyes. Rebekah sat pale and silent, staring at the tablecloth. Mother stared wistfully past the shutters out into the darkness and the cold.

'Be thankful,' Father said.

☉

Emily lay tucked under the quilt. She struggled to sit upright against the pillows when Mother came into the bedroom. Mother placed a tray holding a mug of hot chocolate and a biscuit onto the bed stand.

'Remember. Saint Niklaus won't come until you're asleep,' Mother said, sitting on the bed. 'He knows if you're awake.'

'How does he know?'

'He just does. You want him to come, don't you?'

'Of course! Will he bring lots of presents?'

'We'll all go down to the village tomorrow to get the presents with what Saint Niklaus brings. You, me, your sister, and your father. Together.'

Mother picked up the steaming mug and handed it to Emily. It was hot against her palms and the chocolate smelt rich and delicious. A white swirl of cream crowned the thick, syrupy drink. Emily sipped the cream, and a thought crossed her mind.

'Will he still come if Rebekah doesn't go to sleep? She's not going to bed like me. You said she's staying up until he comes.'

'Rebekah is a woman now. Remember the blood? It's different when you grow up. One day you'll understand.' Mother stroked Emily's brow; the dreamy look from her face had gone, replaced with eyes that crinkled at the edges and lines that crossed her forehead. 'Has Rebekah been telling you things?'

Emily paused, the chocolate and cream coated her tongue, and her sister's pudding was a warm presence in her tummy. 'No. I just wish I could stay up to see Saint Niklaus too.'

'One day, sweet child.' Mother smiled, touching Emily's cheek. 'One day. Now finish your drink and have your biscuit. It will help you sleep.' She leant forward and kissed her on the cheek. 'Goodnight, sweetness. Sleep tight. See you in the morning.'

After Mother left, Emily carefully opened the window and poured her drink outside into the snow. The biscuit followed, spinning out into the drift and disappearing. She shut the window, climbed back into bed and pulled the covers tight against the cold. When Mother returned later that night to close the shutters, collect the tray and blow out the lantern, Emily pretended to be asleep. It was all she could do to contain the excitement that threatened to spill out and announce her deceit to the house. Saint Niklaus was coming!

The night wore on, and Emily's eyelids slowly slipped over her eyes. The comforting, muted sounds of conversation from the living room lulled and soothed her, and sleep came. The bells from the village church had tolled eleven so long ago that Emily felt it didn't matter if Rebekah got to see Saint Niklaus and she didn't. The bed was just too nice and warm, the pillow soft, the tinkling of sleigh bells so sleepy . . .

Her eyes opened wide. Sleigh bells! Outside the window, tinkling and chiming. Emily slipped out of bed and inched open the window, ignoring the cold as it rushed in to feed on her warmth. The bells suddenly went silent.

All she had to do was unlatch the shutters, push them open and she would see him. Fear stayed her hand. What if Saint Niklaus saw her? She couldn't risk it. She closed the window and crept back into bed, snuggling into the blankets. Shutting her eyes, she again pretended to sleep.

A scratching sounded against the outside wall. The bells rang louder this time. Emily heard a stifled scream from the living room. Father was saying something now, but she couldn't make out the words. Emily's breath caught in the bowl of her throat, as she listened for the restless stomping of hooves and the impatient neighing of reindeer. Something scrunched through the snow on the roof, accompanied by a score of bells.

Emily wondered whether Father had put out the fire, so Saint Niklaus could enter. She crawled out of bed, pulled on a dressing gown and crept to the bedroom door. Slipping into the darkened hallway, she tiptoed toward the crack of light under the living room door. She heard her sister's muffled cries and the muted bass of Father's voice.

Easing the door open, Emily peered through. The table lay spread with roast meats, vegetables and fruits. Rich, steaming puddings stood next to bowls of brandy custard and piles of chocolate, amongst flasks of wine and mead. Enough to feed two or three families, Emily thought. Did he eat at all the other houses too? She inched the door a little further and saw Mother, wearing her best evening clothes, sitting on the floor by the hearth. She gazed longingly toward the chimney, and Emily noticed the embers in the fireplace had all but gone out. Something scrabbled inside, loosening soot, and Mother shuffled forward on her hands and knees, weeping and smiling.

'Get back, Marthe,' said Father, still out of view. His voice sounded like it had passed through a throat of thorns.

Another muffled scream made Emily push the door wider. Father sat on the rug in the middle of the room. One hand wrapped Rebekah to his chest and the other smothered her mouth. His legs were coiled around her and Rebekah kicked and struggled against him. Her sister, too, wore her evening's finest.

Before Emily could growl at her father, something large fell into the hearth and a ball of soot billowed into the room. Mother gasped and Father uttered a curse or a prayer, Emily couldn't be sure. Her ears had filled with a rush of blood and her knees trembled.

The thing in the hearth twisted and elongated, and stepped into the room. Its red skin, where it was not coated in ash, shone with sweat and oil. Two long, thin arms stretched out, flexing sinewy muscle and tendon-lined bones. Its torso was small and stout, and a thick, glistening organ hung loosely between its thighs. The head, too large for the body, swivelled on a thin neck, as its snout-like face studied them with pale eyes that reflected yellow in the lamplight. Bells woven into the thick tussocks sprouting from its head tinkled as it moved. A fibrous tongue flicked out between ragged teeth.

It smiled and Rebekah screamed. Emily's scalp crawled and she shuddered. Impossibly long fingers snaked out from its hand, curled and beckoned for Rebekah.

'Aaaahhh,' it sighed, the sound deep and rich, the humming of a choir. 'My blessings have served you well. Look how she has bloomed.'

It shuffled closer and leant forward, nostrils flaring, chest quivering as it sniffed. 'And she is with the moon. Perfect. You have done well, woodsman. Give her to me. My hunger is great and I must taste my fruit.' A leathery finger caressed Rebekah's cheek and she convulsed, her eyes rolling into the back of her head.

Father rocked back and forth, cradling her and sobbing. 'I can't. I can't.'

'Take me, Domovoy,' Mother said, her arms reaching out towards the creature. 'I am ready too. I have waited.'

Domovoy stretched out a skeletal hand and held Mother's chin. Its fingers wrapped around her jaw and splayed up and across her cheeks to her temples. It slowly massaged there, its voice soothing. 'Soon, woman. First I must have my fruits.' Mother slumped back on her haunches, smiling and moaning as she hitched her dress and parted her thighs.

'No!' Father scrambled back with Rebekah limp in his arms. 'I will not yield her to you!'

'You have no choice, woodsman. If not for me, your life would be barren. I bless this house, I bring you gifts.' Domovoy slunk close on spindly legs. 'She,' it said, a long finger pointing at Rebekah, 'would not be here if not for me.'

'Please. I will give you anything. Please, not my daughter!'

'You have nothing left to give. Everything you have comes from me. She is already mine, just as she is yours. Without me, they can never be complete. Now, woodsman, let me make them fertile for you. It is for the good of your village.'

'No,' Father sobbed, as Domovoy's sinewy arms pulled Rebekah away from him.

Emily wanted to scream, to run forward to protect her sister, but her feet would not move. She stood frozen, filled with fear and panic. Nothing worked. No mouth opened wide to yell a warning, and no eyes closed so as not to see.

Her father, a giant of a man, huddled with his knees up under his chin. He sobbed, rocking back and forth. Rebekah's evening dress and petticoat were pushed up over white thighs. Black pubic hair, vaginal lips, fresh with new blood; Domovoy gulped from her sister's thighs. Red, glistening torso expanded, hovering over Rebekah, teeth bared, sinking into her throat while its fingers weaved up and into her sister, sliding into her vagina, throbbing, pulsing with the life it found. Rebekah moaned, slick with sweat, nipples taut and brown, clothing now stripped from her body. Domovoy drank, ate and slaked itself on blood.

Mother spread herself wide. She thrusted up, moaning, bucking against the beast that entered her mouth, nose, vagina and bottom. Domovoy probed, erect and thick with blood and energy. Mother keened, smiling, shining, laughing, ecstatic.

Withering, paling. Wasting away.

❧

Her father, small and broken, wailed; knuckles and fingers bled as he beat the floor.

Emily stood terrified and the room shrank until all she could see was Domovoy's approaching head, its yellow-slit eyes mesmerising, its voice sliding into her to chase the fear from the marrow of her bones.

It kissed her softly on the lips, sending shudders of bliss through her small body and whispered to her lovingly, like a father. *Sleep, daughter, and be silent with this knowledge. Your time will come. I await your flavour with anticipation.*

Emily's eyes closed and she fell, forever and dreaming, until she awoke covered in sweat and burning in her bed.

'It's all fine, my darling.' Father cradled her, rocking back and forth, wiping her head with a damp cloth.

'Domovoy . . . ' The word struggled to pass the dry thickness of her tongue.

'You have a fever, Emily. Domovoy is a dream, a fairytale.'

'No, I saw him! I . . . I . . . ' She recalled red, slick skin, and nearly wet herself. 'I need to go to the bathroom.'

'Come on then.' Father took her by the hand.

She noticed his hand was cut and bleeding. Splinters porcupined the skin.

'Nothing to worry about, Emily. I cut myself chopping down the mistletoe I hung above the hearth.'

They passed the living room on the way to the bathroom. Light shone from under the door.

'Where's Mother?' she asked.

'She's in bed sleeping. So is your sister. Hurry, we don't want to wake them. They're very tired.' He passed her the lantern as she went into the bathroom and waited for her in the hallway.

The chamber pot was cold against her skin, a contrasting relief to the fire burning up her body. She urinated hot and long. Afterwards, she sat there watching the lantern flicker, listening to the noises in the house. She heard Father shuffling in the hallway, the wind rustling the trees. And noises from the living room, hungry and slurping.

Domovoy was still in the house! Her stomach cramped and she vomited into her lap. Father rushed in and she started to cry.

'Domovoy,' she whispered through sobs. 'He's still in the house. In the living room. He wants to eat me, too.'

'Ssshh.' Father removed her nightgown and cleaned her with a damp towel. 'There's no such thing.'

'He's in there. I can hear him!' she wailed.

'Quiet, honey-pie. You'll wake your sister.' He wrapped her in her robe. 'Let's get you back to bed.'

He picked her up and carried her to the bedroom. They passed the living room, and she managed to reach out and push the latch, kicking the door with her feet. The door swung open, spilling light into the hallway. Father cursed. Her mother and sister sat at the table staring guiltily, startled mouths stuffed full of meat, grease running from chins and fingers. Gold coins lay scattered near the hearth.

'Emily!' Mother said around a mouthful of lamb. She looked radiant, her hair black and shining, lips full, cheeks dashed with colour.

Rebekah paused briefly, flashed a smile, eyes sparkling, and began to devour the food in front of her once more.

'There,' said Father. 'Are you satisfied? There is no Domovoy in the house.'

As he tucked her into bed, he felt her forehead again. 'Your fever has almost gone. Maybe you threw it all up.'

'You told me they were in bed.'

'Who?'

'Mother and Rebekah. You said they were sleeping. You lied.'

'No I didn't, my baby. They must have got up when I came in here to look after you. Sshh, now sleep.'

'You lied to me! And you lied about Domovoy!' Emily shuddered and her voice hitched. 'I saw what happened, Father. Domovoy spoke to me. He said . . . he said . . . ' The lingering burn of its kiss ushered forth a new tumbling of tears.

Father sat there, his big hands stroked her brow, and the apple in his throat bobbed up and down, up and down. 'No, Emily, no.'

'He's coming back for me,' Emily wailed. 'He'll go inside me like he did Mother and Rebekah. Don't let him, Father, please!'

'I won't,' Father croaked.

'You lie!'

'No, Emily, he'll never touch you.' Tears slid down the creases in Father's face, and he tucked the sheets tight around her.

'Do you promise?'

'I promise.' He reached for the fallen pillow.

'Father, the sheets are too tight.'

'I know.' He pushed the pillow down hard over her face.

He sat with her, a giant of a man, singing lullabies while she thrashed beneath the sheets. He sang softer and pushed harder until Emily ceased moving, until the last heave of her chest subsided. He imagined that last breath of air, so sweet and innocent, and wished he could hold it alive inside himself forever.

Father heard scuttling on the roof and the tinkling of bells. A thud sounded from the living room and Rebekah and Marthe started screaming. The pact now broken, Domovoy had returned to claim his own.

He left Emily's side and reached for his axe.

THE GARDEN OF JAHAL'ADIN

Jahal'Adin the Wise stood outside on the balcony, deep in thought. If it were another time he might enjoy the warmth of this autumn dusk, with the torrid heat of summer now past, and the promise of rain in the coming weeks. The host encircling his castle, now encamped upon his lands, destroyed any pleasure he may have gained from the serenity of the evening.

Fires began to glow throughout the encampment as soldiers readied themselves for the coolness of the desert night. The smell of roasting mutton drifted tantalisingly on the breeze, an otherwise pleasant aroma. *Unless it happens to be your livestock the enemy feasts upon.* Jahal'Adin had been given enough warning of their approach to stockpile most of the harvest and animals within the castle walls. The villagers had set up make-shift tents in the outer courtyards of the castle, and camped there subdued and frightened.

Jalmyro had fallen three weeks earlier as the Xiatian armies marched persistently on the south and the east, conquering all before them. Jalmyro's armies had outnumbered Jahal'Adin's own three to one, and still they had fallen. It was said those that would not yield had been crucified when Jalmyro finally surrendered. Bodies of women and children alike decorated the outer city walls, thrust up on wood, offerings for the cruel Xiatian gods to feed upon.

And finally, inevitably, red banners emblazoned with a golden inner eye staring towards the heavens announced the Xiatian army's arrival.

Jahal'Adin sensed the approach of Master Nehilo and turned to face his chief advisor. Master Nehilo had served Jahal'Adin's father, and with recent events had finally begun to look his age. He could have been a priest wrapped in the white cloaks of council. Despite his age, a mind as sharp as the blue in his eyes kept him in Jahal'Adin's close counsel.

'What are their terms?' Jahal'Adin asked.

'What we expected, *Murlah*,' said the old man. 'We have until midday tomorrow to decide. All those who take their faith will be spared if they remain. Those who don't . . . '

'And my family?'

Nehilo remained silent.

Jahal'Adin laughed bitterly. He considered the host again. Although they outnumbered him two to one, the castle's defensive walls should have given him a four to one advantage, but he would not have the opportunity to outwait the enemy. Jalmyro's walls had crumbled against the enemy's siege weapons within days. Jahal'Adin did not fear death, not his own. It was well known that the Xiatian commanders executed all royal blood, destroying any family line or claim to an old throne. *Could I die with the blood of my people on my soul?* They would die rather than accept the Xiatian faith, of this he was sure. *Did not the walls of Jalmyro stand testament to the beliefs of their race?* It was better to die than to burn in hell under the enemy's spiteful gods.

Before Jalmyro, the capital city, Onkharo, rich in jewels and spice, the bridge from East to West, the Merchant City, had fallen. Reports claimed the city lay in ruins, the dead haunting the alleys and sewers. His nation's people, Jahal'Adin's entire race, were slowly, systematically being eradicated.

Jahal'Adin traced the fine scar tissue running lengthwise up his forearm, stretching from elbow to wrist. A single line, straight and unwavering, a bloodless vein, dead to the touch; a serpent beneath his skin, waiting.

'Meet me in the Great Hall in two hours time. You shall have my decision then, Nehilo.'

Jahal'Adin made his way to a thick wooden door guarded by two sentries. They wore light robes over which oiled ring-mail gleamed by the light of the torches in the hallway, and were armed with sword and spear.

They opened the door for him and he passed through silently, the heavy clunk of the wooden door closing behind him echoing throughout the stone hallway. He made his way down smooth, spiralling narrow steps until he came to a modest stone room that at first appeared to be a place of worship. A small hand-woven prayer mat decorated the floor before one of the walls. Fixed horizontally upon the wall was the Staff of Isha, the length of a man's arm and the thickness of a wrist, encircled with vines carved from the same hardwood as the staff. The symbol of their God Upon Earth, the laying down of arms, forever peace, never to be raised in anger. It was here his people believed he came for inner guidance and spiritual fulfillment.

Then Jahal'Adin committed a sacrilege, a crime punishable by death as ordained by the High Priests. He broke the back of his God, raising arms against the heaven, as he pushed the staff into a vertical position. The wall to his left rumbled aside revealing a small passageway. *Rules were made to be obeyed, but not necessarily by those who made them.*

He stepped through it quickly and the wall closed behind him. He emerged into a small garden surrounded by high, windowless castle walls, a retreat invisible to all except the birds above and the prying yet uncaring eyes of the gods. Thick green foliage grew undisturbed, fed by an underground spring drawn from the nearby river. Plants with thick, hairy, curling fronds sprouting lush green canopies provided shade, and brightly coloured blossoms of red and blue and yellow grew all year round on rich healthy shrubs that filled the air with soft perfumes. Jahal'Adin knew not the names of these plants; none grew outside of this garden and their names had been lost before his father's father was a boy.

Jahal'Adin felt instantly at peace, as the weight of the world lifted briefly from his royal shoulders. He could feel his muscles unknotting, unwinding, the breath in his body, the blood flowing through every particle of his being, the steady beating of his heart, strong, and one with the earth around him.

A soft velvety moss carpeted the ground, and a luxuriant path, clear of root and leaf, led towards an ancient gnarled tree of pale red wood at the centre of the garden. The Bloodwood.

He approached tentatively, worshipfully, his mind unravelling as he became a part of the garden around him. He knelt before the Bloodwood, his arms outstretched, palms placed outwards, gripping its thick gnarled roots, the veins of the tree. Above him, the limbs of the tree hung low with unripened seeds, its fruit yet to flower amongst dull, silvery scale-like leaves.

The scent of blossom became strong and cloying, thickening his senses, lulling, soothing, and the dread built inside his every nerve.

'Blood of old drink blood of new,
For vision bold and vision true.'

A slivery offshoot peeled from each root he held, elongating and sinewy. They coiled serpent-like around his wrists and thrust in, piercing the skin at the base of the long thin scar that ran the length of each of Jahal'Adin's arms, the initial pain hot and fiery, as if burning coals were pressed to his flesh. The skin bulged as the root burrowed its way towards the elbow, and numbness swept over the pain. It began to pulse and the pale red roots at the base of the tree deepened in colour as Jahal'Adin's lifeblood flowed into the Bloodwood.

His head lolled back lazily on his shoulders, his jaw fell slack and his eyes rolled into the back of his head. The roots cradled him against the trunk of the ancient tree and as it drank, Jahal'Adin passed from this world into a dream.

❧

A falcon swooped in and landed gracefully on one of the Bloodwood's branches. It pruned its rich plume of feathers as it studied the garden and its surrounds. The bird plucked out a tail feather upon which a golden eye shone and the wind caught and blew it towards the north. It plucked another and the wind caught that too, but this time pushed it westward. The feathers swirled upwards and onwards and the falcon, satisfied a sign had been sent to its flock, once again returned its concentration towards the garden.

Unbeknown to the falcon, the feather that had blown to the west was caught by a sudden storm and washed out to sea where it eventually grew heavy and sank beneath the waves. The feather that had blown north suffered a similar fate and, caught by a sandstorm, was buried beneath the infinite sands of the desert.

The fruit on the branches had ripened and as the falcon watched, one by one each dropped and disappeared, swallowed hungrily by the thick green moss. Alarmed, the falcon snared one of the last remaining fruits and devoured it, hoping to finish it in time to eat another.

Before it could finish the fruit, the tree shed its leaves and the garden grew cold; the skies above filled with winter's call. The falcon at first seemed worried but stayed on the branch waiting. For was this not a tree? And did not such a tree bear fruit?

So the falcon waited. And waited. And waited.

No more fruit grew, and the still falcon's flock had not yet arrived, and the falcon worried, thinking perhaps its flock would never arrive. It plucked another feather with a golden eye, except now the wind took it southwards. Another was carried off to the east.

The falcon grew thinner and finally in despair it rose to the skies, deserting the garden, heading towards its true home in the far north. But the falcon had left too late and Jahal'Adin saw it perish on its flight home, its bones eventually picked clean by insects, and then buried by the winds and the sand.

◉

Jahal'Adin awoke on his back in the darkness on the moss beneath the Bloodwood. His arms burned and itched, and his wrists were caked in drying blood. He felt weak and exhausted, as if he had not slept for days, although he knew from the position of the moon he had been asleep for not more than two hours. On his chest rested a fruit from the tree, now ripe and fat with juice. He bit into it, the flavour strong and bitter, the texture like raw meat, juice streaming from the corner of his mouth, matting his long spade-like beard. His body became imbued with an inner strength and he looked up, remembering what he'd seen, futilely searching the night sky for a bird's shadow.

Jahal'Adin knew what he must do, and made his way back to the Great Hall to tell his advisors of the decision he had made. They would think him mad.

☙

Sir Pohl Garrick, Lord Commander of the 7th Southron Army, polished his blade as he studied the approaching rider bearing a white flag. The rider was a small, lithe man with long, oiled, black hair worn freely at his shoulders. He looked as if he had been baked a light brown by the sun, like all who lived in this god-forsaken land. The rider wore little armour, his clothing mainly roughspun cotton, and he bore no weapons.

A heathen come to treat.

Sir Pohl hoped the reply from the city of Khalaja would be somewhat different than that delivered by the rulers of the cities that had fallen before. These people were too proud, stubborn to the point of ignorance. A race of unwilling savages, and if history foretold the truth, this would be no different. Their knees would never bend, and their hearts would never open to embrace the one Lord and accept the True Faith. His men had spent the morning cutting down trees in the village, slashing and binding them into shape, crude crosses for crude religions.

If the heathen did not see sense then the bodies of his people would stake this city for the weeks to come. As had those too proud to see sense in the grand cities of Jalmyro, and Onkhara, and Hunza and Sust before them. Women crucified and wailing for their children, thrust up on wooden stakes, blood leaking from bodies burnt and crisp, as flesh slowly cooked, and carrion birds ripped meat from their dying carcasses. The stench of decay and blood and fear. At first he had been sickened by what was required of him, but his devotion to his God fed him strength, and now there was nothing he would not do for the cause.

The rider stopped and planted the flag into the ground and waited. He looked proud, defiant, and ready to die. *And all the better if they are ready to die. It makes it so much easier for them to accept it.*

Sir Pohl signalled and Sir Eldric, a young knight gifted in the languages of the East, rode out to treat with the rider. They talked briefly and a piece of parchment was handed to Sir Eldric, who studied it quickly, before returning to Sir Pohl. The rider remained motionless, awaiting Sir Pohl's reply.

Sir Eldric pulled up and dismounted, a strange smile upon his lips. Sweat was already dripping from the knight's brow, his chainmail and helm serving more as oven than protector in the heat of day. 'This is most strange, my Lord. They are willing to yield us the castle. On one condition and on that condition they must have your word.'

If Sir Pohl was surprised his face showed no outward emotion. *They would yield the city? Do they not realise the strategic position they would hand over?* Although not a coastal city, Khalaja had been founded upon the mighty Kunjerab River, fed from the mountains far to the East. The Kunjerab's mouth kissed the ocean not more than half an hour's sail from the city's port. With Khalaja secure, the kingdom need no longer rely on the Merchant City of Onkhara as its staging area for its southern campaign. Supply lines could be established with the West, reinforcements, weapons, and food, delivered in easier abundance by the tides of the sea.

'And what would that one condition be?'

'That the Golden Eye of the West let them leave the city unharmed. They will leave provisions in the castle and only take what they need to aid them in their travels south.'

'So they can reform and strengthen their allies walls I'd wager. Yet they would give us this rock not realising it hastens their defeat.' Sir Pohl weighed it up carefully and finally, like the sun unfolding in the dawn, he smiled for the first time that morning. 'We will grant them this mercy. They will be allowed to leave the city unharmed.'

Sir Eldric nodded and mounted his charger. 'Very good, my Lord.'

'There is one more matter that needs to be attended however,' said Sir Pohl as the young knight made to return with his commander's reply. 'Jahal'Adin and his heir—I believe he has a trueborn son of ten years—must present themselves. They know of the Xiatian custom regarding bloodlines.'

❧

Within the hour an honour guard on horseback rode towards Sir Pohl's encampment. A man in golden silk robes and pale blue pantaloons rode in the centre of the guard. Encircled upon his head a band of gold sparkled in the dying heat of the afternoon sun, the gemstones embedded in the crown flashing blue and red fire as he rode closer. On a smaller destrier next to him, rode his son, a boy not yet a man. *A man not yet to be.*

Sir Pohl Garrick studied Jahal'Adin the Wise as he approached. A tall, well-built man, his hair long, black and worn in a thick braid that hung halfway down his back, younger than Sir Pohl would have expected for a ruler called The Wise. Was that not a title fit for older men, those who had ruled for decades and prospered peacefully? For sages and librarians? Not this warrior still in his thirties. Although young, Sir Pohl noted, the man's face was hard, his eyes a cold blue and harder still. A long, thin moustache drooped below his chin, as was the fashion of these Easterners. Jahal'Adin showed little emotion as his entourage pulled up next to Sir Pohl and his guards. Unlike the son, whose eyes were red and raw, though to his credit no tears flowed now. Sir Pohl could see the flowerings of the father in the boy, the strong chin, the same long, thin nose.

Jahal'Adin nodded to his honour guard and he and his son dismounted. They were unarmed. The honour guard milled nervously, horses whinnying, until Jahal'Adin bid them farewell. 'When it is over and the people cannot see,' he commanded, 'lead them safely to freedom. This must be done.'

The captain of the honour guard, another strong looking man, this one with a spade-shaped beard, nodded curtly and led the horsemen back to the castle. 'As you command, *Murlah*.'

Jahal'Adin stepped forward and the two leaders stared into each other's eyes, Jahal'Adin's the bright desert blue oasis, Sir Pohl's a deep impenetrable brown.

'Jahal'Adin, well met,' said Sir Pohl. *This man does not fear death even now. His eyes burn with pride. No matter, such a fire shall soon be quenched.*

Jahal'Adin knelt before him, his head bent forth, the neck offered. Sir Pohl could see fine black regrowth where the hair had been shaved clean not too long ago. Sweat shone, glistening on the skin. Goosebumps despite the heat.

'Do not let us wait. Be merciful, be quick. Praise Isha,' said Jahal'Adin.

Tears ran freely down the boy's face.

It took three swings of the blade to sever Jahal'Adin's head from his body. The boy needed only one. The same chin, the same long thin nose, and now the same blood pooling in the desert sands. A feast for the flies over which they once ruled.

'Mount the heads on the side of the road for all who leave the city to see,' said Sir Pohl, before retiring to the shade of his tent to prise the jewels from the crown.

❧

That evening the 7th Southron Army of Xiantia celebrated with spiced mutton, fresh breads, olives, dried fruits and the rich peppery wines left behind in the great desert city of Khalaja.

Sir Pohl Garrick found the royal chamber much to his liking, the carpets and tapestries intricate and colourful, and the bed large and spacious. The only softness it lacked was the flesh of a woman. Perhaps he had been to hasty in letting *all* of the heathens flee.

The castle taken without a drop of blood spilt. *Well almost.* Sir Pohl laughed at that. *Jahal'Adin the Wise. What was it that had earned the man his title? Of course. Had not the man been attributed prophecy? Perhaps he had foreseen his own death.* He laughed again lounging back upon the bed, the cup pressed to his lip. *Jahal'Adin the Foolish.* This would surely earn him high favour in the King's court. The messages had been written and the birds would be released at dawn to convey his triumph home for all to hear. All Sir Pohl had to do was wait for the reinforcements to arrive. This land was already conquered.

❧

As Sir Pohl Garrick slept on a dead man's bed, Jahal'Adin sat with his advisors around a campfire planning their next few months. Riders had already been dispatched to the cities further south and east, and to the Holy City in the eastern mountains that gave birth to the Kunjerab river. Archers had been deployed to the north of Khalaja, instructed to watch for Xiatian outriders, messengers, and birds, especially birds foreign to these lands.

Death was no stranger to a man such as Jahal'Adin. Men had willingly laid down their lives for him before, and it was no different now. It had pained him to see the heads of those who had sacrificed themselves staked upon the road as he had left the city. A ruler, a *Murlah*, had to be strong. Such decisions always were to be made, and to be made quickly.

With their harvest ready for the winter, and with the aid of the monks in the mountain, Jahal'Adin and his people had only to wait for Isha to return to them what was once theirs.

❧

On the third day of their conquest Sir Pohl discovered the altar room. He looked upon the staff on the wall with disdain.

'Shall I remove it, my Lord?' asked Sir Eldric.

'I'm surprised you even asked,' said Sir Pohl, studying the rest of the room. *This room seems sparse even for Eastern standards. Very pious.*

Sir Eldric reached up with a solid hand and pulled hard upon the staff. Nothing happened, and Sir Pohl noticed the knight's neck redden with hot embarrassed blood. Sir Eldric pulled again, and still the staff did not move. Cursing, he grasped the staff with both hands and twisted hard, the staff sliding on its axis, overbalancing the knight so he tumbled forward against the wall. The wall grinding open hid any dignity Sir Eldric may have lost in his attempt to remove the staff. Sir Pohl instinctively drew his sword. Sir Eldric's blade unsheathed a second later.

Sir Pohl motioned Sir Eldric forward, who moved cautiously into the passageway. He inched forward, glancing back and nodding the all clear. As he moved further into the passageway the wall began to close between the two men, and Sir Pohl glimpsed Sir Eldric's concern before the ancient brick shut between them.

If Sir Eldric called out in alarm, Sir Pohl never heard. The walls were thick and soundproof, as deep as they were long. The staff on the wall was again parallel with the earth, and smiling, Sir Pohl turned the staff skyward and the wall rumbled open. Sir Eldric was nowhere to be seen.

So beyond lies the real truth. Sir Pohl followed the passageway slowly, his body one and alive, senses reaching out into the air around him for any possible threat. The paving beneath his feet moved slightly, and the plate beneath the path set the wall rumbling behind him again. He turned and ran back, slipping easily between the closing stone, and into the safety of the altar room. He would need others to help with this task, at least someone to turn the staff when the walls closed again. And others to face what lay behind the walls.

Sir Pohl Garrick returned with three soldiers. As he made to turn the staff, it spun before him of its own accord and the wall slid open. Sir Eldric staggered out, his eyes sunken, cheeks hollow. He looked like he hadn't slept for days. One hand held his sword, dragging the point behind him, the sound slow and piercing as the blade scraped across the stone floor. His other hand was drenched in blood, it had run to his elbows, and now dripped steadily onto the floor. Sir Eldric's gaze found Sir Pohl's, and hung there burning. He flung something red and pulpy towards the staff, and it hit the wall with a sickening squelch, smearing and sliding down to the floor. It looked like a heart, though not of human origin.

'We must leave here,' Sir Eldric choked out before he collapsed into the arms of the nearest soldier. 'I have forseen our death.' His eyes rolled into the back of his head and he spat through foam on his lips, 'The Devil is within these walls!' His body shook and went limp, and the sword clattered onto the stone floor, punctuating his words with an empty clanging echo.

'Take him to the healers and bring more men,' Sir Pohl commanded the soldier who held Sir Eldric in his arms. 'Nyman, I want you to keep turning the staff upwards every time the wall slides shut again. Olliver, you come with me.'

Nyman opened the walls, and Sir Pohl and Olliver moved through quickly, weapons drawn. They emerged into a low green canopy, thick with fronds, the air cool with moisture and laden with perfumes. Sir Pohl felt the anger and tension seep from him, and he lowered his sword before him, his muscles loosening and relaxing. Birdsong could be heard, although none of which he recognised, and the burbling of water and buzzing of insects calmed him. Next to him Olliver apparently felt the same, his sword limp in hand, his mouth awash in a smile.

'It's beautiful,' the soldier whispered. 'An oasis.'

'Be on your guard,' said Sir Pohl, although he wanted to sit and rest in the serenity of the garden, to savour the simple delights of nature, the cool soothing blues and greens, a sharp contrast to the hot harsh browns and yellows of the summer past.

The two men crept through the garden, following the pathway towards an ancient, gnarled tree that dominated the centre, its roots thick and twisting, the branches heavy and strong, reaching up towards the sunlight, which glinted off the silvery leaves. The wood was a deep red and seemed to pulse with life.

As one, both men sheathed their blades, without questioning why.

Though they searched the garden thoroughly, they found no sign of a struggle, and no sign of the body to which the heart Sir Eldric had flung upon the wall belonged.

◉

A week later Sir Pohl stood in a cool chamber within the castle that had been converted into a place of healing.

'Will he recover?' Sir Pohl asked the healer, an elderly man called Tomas.

'His fever grows, my Lord,' replied Tomas. 'His muscle wastes away with every day that passes.' He pulled back the damp bedsheet that covered Sir Eldric's sickly frame. Sir Pohl could see the sinew and bone beneath the skin, stretched pale and taut, the colour of his flesh leeched by the sunlight. Thick, white scar tissue ran the length of his forearms.

'What are these?'

'I know not, my Lord. They appear to be quite old. Perhaps something he gained in his youth?'

He is in his youth. What sickness is this?

Sir Eldric had spent the last week in a fevered state, his sleep haunted and broken, sweat pouring from his skin. No amount of salves and cooling cloths managed to reduce the man's temperature, and his body slowly wasted away, no matter what sustenance they managed to force into him.

'Have you made any sense of his rantings?' Sir Pohl asked, leaning over Sir Eldric, studying the sallowness of the skin on the man's face, the waxy sheen that coated his skull. The knight's hair lay plastered to his skull and lacked all lustre. Sir Pohl fancied he could snap the strands between his fingers; it looked like faded black, brittle straw. *What beast did you find there, Eldric?*

'Only that which you already know, my Lord,' said Tomas. 'The Devil has shown him his own death. That, and the tree, although mostly we cannot understand him.'

'I do not think it was just *his* death he saw,' said Sir Pohl pulling the blanket back over Sir Eldric's palsied frame.

''Tis the Devil!' said Sir Eldric, sitting bolt upright, his skeletal hand grasping Sir Pohl's wrist and squeezing it with the strength of a man damned. Sir Pohl could feel the knight's fingers burning through the sleeves of his tunic. 'Eat not of his flesh!' Sir Eldric's eyes rolled white and his body spasmed, and Sir Pohl grunted in pain. Sir Eldric fell limp, and his body seemed to cave in, the last of his lifeforce sucked dry.

Tomas placed his fingers on Sir Eldric's throat. 'He's dead, my Lord.'

Sir Pohl didn't hear him, he was too busy trying to prise the dead man's fingers from his bleeding wrist.

❧

Towards the end of the second week, three days after Sir Eldric's death, Sir Pohl was interrupted as he pored over his plans. He pushed the maps and scrolls away as Orson Ryberg, a thin man with a thin lip and hooked nose shuffled forward. A man as nervous as he was good with numbers and supplies.

'There is more bad news, my Lord.' Ryberg cringed.

Sir Pohl stared impassively at him. *The faithful cur awaiting the back-hand.* 'And?'

'Most of the provisions left us in the city have spoiled. We have found the carcasses of dogs, cats and other vermin buried amongst the grains, fruits and cured meats. The rot had set in well before we noticed the smell, my Lord. Much of it is unsalvageable.'

'How much do we have left?'

'Less than a month on full rations.'

Sir Pohl dismissed Ryberg with a wave of his hand and stared at the maps spread before him on the table. They could hold for at least two more months, they still had the river and that could be fished. By then supplies and reinforcements would arrive. *Was this Eldric's warning? Eat not of his flesh? Had he foreseen the spoiling of their supplies?*

A dying man's curse would not force him to give up this prize. Sir Pohl wandered over to the balcony and stared out over the desolate city, empty of people and noise and life.

❂

Sir Pohl Garrick began to spend the evenings contemplating in the gardens of Jahal'Adin. There he felt at peace, his thoughts truer and clearer away from the noise and the heat of the rest of the palace. Birds with strange colourful plumage flitted between the branches of the trees, suckling on the nectar of the blossoms that still bloomed. It did not dawn on Sir Pohl that spring had long past this part of the world and autumn had nearly finished.

The air was cooler in the garden, and his mind and body felt constantly renewed and revived after his visits. He had plucked fruit from the ancient tree, and sniffed tentatively at it. The fruit itself seemed dried and with-ered, like large prunes, only coppery to the nose, and salty to the tongue. Needless to say, the fruit was unappealing even though hunger had crept its way into the diet of his garrison. *Such a pity nothing else edible grows in this place. Soon I will have to place the men on half rations.* The tree did not seem so deep in colour as it had when Garrick has first set eyes upon it, but he paid that little attention. Things often changed when seen through accustomed eyes.

Of the beast Sir Eldric had encountered no sign was ever seen. Perhaps it had been the only one of its kind, an unwanted pet, left behind in the exodus from the palace.

Although the temptation to sleep the evenings in the garden was great, Sir Pohl always retired to Jahal'Adin's palatial suite. Something inside him warned against spending a night of slumber under the old tree.

◉

'Is there still no sign of the birds?' Sir Pohl Garrick asked wearily, his features grown gaunt and thin.

Eoman Winton, the Master of Bird, shook his head and pointed towards the empty cages. The last birds had been sent more than three weeks earlier, the first birds almost two months. Eoman, once fat in the face, his jowls hanging loosely now from his cheeks, the meat once contained within burned away through hunger, smiled sadly at his commander.

'If they had made it back to the kingdom, would we have had word by now?' asked Sir Pohl.

Eoman nodded his head weakly, afraid to meet Sir Pohl's eyes.

Sir Pohl wanted to smash his hand across the slack face. Restraint became harder with each passing day. None of his riders had returned from the north either. He had even sent them in numbers for fear of retaliatory attacks, but it seemed even they had failed them.

The food had almost run out; they had been on half rations for two weeks, and the once mighty Kunjerab barely trickled through the drying and cracked mud of the riverbed. The stink of rotting fish assailed the evening air. Men had cramps and sickness from drinking the water. He had sent scouts further up the river in hope of finding the source of its staunch. They had ridden for three days before returning, removing decaying and rotted goat carcasses as they went. Gifts from their former owners no doubt. The river flowed no greater further upstream. As it slowly dried away, so did their strength. If they did not return to the north soon, they would be too weak to make the journey. Things could not be worse than they were now. *What shame shall adorn my shoulders on our return? There will be no gold and honour as my reward. If we make it home.*

Sir Pohl left the Master of Bird, and made his way up to one of the sentry towers. The two sentries stood to attention as Sir Pohl came through the doorway, out onto viewing platform. No doubt they were bored, tired and, most of all, hungry. From here they could see the flat, dusty land stretching far to the east and south, the landscape almost barren except for the now-abandoned city that lay to the east of the castle walls. And the bands of nomads lurking just within their vision, at least a day's ride away.

'Have they come any closer since this morning?' he asked.

'No, my Lord. It appears that they are setting up camp around the southern and eastern peripheries. They should have made the city if they had continued their march.'

Sir Pohl nodded. *They're waiting.* 'And their numbers?'

'Close to your initial estimates, my Lord.'

He could feel the frustration building inside, eating away at his dignity. Sir Pohl wondered if any of his men had realised just who lay encamped in the desert. *They're waiting for us to leave so they can have their city back.* He had been made a fool, and his head would be the price to pay on his return to the north. *And if we don't leave now, there is a good chance all of us will die.*

He made his way down to the chamber they had converted into their war room. Once it feasted royalty and guests, where now the large tables seated his captains; soldiers foreign in blood and tastes.

'We leave the day after next at dawn. Send riders to the largest encampments to tell the Easterners of our intentions. Khalaja is once again theirs.'

The room remained silent, though Sir Pohl could read relief in the faces of his men. He retired to the garden to contemplate his fate. *If I could sew shut the mouths of all in my command, perhaps no-one would hear of this humiliation. The blade awaits my neck as surely as it did Jahal'Adin's. I could desert, although better the blade than the sun my executioner.* And in the serenity of the garden other ideas came to Sir Pohl, unbidden and furtive. *Yet there is still a way to redeem my honour . . .*

👁

Jahal'Adin rode the length of the Xiatian lines searching the retreating soldiers for a face that had intruded upon his dreams over the last few months. Few returned his gaze, and those who did looked back with disinterest and fatigue. Skin stretched tight over jutting bone, skin yellowed not with sun but sickness and hunger, clothing that hung poorly on emaciated frames. *The falcon's feathers have indeed become bedraggled, but where is the falcon?* The face Jahal'Adin sought eluded him.

He rode again to the front of the line, accompanied by a troop of his own soldiers.

'Where is your commander?' he yelled.

A man with thick curling hair the colour of copper, and skin continually burnt red from the sun replied. 'I command now. What concern is it of yours?'

Jahal'Adin recognised the man from their initial encounter, when he had given up two of his own people to appease the Xiatian bloodlust. 'You are not the Great Eye of the West, your armour marks you as a Captain of the Guard. I will ask you again. Where is your commander?'

'As I said, I command now. If you refer to Sir Pohl Garrick, he has given his life to the gods to grant us safe passage home. What is it you want?'

'Nothing,' said Jahal'Adin. *And so the prophecy is fulfilled. The falcon has gone. His feathers lost in the winds.* 'May your gods grant you speed and safety.'

Jahal'Adin the Wise led his people triumphantly back into Khalaja.

👁

The pull on his veins was strong, and he succumbed that evening. Jahal'Adin went to seek solace and comfort in the secret garden. At first he was nervous, fearing the invaders may have desecrated his holy ground beyond all that was considered holy. It was not the Staff of Isha who Jahal'Adin prayed to, but to the Bloodwood, a tree so ancient it was said its roots had grown to the core of the earth itself, and with the core tapped, all knowledge could be gained. It exacted a price of course, but to Jahal'Adin that price was small in exchange for the wisdom he had received during his reign.

Jahal'Adin felt relieved to see the altar room intact. He pushed the Staff upwards, and moved through into the passageway beyond. His arms itched and the white scars that ran from wrist to elbow stood stark and proud against his skin. The *Murlah* entered the garden, an immediate flood of relief sweeping his body and psyche, and went to feed the Tree.

He felt weak and his legs trembled as he neared the Bloodwood. Always the fear, and the anticipation, overriding his senses, and he sank to his knees in the soft green moss. His hands curled around the thick twisted roots and as he did so, he noticed the colour of the wood throbbed a deep red. *Something is wrong.* Slivers of wood, thin and snake-like, coiled from the ground around him, entwining his wrists. The hot stab of pain as the roots of the tree pierced his veins. *The tree has been fed! Someone else is in here.* As the tree began to drink greedily from his body, Jahal'Adin for the first time noticed the oil smeared over the trunk of the tree. The moss glistened, soaked too in the oil from the armoury, and as Jahal'Adin looked down he could see the oil soaking into the silken pantaloons he wore. The first hint of smoke revealed the intruder before he stepped from behind the Tree.

'The falcon,' whispered Jahal'Adin, his body trapped within the root system, too weak to move as the Tree drained his life from him.

Sir Pohl Garrick stood before him, naked, his body slick in oil and the dark red ichor from the fruit of the true. In one red-smeared hand the pulp of the fruit dripped steadily, crushed and half devoured, in the other a flaming torch.

Sir Pohl grinned carnivorously, red flecks of meaty pulp strung between his teeth. His eyes glowed and sweat poured from his face, as if in every action he undertook he fought the tide.

'I know your secrets. I have been shown it all,' he said. 'A man could live forever here.' He threw the pulpy fruit and it splattered against Jahal'Adin's chest. 'You need only eat your own flesh, heathen, to survive. It might have saved poor Eldric had he known.'

'Nooo . . .' Jahal'Adin moaned, fighting the overwhelming blackness as the Tree drank deeper. He could not move while in the clutches of the Bloodwood. Above him a fruit begin to swell and pulse.

Sir Pohl plucked it from its branch and bit into the fruit, and juice poured down his chin, red and sticky. 'You won't be needing this, heathen.'

'Why have you betrayed me?' Jahal'Adin whispered to the Bloodwood.

'I have done nothing of the sort. It is you who has betrayed the world,' said Sir Pohl, mistaking the direction of the question. 'And the Devil's work ends here.' He dropped the torch and the oil burst into flame, engulfing the knight's body, spreading into a lake of fire around the tree. Jahal'Adin's legs caught alight, and the flames licked at his body.

'Why?' he whispered, as the pain screamed through him.

Something long and serpentine uncoiled from the branches high in the Tree and slithered down into the flames. He had never seen it before, it looked carved from wood, though its body twisted and shone in the heat, alive and sinister.

Jahal'Adin could see the knight staggering and screaming and laughing, his body blackened and burning, white teeth bared in anguish and madness. Jahal'Adins's hair ignited, popping and sizzling with his flesh. Through the flames he saw the Golden Age of his people descend into a thousand years of darkness, while the Xiatians flourished, conquering and converting all before them. Steel birds swept the skies spitting fire, and the heavens opened above and rained down hell. And when Xiatians finally ruled all, their faith slowly dissolved until darkness smothered the world, and from the ashes a new lord rose, dark and twisted, ancient and familiar.

'No,' he sputtered, his lips and tongue melting away.

The wind eddied around the garden, fanning the flames into a pyre, and carrying sparks and embers into the surrounding countryside. And as the castle and the city burned, the Tree stood healthy and resplendent, a rich red wood shrouded in a silvery sparkling green veil, growing tall and strong amongst the raging flames.

THE PUNJAB'S GIFT

The scents of cardoman, spice and sugar hang heavy in the air. Strange, misshapen lumps, brown and red and white, some chalky, while others sweat in the dry heat. The square, dense shapes towards the back of the display could be fudge.

The man behind the counter smiles, wiggling his head from side to side, urging us to sample the delights of his wares. His moustache is oiled and his teeth look like they have seen too much of what he has to offer. On the wall behind him, Vishnu smiles benignly, in colours exploding. Eat, he whispers, and the colours swirl.

I glance at Mike, aware the café is silent, all eyes upon us, the ignorant tourists off the beaten track. We can almost hear the shuffle of dirty rupees passing discreetly below tables, behind backs and under hands, as the locals bet on us staying or going.

'*Namaste.*' Mike's finger begins pointing. 'I'll have one of those, some of those, and that one, no, that one.'

The shopkeeper grins. Time resumes inside the café.

I choose whatever Mike hasn't.

We sit at a table towards the rear of the cafe. Its colour is not unlike the food.

'What the hell is this?' Mike sniffs an oily biscuit.

The café is again silent. All bets are back on. Double or nothing.

I bite into something unnaturally red, and sweetness fills my mouth.
Mike's head tilts forward, eyebrows raised, and then he eats his biscuit.

'Is good?' The shopkeeper leans over the counter. I don't think his feet
touch the ground.

'Is good.' Mike grins and finally the café goes about its daily business.

An elderly Sikh, resplendent in white cottons and silk, his turban
adorned with exotic feathers, nods and smiles at us from a far table. His
beard is woven up into his turban. He whispers something to a man at his
table and they laugh.

'Where are you from?' he calls.

'New Zealand.'

Nods of approval; at least here, in the Punjab, our cricketing nation
commands respect.

'Do you like India?'

We nod back enthusiastically, finger to mouth, savouring the sweet
delicacies. Indian heads bob, white teeth in brown faces.

'We're off to Amritsar,' says Mike.

'Oh.' The room falls quiet. The Sikh looks at the others around him. A
heartbeat passes. 'Then to Pakistan?'

'Yes,' says Mike.

'No,' I say too late.

Mike glares at me until he realises. A war is still being fought here and
Amritsar lies in its heart. A border town built on passports and guns,
looking fearfully, contemptuously west.

'Wait here. I have a gift for you.' The Sikh disappears into the haze
outside and conversation returns nervously to the café.

We finish our meals and step outside into the heat. The street teems
with people working, loitering, begging and scamming, the babble loud
and chaotic. Crowds push past, eyes staring and fingers groping. The
heavy smell of spice and unwashed bodies assails us. Two scrawny
donkeys pull an overladen cart of baked dung and the small boy aboard
pauses in his whipping to flash us a grin.

'Wonder what he's getting us?' says Mike.

'Dunno. What time is it? We leave in ten minutes.' Sweat drips from my armpits, trickling coolly down my sides.

'Why would he want to give us something?'

'Perhaps he likes us.'

Time ticks and sweat drips. Flies descend and eat the salt off our skin. I can see the truck from here. The rest of the crew mill around it, ready to board.

'Where the hell is he? We gotta go.'

'What if he wants us to carry something over the border?' Mike's eyes shine. 'What about those stories in the paper?'

'You thrive on that crap. You stoned?'

'I'm serious, man. All those bombings recently. They're not far from here!'

'You're paranoid, Mike.' But the headlines are still fresh. Dozens of them. 'Let's go.'

'Ah, Kiwis!' The Sikh emerges from the crowd, his white silk bright and clean in the sunlight. 'I hope you still here. Here is your gift.'

He hands Mike a plain cardboard box, twice as wide as a shoebox though not as deep. The Sikh's hand stops him from opening it.

'Not now,' he smiles. 'Your truck waits. Go.'

He ushers us forward. Our legs jerk back towards the truck.

I look back and he's standing there surrounded by villagers, all smiling and waving. 'Remember the Punjab!'

Mike shoves me the box. 'Here, you take it.'

'I don't want it.' The box is far too heavy for its size. Something large slides within. Too heavy. *Bus torn to pieces. Twenty dead.*

'What if it's a bomb?' says Mike, our thoughts riding parallel paranoia. His eyes no longer shine; they burn and his face is slick with sweat. He looks sick.

'Don't be stupid, man.' People on the street avoid us. The seas part. Everyone stares. The Sikh has disappeared. I try to hold the box level. No more sliding. Too heavy. I've seen the headlines.

Mike's walking ahead now, his pace faster. Black stubble upon paling face. His shirt sticks to his back. Like mine.

The box is too heavy. Too much noise in my head, though no one is speaking.

'What have you got there, Richard?' One of the girls climbs up into the truck. The street around us is empty.

'Open it!' hisses Mike. He puts the truck between us.

How did I end up holding this? I can't take it on board; I know these people. Just put it down. Leave it. It's just a cardboard box. That's why the street is empty. In India. Where you are never alone.

I think of only one thing. Will I feel it? My eyes brim with sweat and I reach for the lid. I try to prise it off, but it sticks, so I work at it slowly. Time has stopped. I hear nothing for the blood in my ears. I've wandered away from the truck, my back to them, using my body as a shield. I hope Mike has made it far enough away.

I pull off the lid.

Indian fudge.

THE GIFT OF HINDSIGHT

I cleaned my blade with the shirt of one of the dead men.

'Thank you, thank you,' muttered the old man sprawled on the cobble-stones in the alleyway. In the failing light of day, his robes appeared sewn with gold thread—or at least I hoped they were; it was why I had bothered to interfere.

I pulled him up from the stones easily; he wore little meat on his bones. 'I heard your screams, old man, and came to see. It was a measured risk.' I indicated the three bloodied bodies of his assailants, then stared into the old man's inky eyes. 'Very measured . . . '

He studied me, the wrinkles in that furrowed brow deepening. 'Ah,' he said, his eyes suddenly widening. 'Yes, of course.' He fumbled in the folds of his robes and reverently produced an orb the size of a large apple that he cupped in the palms of his gnarled hands.

One of the bodies groaned.

'A reward for the kindness of strangers,' he said, proffering the orb.

A mere bauble; maybe twenty coppers, maybe more if I conned someone. 'I see. The measure of the value of your life.' I regarded the thread in his sleeves. It was indeed gold. 'Thank you.' I took it; the weight felt cold and heavy in my hands. I felt like killing him and taking his robes instead.

'No, no, you misunderstand,' the old man said. 'With this you can change your past.'

'Indeed,' I said. I should have left him to join his mind. In the after-life.

The old man cackled. 'You don't believe me, do you? This is worth so much more than gold. Here, let me show you.'

He moved my hands into position and guided them in circular motions over the orb. 'It uses the heat of your body.' He laughed again. 'Can you feel it?'

I smiled. The orb tingled in my hand, the opacity lightened and tiny figures swirled in the milky pearl, coalescing into what appeared to be a view of this very alleyway. I could see the old man backing slowly away inside the orb as three men appeared from the shadows.

'You can only see what the orb has seen of you,' said the old man. 'You can only change what happens from now on. Use this to your benefit, friend. You can grow rich and powerful if you use this wisely.'

I watched myself enter the alleyway, startling the thieves.

'How do I perform the change?'

'Tell yourself what you should do.' And he laughed, the sound stretched and painful, as if he mimicked those he had heard laughing around him but had never heard the mirth within.

His eyes shone too brightly in the twilight. I saw now that he was truly mad. The orb dulled in my hands, once again white and lustreless. *What trick was this charlatan feeding my mind?*

Something grabbed at my leggings. My sword was out and poised on the hand tugging upon me. Evidently one of the dead had survived.

'No,' the wounded man gurgled. 'Stop . . . you must—'

The old man silenced him with a kick to the head. I relieved the bodies of their purses and left the old man in the alley kicking the wounded man to death. I heard his cackling slowly fading as I retired into the evening and the pleasures the city of Perasha contained.

◉

In the following weeks I soon forgot the old man, and the orb sat locked in a small chest with my other possessions back in my rented room. I busied myself in spending the coin I'd earned escorting caravans, by indulging in women, drink, gambling, and blowing the Black Lotus Perasha was famed for.

It was on such a night my troubles began, though I didn't realise to what magnitude.

I took another swig and signalled for the barmaid to refill my mug. I pushed two sovereigns into the centre of the card table.

'I'm in. I'll take two.'

The man dealing—a swarthy, sweaty dark-skin with a gut like an ox—grinned and flicked me two cards. I slid them into my hand and tried not to smile. Three Royals and the Harlequin. Luck smothered my brow with her kisses this evening. I hoped she continued to favour me, for tomorrow night the Black Pig Tavern was hosting a much richer game. I was just warming up, honing my skills. The guards I'd worked the caravans with had been little sport and with less coin.

Four others besides the dealer sat at the table, and the man to my right threw his cards down, muttering he was out as he exhaled a thick cloud of liquorice-smelling smoke.

'I'll take one,' said Dravid, a lithe man who wore his hair slicked back with the same oil he used to preen his thin moustache. He tossed some coins into the kitty. He had the look of a desert nomad, though I couldn't be sure.

Elyse, the red-headed woman, smiled and took two more cards. She glanced at me from the corner of her eyes and smiled again. *Not about the cards, either.* When I won enough this evening, I'd have her in my bed.

'I hear you have come from the northern province,' said Dravid, studying his cards.

I nodded. More coins were pushed into the middle and we played awhile longer in silence.

'I take it you came with the caravans,' said Dravid. 'From the look of you I'd wager you were a sell-sword.'

'I wouldn't wager too much if I were you,' I replied as we revealed our hands. I swept the kitty towards me as Dravid glared, the Harlequin laughing silently from the deck. 'But be my guest.'

'Fortune is with you tonight,' Elyse said. Her eyes suggested something more pleasurable than cards.

The dealer belched. 'All in?' He shuffled and re-dealt.

As we studied our hands, Dravid said, 'Any trouble on the journey? I hear the raiders have struck hard these past few months.'

I didn't spare him a glance as I gulped a mouthful from the mug that had been set before me. 'You ask a lot of questions.' He looked like a raider.

'Just being friendly.'

The game progressed and Dravid, thankfully, sat sullenly watching his pile of coins dwindle. I won two more hands, called it a night with little protest and in doing so won the third hand: Elyse's. She wrapped her cloak tight and joined me, slipping her arm though mine as we stepped into the murky night.

'Where can I take you?' I asked.

'Depends on whose is closer.' She snuggled into my side as we walked from the tavern.

Perfect. Good beer, good winnings and hopefully a free woman to spend the night in. 'I'm staying at the Vale. It's not far from here.'

Elyse stopped, pulled me to her against the stone walls and kissed me. Her lips were warm and soft, her tongue tasting of the honeyed wine she'd been drinking. I moved my groin into and against her, letting her know my need. She nipped softly at my lips then kissed deeper.

'I hope it's not a long climb to your room,' she said.

'Not at all. I'm on the first floor. I'll carry you.'

She smiled and something tugged my hair back hard, jerking me from her embrace. As I spun I grasped for my blade but Elyse's hands entwined mine, twisting me off balance. The hand in my hair yanked my head down and something cracked into my temples. The world sang blackness.

A blur hovered over me, spouting thick words, fuzzy, not making sense. My eyes skipped in my head and suddenly focused as my ears popped. Dravid leaned over me, his grin dripping vile and loathing. Over his shoulder, Elyse stood cold and scornful.

'Kill him,' she said.

Dravid laughed and thrust ice into my side, a knife for sure but not deep enough to mortally wound. 'No, let the blade do its work. If only we had the time to watch him die.'

His boot caught me in the face and when I came to I was alone.

Blood had congealed under me as I gingerly fingered the ragged lips of flesh above my waist. I prayed he'd missed my kidneys. He hadn't missed my purse or my keys, though. I lurched to my feet and the wound gushed hot over my hand. Fighting the urge to vomit I reeled though the empty streets towards the Vale. The thick oak doors were bolted and few lights burned in the windows. I pounded the door as bile threatened to choke me and the grating sounds of the bolt being pulled brought little relief. The nightman swayed in the doorframe, the whiskey sour on his breath.

'What?' he grunted. I tried to push past him but his stalwart bulk broke me and I fell at his feet. 'Bloody drunks. You staying upstairs, ain't you?'

I managed to nod and his rough hands dragged me in.

'Oh, shit.' His face paled. 'Look at your face. You hurt bad.'

'No, no, I just need it cleaned and bandaged.' As I said it, I knew something was wrong. The wound burned and an incessant tingling spread through my body, itching from within the skin.

'Oh shit oh shit oh shit.' The big man stood staring into nothing. What the hell was he panicking for? He stared at me with a face lost and whispered, 'Your skin.'

'What?' I pulled up a sleeve. Veins bulged, pressed up tight under the skin ready to explode, blue and yellow splotched through blood-red, patchworked flesh around the elbow. I could see it creeping slowly, ever so slowly, down the length of my arm.

The nightman scooped me up in his arms and staggered up the staircase. 'You need rest. I get help.'

I'd seen this poison before. Favoured by the raiders in the desert to the north of Perasha, it would burn through veins and arteries, and I would eventually drown in my own blood. By the morning.

My door stood ajar, and the nightman whirled me into the room and onto the bed.

'Back soon.' He left me lying, dying in the darkness.

How had I been so blind? Too long on the road, I told myself. Too long with the simple company of camels and horses, and quiet caravan guards and invisible caravan masters. Too soon I'd forgotten what I hated about the cities: their confines and treacherous peoples. At least in the desert you knew who was trying to kill you. I swore then and there to any of the gods who'd listen that from now on my time in the cities would be minimal. The country and the road would keep me safe. If I lived through the night.

The urge to scratch, to rip my nails through my itching flesh became intolerable, but I resisted. I'd seen men hasten their own deaths by tearing open their skin and pouring their life into the soil of a world only too keen to soak it up. The cure existed somewhere in the depths of the desert, safe with those who concocted the poison. My friend, the nightman, would find no antidote for me here.

My eyes adjusted to the darkness, and the moonlight from the window cast its glow upon my room. I could make out my pack tossed and emptied upon the floor, drawers opened and turned. The chest was gone. They'd robbed me good.

A soft luminescence emanated from near one side of the bed and as I noticed it, the light seemed to flare. I rolled to the edge of the bed and fresh blood oozed over my hand. Beneath the bed lay the orb, luminescent in the dark. Hadn't I locked it in the chest?

I reached for it and as my hand touched its smooth, cold façade, I thought I felt it stir. *What had the old man done?* I moved my hands slowly over the orb as it warmed, the milky whiteness swirling into a crowded room, smoke and cards.

Tell yourself what you should do . . .

◉

'I'll take one,' said Dravid, a lithe man who wore his hair slicked back with the same oil he used to preen his thin moustache. He tossed some coins into the kitty. He had the look of a desert nomad, though I couldn't be sure.

The red-headed woman, Elyse, smiled and took two more cards. She glanced at me from the corner of her eyes and smiled again. Not about the cards, either.

I didn't study my cards; I didn't need to. And I watched them—Dravid and Elyse—exchanging glances and smiles when they thought I wasn't watching.

I resigned from the table and Elyse joined me as we stepped out into the murky night.

Elyse stopped, pulled me to her against the stone walls and kissed me. Her lips were warm and soft, her tongue tasting of the honeyed wine she'd been drinking. She groped my groin, hoping to induce urgency in case her kiss failed.

'I hope it's not a long climb to your room.' This time I heard the padded footfalls of the desert raider.

'It won't be.' I spun her as I spoke, twisting her legs from below so she fell. Dravid faltered in his attack and my blade severed his head, the surprise frozen on his death mask. As his body dropped, I heaved Elyse to her feet and dragged her back towards the inn and my room. I'd have her either way; she'd earned it.

◉

. . . the world swirled and I was back in my room, the orb heavy and dull within my hands. My eyes felt as if I'd spent the night riding through sand and sleep hung heavy behind the lids. Of Elyse there was no sign. I didn't know if I'd brought her back here. In fact, I didn't know what had happened at all. My hand moved instinctively to my side and found the cotton of my shirt intact. No blood. No wound. No scar. My pack, again full, sat propped in the corner next to the chest and a fat purse spilled coins over the bed.

I laughed aloud. What gift had that old fool bestowed upon me? This was magnificent, this was the start of dreams yet undreamt. I collapsed exhausted onto the bed, and sleep claimed me before my head touched the mattress.

The sound of heavy boots in the courtyard outside tore me from my slumber. I leapt from the bed and peered out the window. Torches bobbed in the half-light of dawn and a woman handed out coins amongst six of the city guard.

'The rapist and murderer is in here,' Elyse said.

She pointed to my window and for an instant our gazes locked, her eyes like that of a hunting hawk, burning through the early morning haze. She sneered and I heard the door downstairs splintering as the guards kicked their way through.

Where to flee? Where indeed?

Could I still use the orb? Would they find me in this room, lost to thought and time, and murder me while I sat gazing into the orb? Footsteps pounded up the stairs and the blades unsheathed sang terror songs. I knew I had little choice.

The orb on the bed glowed softly and my hands were upon it and my bedroom door bounced from the frame as the guards thundered in and . . .

◉

I sat at a table drinking mead and lifted a Harlequin from the two cards dealt while a red-headed woman eyed me surreptitiously. Coin filled my purse and I left alone with my winnings. I clubbed Dravid unconscious as he trailed me and I slipped home.

◉

. . . the world swirled and the orb fell heavy from my hands. I reeled in exhaustion and slumped to the floor to awaken with the sun streaming in across the room.

It felt like I hadn't eaten for a week. Still tired, I dragged myself downstairs, the orb tucked away in an inner pocket of my coat. It was too valuable to leave in the room, far too valuable.

The innkeeper raised his eyebrows and muttered, 'Thought you was dead.'

'What?'

'Just haven't seen you awhile is all. Hard night?'

'You could say that. What do you mean you haven't seen me for a while? I saw you yesterday.'

'Nuh. I ain't seen you for about three days. Must a been a real hard night, eh?'

I laughed and nodded and walked out the door. I wasn't sure what he was insinuating or whether he knew something, but he wasn't getting anything more out of me than my board.

'You owe me three days!' he yelled from the doorway as I headed off to find meat and mead. He was definitely trying to blackmail me, but how did he know what had happened? I hadn't killed anyone, at least not this time. I hadn't done anything. What could he possibly have on me?

I found a place still serving food—it seemed I had slept through into the afternoon, as many of the kitchens were shut and preparing for the evening meals—and began devouring a roast chicken smothered in herbed butter. I couldn't stop grinning as I ate and had to wash away the smile with several mouthfuls of the house brew. There was no way I could lose the games at the Black Pig Tavern tonight. I'd play it through, win or lose and then go home and use the orb to win a fortune. The stakes tonight would make last night's winnings the tip I threw the barmaid.

Eager to get a place at a table, I decided to make my way to the Black Pig early. The place was empty. I ordered a spicy pimento ale and sat at one of the tables to wait for the other punters. After an hour a few patrons shuffled in and made their way to the bar and stayed there. By my reckoning the games should have been starting soon, but no-one was here. There weren't two Black Pigs in Perasha, were there?

'Hey,' I asked the barman. 'When are you expecting everyone?'

He shrugged. 'Gets a bit livelier when the sun goes down. Usually a quiet night tonight.'

'What? A quiet night?'

'That's what I said.'

'What about the card games? It's all over town that they're at the Black Pig tonight. Have they been cancelled?'

The barman snorted. 'Afraid you missed that, son. Some desert lad cleaned up the big one a couple of nights ago. Weaselly-looking fellow, shiny hair and moustache. Reckon he cleared a couple of thousand gold pieces, most of it in paper chits, mind. Couldn't carry all that . . . '

I leaned over the bar and grabbed the man by the throat. 'What do you mean "a couple of nights ago"? If you're—'

A blade at my throat. 'Let go, son. We don't want no trouble here. Now get out.'

I left confused, the sting of steel still on the skin of my throat. I found myself back at the Vale and the innkeeper demanding three days board. Reluctantly I paid him and retired to my room. I'd missed the Black Pig games.

And three days of my life.

Dejected and worried, I smoked Black Lotus to pass into a fitful, broken sleep.

In the morning I awoke calm and refreshed. It was too easy. All I had to do was use the orb to go back and make sure I made it to the Black Pig. My hands hovered and tingled and then I was inside, moving back over my actions, Elyse, a card game, Dravid, an alley with an old man then nothing. Then blurring forward, the Vale looming up in time and blackness.

The orb sat heavy in my hands. Fatigue crept into the room and sat with me. Determinedly, I induced the orb and moved back and forth within the time I had spent that evening playing cards, but I never managed to see the dawn of that following morning. It ended before I entered the inn, a sudden nothingness swooping in and spitting me back into my room. I really had lost the three days. And I assumed I'd just lost a few more trying to find them.

When I next woke, I dived straight in. I decided to maximise the time I'd lost and take as much gold as possible from the card game. I was stabbed twice, robbed at least a dozen times on my way home, killed Dravid and Elyse and a few of the other players several times over before I realised I could only ever make two hundred gold pieces. Once more upon my return, I slipped into the slumber of the dead.

The sound of splintering wood tore me from dreams of where sun-spotted skin shrivelled on bone. I shot out of the bed, the dagger from underneath my pillow in my hand.

The innkeeper stood confused between two thickset heavies in the doorway, one of whom brandished a dull-looking axe.

'Why didn't you just bloody knock?'

'Why didn't you just bloody answer?' The innkeeper's face purpled. 'Thought you were dead, you damn fool!'

I pulled on some clothes. 'Haven't you got a master key? Just unlock the damned thing.'

Rough hands grabbed me and thrust me up against the wall. One of the hands, as big as my face, ground my head into the wall.

'Don't fuck with me, boy,' the innkeeper growled from the back of the room. 'It's been four days since you last paid me. I dunno what you're playing at or where you go or how you locked the door from me.'

The hand ground some more. I tried to pull it from my face and one of them smashed me in the stomach. The hand cracked my head against the wall for good measure then let me drop. I collapsed onto the floor, curling my knees up to my chest as the first boot connected.

Coins clinked on the bed, gold on gold.

'This is for the board, this is for damage to the door, and this is for changing the lock on the room.'

I managed to spit out, 'I haven't changed the—' before the boot advised me to keep quiet.

'I want you out in an hour. Your kind ain't wanted here.'

This time I anticipated the incoming boot and caught it before it struck.

'You're dead,' I snarled into the brutish face sneering down at me. He laughed and the second heavy, who I couldn't see, punched me in the head.

'Magician,' one of them hissed as they left the room.

I struggled into a sitting position, wiping blood from my nose on the sheet dangling from the bed. What the hell were they talking about? Magician? There were no magicians these days. Not this far south. I crawled to where the door lay in pieces and pushed my key into the lock. It turned easily. What in hell was the innkeeper talking about? My eyes were drawn to the orb where it had fallen to the floor.

I washed the blood from my face and in the grime of the steel mirror I noticed lines on my forehead and tiny crow's feet at the corner of my eyes. A lack of sleep, I thought. Hastily I collected my things—the bastard had taken almost a third of my coin, ten times what he should've—and limped out.

I decided to leave Perasha and signed onto a spice caravan heading west in the morning. I laid awake with the orb that night, terrified, resisting the urge to go back to the Vale to murder the innkeeper. What in the seven hells had happened to me?

☽

One month later we arrived in the seaport city of Teranui to find we were the third caravan to arrive carrying the same spices.

'But this is less than I paid for it,' argued the caravan master.

'We can take these silks off your hands,' said the representative from the Merchant Guild. He ran his fingers across the textile rolls. 'You've come from Perasha, yes? Now if you'd brought Black Lotus . . . '

'And risk being caught?'

The representative shook his head sadly. 'How slow word spreads to the backwaters. Why, only a week or two ago it was legalised here. The port here is most lucrative at present.'

'How could we have known?' argued the caravan master. 'We have been on the road for almost a month!'

The representative dipped his hand into a barrel of red spice and watched it fall between his fingers to be caught upon the soft breeze drifting away through the docks. 'This, I'm afraid, is almost worthless. You've come too late and we've already plenty. Of course, if you *have* to sell it, then by all means we can come to some arrangement.' He laughed softly and walked off.

Dissent spread like lice amongst the caravan. There would be no bonuses but I didn't care. I took my pay and found the nearest inn, shaking with excitement. I paid for a room with enough gold for a month upfront and left orders not to be disturbed.

Sitting at the small table in the corner, I studied the orb once more, my fingers stroking the warm surface as my body tingled and I was moving over the desert, the caravan a backwards blur and I was back in Perasha with a bruised and bloodied face looking to sign on for work.

It took a score of failed attempts. I fought off sleep, eager not to lose any more time than I had to, and entered the orb again and again until I managed to succeed. The path I took was not the most honourable, but as I soon found out, the path to wealth and power never was. Inevitably I had to murder the caravan master on the journey west; it seemed to be the only way the Black Lotus made it to Teranui.

And the more I slipped into the orb, the easier murder became. My life didn't seem real and neither did those around me. What did I care for them? I had absolute power over fate as long as I didn't get killed in the process. I took what I wanted and who I wanted as the world became mine to control.

◉

I reached up for the sun, sprouting branches and leaves, but before I could blossom, I withered, the sap sucked from my bark. I dug deeper, searching for water, pushing roots through parched soil. An axe bit deep into my trunk and dried blood powdered onto the land. And the land shook . . .

. . . me gently awake. My eyes peeled open, thick with crusted sleep, the dream of decay still etched in my mind.

'Sire. It has been two days.' Agota stepped back quickly from the bed. She hadn't been able to successfully disguise the look on her face.

I struggled from the bed still clutching the orb, the ache in my bones worse than before. 'Two days?'

'Yes, sire.' Agota reached forward to help me stand, remembered my orders, and resumed her standing position.

'I can't afford to lose more than one day.' She removed my bedclothes and began to dress my sagging, wrinkled frame in ceremonial robes. 'Why did you let me sleep?' I had suspected she had been letting me sleep longer than I could allow myself.

She said nothing, her lithe fingers weaving together my buttons. Her smooth, young fingers, free of swollen knuckles and splotched skin. Agota reached for the sash to tie around my waist.

'I asked you a question. I am still king and you will answer me.' Once, only a year ago, I could have summoned anger into my demands. Now it rasped from my wheezing throat.

As Agota adjusted the crown on my pate, she spoke evenly and quietly. 'The orb costs you too much with every waking.'

'I have no choice. The kingdom needs me.'

She said something I couldn't hear.

'What? Look at me when you speak.' I didn't need to say my hearing was failing.

Agota's slender frame suddenly shook. She looked up at me, her eyes red and watering. 'Look at me. Why don't you look at me instead?'

What the hell was she going on about? I paid her well, and had even let her share my bed when I was able. Once I would have killed her for such an outburst, but now I simply cupped her chin in my palms. Her face, the skin soft, hot and alive, shuddered with my touch.

'You are beautiful, Agota. You are young. You serve me well and will not go wanting. What is wrong?'

'This life! This prison I live in, watching you obsess with that cursed orb! Day after day I sit by your side counting time. Trapped in this room until I awaken you and the orb's bonds are broken. Watching you visibly age every time I rouse you early from its imposed slumber.' She yanked her head from my hands, pointing to the corners of her eyes and mouth. 'And now look what it's doing to me!'

Crow's feet crept delicately through her skin, the lines so fine I'd missed them in the curtained light of my bedchamber. The orb had begun to steal from Agota as well. I felt a surge of hope. Perhaps the orb's power could be sustained on her youth, instead of the little life left in me.

She composed herself. 'You will be dead soon, sire. The orb knows this. You must stop using it.'

Agota helped me to the doors and we passed through them into the hallway leading to the throne room. I shuffled past massive paintings mounted on the walls; of battle and glory, of monarchs and their families, of ancient cities and landscapes blessed by even older gods. I shuffled past things I would never see, the lands of my kingdom I would never walk in. Shuffling to a cold, hard seat to listen to a dozen advisors and petitioners, only to shuffle back to my room and wait until enough time had passed before I could use the orb to explore the right decisions to make. How could I stop using the orb? My kingdom would disintegrate. I needed the orb to keep it together, to keep me in power. To keep me alive.

As Agota led me to the throne, she whispered, 'The Ageing King will be no more and the kingdom will fall once more to war.'

I sat there, the frail beat of my heart shuddering in my skull, listening to the last wheezes of air escape my lungs, as men I didn't know advised me of things I could never fully understand, while others requested audiences and alliances where I could never count the cost until it had come to pass.

And at the end of the day, like every other, Agota led me back to my room. I sat at the table, my hands paused over the orb. What if, on my return, the orb had stolen my last breath and I found myself trapped inside a cooling corpse?

But then, I was already as good as dead, wasn't I?

◉

I know how to end this madness. I know how to finish it before it even begins. My wrinkled hands stroke the orb once more, its tingling feeding on my flesh, the remains of my soul.

And once more I'm inside this curved, sometimes opaque, now swirling prison.

I step from the light and music and smoke of the tavern, out into the cobbled streets of a twilight Perasha, my thirst from the desert now sated and my purse full of coin. This time the scream doesn't startle me though I still creep to the mouth of the alleyway. I need to make sure and I don't want to interrupt them.

It was as it was that night, a lifetime ago. My lifetime. Three men menace an old man dressed in robes sewn with gold thread. One of the assailants shoves the old man to the ground and he squawks as he hits the cobblestones.

'No,' the old man pleads and then his eyes light upon me. He grins as if he has been expecting me.

I wonder if the old man is me. He could be, but if he isn't, I care not. He can keep the cursed orb and its vision of second seeing. I'll keep everything I have lost since.

I ignore his screams and walk on by into the rest of my life.

SHOT IN LORALAI

The news preaches terror and the world is closing its borders. Hatred and mistrust printed across dark skin and long beards, tattooed in blond hair and blue eyes. For me it was a Western ignorance buried deep in the fear of a different skin, a foreign culture. For them? I can only guess. I thought envy, I thought fear, I thought awe. If you look back further than my life, that misnamed thing masqueraded as a battle fought with religious steel. And if you open your eyes and ears we're told it does once again. When wars are best viewed on digital wide-screen it's hard to believe Hollywood does not have a guiding hand.

The photos in my hand show a version of the truth from the spring of 1998, after the thaws, before the heat cooked the earth again. See this one? With the woman dressed in *purdah* pointing an automatic handgun at the tall, white man with the short brown hair. See the liquid eyes of the dark man with the moustache, muscled and sweating in the background? See how they shine? He wants to kill the white man whose name is Simon. I travelled with Simon for a while.

And this photo here? You can still see the handgun in the corner pointed at Simon's head. He's half-sprawled on a stretcher, trying to prise the dark man's hand from his throat while his other arm pushes up against the wrist bearing down on him with a thick steel blade. Why doesn't the woman just shoot him?

And what am I doing while this is happening? I'm standing watching. Someone else took this photo. Could I have helped? Perhaps, but I wasn't big enough and the dark man was a Pakistani policeman.

Yes, there is truth here, in these photographs, but what is that truth when you are shown what people want you to see? Here is part of that truth.

❧

Dusk settled upon the desert as our truck pulled into Loralai—a seedy, frontier village choked with dirt and grimy used-car parts that littered the roadside through Pakistan. The narrow street flooded with dark shapes and white, peering eyes.

The *shalwar qamiz*-clad crowd surged towards us—our welcoming committee. Few white men stopped overnight here, even fewer white women. They liked white women, we knew, and our truck carried fourteen of them. One of the younger girls, Steph, shuddered as she peered out the window. She'd been molested in her hotel room the night before when we had stopped over in Dera Ghazi Khan—a dirty, cluttered city banking the Indus River. The hotel we stayed in had been the most expensive in town, but in this part of the world, money does not mean safety, though sometimes it buys it for a while. There had been blood on the walls of my room but the bed had been free of lice. I had slept well.

Tonight we had arranged to make camp in the police compound near the outskirts of town. Apparently we would be safer there, but we all knew if anyone would fuck you over in these countries, it would be the police. The compound looked like cheap army barracks made from wonky, lilted prefabs.

A few lightbulbs strung up on poles cast a dim light, and we were directed to a large enough area to park the truck and pitch our tents.

'Okay, girls,' Chris the driver said, bringing the truck to a stop. 'Time to put on the robes. You know the drill. Just because we're with the cops doesn't mean we won't have a repeat of last night. The repercussions will be a lot harder on the offender if they try anything within the compound. You should be safe. Just follow the rules and obey the customs.'

The women muttered and mumbled as they pulled on their *chadors*; tempers frayed with restrictions, continual groping hands and probing eyes. I watched with male amusement, immune to their complaints. They'd been bitching amongst themselves for the last two weeks about the conditions and it was only going to get worse. What did they expect from a tour of the Middle East? Greenie feminists, political correctness, beer and kebabs?

'One last thing, and I shouldn't need to say this.' Chris leafed through his guidebook. 'No booze or drugs tonight. It's too risky.'

Bill slumped in his seat. A small, scrawny man who looked a little like Willie Nelson, he had left the mines in Western Australia, shouldering a twenty-year-old alcohol addiction in search of greener pastures. 'Ah, Christ,' he moaned. 'Not that it matters. That Paki whiskey is killing me.'

Although a seasoned alcoholic, Bill's liver preferred a constant soaking of five percent alcohol. He'd stood silent as we gave away the Indian-brewed beer at the Indian/Pakistani border. Not that he could drink that either—it made you sick before the alcohol entered the bloodstream. Probably why he'd been silent. If it had been San Miguel, he would have attempted smuggling it across the border. The whiskey he'd purchased since in Peshawar, a smuggler's paradise of a city, *was* most likely killing him—if it didn't make him go blind first. We all knew he was struggling with his newfound sobriety.

As the women disembarked, police numbers swelled, emerging from the shadows. But unlike the villagers the night before, they kept a respectful distance. A sergeant moved amongst them, waving his arms and talking quickly in a tribal language. Most of them soon moved back to their huts, leaving us to pitch our tents in relative peace.

Being last off the truck left Steve and I with a rough, uneven patch of rock near the toilet block to stake our tent claim. The smell of shit and urine wafted over the dry, stale, evening air. After struggling in the dark to find a softish, somewhat level area to lay out the tent, Steve stood up quickly.

'Gotta take a dump,' he said, and walked carefully and slowly to the darkened toilets. I heard him take a large breath of comparatively fresh air before he entered. No lights came on.

I struggled with hammering the tent pegs into the ground and fixed the poles upright inside the tent before Steve returned.

'Jesus fucking Christ,' he gagged, 'those are the worst so far!' His face shone with sweat in the dim light.

'You hungry?' I pointed toward the truck, where the group on cooking duty was unfolding the tables and attaching the gas bottles.

'Nah, but I gotta get away from this area. It stinks too bad.'

The sergeant stood in discussion with Chris as we approached the truck.

'I don't know, mate. It's not up to me,' Chris said.

'But you must,' the sergeant implored. 'Please. It would be great honour.'

'What's going on?' I asked.

The sergeant turned to us and grinned, his teeth white beneath his black moustache. 'You are come dinner at my house. All of you.'

'Hold on.' Chris rolled his eyes at us.

'Is ten minutes walk from here. Very close.'

The sergeant was almost six foot—tall for a Pakistani—and his uniform appeared packed with muscle. I was pretty sure he could beat the shit out of any one of us, if he chose to. Or perhaps just open up with the Kalashnikov dangling from his shoulder. His eyes oiled over the two women pulling out the food baskets.

'Please. Is Muslim custom. I must offer you.'

I watched Karen remove potatoes and cauliflower and put them on the table. Nothing else came out of the baskets. Alicia reluctantly began to chop. It looked like another minimalist effort.

'I'd be keen,' said Steve. 'Let's do it.'

Chris scowled for a second and then called us all over and explained what was on offer. Nine accepted; five guys and four girls—less than half of the tour. Steph, wisely, had decided not to join us, and took over cooking duties from Karen and Alicia.

'Just remember. You'll be outside the compound. Be careful.' Chris climbed back up into the cab of the truck and lit a cigarette.

'You're not coming?' I asked.

'Not fucking likely.' He pushed The Chemical Brothers into the cassette deck. And then in hushed tones under the beats, 'Watch yourself, eh? These guys are corrupt as hell.'

And so I found myself wandering up a road in the dark with a bunch of Kiwis, Aussies, Poms and a Yank, accompanied by several Pakistani policemen and students.

We had women. They had guns.

☮

We introduced ourselves to two young, non-uniformed men, who had attached themselves to our group as we walked towards the house of our honourable host: Officer Mirza Khan.

'I am Rashid,' one said, trying not to look too much at Alicia, who walked between Steve and I. He sprouted a thin moustache and looked to be in his late teens.

The wiry fellow next to him spoke up, his eyes skimming over Alicia before settling on me. 'I am Omair.' He too sprouted a thin moustache, and was of a similar age to Rashid. He glanced once more at Alicia, and then looked ahead.

I smiled at Alicia. Even though she wore her *chador*, dressed in *purdah*, there was no mistaking the mountains her breasts made. She nodded and gave me the 'what-can-I-do-about-it-look'. She knew. Blonde with big tits. Thank God she was sensible enough to follow custom. At nineteen, Alicia was the youngest on the tour, but she handled this part of the world a hell of a lot better than the rest of the women.

'I am a student here,' said Rashid. 'I am study English, Drama and Political Science. I am wanting to be a romantic actor.'

'I too study,' said Omair. 'The same things. However, I will be wanting to be an emotional actor.'

'Right,' I said. What the hell were they studying in a Loralai police compound?

98

I'd already met a lot of young men who were studying English and Political Science, but not too many actors. How to act like a Hard Cop? A Hard, Romantic, Emotional Cop?

'Which actors do you like?'

'Leonardo Di Caprio.' They beamed.

Steve laughed and Alicia elbowed him in the side.

'What about Pakistani actors?' she asked.

'You would not know the Pakistani actors.' Rashid shook his head sadly. 'Pakistan does not make many movies. The government does not approve. We are thinking of going to India. They make many movies.'

'Yes. Bollywood,' grinned Omair.

At that moment, I'd swear the road lit up from the sparkle in their eyes.

There are three questions you will be asked when travelling through Pakistan. The first question is, 'Where you from?' And now, feeling a degree of comfort between us, they asked the second question.

'Have you got any alcohol?' Rashid said quietly.

'No,' we lied in unison.

The sparkles died and we walked in relative silence until we arrived at Mirza Khan's abode.

❧

As custom required, the girls were taken into the interior of the house to be with the women and children, and we were led into the Muslim equivalent of the entertaining room. Wall hangings draped the white, earthen walls, and tribal rugs and cushions adorned the floor. A big-screen television, with accompanying video recorder, sat displayed on a cheap shelving unit against the middle of one wall. A small cassette recorder sat meekly next to the television.

'Welcome,' said Mirza, his mouth a wide grin. 'Make comfortable.' He indicated the cushions and then pointed at the television. 'Home theatre.' He glanced at the other tribesmen and then said to us, 'Back soon.'

We sat down on the cushions, five tourists, two policeman and two students, eyeing each other nervously. Steve began picking at the rug he sat on, lifting the corner, examining the tightness and number of knots.

'Very good,' he said.

They nodded and grinned.

'This is the real thing, mate. No tourist shit here.' Steve picked up a cushion, studying the weave and pattern. 'How much?'

Rashid laughed. 'We pay maybe five dollars US. Tourist, maybe ten, fifteen. Depends.'

Brief silence.

'Well,' said Bill. He lounged back, stroking his beard. 'You guys got any hash?'

My stomach lurched. Steve dropped the cushion. Jeff, Simon and I stared at each other in horror. Passports confiscated. Money drained. Big, blunt cleavers, chopping off hands. Fucked up the arse by sweaty soldiers in the shit-reeking toilets of the Loralai compound.

Rashid glanced at the two remaining policemen. 'Do you want some?'

'No,' said Simon.

Bill looked at Simon disinterestedly. 'Yeah,' he said to Rashid. 'If you've got some. I heard you guys got pretty good stuff.'

'Is very good,' said Rashid. He flicked his hand and a policeman stood and left the room. 'Some of the best.'

'Bill,' Steve warned.

'Is okay,' Omair said. 'We are allowed not much, but this is . . . gift of Allah.'

Bill laughed. 'What about alcohol? You got any of that?'

'No,' said Rashid.

'We hope you have some,' said Omair. 'Perhaps whiskey?'

'Nah,' said Bill, making himself comfortable on the rug. 'You got any beer?'

'Not much beer in Pakistan. Can get Indian beer maybe. You want I get?'

Bill shook his head and began to talk about the beer in India, the beer in Nepal, Australian beer, pubs, beer in pubs. And drugs. The Pakistanis crept closer, fascinated by this weathered, hairy little man, who spoke of things banned in their country.

'This could be bad,' whispered Steve.

'No kidding,' Simon replied, his six-foot-three frame coiled and ready to spring.

Jeff and I sat in stunned silence, listening to Bill's tales, waiting for God knew what to happen next.

Mirza came back into the room with the policeman who had left. Mirza had changed from his police uniform into a dark blue, *shalwar qamiz*. They both carried large serving trays that contained bowls of *dhal bhat* and unleavened breads. They placed them on the floor and we huddled around, dipping the bread into the thick, spicy soup. Mirza did not eat with us. He stood apart, smiling, resplendent in traditional dress, his eyes continually flicking between the door and his guests.

I couldn't tell if he was happy or nervous. At least the hashish request had been politely ignored. What the hell was Bill thinking, asking the cops for drugs? I mopped up another mouthful of soup.

'Is good?' Mirza asked.

We nodded.

'Good!' Mirza's smile widened. 'I bring mutton curry next. And hashish.'

Simon spluttered into his bowl, and Bill yelled 'Yeah!' through a mouthful of bread.

'How come Mirza doesn't eat with us?' Steve asked, oblivious to what had just been said. He wiped up his second serving of *dhal bhat* with a pita.

'He will not eat until guests finished,' said Rashid.

'Oh,' Steve said, his initial onslaught on the meal slowing guiltily. 'I see.'

He put the bread in his hand back on the tray. Omair tore a chunk off and dipped it into his bowl.

'There is more. He is Mirza Khan. Don't worry.'

'Be 'appy.' A policeman laughed, soup dripping from his chin.

Steve looked quizzically at me. I knew what he was thinking. I was asking it myself. Just who was Mirza Khan? And how high up the ranks was he?

Mirza returned with a tray, carrying a huge bowl of curry and a mound of steamed rice, and placed it on the floor in front of us. As we dug in, Mirza sat down and produced what appeared to be a large braid of liquorice from the folds of his *shalwar qamiz*. He sliced off a chunk and briefly held a lighter to it. Satisfied it was heated enough to crumble easily, Mirza mixed it with tobacco and rolled a fat spliff. He passed it to Bill and gave him the lighter.

'Thanks, mate.' Bill pulled a bit of goat gristle from between his teeth. 'Smells good.'

The room fell quiet, and I noticed all eyes in dark skin were staring intently at Bill. So were the eyes in white skins. I could have walked over and left the room. No one would have noticed. Walked back to the compound. Fucked off out of there.

And with a flick of the lighter, Bill pulled us across the threshold, whether we wanted to or not. He dragged deep and exhaled. Mirza grinned slyly, and Omair nodded to Rashid.

Bill dragged again, smoke curling from the end of the spliff. 'It's fucking good gear.' He passed it to Mirza, who declined. Rashid and Omair also refused. We started to get a very bad feeling. Even Bill's eternal optimism seemed to waver. 'What? You . . . you don't want any?'

Mirza shook his head.

Bill tried to palm the joint off to Steve—easy, swayable Steve. He didn't want a bar of it. Bill tried Simon. I don't know why, I guess he was nervous. Simon hadn't smoked a joint on the whole trip. We suspected him of being a Christian, we'd even accused him, but he denied it. Naturally, he refused the spliff.

'What's wrong?' The smile leaked from Mirza's mouth. 'Is good hash, yes? Is best.'

'It's good, alright.' Bill leaned back, somewhat pale. 'Looks like nobody wants it.'

'Why aren't you having some, Mirza? Rashid?' I asked.

'You my guests. I cannot. You must go first,' said Mirza, visibly stressed.

'Like the food,' Steve said, understanding dawning. 'Here, giz a go, Bill.'

Steve sucked greedily and passed it me. I took a tentative drag, worried the tobacco would rip my throat, but found it pleasantly smooth. I took a deeper toke, inhaling the spicy aroma and passed it on to Jeff. He took a small hit and then the Pakistani boys devoured the rest of it. All except Mirza, who sat nodding and smiling and watching. Bill was right. It was good. Fucking good.

Too good.

My tongue felt thick and heavy inside my cheeks and the corners of my eyes, along with my temples, buzzed comfortably. I was a little too stoned to talk. Bill lay on his back grinning at the ceiling, his conversation rambled to a stop. Mirza left the room with the empty trays. Luckily, reliable Simon had taken up the reins and had thanked our hosts for the dinner, discussed physiotherapy and had begun edging around the fundamental differences between the Bible and the Koran.

'Safe topics for dining conversation, eh?' I whispered to Jeff, who had been silent and immovable since we arrived. He sat staring at the floor. I wondered if the metal plate in his head—he'd had his head caved in when boxing at university—combined with the strong hash, was fucking him up. I elbowed him. 'Jeff?'

'Yeah, sports and sex,' he drawled in his Mississippi accent. 'Stick to sports and sex.'

'What was that?' Rashid said, staring at me. He was frowning. 'Who said that?'

'What? Sports and sex?' said Jeff.

'Ah!' Rashid declared, as if he'd caught his best friend sleeping with his mother.

In a flurry of knees and robes, Jeff and I were surrounded by the two students and the policemen. They almost sat on top of us.

'You!' said Omair, his face now dark with blood.

'Him!' Rashid glared at me, jabbing his finger at Jeff.

'What?' I asked nervously. 'What's wrong?'

'He,' Rashid's finger jabbed again. 'He speaks like Bill Clinton.'

'He has the same voice,' accused Omair.

'What . . . what the . . . ?' Jeff whispered to me.

Rashid glared at me once more, as if I were the one who led his best friend between his mother's thighs. He turned to Jeff and spoke in measured tones. The voice of a man who had waited years for the opportunity to interrogate the Infidels. The dreaded third question.

'What do you think of American Foreign Policy toward Pakistan?'

'Oh, shit,' Jeff moaned. 'Mississippi borders Arkansas. Same fucking, Southern accent.'

'What . . . do . . . you . . . think . . . of . . . American . . . Foreign . . . Policy . . . toward Pakistan?'

Rashid's finger hovered in front of Jeff's face, stabbing every word.

Jeff retreated from the finger, his eyes red and pleading for help. 'What?'

'We don't know anything about it,' I cut in. 'We don't see much about your country at all.'

Their heads swivelled, a look of incredulity briefly rising over the anger. 'You don't know?' Rashid said. 'You don't know what they have done?'

'About all we get is cricket, mate,' I placated.

'He knows,' spat Omair, his gaze directed back at Jeff. 'He is American.'

'Omair!' Mirza stood in the doorway glaring at the students. He barked something sharp in dialect and they backed away from us, eyes downcast.

Once more, the smile spread across his face and he waved a video-cassette in front of us. 'Movie! You like to watch?'

And just like that, the mood lightened, the impending conflict—we hoped—forgotten.

We all nodded, relieved, keen to distance ourselves from foreign policies. I was also interested to see what was on offer at the local video shop out here on the edge of the Baluchistan desert. What was a Pakistani movie director allowed to film?

Bollywood-style musicals, perhaps?

'This just started in movie theatre in Lahore.' Mirza grinned. 'And I have copy already!'

The tape started, grainy, lots of hiss. Suddenly the score wobbled distortedly out the speakers, and the opening credits flickered onto the screen.

Rashid and Omair both cooed and clapped their hands.

'I love this movie,' said Rashid. 'Have you saw it?'

'Yeah, I've seen it,' I replied.

'Isn't he wonderful?' said Rashid. 'I am wanting to be an actor like him.'

'And me,' said Omair. The sparkles were back. With brief attempts at political and religious discussions over, the sporting achievements in cricket acknowledged and the hints of sex with western woman cleverly by-passed, we moved into the greatest unifier of our times—the television. Mirza rolled another huge joint but did not partake. We laid back and watched the latest, pirated movie to hit the sub-continent: James Cameron's 'Titanic', starring everyone's favourite cunt: Leonardo Di Caprio.

❧

I staggered out of the tent toward the toilet block, as the crew was packing up breakfast and loading the truck. The rich stench of shit assailed my senses and I decided I'd break my bladder on the first piss-stop of the morning's journey. I didn't want to face my imagination in those damp, dark toilets. Instead, I packed up the tent.

Karen gave me a dirty look as I passed up my tent to be stacked on top of the truck. She was still pissed with us guys taking drugs the night before. They'd been offered but had refused.

'You're supposed to be representatives of the tour! What sort of example are you setting for these people about us?'

I reckoned she was bitter because we'd gotten into it and they hadn't.

Mirza whipped past in his uniform, clapping hands, smiling. 'Salaam Aliehkum. Good morning, good morning. See you soon.' And then he was gone.

We climbed onto the truck and I took a seat next to Steve. As we pulled out of the compound, flanked by white-toothed smiles and waving, dark-skinned hands, I asked Steve if Chris knew what had happened last night.

'Yeah, the girls spilled their guts. He didn't care.'

I nodded. 'Cool.'

'Yeah, that Mirza's one crazy bastard. He's invited us out to his mother's place for a Muslim breakfast.'

'Eh?'

'Some place about five kilometres out of town. What do you think?'

What did I think? He was a cop we'd accepted drugs from. 'I dunno. There's nothing on the truck, is there?'

'Can't remember.' Steve scratched the stubble that smothered his face. 'Do you think he's going to fuck us over?'

'What do you mean?' I tried not to think too much about the answers that came to mind. I realised we were following what passed for a police car here on the desert fringes.

Steve just stared at me. 'Nothing,' he said after a while.

I knew they'd beheaded tourists in Kashmir. People in the wrong place at the wrong time. Did they take hostages in Pakistan?

☉

Mirza's mother's house was a low, flat complex the colour of the desert. I'd guess it was a farm but I couldn't tell what it was they grew or husbanded. Camels probably.

More importantly, I noticed Mirza's mother had no neighbours. Steve made sure I knew this with a quick statement hinting of imminent betrayal, but then he'd been a paranoid bastard for weeks. His evening hash intake kept that fire fuelled. Once again we were split by sex, the women taken into the interior of the house and the men into the guest rooms. This one was barren compared to last night's. A thin rug spread over the floor and several camel-bags served as cushions. Simple weavings hung on the wall covering alcoves and recesses. A couple of elderly faces poked through the door leading to an interior courtyard, and shortly four other, younger faces peered in. They scattered when Mirza entered, carrying a tray of chai and hard-boiled eggs. He placed it on the floor.

'Welcome, welcome. This is where I grew up,' he said, before leaving the room again.

Simon poured the chai into cups and Steve passed the eggs around. They were still warm.

'Full-on breakfast, eh?'

'Continental-breakfast, Muslim-style,' I said.

Mirza returned and handed Bill a cheap, plastic, photo album. 'Is of me,' he said with a puffed chest. 'I be back soon.'

We huddled around Bill as he turned the first few pages. They were blank. He flicked the pages quickly and discovered that there were indeed some photos in the album. We, being the ignorant bastards we were, had forgotten that not all nations read from top to bottom, front to back.

'He wasn't kidding, was he?' I said. 'It is of him. Just him.'

The first photo showed Mirza taking a shower from the chest up. He gazed into the camera's lens as water poured down his face, spray cascading off his chest, flexing a bicep dramatically, his fingers running through the black hair sculpted to his skull.

There were five similar photos on the first two pages, one daring enough to show a full length shot, his back toward us, buttocks tensed.

'Maybe he doesn't want the women.' Steve prodded Jeff in the ribs. 'Maybe he wants a fine piece of American 'ass'. Some tight, Bill Clinton butt.'

'Don't joke about it,' Jeff said.

The next page showed Mirza in cowboy boots and denim jeans, bare-chested and gleaming in the sun, cresting a desert dune and staring through dark sunglasses. He had shaved his moustache in this series of photos. Another man stood next to him, similarly attired, striking an equally heroic pose.

Mirza in combat gear; Mirza swimming; Mirza disassembling Kalashnikovs, firing weapons; Mirza smiling and laughing; Mirza swirling long, mean blades overhead; Mirza, Mirza, Mirza.

'What the fuck is this?' I asked.

Chris had started laughing. 'Does this guy love himself or what?'

And, as if Chris's laughter was an infection, we all caught it.

'What's so funny?' Mirza said from the doorway. He had changed from uniform into blue jeans and a white singlet, but it was the automatic pistol he brandished in his hand that choked the laughter in our throats. A boiled egg and a cup of tea didn't seem like much of a last supper.

'Nothing,' I said, perhaps too quickly. Mirza's forehead furrowed. I quickly spouted some shite from the movie we had watched last night.

'Ah,' he said, unconvinced. The handgun jerked carelessly around the room. The room fell silent for what seemed an eternity, but was less than half a minute. Mirza swallowed. 'I have other reason for bringing you here.'

Silence. Thick and penetrating, when one can hear Adams-apples grinding up and down in dry throats and the trickle of bladders filling.

'What reason?' Chris asked, taking control. 'The tour company knows we're here.'

The edges of the room seemed to take on an unreal quality, slightly out of focus. Did he want money? Passports? The women? Our American?

He pointed the gun at Bill. 'See the photos?' Mirza then pointed at Simon. 'I want with him. He is the biggest.'

Good old six-foot-three, country boy Simon. Tall, strong, Christian-like and clean.

'I dunno about this.' Simon shook his head, sliding back on his haunches.

'Is for photo!' Mirza stared at our faces and laughed. 'You no understand.' He knelt down next to us, put the handgun down and flipped through the photos. I saw Steve eyeing up the gun. 'See me here. And this? I want to be action star. Movie hero like Arnie or Stallone. This is my . . . what is the word . . . polio. Is for Bollywood, yes?'

'Your portfolio?' I could hear the breath exhaling from around the room.

'Yes!' he cried. 'My portfolio. And with you here, I get great photos. Me against the West! Such advantage I will have! You no mind?'

We started laughing again, and this time he laughed with us.

'When you came in with the gun,' Steve said, 'and after last night . . .'

Mirza smiled and pushed the gun toward Steve. 'You have been my guest, you have eaten in my house. No harm would come to you, *Inshallah*. It is the way of Allah, my friend. Please photos, yes?'

'Jesus,' Steve said, removing the clip from the chamber. 'It's loaded.'

'Is it?' said Mirza. 'Forgive me; I am very excited of this.'

We went out to the courtyard where the women were waiting. Mirza's family and friends clustered around the walls, cameras and smiles ready. Suddenly in his stride, Mirza assumed a Scorsese-like role, directing positions and cameras and barking orders.

Alicia accepted the handgun and struck poses, holding the gun against Simon. Mirza whirled in the morning light, blades flashed in the sun, guns were cocked, muscles flexed and strained. Sweat was applied from a small bowl to the skin of the warring combatants, and cameras clicked, whirred and popped.

❧

Under a blue sky on the edge of the Baluchistan desert, I watched Mirza begin to realise the first of his dreams. An escape to a better life. A life most of us in the 'civilised' West wanted to be a part of, where men and women altered their bodies, lessened their minds and soiled their spirit to achieve fame and fortune, Hollywood-style. Where truth is a world of plastic gossip and entertainment, where role models are shallow, selfish fucked-up puppets that we adore and worship. The new faces of the gods of the Western world presented in all their wide-screen glory in surround sound. Which version of the truth would you like today?

I'm meeting Simon in a café in St Kilda shortly. He's just passing through. I haven't see him since the tour ended more than three years ago. I want to ask him how he's changed since his travels, through what he's learned. I know I've changed. I want to ask him what he thinks of this war on terrorism, the shame of Islam and the scourge of capitalism.

So I take a tram down to meet him, noting the way people avoid each others' eyes, careful not to touch, strangers afraid to speak to strangers,

God forbid if someone asks for help, lest they rob and rape and kill each other through an ill-conceived invitation.

But, as I said before, this is just a part of that truth.

HAMLYN

To see townsfolk suffer so

Winter lingered over Hamlyn.

It smothered spring like a wet cloak left on the ground, blanketing the spirits of the townsfolk, keeping them cold and weary. Whispers of the Apocalypse crept through the town, while rumours of a plague spreading throughout Europe scurried between the ears of the townsfolk like vermin.

Frau Heschlinger sat vigil next to the bed of her only son Pieter, the room lit by flickering candles. She dipped a cloth into the bowl on the bedside table, wrung the icy water from it, and placed it over Pieter's brow. The cloth turned warm beneath her hand in seconds.

' . . . no . . . don't . . . he comes . . . ' Pieter moaned.

'Ssshhhh.' Frau Heschlinger dribbled water over his cracked lips. 'It's alright. *Mutter* is here.' But she knew it wasn't alright and when he fell into a restless slumber she would go upstairs and pray until sleep claimed her too.

Pieter's eyes flicked open, bulging and white in a face leeched of blood, the skin drawn taut over the skull. Dark hollows swallowed his cheeks. His arm shot from the bed, the skeletal hand clamping his mother's arm. The strength of the dying, she thought, before trying to banish such a thing from her mind. His fingers dug into her flesh, his veins a purple lacework tracing from wrist to elbow, through raw, seeping punctures that peppered the otherwise pale skin. The cartilage in Pieter's throat bobbed furiously as he tried to speak.

'. . . biting me . . . everywhere . . . '

'No, my love. You are safe.'

His eyes turned sightlessly upon her, through her. They shone with the light the rabid dogs in the streets had had before the men put them down. Pieter grinned, the broken lips peeling back from the teeth, saliva thick and gummy in the cracks at the corner of his mouth. And he screamed:

'Rats!'

☮

They fought the dogs and killed the cats

The stench hit Günter first.

The smell of hot, furry bodies; of ripening cheese; of festering shit and decay. The torchlight sputtered in the draft from the trapdoor above him. He descended further into the cellar, peering into the darkness, listening to the scurrying and squeaking around him.

'Can you see them?' said Helmut, Hamlyn's master cheese-maker, from the safety of the shop above. His nine-year-old daughter, Anna, with a head of red curls clung to his leg, peering between her fingers.

'*Nein*, but they are here. I can hear them.' Günter swept the torch before him, straining to see past the flames. Shadows scampered from the light. 'How many did you say there were? A dozen?'

'No.' Helmut paused.

Günter unclasped the traps from his belt. He had smeared them with a concoction of chocolate and poison. 'How many?'

The scurrying had stopped. Tiny, shiny eyes reflected the torchlight in the cellar. Two, then four, and eight then twelve pairs of eyes.

'I said dozens of rats. Not a dozen. Dozens,' Helmut called.

Something scurried over Günter's boots. He looked down as the rat clawed its way up his legging, its whiskers pricking and eyes gleaming. He swung the steel trap down onto its body, hurling it into the darkness beyond.

112

'The cheek of the thing,' Günter muttered. He'd been trapping rats too long to let the bravado of one unnerve him. He turned slowly, the torchlight reflecting from hundreds of eyes surrounding him. The air grew dank and heavy as the torchlight shrank with the weight of a legion of rodent bodies.

Razor teeth sank into his wrist and Günter cried out more in surprise than pain as another rat clawed at his hair. The torch fell to the floor, the flames extinguished by the mass of bodies that swarmed over it. Günter stumbled back towards the light from the trapdoor, swinging the traps around him blindly. He felt it connecting with bodies, smashing them away. Jagged incisors gnawed and ripped at his arms and legs and face. He staggered up the steps into the shop, blood stinging his eyes.

'Shut it! Shut it!' Günter screamed.

Helmut slammed the trapdoor shut, his eyes wide and mouth open. Günter collapsed to the floor, his chest heaving, blood flowing from myriad cuts over his body. He sat there shaking as Helmut backed slowly away, his daughter wide-eyed behind him.

Not a single rat, as if fearing the light, had come into the room with Günter.

☙

For a guilder I'd my ermine gown sell

The council sat in silence.

The Mayor stared glumly at the liver-spotted folds of flesh his fingers made around the gold rings he wore. My, how the rings had grown tight over the years, he thought, trying futilely to think of something to say. The scurrying of clawed feet could be heard above them in the rafters of the town hall. Busy, hungry, tireless feet disrupting any train of thought he could compose. The townsfolk sat before him, waiting for an answer. A solution wasn't forthcoming.

'We've lost our export stocks, you say? I knew we'd lose the cheese, I knew that at least. But they've split open the kegs of salted sprats?'

The council nodded wearily.

'This will be a lean year,' the Mayor said, and in protest, his mutinous paunch grumbled. 'The winter has already hit the lands hard and our coffers are on the edge of empty.'

'What of the coffers? My husband Günter lays dying!' Frau Heuchert cried from the crowd.

'And my son Pieter!' wailed Frau Heschlinger. 'The rats bear the plague! They've come to destroy this town!'

Voices rose in cacophony and spat anger and fear at the Mayor and his council. The councillors responded, fingers pointing blame and accusation, an undercurrent of inevitable violence creeping into the room, marching step for step with the rise of hysteria. The Mayor sat there, willing his ermine-lined robe to swallow him in his old age, to take him elsewhere, to a Hamlyn of times past with pickle-tub boards and hoops of butter-casks, of cider-presses and the crisp smell of summers remembered.

A rat rose on its haunches on the council table in front of him, snapping the Mayor out of his reverie. With long-dormant reflexes once schooled in war, he smashed the gavel down on its body. Blood splattered his robe.

'Enough!' he roared.

In the shocked silence that followed, a gentle tapping could be heard at the chamber door. Heads turned, as the great doors creaked slowly inwards, the wind sweeping into the hall, chilling its occupants. A tall, thin man stepped into the room clad in a pied cloak of ruby red and yellow sun. Light, loose hair hung down to his shoulders, his face smooth and tanned. He smiled and with it came the scent of spring in the warmth of a lover's embrace. He strode towards the council, his sharp blue eyes drinking in the faces and emotions of the gathered townsfolk. When he reached the council-table, he spoke with a voice rich in the timbre of orchestras, a texture of honey for the ear.

'Please your honours.' His accent betrayed hints of the older Europe, where the gypsy still held sway. 'I believe I can help. But,' and he smiled again of gold, 'there is a price.'

'Name it,' said the Mayor, with the voice of the town in his throat.

'A thousand guilders if I can rid your town of rats.'

With empty coffers and a gilded lie . . .

'Done.'

. . . the pact sealed.

❧

Into the street the piper stept

Hamlyn waited in thrall.

The stranger took free lodging in the inn, needing some little time to survey the town and its denizens before he could take action. The clouds lifted a little, allowing the sun to dribble through, and the stranger was seen strolling along the banks of the river Weser in the afternoons. Sometimes he could be seen talking to the children at the school yard, the squeals of laughter a boon to the heart as they played in the folds of his pied cloak, chasing after him as he led them through the barren trees in the parks. And though the Mayor and council and a number of eligible women offered, in different ways, companionship he politely refused them, spending the evenings supposedly alone. Rumours abounded he preferred only the company of children, their simplicity and honesty —their innocence —or so it was said.

And all the while the town waited, the rats held their vigil.

Frau Heschlinger thought her prayers had been answered. A day after the stranger's arrival, her son Pieter found the strength to sit and call his mother for nourishment. The colour has crept back into his cheeks and his eyes glowed with the beginnings of a new-found health. And though spring could not yet be found in the buds upon the trees and bushes, it could be found in her step.

One morning she found Pieter's bed empty. At first she was overjoyed, thinking he was on the way to a full recovery. When she couldn't find him, worry gnawed at her like the rats on Helmut's cheese. Had Pieter wondered off in delirium? Perhaps even now he lay outside in the cold with the little strength he had left whittling away. Frau Heschlinger ran from neighbour to neighbour calling for her son, though none claimed to have seen him. She ran faster, her voice rising in pitch and temper while dark birds careened above and the clouds roiled, their bellies pitching black and threatening to roar. The wind slid over the river, slipping behind her back to urge her forward. Dead leaves swept over her feet as the panic whispered louder and louder in her head. Her son, her darling, only, beloved son. Could rats now be swallowing his tender flesh as they had Günter's? And as quickly as the madness rose it vanished. There in the shade of a twisted elm near the verge of the forest sat the stranger wrapped in his cloak of ruby red and yellow sun. Surely he would know where Pieter was, she thought. He had befriended many of the children here in Hamlyn. Dear God, please let him know she prayed. The stranger's head turned towards her as she approached. His eyes blue and as sharp as pins, this time his face offered no smile just the stony countenance of one who has had his concentration interrupted.

'Excuse me, *Herr*,' Frau Herschlinger began. 'I . . . I . . . have . . . '

The folds of the stranger's cloak bulged and shifted. He tried to cover it with his arm. The cloak parted and Pieter's head emerged.

'What is the matter? Pieter asked the stranger. 'Don't you . . . '

'Pieter!' Frau Heschlinger felt her heart rip. 'What are you doing?'

And with her son's hateful stare, his face rippling in shame, she felt her soul then stripped of innocence. He leapt from the stranger, his shirt undone and tore into the woods. Upon the lips of the stranger a slight curl, a little smile for a little evil. Where was her God? The clouds whirled about her then, the streets a blur until she staggered outside the Mayor's house, the gold door-knocker firmly in hand, thumping hard against the cold wood.

'What is it, woman?' Folds of wrinkled fat sprouting coarse, white hair hung from the Mayor's cheeks. His breath smelt of brandy. He pulled his ermine robe over his swollen gut. 'Why do you disturb me so?'

'The stranger! He was with my son! A molester of children, dear God. I swear!'

The Mayor's eyes widened. 'What? I don't believe this . . . ' His voice trailed off.

'He is preying on our children!' She noticed he was looking over her shoulder. Perhaps he was too stunned from such a revelation, she thought. 'In the name of God, you have to do something!'

He pushed her aside, stepping slowly into the street like a cripple healed and taking his first step. 'Here is your God at work, Frau Heschlinger. This is nothing short of a miracle. We are saved. The piper, look!'

She followed the line of his outstretched arm, down to the high street leading towards the bridge over the river Weser. The stranger—a long, thin, ivory pipe to his lips and if a tune he played she could not hear it—marched through the town, the folds of his cloak dappling red and yellow. And flowing behind him a sea of rats, pouring from the sewers and gutters, tumbling from windows and houses, swarming, seething, squealing and shrieking.

And the piper led them, each and every one, to their deaths in the waters of the Weser.

And what's dead can't come to life, I think

'Perhaps if you were to come after next year's harvest?' said the Mayor, examining the lining of his robe. The town hall was empty except for him, the councillors and the piper. 'I'm sure you understand. The winter has lasted long in Hamlyn. We simply cannot afford to pay you at this time. Come next year who knows? I'm sure we can at least provide you with, say, fifty guilders until then.'

'We agreed upon a thousand guilders,' said the piper. His face showed less emotion than the dead.

'Yes, we did.' The Mayor smirked. 'But we did not say when. Did we?'

The council remained silent, as did the piper, standing impasse.

'Fifty guilders, friend,' continued the Mayor. 'That is good trade for a gypsy in these parts.'

The piper leant forward on the table, his knuckles white. The ivory pipe hanging from his neck by a red and yellow scarf swung towards the Mayor. Hundreds of tiny skulls were carved into its surface, their eye sockets and teeth a mottled, yellowed bone. The room grew cold. The blue of the piper's eyes stung the Mayor's attention.

'I will not be cheated and I suspected as much. Perhaps we can come to some other arrangement.' The piper leaned even further forward, his mouth inches from the Mayor's ears. 'Give to me one of the children and you will never hear from me again. You and I, we share a common interest, do we not? No-one else needs to know.' He inclined his head minutely towards the council out of earshot.

The Mayor laughed, though fear as cold as a sharp blade sliced through his gut. How could this man know his secret, his vile lust? The words of Frau Heschlinger resounded suddenly in his ears. Had she accused him as well as the piper? 'Get out of here, gypsy. You are not wanted here. For helping our village you are lucky to have your life. Consider yourself rewarded.'

'You have till dawn,' spoke the piper standing straight and tall. 'One thousand guilders or one of your own. The choice is yours.' And strode from the hall.

That night, four of the night guard entered the inn and murdered the piper, cleaning their blades on his cloak afterwards. They dragged his body through the cobbled streets after midnight and dumped it in the Weser.

The following morning winter broke and birdsong rose with the spring dawn.

◉

Alas, alas for Hamelin!

Frau Heschlinger woke from a nightmare where Pieter hovered outside her bedroom window, his face pale in the moonlight, his eyes haunted and longing for love —her love. Her curtains had blown open during the night and a cool breeze entered the room, chilling the sweat on her skin from the dream.

She decided to go downstairs to check on him. He'd been withdrawn and sullen since the day in the park and they had hardly spoken since. His silence now hurt her even more than the hatred she'd seen in his eyes that day. She'd tried to tell him it wasn't his fault, that the piper was an evil man who lured children with false promises and seduced them with lies, but Pieter would hear nothing of it, staying in his room for days.

She opened his bedroom door and slipped into his room, hoping to catch at least some peace on his frail, sleeping face.

But his bed was cold and empty.

Frau Heschlinger would never see her son again, though night after night she would hear him tapping at the door or the window crying to be let in. When she woke, she knew it was simply her loss manifesting itself. Soon she would lose herself and embrace her son in the only way she could—in her dreams.

And while Frau Heschlinger descended into the madness of grief, one by one the children of Hamlyn began to disappear. From beds and cradles; from the arms of loving parents as they slept trying to keep them safe; from windowless rooms with only the crack under a locked door to provide air; slowly and surely by summer's retreat the children vanished. Parents swore on God's name they'd seen their missing children in the streets after dark or hovering at the forest's edge in the late afternoon or playing by the river in the early morn, but call and search as they might, their sons and daughters could not be found. Though the seasons changed from green to gold, it remained forever winter, frozen in the hearts of Hamlyn.

They found the Mayor dead soon after. He had slit his wrists and bathed his last in a bath of blood with a cask of the finest claret to help ease the pain.

And Günter, once-strong Günter, with puckered flesh from the rat bites that had almost claimed his life last winter, prayed for strength through the nights in the church alcove he had taken for residence. When he could pray no longer, Günter would ascend to the bell tower to watch over Hamlyn and wait for the dawn. Though his body had now healed, his mind lay scarred and devoid of the reward of sleep. And with what he saw each night— a flickering cape of blood red and yellow moon; of pale skin and long teeth—the horrors crept in to haunt his soul. So Günter prayed.

And prayed.

☻

Out of some subterraneous prison
Autumn lay in its death throes.

Günter slipped the rabbit into his sack, cleaned and reset the trap. Up here in the hills above the forest, the air was clean and cool. The first chill of winter could be felt in the air. He would lose the sun soon, so he decided to set back towards Hamlyn, unwilling to spend any portion of the night outside the confines of the church.

The sound of rocks slipping and tumbling off to his left. Too big to be a rabbit, he thought. He traced the rocks' fall upwards over the surface of slope until he came to a small mound thirty feet up on the hill. A head ducked down behind it. Günter crouched, nervous, and waited. The head poked up, saw him, then ducked again. A second later a boy darted away, pulling a girl with a mass of red curls by the hand after him.

'Pieter!' shouted Günter. 'My God, Pieter!' And the girl—surely that was Anna, Helmut's daughter. He dropped his sacks of rabbits and traps and raced up the hill after them. They moved fast, much faster than he gave them credit for, and Günter couldn't make any ground on them. Impossible, he thought, but the backward glances of the boy confirmed that it was indeed Pieter. They were alive! The children were alive and living up here in the hills! Günter stretched his muscles, the thin air burning in his lungs. God give me strength, he prayed, and as if he had been heard, he felt the power flow through his legs, his stride lengthening and pace quickening. He began to close on the children.

Pieter veered suddenly around a massive boulder sunken into the side of the earth, dragging Anna with him. She glanced back, a smile playing at the corner of her lips. Günter tried to slow down as he made the corner but he was running too fast and slipped, tumbling down into a grass-shrouded tunnel leading into the hill. He sprawled headfirst into a large cavern. The stench hit him first. The smell of hot, furry bodies; human sweat and the stale scent of sex. A rat scurried in front of his face, stopping briefly, its snout twitching, fur bristling. Günter rose to his knees, a feeling of dread eating its way into his bones. Torches lined the walls of the cave and rats scurried along ledges high up towards the ceiling. Children stood, sat and sprawled around the floor staring at him. Günter recognised them all. Anna stepped forward and kissed him with an open mouth as she helped him to stand. Günter shuddered.

'You don't like?' she whispered hotly into his ear as he stood.

Towards the rear of the cave, on a crude earthen throne, sat the piper, his ruby red and yellow sun cloak tattered and slashed from his murder. A young boy, Otto, sat naked on his knee, kissing the piper's neck. A girl of no more than five straddled the piper's thigh. Her eyes glittered menacingly, seductively.

'Ah, Günter, my child,' said the piper, his voice a languid measure of silk. 'Such strength to resist the desires my vermin servants secreted into your blood. And now here you are, returned to the fold. Such timing. Now that winter begins, we were just about to go hunting in Hamlyn for provisions for the journey back to Romany.'

The children advanced on Günter, their mouths wet and shining in the torchlight. He made the sign of the cross.

The piper grinned, his lips peeling back over glistening vampiric fangs. 'You can join us if you like.'

THEY SAY IT'S OTHER PEOPLE

I haven't had much luck with women. Not since the accident anyway. Tonight was, well, not great; but it was going good until *he* turned up.

Her name was Marie—short and curvaceous, shoulder-length, blonde hair and large, blue eyes. She worked for a PR company and painted abstract expressionism in her spare time. Best of all, though, she laughed at my jokes (most people don't). Over dinner she'd touched me on my hand three times as we talked. We were sliding into each other's eyes in one of those electric moments—you know the ones, where your peripheral vision ceases and the focus narrows and narrows until all you can see is her eyes, her mouth—you can no longer understand the noises each of you are making. Words? What words?—and your skin is crackling with an urgency that screams: *lean over and kiss her.* They don't happen often in your life but when they do, the world feels fresh and new, and you *know* how it all works and what to do . . .

. . . and the electricity arcing between us suddenly felt wet and slimy and

(it's the oysters)

nausea poked its head into my stomach for a quick peek.

'What's wrong, Will?' Marie asked.

'I, uh, nothing.' And just like that the world crashed back in, with the noise of the restaurant cacophonic in my ears, the smell of the tortellini bolognese rich as spoiling meat.

She reached out to touch me and my hand jerked away, knocking a wine glass. It teetered for a second, the wine sloshing against the rim, then Marie's hand caught and settled the glass.

'Are you okay?'

'Yeah, just feel a bit weird. Must have been those oysters.' I attempted a laugh, though it sounded more like phlegm catching in my throat.

'Oysters? We haven't had any oysters, Will. You look pale.'

Her hand reached out again and this time her touch was reassuring, not like the sickening jolt I'd experienced before. By this time though, nausea was no longer having a peek inside my stomach—he had climbed right on in. It felt like he was unhappy with the walls and had decided on a little redecorating.

'Excuse me.' I rose from our table, eyes searching for the bathroom. 'I'll be back in a minute.'

I was on my way to the door with the shiny top hat on it when I saw him: Hustlin' Hawkins. Sauntering past the restaurant window in a long, black coat, with his shiny, leather shoes impervious to the rain and his hair rejecting the breeze. He waved to someone inside and disappeared from view behind the wall. Then he came through the door, the maître d' welcoming him with a wide grin. I'd moved universities, cities, even goddamned countries, and here he was in the same bloody restaurant!

I barely made it to the bathroom. In hindsight, using the basins would've been better—no splashback on my clothes—but I never saw them in time and the cubicles looked too hard to negotiate—doors, handles, locks—so I staggered onto the urinal and threw up.

Where do I start with Hustlin' Hawkins? He's been following me all my life.

To say he was my nemesis would be wrong. An agent of retribution and punishment? How could a fourteen-year-old boy be my nemesis? Why would a fifteen-year-old boy, as I was when we first met, deserve one? To say I hated him and always hated him would be true. To say I was equally envious is also true. Do we have a word that expresses both hate and envy? Resentful. Bitter. They can be used for both but neither word conveys the depth of feeling, that intense hatred and, worse, the envy I had for Hawkins back then, even before he'd earned his millions and the Hustlin' tag.

He'd been big for his age and had the looks that drew the girls. He inspired male friendship because we knew he drew the girls, and if you hung out with him then they might notice you, too. After all, he'd have more than enough to go round. He wasn't smart but he wasn't dumb enough to be kicked out of school either, and, due to his physical prowess, he excelled at sport. I could see what people saw in him but I couldn't understand why they'd flock to him. Did I feel threatened? Sure, I guess, who wouldn't? It was a stage of my life where hormones were running rampant, confusing everything, pumping testosterone, producing sperm, with no outlet except my hand.

Hawkins began to woo my friends from me, slowly and surely and I never noticed until it was too late. I'd started seeing Katie, one of the more popular girls in school and who had good-sized breasts for a girl that age. (Back then that seemed to be the mark of a good girlfriend. Back then when we didn't know anything at all). We did a lot of kissing and that was it. No touching, no feeling. No sticky fingers or hand-jobs. Our dates would leave me beating off in the bathroom late at night. She wanted it to be right before we did it, saving herself for when that time came. She promised me it would and with that promise I knew I could wait.

I threw the end-of-year party at my house because my parents had gone away for the summer holidays. It was shaping up to be the party to end all parties. My older cousin, Fraser, jacked up the booze. (It only cost a bottle of Jim Beam and an invite to him and his black-jersey mates).

And even better, Katie lied to her parents that she'd be staying at Tracey's place overnight. I'd been walking around with a hard-on for most of the day, even beaten off a couple of times to make sure I wouldn't rush the moment when it came.

The party heaved, music pumped loud into the night, beer flowed from kegs and crates, wine coolers and Malibu and Southern Comfort. The hard men of school drank Jim Beam and smoked cigarettes and talked V8 engines in the corner of the kitchen. Knives heated on the stove element, ready to burn 'spots'—tightly rolled balls of dope—under a cut-off milk bottle. The smell of marijuana drifted easily through the house, couples danced and air-guitared and kissed and necked and I walked in on Hawkins busily fucking Katie in my parents' waterbed.

They lay naked on the bed, the sheets thrown back onto the floor. Her legs were wrapped around his waist, her white lace knickers—the special ones—hung from one ankle, so eager had she been to have him in her. She peppered his neck with kisses. I saw the wet trails her saliva made on his skin. (Sometimes, late at night when I'm alone, I can still hear her soft moans. They make me feel sick and aroused. What's the word for that?) His arse pumped up and down like the pistons in those V8 engines my cousin always talked about, the hard line of muscle flexing with each rapid thrust. I remember him raising his head and looking at me, sweat shining on his brow and the veins in his temple and neck bulging with the blood pumping through his body. Pumping inside Katie. He grinned and pushed harder into her. The groan from Katie, deep and animal, was the last thing I really remember.

I found out later they'd been fucking each other for about a month. My friends knew, her friends knew (hey, we were all friends!), but no one had bothered to tell me. I confronted him and he beat me up. End of chapter one.

I tried to wipe the splashes of vomit off my trousers, but the paper towel disintegrated, leaving a damp stain stippled with white paper dots. The mirror showed red, watery eyes and my skin had taken on a sallow appearance.

What are the chances? When does coincidence become pre-ordained? I couldn't believe Hawkins was here in this restaurant. I hadn't had any contact with him or his friends

(my friends, they were my friends)

in years.

I splashed cold water onto my face, chanced another glance in the mirror—still looked like shit—and braved the interior of the restaurant again. I hesitated

(he'll be at the table with Marie. She'll be laughing, touching his hand)

at the door. Paralysed by an inability to face Hawkins, dreading the 'Hi, how you going? Great to see you. What brings you here? We must catch up' charade we'd been playing our entire lives. Where really I wanted to choke the bastard and smash his head open on the floor, with a crack of the skull for everything he'd done to me, until there was nothing left but a dead, lifeless fuck that didn't deserve to . . .

'Oh, sorry,' said a man entering the bathroom as the door hit me.

'My fault,' I said to the floor, terrified for an instant it was Hawkins but knowing the voice wasn't his.

I stepped into the restaurant and walked back to my table, eyes still on the floor. I expected to see shiny leather shoes stop in front of me and that drawl say 'G'day, Will. Long time no see. You dating anybody I can fuck?'

By the time I got to the table, my shirt stuck to my back. Marie sat there with

(his saliva still wet on her skin)

a smile on her lips; her eyes widened when she saw me. She stood up and came round, taking hold of my arm.

'You look terrible,' she said. Her perfume, Chanel No. 5, I think, filled my nostrils and for a second I felt better. 'Perhaps we should go, take a raincheck perhaps.'

'Yeah, look sorry about this, Marie.' I kept my voice low and stared at the table. I could *feel* him sitting somewhere in the restaurant. 'I'm just, uh, yeah . . . '

'It's okay.' She guided me gently towards the bar. 'I'll fix this up and we'll get you into a cab.'

As Marie paid, I noticed a long, black coat draped on a stool at the bar. It was still damp from the rain outside. On the bar next to the stool lay a black leather folder with a business card on it. A glass of whiskey on ice sat next to the folder. My gut churned and I lurched out into the street, sucking in lungfuls of air, trying to quell the nausea. I collapsed to my knees, the wet concrete biting beneath my trousers, and tried to vomit. My stomach racked and a trickle of bile splattered the pavement. The world around me roared and blurred, Marie had me, then I sat alone in the back of a taxi as it slid through the empty streets.

The business card had been Marie's.

I sat nursing a bottle of vodka in my one-bedroom apartment with the music turned down low so the neighbours wouldn't complain. I'd tried calling Marie but I kept getting her voicemail. I couldn't keep

(his sperm on her skin)

the worm of worry from burrowing into my thoughts. I hadn't been with a woman since the accident and this was the first chance of intimacy I'd had. And bloody Hustlin' Hawkins was here. They say history repeats and no matter how I've tried and what I've done, it looked like it was going to repeat again. He would steal her off me, use her and discard her like all the others. How could I be with her then? After *he'd* been there?

I called Marie's mobile once more but it rang out. I sculled long from the bottle and hit the bed, hoping the booze would pull me under and wipe his face from my mind. Instead I lay on the bed in the dark, the jumble of memories left to me since the accident a sour reminder of his life in mine. Why couldn't the bad memories have been scrubbed instead of the good ones?

The jugs of beer are lined on the table and the chant of 'down down down down' reverberates through the entire uni pub. Hawkins staggers onto the table, a jug in hand. Cheers and whistles pierce the chant as he begins to scull from the jug.

'You think he'll do it?' Carla whispers in my ear. She sucks quickly on my lobe and squeezes my arse before I can reply.

Then Suze, Carla's best friend, has her and they chatter away, eyes fixed on the man in the spotlight. Suze had switched universities and ended up bringing her boyfriend with her. Hawkins.

Someone elbows me. 'Come on, mate. Down down down down!' They elbow me again and I start chanting, wishing Hawkins would attempt an open-throat and choke to death on his twentieth birthday.

Hawkins lifts the empty jug high in the air then turns it upside down over his head. The pub cheers in adulation and the girls are clapping and screaming. I grab a jug from the table—I'll drink his money.

Later on, a catfight breaks out. One of the guys pulls Suze off one of her friends, a girl called Debs. Suze is screaming at her, but Debs gives her the finger and wipes the blood from the scratch on her cheek. Rumour has it that Debs fucked Hawkins behind Suze's back. Beats the hell out of me why Suze stays with him, then I remember high school and me and Katie. I was the last to know then, maybe it's the same for Suze. Hawkins cares for no one but himself, but no one seems to care.

I push through the crowd to the toilets. Someone's kicked in one of the toilet bowls and the floor is flooded with water. Guys stand in the doorway, pissing into the room. I try for the women's toilets instead and miracle of miracles there's no one applying makeup or exchanging gossip inside. The two end cubicles are engaged but the middle one is vacant. I go in, wipe the lid, and start taking a dump.

I hear something knocking against the wall in the cubicle next to mine, a rhythmic banging. And the occasional grunt. I grin. Dirty bastards, I think. By the time I've finished squeezing out the first log, the banging is louder, faster. The woman is whispering 'harder, harder' and I know her voice.

'I'm going to cum,' says Hawkins.

'Hold on hold on,' Carla keens.

'I'm fucking cumming, bitch!'

Then she's moaning high and loud, as her first ever orgasm rips through her.

I lay awake for the rest of the night, scared the next set of memories would also decide to spend the night with me. By the time the alarm went off in the morning the bottle of vodka was well empty and my head well full with the relentless gnawing paranoia that Marie was rising weary and sore from Hawkins's bed.

That night, a Sunday, Marie called and invited me out for a drink on Thursday evening. The sound of her voice calmed me but I wanted to ask her if she knew Hawkins. I *needed* to ask her, but I knew if I did that the hysteria dwelling within would show. Instead I blocked it out.

I spent the following days in a blur—since the accident it gets hard to remember details sometimes. And then, finally, it was Thursday evening.

Ciccolina's was one of those exclusive bars where you had to know the bouncers to get in. And they sure as hell didn't want to know you. A big, black guy in a Hugo Boss suit stood sentinel, massive arms folded, gold gleaming on his fingers. He opened the door before I even approached him and

(blood pooling on the floor)

ushered me through to the bar.

Inside, the room was lit sparingly with art deco lamps. Dark wood took precedence, while huge ceiling fans turned the air from the wall heaters around the room. The bar itself was long, perhaps fifteen metres, and people in designer clothing and hairstyles, suits and leather and flesh, clustered around mostly taken seats. Music slipped from concealed speakers, the volume comfortable enough to allow the steady rhythmic bass to ride with the patrons' heartbeats. I spied Marie and began to ease myself through the crowd. But as I tried to move closer to Marie, the crowd pressed tight, forcing me to push harder. The music throbbed in my ears and sweat broke under my armpits. I thought I heard my name chanted in the music, all twisted and metallic. Elbows jabbed and I tripped. I staggered forward, then hit the floor. The crowd closed over me, oblivious to my presence. I lay there for a second on the polished floorboards among high-heels and leather boots, the breath hitching in my chest. I knew what would happen next. I'd been here before. Before the accident.

Rivulets of liquid oozed from the wall of the bar down to the floor, then snaked through the forest of legs towards me. Dark and thick, the stink of copper. When it hit my skin, matting in my hair, it was warm and sticky.

I wanted to scream, *needed to scream,* so I opened my mouth. The blood poured in, hot and rancid, choking me, suffocating . . .

'What would you like to drink?' Marie asked.

I sat at the bar with her. There was no blood in my hair. I didn't . . . what had . . . ?

'Shiraz okay with you?' She refilled her glass and looked at me, a slight smile on her lips. I nodded and she filled the clean, empty glass before me.

She put the bottle down and rubbed a finger over her lips. 'You've got some of my lipstick on the corner of your mouth.'

'Sorry? I don't . . . '

She leant forward, her hand sliding along my thigh, applying a gentle, persistent pressure. 'Perhaps I'll even it up with another kiss.' Then her lips, soft and slightly parted, were upon mine.

Marie took another sip of her wine, her eyes sparkling. She placed her glass on the bar and stood up, smoothing her dress. It clung to her curves and cut deep to reveal her cleavage. 'Excuse me for a minute.' As she left, she leaned close and whispered, 'I loved last night.'

I sat there stunned. Last night?

My eyes were drawn to the massive mirror on the wall. My reflection sat alone in a decrepit bar, long since empty and now cobwebbed. Dust coated the bar and swollen, hairy things scurried in the dirt on the floor. Clumps of hair had been ripped from my scalp, my clothes torn and dirty, the flesh hanging from my face a mockery of life. In the mirror I held a long, discoloured blade, its tip wet and shining. I looked down at my real hand and saw only the wine glass. I turned my head slowly to my right, to where a young, professional couple sat flirting over martinis. No dust, no cobwebs. I stared back into the mirror. The place was deserted. Then slowly, as if the light played tricks in the warp at the edge of the mirror, shadows the colour of rotten fruit began to form, swirling and coalescing towards my reflection. They loomed over me, swelling and substantiating, until Hustlin' Hawkins's face leered from the mirror. Arms slipped from the shadows to rest on my shoulders.

'*Good to ssseeee you, maaate.*'

Blood rushed to my head as the wine in my stomach rushed to meet the bar. Someone pulled me by the arm. The smell of Chanel No. 5.

'I'm so sorry, Johnny.' Marie's voice.

I tried to lift my head and the muscles in my neck screamed in protest. Marie slipped an arm beneath mine and lifted. I staggered to my feet as the room spun around me. *She's spiked my drink.*

A long, black coat. 'Don't worry about it, babe. You're always welcome here.'

The voice, that sardonic drawl, smashed into me, the room suddenly turning into a blurred tunnel dropping down fast and away, twisting and turning until the light came crashing into his face. Hawkins grinned and winked at me.

'You . . . I . . . ' My tongue turned traitor and my throat closed in the rebellion of my senses. It was *him*. He'd done it, slipped something into my drink so he could steal her from me.

Hawkins

(a blade in his stomach, his fingers shiny in blood clutching the handle)

leaned forward and kissed Marie on the cheek. He winked at me again as his hand ran down the small of her back to the curve of her arse.

'Thanks, Johnny. I'll fuck you later,' she said.

'See you later then,' he replied. And then to me, 'Good to see you again, Will. We must catch up.'

He clapped me on the shoulder. When he touched me, it felt as though I'd been pissing on an electric fence. I remembered screaming, then not much else.

I woke up in a bed feeling disoriented. It didn't think it was my apartment. The room was dark, except for a crack of light creeping in from where the curtains met.

Someone lay asleep next to me, an arm curled around my waist. I moved my hand down tentatively over the body, the feel of soft, warm, skin and the curve of a breast. She was naked and so was I. What the hell had just happened? I groped for a light switch at the bedside table but found none, so I waited as my eyes adjusted to the darkness.

A light in an adjacent bathroom flicked on, flooding the bedroom with enough to see by. Marie snuggled closer and murmured something soft. Had I slept with her and not remembered? My thoughts snapped back to the bathroom. I heard movement, the slap of bare feet on tiles. Someone else was in here with us. Then the sound of a hard stream of urine hitting water.

I crept from the bed, careful not to disturb Marie, and approached the open bathroom door. Inside a man with a muscular back stood pissing into the toilet. His arse muscles flexed with

(each rapid thrust)

the final squeeze of drops. Hawkins turned slowly to face me, and for an instant his cheek appeared sunken, the skin withered and decayed. Bone shone through under the fluorescent lighting. The room wavered and Hawkins looked normal again. Handsome, arrogant, strong. He grinned then shook his semi-hard cock. Drops flicked from its glistening end, the spatter on the tiles loud in the silence of the room.

'How's your bride, Will?'

'What?' Inside me, I felt something building, ready to erupt.

Hawkins swaggered towards me, still shaking his cock. 'Wonder if she wants some more of this? She loved it on her hen's night.'

'You're lying!'

Marie's voice behind me. 'Will, honey, what's wrong?' Her hand on my trembling shoulder had a gold ring on the wedding finger. Something was wrong here, *really* wrong. *A drink.*

(a needle, cold, as cold as death itself)

They spiked my drink.

I turned to face her, throwing her hand from my shoulder. 'What the hell's going on?'

Her face screwed up in confusion. She was good, I'll give her that. I almost bought the look of hurt innocence in her eyes.

'I don't know what you mean,' she said. Her voice trembled as much as my body. She stepped back into the shadows of the bedroom so I couldn't see the deceit plastered over that seductive face.

'You two drug me and bring me back here! Messing with my mind. What do you hope to achieve from this? I don't have any money. You fucking slut!'

Marie started to cry. 'Will, listen to yourself. Please, you're scaring me.'

'Did he put you up to it, you bitch?'

'Who?' Her sobs hitched the word into broken syllables.

I pointed back at Hawkins. 'Him! That evil bastard!'

'Who, Will? There's no one there.'

The bathroom was empty.

The edges of the world blurred and melted, rushing around my peripheral vision like a whirlpool. The light merged with the dark and the sudden silence howled static in my ears. The cold tiles under my feet provided a focus as I tried to bring myself back in. He'd been here, I'd seen him. *Concentrate on the tiles. He was in here pissing into the toilet.*

I staggered towards the toilet bowl. 'Fuck you both!'

The smell hit me first, so strong it almost clogged my nostrils. The water in the toilet was thick with congealing

(oysters, it's the oysters, they taste like)

sperm. I gagged and reached for the flush, pushing hard down on the button. The cistern gulped hungrily, then spat the contents of the bowl up and out into the room. Sperm and water coated my face, stringing through my hair, slapping against my sealed lips. I slipped as I jerked back and crashed onto the tiles. I tried to turn and crawl towards the doorway but what I saw froze my heart.

Marie stood naked in the doorway, her legs spread wide. Hawkins stood behind her, his hands pawing her breasts. Her nipples were large and erect, and his fingers pinched them cruelly. He looked at me over her shoulder as he thrust up beneath her, sliding into her. He laughed as she gasped, then gave me a wink.

'Nooooo!' I screamed and, as my mouth opened, Hawkins's sperm poured from between her thighs, filling the room. The last thing I remembered was the taste of thick, salty glue tinged with urine and the scent of Chanel.

Darkness.

I awoke dry and shivering on the bathroom floor. My head hurt and there was a trickle of blood on the otherwise clean tiles. I turned on the lights and checked my apartment—it was my apartment—the one room, the kitchenette, the double-bed. The blankets were disturbed on one side only, the side I normally slept. I had been in it alone. This was something to do with my accident, I

(killed him)

was sure of it. I had had times like this before, though I couldn't clearly recall them. But I *knew* I had. I think my accident affects my memory when I get stressed or nervous. Like a benign brain tumour, every now and then it kicks in and I get a little haywire.

I sat down on the bed and as I did I noticed the photos on the bookshelf opposite. Wedding photos. Of me and Marie. Christ, I didn't even remember kissing her, let along making love to her! Married? Instead, burning in my brain, the only clear image we had of our relationship. Hawkins behind her, smiling and thrusting, filling her with his poison. And the sound of her soft moans. My head throbbed and the world sang darkness.

So I followed its tune.

The bouncer in the Hugo Boss suit glared at me, his massive arms still folded over his chest.

'He's expecting you,' he said. 'When you go in, take the staircase on the left. His office is at the top, second door down.'

Ciccolina's buzzed, the bar five deep, the music loud and intoxicating. I ignored it all and strode up the stairs, my eyes focused on every step. I blocked everything and everyone, the roiling ball of nausea in my stomach growing as I neared the top. I approached his door, the urge to vomit increasingly strong, but this time I knew what was happening. It was Hawkins who made me feel sick. Every time we were near each other I'd feel this way. It had to be Hawkins, and I suspected he'd had something to do with my accident.

I stood outside his door, summoning the strength to turn that handle, to push

(the needle into the skin of the bag)

the door open and confront him. I had to do it. I'd been too weak before and he'd walked all over me all my life. Stolen my friends and lovers, turned me into this erratic animal. *I had to do this. It had to stop.*

But I didn't open the door.

Instead it swung slowly inwards and there, lounging in a large, leather recliner, his bare feet on the mahogany desk beneath a massive glass window overlooking the bar—my nemesis: Hustlin' Hawkins.

'Hi ya, Will. Come in and shut the door,' he said. 'You got here sooner this time.'

I walked into the room and the door shut silently behind. The room stank of stale cigarettes, but there was something else, some other smell, hidden beneath.

'Stay away from my wife.' I had meant to say Marie but it felt right anyway.

Hawkins raised his eyebrows, his blue eyes sparkling. 'Come in, old buddy. Take your weight off, have a drink. Good to see you.' He sat forward and placed the long letter-opener he'd been turning over in his hands on the desk. 'Don't you just love the way your memory fucks with you. You know the best thing about this, don't you?'

'I'm warning you.'

'I only feel the pleasure, Will. Not the pain.' He laughed and leant back. 'But not you, eh, Will? You don't get to experience the pleasure. She's a great fuck but you'll never know, will you, Will? Do you like that? "Will you, Will".' Hawkins laughed again.

It was no longer nausea I felt, but something dark and thunderous ripping from the embryo of hate I'd been nurturing.

'Stay away from us or I'll kill you.'

Hawkins stopped smiling. He stood and leaned over the desk. His cheeks suddenly looked dry and sunken, but his eyes burned. 'This is the moment I look forward to the most. I can see it there, I know you've almost grasped it, but you never do. Get it over with, arsehole. Let's do it again.' And he grinned a grin full of decayed, yellow teeth.

I realised the smell hidden beneath the cigarette smoke. Chanel No 5. He'd had her in here, probably on his desk while he looked down at me sitting at his bar. It all unravelled, the years of pain and hatred, pummelling out in the shape of my fist, smashing into his jaw. His head rocked back and he blinked, his eyes dazed, the young, arrogant Hawkins back in my view.

It felt like elation, the first orgasm, creation!

I punched him again and he collapsed into his chair. It rolled back on its wheels into the wall. He shook his head dazedly and laughed. I leapt over the desk, grabbing something from it to really hurt him, to wipe that stupid grin from his pin-up-boy face. Hawkins tried to stand and I punched him hard in the stomach, again and again. Something hot and wet gushed over my hand. The coppery stink of blood. The letter-opener dropped from my hand to the carpeted floor. Hawkins stood there, smiling and still. Blood oozed from the cuts in his stomach. The room grew hot.

'You can only kill me once, Will,' Hawkins said.

And I remembered, oh yes, I remembered it all. It came crashing back into my brain, all those fractured memories of my life. My real life, the life before my accident. Eating his oystery sperm from between her thighs. The blade in his gut held by my hand. His body in a pool of blood. The trial. Before the needle. An IV Tube leading from my arm to a bag where a man injects a lethal needle.

'Normally we go through a lot more before we get to this point,' Hawkins said. 'And frankly I'm glad you came earlier this time. I was sick of fucking this one.'

'No,' I said, the sound low and hollow, an empty whisper.

'Who'd have thought? Sartre was right.'

'No . . . no . . . '

'This is the part I love!' Hawkins spun on his feet, clapping his hands. 'You know! You remember!'

'No . . . '

Hawkins winked at me. 'One man's heaven . . . '

◉

I haven't had much luck with women. Not since the accident anyway. Her name's Irene—tall and slim with legs to her neck; long, black hair; and large, blue eyes. Works in marketing and sings jazz on the weekends. Best of all, though, she laughs at all my jokes . . .

BURNING FROM THE INSIDE

Now

I'd like to say I feel unsettled here, but I don't.

From my hotel room I can see the river Torrens snaking through the park, the lush of leaf in contrast to the desert sands that lap at the shoreline this city makes. The sun is settling on the horizon, finally a thing of beauty rather than the raging father in the sky, now its urgency is almost spent. One can imagine the river, that gurgle of water, a searing temptation for the heat bursting forth from the dead heart of this red island continent. A thirst to be quenched? Or something to be destroyed, the last bastion of hope holding back the inevitable conquest that shapes this dry land? Ornate spires reach for the heavens, dozens of them, over trees, nestled between crossroads and office buildings, the cross of Christ thrust up bold and true. One only has to glance in any direction to find the house of God here. From this spot alone I spy the Holy Trinity, Scots, St Patrick's, St Peter's, Christ's, Brougham Place and Immanuel. And here I am. In the City of Churches. Adelaide. My new home for the foreseeable future. The murder capital of Australia.

My window looks towards the west, over the grand boulevard that is North Terrace, a street lined with massive sandstone monuments—libraries, museums, art galleries, parliament—proclaiming the greatness of the only settlement to be founded without the stain of convict blood. These buildings humble the rest of the city, not so in size but in grandeur, as if they were built for a time when the streets prospered and the anticipation of unbridled growth reigned. For an Adelaide where the young didn't leave as soon as they could, and the old stayed not to die.

If my room were on the other side of the hotel, I would see darkness rushing from the east, for once the sun descends beneath the lip of the desert, night blankets the city. And so, soon, it will be time to leave my room and explore the streets. To see if the city lives by night as it does, barely, by day.

I shower and masturbate listlessly into the drain. The life that spills onto the floor is quickly cooked and hot water tears it into swirling strings of muck. I always do this before I go out. Helps me to quell any premature urges—to keep some modicum of control.

I dress and take the elevator down to reception. The concierge approaches with a friendly smile and small pleasantry. With his well-groomed body, sharp and spick, he urges me towards the restaurant.

I decline. 'Where's a good place to go in the city?'

'Ah,' he nods effortlessly. 'East Rundle Street has a good selection of cafes and restaurants, you know, if you like the café sort of thing. It's just around the corner, just after the mall ends. Where are you from, sir?'

'Melbourne, originally.'

He grins and laughs something polite. 'Ah, the Paris of the south. Well, the East End's not quite your Acland or your Brunswick streets, but the food's good and the prices affordable. Chinatown is not far from there either, but,' he grins again, 'if you've been to the one in Melbourne . . . '

'Sounds fine. How do I get there?'

He shows me a tourist map—the city centre is only a small grid—and offers it to me as I leave. I decline. I don't think this place is big enough to lose myself in.

I take a small piss-stained and stinking alleyway near the hotel and emerge into the neon porn of Hindley Street. It's not like Sydney's King Cross—there are no hookers, the pimp's menace is noticeably missing, and pushers are nowhere to be seen. Club X, the McDonald's of Australian porn, proclaims "Cyber Sex here!". Black doors with red fluoro lead to dark hallways for Gentlemen's Clubs. Mostly, though, pubs advertise live nude dancing with the allure of pokies. It seems the plague of poker machines has decided to nestle comfortably in this part of town. It shouts louder from the signs than silhouettes of long legs and pert breasts. And what could be better than a bit of tit, a cold beer and a pull—not on your cock, but on a pokie machine? Or so it seems. At least these places have patrons; the niche restaurants and bars along this stretch of road look decidedly forlorn.

A scraggly-haired guy who looks in his late thirties staggers towards me. 'You goddenny blowie, mate?' Stains on the shirt stretched over his paunch are stale. 'Caarrmon, mate, just some fucken blowie, fer Chrissakes!'

A young drunk, standing sentinel over an old drunk collapsed in a puddle of piss, howls into the night as I pass—some wordless, tuneless sound that had perhaps once been a song he'd known in better times. A scrawny middle-aged Aboriginal man argues with his haggard-looking wife over cigarettes as they enter through a doorway crowned by a TAB sign. I pause in the doorway and glance in. A reflection in the mirror over the bar shows a woman gyrating against a pole. She's wearing jeans and a tight T-shirt. An old song blares from the pub. *This is not my beautiful wife, this is not my beautiful life.* I wonder how this can be considered a song for erotic dancing then realise no one really cares. They're just waiting for her to get her gear off. The singer wails again. *How did I get here?* The dancer's young and bored, and it looks like she's going to disappoint her customers. Her clothes are staying on.

This is the red-light district in the City Of Churches. Tame, really . . .

How did I get here?

❧

St Kilda—Before

'Nah, I grew up in Brisbane.' He takes another slug of whiskey and coke. He's dressed in black, with soft, expensive-looking leather shoes. Beads have been braided into several strands of his long, black hair. A spidery hand, dripping with ornate, silver rings strokes his goatee. 'Came here about four years ago.' He laughs. 'Usually the other way round. All the Melbournites are heading north for the sun. Me? I like the dark.' He offers me his glass again. 'You sure you don't want a drink?'

'No thanks.' I'm waiting for the girl I was kissing in the pub to come back from her bedroom. I'm hoping she's making herself more presentable for the rest of what the evening has left.

'St Kilda's got this vibe, you know,' the drinker continues. 'An amazing sort of vibe.'

I can't remember his name. I'm not sure the girl I'm with introduced us. I guess that means I'm disposable and that suits me fine. I can't remember her name either. Meeka? Mica? Michelle? Who knows? I cast a glance towards her doorway. She told me she'd be back in a second. Should I just go in?

A dreadlocked girl passes a joint from a tired beanbag she and her boyfriend are nestled in. I pass it straight to the whiskey drinker who's changing the CD. The Church's *'Magician Amongst The Spirits'* resonates eerily into the lounge room from speakers hidden in crammed book-shelves sharing space with statues of Buddha and Chinese dragons, crystals, incense burners and paraphernalia for smoking.

Her door is still shut. How long's it been? Ten minutes? Is that too long?

'You been living in St Kilda long?' The drinker washes down the smoke with his drink.

'About a month.'

'Not long then. Enough for first impressions only. What do you think?'

'Seems pretty cool. Good pubs and cafes and things. The beach is a bit rough.'

The girl in the beanbag laughs, a smooth smoky sound. 'Too many needles.'

The drinker swallows the contents of his glass and refills it, more whiskey than coke. 'And what else?'

I glance at her door. It's painted a seductive green, the brass door handle shining, calling my hand to turn it. 'I dunno.'

'She'll be a while, mate,' says the drinker. 'Micana likes to take her time. This place is more than just pubs and restaurants. It's more than a beach. Why did you come here?'

'Micana. She invited . . . '

'Not here, mate, not to this house. To St Kilda.'

'The drugs, the prostitutes . . . you know, why everyone else comes here.' I laugh and the drinker smiles politely, though the edge of his smile waits for the real answer. 'I heard it was a good place to be. All the travel guides say to check it out. Lots of people. Like you said, it's got a good vibe.'

'Why do you think?'

This isn't going the way I thought it would. Micana's door is still shut and I'm stuck talking to some bohemian "intellectual". I shrug.

The dreadlocked girl exhales a blue cloud between me and the drinker. The cloud shifts and swims, curling in swirls to break across the ceiling. Tiny stars glow beneath the dissipating smoke, where little moons and planets rise, an artificial constellation glued to the ceiling.

'What about all this?' the drinker indicates the incense and crystals.

'Sure, there's a lot of that around here. Lots of yoga and massage. Spiritual healing, that sort of thing.' I don't know if he's for or against it though. If he lives here then maybe I should stay tight-lipped. 'Good energies, right?'

'Ever felt drawn to a place?' The drinker asks. 'Ever wondered why all these spiritual—shall we say *magical*—things congregate in the same place?'

A soft breath of perfume and an arm slips round my shoulder as a warm body snuggles in against me on the chair. Micana strokes my cheek with a gentle finger and smiles.

'You talking about your magical nexus again, Dave?'

'A nexus?' I ask.

'Don't get him started,' Micana says.

'A nexus is a connection.' Dave takes another slug; he's started already. 'And St Kilda is one of them. And it's not just sweetness and light, it's not all that Moonstar massage and crystals and dragons and meditation shit you see down Acland St. Sure, that's part of it, but it's only a part. You heard of Aleister Crowley?'

I haven't, but I don't get a chance to answer.

Micana whispers in my ear, her hand inside my shirt. 'Come into my room. Let's play.'

�

Now

The river Torrens slithers past the zoo and Adelaide Oval, beyond the airport to spill into West Beach, where the water is unseasonably warm this summer. A few minutes south lies Glenelg beach, where the first South Australian colonists landed in 1836. A site steeped in historical interest, a beach famous for its gentle waters and clean sand, where predators lurk a little further out in the deeper waters. Shark attacks are not uncommon in such places, but this beach in particular is famous for other reasons. Perhaps famous is not the right word. Children go missing here.

Dusk falls late this time of year, the sun still high, the early evening softening its blows, allowing people to spill out from the four-star hotels, the seafood restaurants and noisy bars onto the warm sands where the water sucks at the shore. The skins adorning the sands are mostly white, though a tan cannot hide the ancestry within the genes. The Aboriginal community appears to be missing here in this rich vacuum of holiday-makers, though their traces can be seen littering the parks and alleyways of the city, half-empty bottles cleverly disguised in worn paper bags.

The smell of tanning oils and fried fish mixes with the fresh salt of the sea as I meander along the beach. In any other beachside town of a major city —say a St Kilda or a Surfer's Paradise or a Fremantle—the new-age shops, the experiential, celestial, spiritual side would have moved in to celebrate such a place, such a nexus. But not here. This is not a soulless place of cheap tourism and cheaper T-shirts—the things that epitomise the southern coast of Queensland—it's subtler than that. Almost relaxing, calm. I don't know why, but this feels *good*. And as soon as I realise this I feel nauseous.

Something flashes behind my eyes, a quick, sharp bolt of light, and a shudder crawls over my skin. The colour of the sand shifts from dull white-yellow into a brighter spectrum where the sunbathers fade into the background. I turn slowly—or is it the world spinning around me? An Aboriginal man emerges from the water like a silent hunter from a jungle river stalking his prey. He clutches a tall, jagged spear in one hand. His face is smeared with ochre, and white dots encircle his armpits and genitals, linked by undulating red-dotted lines to the centre of this chest. His eyes are black holes, his thick lips pressed tight and heat coruscates from skin resembling ebony, skin that is hard and unforgiving. The stench of wet, bloated flesh envelopes me as he steps closer. I can't see anything but his face—his emotionless, ochre-cracked face. The beach is gone, dead and buried in another time. Raw meat seethes between those cracks, oozing pain and hate like heat shimmers from the baked skin of the desert. How can this be? He should be wet, I think, trying to back away, but my legs won't move. The sand has crept around my ankles, drifting up my shins, clutching me tight in its embrace. Tiny, animal teeth line the ridges underneath his dead eyes, bright white and sharp. His mouth opens wide and a terrible heat pours from his maw, burning the breath in my lungs.

'Open your eyes. Look at my past.' He thrusts the spear into my stomach and twists, the pain ripping through the veil, and I collapse onto the beach falling on something warm and soft, something that yells in surprise.

'What are you doing?' A woman, a sunbather, something real. 'Get the hell off me! Hey, are you . . . '

And the pain twists again and sweeps me away . . .

❧

A giant heart pulses one last time and serpents spill from its hardening flesh. They weave through the desert sands towards the north and the south, eastwards and westwards, radiating from the dead heart, over desert and mountain to the distant coasts. Their trails fill with moisture, the moisture grows to a trickle, and as the trickle gains momentum, the rivers fill with life and spill into the sea.

The pain twists again . . .

❦

'Take my hand.' My voice. Not my voice. A voice. 'It's not safe here.'

Her skin is soft with youth, nine years of innocence. She holds her younger sister's hand, who in turn takes their even younger brother's. They'll be more than enough.

The nation celebrates. The turning of the land. The taming of the beast. Birth anew.

It's Australia Day, 1966.

And it twists again . . .

❦

The serpent heading south, fat from consuming the land, struggles as it burrows through the last mountain range barring it from the sea. A thin trail of blood lines its passage. Something deep within the serpent has ruptured, and the poison slowly seeps throughout its body. It eats everything in its path, hoping to devour the pain burning from the inside. And by the time the serpent slides dying into the sea, its wake has swollen with blood and rot. And something dark and twisted crawls from the serpent's corpse and secretes itself into the riverbed.

And again . . .

❦

The house screams of excessive late '70s architectural lauding. Sharp, angular roofs point inwards, the walls bending to the whims of the designer. It could be the house for the curator of Sydney's Opera House, if there were such a thing, where the sails are pointed not curved. Sun shines on large windows, reflecting back at the bluestone neighbourhood that surrounds it. The doors slide open and an evil heat emanates from within, drawing me closer, no . . . not me . . . someone else.

❦

. . . the pain twists once more—a bright flare of panic and primal fear, the brain in the stomach screaming to run and run and run, to go back where it was safe—and then darkness.

❦

Byron Bay—Before

I don't know what I was expecting. I guess it was this.

Johnston Street leads north to the bay, where the surf rolls easily onto Main Beach. Backpacker hostels line the street, cafes proclaim vegetarian and vegan meals, independent fast-food joints spit out kebabs and fish and burgers. Bars, nightclubs, surf shops, and then what we're all here for—healthy living, spiritual living. In touch with nature and oneself. The rediscovery, the kindling, of the godhead that lives within us all. The counter-culture embracing the alternative lifestyle. Learn yogic dance, take a massage, a submersion tank, some naturopathic therapy, open your chakras, have your stars read while you immerse yourself in reiki or shiatsu. Ferals firedance on the beaches at dusk; marijuana drifts on the evening breeze; the sound of music and tribal drums; laughter; warmth; beautiful happy people; cultures within cultures; a hundred different tongues spoken and united by the one tongue of the body and mind.

St Kilda has nothing on this place. Dave the Drinker and his nexus. His hints of dark magic and occultism nothing more than a thin excuse for free sex. No real connection at all. But here! A land of light and positive energy, revitalising the potency within the lacklustre blood of all newcomers. Fuelling them, providing nurture, a place they can call their own, a place to find themselves, a home.

Except I sit alone at a table eating a dry lentil burger. The satay sauce is strong but can't moisturise the meal. It lodges in my throat. At the table next to me, two couples with their pre-school children finish off their salads, chickpeas, lentils and unleavened breads. One of the women must be in her late twenties. A tie-died sash binds her dreadlocked hair behind her head. The dreadlocks fall to the small of her back where a tribal tattoo creeps down to the top of her hips before disappearing behind the waistline of her skirt. Her nose is pierced; leather thongs and beads adorn her wrist. A Polynesian bone carving hangs from her neck. Her partner, dressed in loose Indian cottons, produces a small colourful bag and begins to roll a cigarette. He rolls thin and tight, one cigarette for each of the adults and passes them round. He lights a match, then lights each of the cigarettes in turn, leaving his own till last. They smoke and lean back, a relaxed enjoyment clear on the turn of their lips, the angle of their eyes. The nicotine unravels their brows and calms their nerves.

The smoke wafts over my table and across the tables of other diners. No one minds, or if they do, nothing is said. I want to get up and shout at them, scream their hypocrisies in their lifestyle-faces. But I guess you choose what you want to believe. Tobacco is part of nature. The leather thong is not really from an animal. The Polynesians never settled Australia. So I finish my burger in silence, as they cast smug looks at me sensing I'm new here, just another tourist. One of the backpackers here to get stoned and laid and show their friends and families back in Europe photos of how they lived this other life for a brief instance. Of how they belonged.

Maybe I'm out of touch.

☻

A water fountain trickles soothingly. Chillout music plays softly from hidden speakers. Incense burns—Tibetan sandalwood, so I'm told, but I can't tell the difference. I lie naked, facedown on a massage table, a towel draped over my arse.

'You need to think about what you wish to invite to this session,' Astra had said before she left the room.

I just wanted an hour-and-a-half massage for forty dollars. She'd been gone for half an hour and boredom was turning into frustration. There's probably mosquitoes breeding in that fountain.

'How'd you go?' Astra smiles as she walks back into the room. She looks early thirties, wears minimal make-up, clean, shiny hair, good breasts—though I shouldn't be noticing, after all this is about spiritual development—and is a little too friendly. Not in a sex way, rather an insincere way.

I shrug.

'I think you're very lucky,' Astra continues. 'You have lots of support. I can see the angels all around you. You've not had a healing massage before, have you?'

'No.'

'Like I said before, the more you invite to this session, the more you'll get out of it.' She rubs oil into my back and begins to gently massage, moving her fingers through the muscle. 'You're very tense.' She pushes a little harder, kneading the knots out with her fingertips. Her bare stomach touches briefly against my elbow. And a little flicker stirs below.

'You always lived here?' I ask.

'I don't think that's relevant for this session, do you?'

'I wouldn't have asked if it wasn't.'

She works her way down to the small of my back, her fingers against the side of my waist as her thumbs work against my spine. I try to detach from the hardness she's shifting from muscle to gland. I'm not attracted to her. I don't know why it does what it does.

'I came here ten years ago for New Year's,' she says. 'When I got here, I had this instant connection, you know what I mean? I loved the place and it just called out to me. Sounds a little hippy-trippy, but it's true. I feel like I belong here though. It's where I should be. You know, there's a huge, positive energy flowing through this place. You can feel it, can't you?'

'Yeah, sort of,' I lie. My erection deflates.

I've been here two weeks and I'm not connecting to anything.

She massages my neck, her stomach again coming into contact, this time against my waist. There's no flicker this time.

I don't belong here.

❧

Now

The river Torrens slides beneath King William Road and if I were to follow the road south to where it becomes King William Street, I'd see the city shut down quickly and silently after 5pm. Shops close, shutters pull down, roller-doors declining an invitation to hurled bottles through windows. People hurry home, bus stops fill and empty and the streetlights come on early. It won't be dark for another three or so hours, and yet the city curls up tight into a ball, ready for the night, waiting to unfold again for the light of a new day.

And what promise does it bring?

There was a time when it brought relief to the hearts of parents, to find their son or daughter at the breakfast table. Alive and well. Where the words 'Be careful' spoken from father to daughter or mother to son when the children left the house for the evening were pregnant with things unsaid. Where those things unsaid invariably wound up in the headlines of the news the following day. Where parents finally slept after hearing the door close quietly shortly after midnight as their children returned safely.

I wander into Chinatown, where there appears to be more life than in the other parts of town. Fat, red lobsters swim in the windows of the restaurants, paper lanterns glow, delicious smells of spice waft from open doors. Perhaps the Chinese are oblivious to the unspoken evil lingering beneath the skin of this city. Perhaps their gods are so long gone and forgotten, or maybe so remote from those that inhabit the churches holding this carcass of a city together, that it does not affect them.

A group of Chinese on the other side of the road push past a drunk Aborigine with his hand out for money. They don't even glance at him, and he curses after them. Then he fixes his eyes upon me. I can see right into him, though I know it's impossible; he's too far away. And suddenly I'm back on the beach, a medic with salts under my nose. The medic says nice words—sunstroke, dehydration—explainable words. But how do they explain what's been happening to me since?

The Aborigine across the road stares at me, his eyes widening, his mouth falling open into a small round 'o'. I'm moving across the road. The squeal of brakes. Honking of horns and angry voices. He backs away from me, hard up against the bluestone wall.

'I know you.' His eyes are so wide, the pupils have eaten away most of the white. He trembles slightly. 'You come back.'

'I've never been here before.'

He squirms against the wall, trying to slide away. 'You always come back. Always hungry.'

I reach out

(don't do it)
and touch him . . .

⊚

From the sky, the river runs like a blue vein through a land of dried blood. Small, black blossoms bloom along the green fringe between the blue and red. As some wither, more again bloom, a cyclical flow of flowers, a nomadic journey along the river's edge. Soon a milky fungus sprouts where the vein hits the sea, spreading inwards, and, like a weed, strangles the black flowers by their very roots.

And as the sky falls or the river rushes upwards, I'm lying amongst hundreds of black bodies. I can't move, I can't breathe. My tongue has swollen and shut my throat. Blood runs from bullet wounds, slicking the grass red, a stream of human water pouring into the river not yet called the Torrens. Flies swarm as the dry wind sends out its call to the carrion that here lies a feast.

A white man stands nearby, reloading a rifle. 'Burn them.'

Flames roar into the sky and the river opens wide its mouth to devour what it can.

⊚

. . . and I'm standing alone on Grote St, a puddle of urine at my feet. It's not mine, it must have been the Aborigine. I'm trembling and nauseous, but in that moment I also find a strange pleasure in this. And it is this pleasure that disturbs me most. *What is happening to me?*

⊚

Next to a roundabout near a park, perhaps ten minutes walk north towards South Terrace stands the house of my dreams. There's a 'For Lease' sign on the high fence. The afternoon sun reflects from large windows onto the sandstone building neighbouring it. The house looks snug here, its angular roof and walls a statement of modern comfort, nestled in the antiquity of an older, more traditional Adelaide. Some might say it looks out of place here, another might say something else entirely.

The real-estate agent pulls up in a navy BMW, leaps from the car, smoothing his suit and hiding a mobile in one fluid movement. Shark grin and pumped handshake and he leads me through the gate towards the door.

(an evil heat emanates from within)

And we step inside, the room full of light, comforting and warm. The real-estate agent looks around nervously, as if expecting something.

'Lovely,' I say. 'If you don't mind me asking, why is the rent so low?'

'It's been empty for a while. The, uh, family think that at this price they'll get the right tenant.' His smile falters, there's no hard sell from this man today. 'You're not from round here, are you?'

'Brisbane, originally.' I know he's not telling me something.

'Oh,' he nods. 'Then you wouldn't . . . ' His conversation falters with the smile.

'No,' I smile. 'I wouldn't.'

We walk into

(welcome home)

the empty bedroom; a huge, spacious, lofty room. A man stands motionless, blending into the corner=, clothed in a grey suit. It matches the colour of his skin. We step towards each other and the walls swirl, washing away the brittle words the real-estate agent had begun to say. There is nothing. There is only us. The man in the suit has black holes for eyes and small hooks and razor blades dangle from his cheeks. The suit smoulders on his skin as we walk towards each other, and the reassuring aroma of cooked flesh consoles me. His mouth opens and the heat rushes out to embrace me.

'Children are our future. Their energy burns so much brighter,' he hisses until the words come from my mouth. We are as one and the world shifts . . .

◉

A young man, barely twenty, in his late teens if we're lucky, lies drugged and naked on the king-sized bed. I look towards the mirror on the ceiling but it's not me looking back. An older man, naked and erect, a scalpel in one hand. There's blood on the sheets, though red satin hides the stains.

Other naked men stand in the room, more wait in the lounge drinking whiskey and laughing. Everyone's eyes are black and empty.

And we shift again . . .

The river Torrens glides by, the water hungry, even here from the safety of the car. The man in the passenger seat next to me opens the bottle and soaks the cloth in his hand with its contents. He wear gloves and is careful not to spill any on his suit. A strong chemical smell permeates the car so I wind down the window.

'Go and get him,' the passenger says.

I step out into the early evening and walk towards a man sitting on a bench overlooking the river. He turns expectantly as I approach. This is a popular haunt.

'You looking for company?' I say, though it's not me talking. It's someone else.

'Sure,' he says. His hair is long and soft. His face yet unlined, maybe late twenties.

The Torrens slaps louder and louder against the riverbank, in time with the blood pumping in my ears.

I nod towards the car. 'Follow me.'

And we shift again . . .

The Adelaide Oval erupts as the crowd roars approval for the goal kicked. Two young girls push through the crowd towards the toilets for the second time that day. The youngest is four years old and her energy is almost blinding. I step forwards, not me, someone else, and take them by the hand. The twisted darkness in the river howls nearby.

And we shift, again and again, back through the years and the decades and the tribes . . .

. . . 'Are you okay?' The real-estate agent shakes my shoulder.

I blink. The room is empty; the man in the suit has gone. The real-estate agent has small beads of sweat shining on his forehead. My skin crawls with invisible lice, tearing at my skin with burning maws. Rot swirls inside my stomach. I need to be sick but I can't move. Instead I smile—or at least something dwelling within moves my lips for me—but the real-estate agent doesn't smile back.

'Tell the Family they've found the right tenant,' says the creature with my voice.

I hadn't expected to see him again and that's got me thinking. Maybe the nexuses are all connected and they have brought him to me. The nexus to a nexus.

'Same again?'

'Yeah, make it JD on ice. Jim Beam's too sweet.' Dave the Drinker runs those long fingers through his shiny, black hair. He points another finger at the teenage girl gyrating against the pole. 'She take her clothes off?'

'No. Others will, but much later. Closer to midnight.' I wink. 'God won't be watching close to the witching hour.'

He laughs and shakes his head, staring down at his sleek, black boots resting on his backpack. 'Fancy running into you here. Last I heard you were up Byron Bay searching for free love and the new age. What the hell brought you to Adelaide? This place is dead, mate.'

'I could ask you the same thing.'

'I'm just passing through. On my way back from Perth.' His boots tap the backpack. 'Bit a quick cash, if you know what I mean.'

'You still dealing?'

'Hey!' His eyes widen in mock surprise then he grins. 'Simply spreading the word. Checked out Freo while I was there. A bit of a happening vibe going down. You'd like it.'

I realise Dave has no idea. He never has and he never will. Unless I show him.

'I don't think Fremantle would be my scene, Dave. You're not going to believe this, but I can feel something happening to me here. I feel, I don't know how to say this, like I can become complete here. I'm not yet, but I can feel it. I think Adelaide is *my* nexus.'

'Adelaide? You kidding me? I spent a year here working the vineyards after uni. Mate, there's nothing happening here except serial killing. Been going on since the mid-'60s, and I'll bet you a kilo of heroin it goes back a hell of a lot further than that.' He slugs the drink the bartender places in front of him, then wipes the corner of his mouth with the back of his hand. 'Urinate I must.'

Dave saunters off to the toilets giving the dancer an approving look on his way past. As soon as he disappears through the door

(he is the one)

a tingling starts in the pit of my stomach. It feels like a barely contained nervousness, a nervousness building from anticipation and excitement. I haven't felt this often, maybe twice in my life. The first time moments before my first tongue-kiss, the second the night I knew I would lose my virginity. And here it is, back, burning away inside me. And I know, as surely as one day I'll die, I know. Tonight Dave will be another of my firsts.

I tell the barman to make my vodkas weak and to double Dave's drinks.

❧

'You okay to drive?' Dave's voice is thick with drink. 'Don't want you getting pulled over.' He indicates his backpack, heavy with hammer. 'Can't risk it, mate. You know what I mean?'

'This is Adelaide. There's nothing to worry about.'

I start the car and we pull out onto North Terrace. The city here shines at night, the splendour of the sandstone giants lining the road. I can tell Dave is caught up in it, the alcohol seeping through into his softer side. I'm finding it hard to concentrate too—though for different reasons. I've had a hard-on for the last hour. Rock solid.

'See this,' says Dave. 'All this fucking grandiosity. Two girls went missing at the Oval back in '73. You know that? Just over there!'

The alcohol is pouring from his body, filling my car, and steaming the windows.

'I know,' I reply. Oh yes, I know.

'This place doesn't stop. Seven women went missing over the Christmas of '76, found them out in Truro. The Beaumont kids on the beach—the beach for Christ's sake. And then there's the Family. You heard of the Family?'

'No.'

'Lawyers, doctors, secret society shit. Abducted, drugged, raped and killed young men. And you say you're getting some sort of connection here?' Dave looks at me, his eyes wild. The spittle is shining on his lips. 'And Snowtown's bloody acid vats were only uncovered a few years back.'

We sit at the lights, the engine idling softly.

'Do you remember telling me about Aleister Crowley, Dave?'

'That's not the same thing.'

'Damn right it's not the same. He was a charlatan. There's something here in this city, Dave. Something real and I'm becoming a part of it. I've been touched.'

The lights change and I accelerate quickly.

'You can too if you want,' I say. The feeling inside me screams to burst out, to rupture my veins and explode. I realise even my voice is trembling.

Dave sits there staring at me. After a while he turns to face the road. 'Micana always said you were *too* weird.'

I want to drive faster, the need is growing unbearable, like an orgasm past release and if I were to ejaculate I'd shoot blood. But I can't risk it, not with Dave in the car. Not now, at the start of my new beginning. And part of the beauty of this city is that nowhere is never far. Soon, within minutes, we are in the driveway of the house. Its lights, like the walls and roof, are angular and stab into the darkness.

Dave steps from the car as if he's wading through glue. 'This is the house.'

'Yes it is.' I take his pack from the car. 'This is the house. My house.'

'No, no, no, you don't understand. This is *the* house! *This* is the place they caught the guy who took the rap for the Family.' His face is pale in the moonlight. It looks like the blood has gone to sleep inside his body. 'I don't know about this.'

'Sweetness and light, Dave. Moonstones and crystals. You won't find them here.' I take him by the arm and lead him to the door. He is like a leaf and I am the wind. 'You want magic?'

He nods dumbly.

'Behind this door, the magic's real.' I turn the key and the falling of the lock is thunderous in the silence of the night. 'Go ahead, open it.'

And he does.

I follow.

I cannot remember the exact details of my first kiss. I can still remember the sudden press of lips and the tentative, gentle touch of tongue that soon made way for a thrusting exploration for fear the kiss may soon be over, never to be experienced again. Of standing in a dark room and never wanting it to end but knowing it would never be enough. Yes, I remember that awful, excited rush before the first kiss, and the burning feeling lingering on my lips—the burn of her lips—for the week that followed. My first fumbling attempt at sexual intercourse I remember even less—warm and wet and over. But the feeling beforehand was, until now, the defining moment of intense unyielding unease. A moment more powerful than the act or the orgasm, and so too afterwards the feeling of invincibility that lasted for days. These thresholds I've crossed are nothing to this one and although it's happening now I can barely comprehend a thing.

A spear in my hand. The wooden shaft has a serpent carved into it, circling upwards to bite the head of sharpened stone. A gift from the grey-skinned man with the ashen eyes and fire mouth who even now lies sprawled upon the ceiling, heat pouring from his maw.

'Where did you get that?' Dave's sprawled on my couch. He tries to rise.

The river Torrens winds gently towards the ocean, fourteen of the thirty-two major churches in the inner city within sight of its waters. Where would a settlement, a city, be without its lifeblood? Especially in the driest state of the driest continent on earth? Colonel William Light built this city with foresight and intelligence, a vision of city squares and wide streets, lined with open gardens and surrounded by parklands.

I stand next to his statue overlooking 'Light's Vision'. His face is set in stone, gazing down upon the parklands and the river running through. It's a beautiful city; a calm and civilised city. There is no communal cluster of spiritual, new-age shops in this city offering guidance and healing for the lost; they are spread few and far between the suburbs, their unity destroyed by unyielding bluestone and sandstone churches whose foundations run deep in an attempt to staunch what they discovered. Dave the Drinker recognised the nexus here. Could he have embraced it as I have done? I think not. He was not made for places such as this. Not many are. Colonel Light staring valiantly over the darkness beneath the veil. I wonder what he thinks of the sights he has since seen?

I give him a wink and wander down to the university. It's a beautiful afternoon here in the City of Churches and there'll be plenty of people relaxing beside the river.

THIS IS THE END, HARRY, GOOD NIGHT!

The lights dimmed and conversation hushed. Butler sat amongst the audience, dread creeping into the pit of his stomach.

What the hell am I doing here? Death is a part of life, he thought. A huge part of mine. There are too many cameras; someone might recognise me. This is stupid. I should leave.

It wasn't just the TV cameras that were unsettling Butler; he'd noticed other cameras, hidden from the audience, and he suspected microphones were also concealed in the studio. Heavy-set minders moved amongst the aisles hushing the noisier in the crowd.

'Do you think it will be Dad?'

'Aunt Martha?'

'John?'

'I hope it's Grandad.'

Butler sat silently. He wiped his hands on his trousers. Third time.

If I don't believe in God, why believe in this? No matter what he said to convince himself, it didn't work. It ate away at him, gnawing his confidence and his ability to act. Making him useless. He felt it, and in this room with cameras and lights he felt something else too. Everyone here clung to it, their essence or aura—Butler didn't know how to explain it—and it intensified, building like a slow, dark storm until someone said

'Action' and the man in the black suit strode like thunder to the centre of the stage.

◉

Butler tightened his grip on the automatic as Hill kicked in the door. The sound of the television spilled like trash into the hallway—*'They're either trying to tell me someone has a name like Katrina . . . or they want me to acknowledge a name like Katrina'*—and Hill stepped through the doorway, his gun barking, muzzle-flash chasing the shadows from the room.

Sometimes, when it was like this, Butler didn't remember anything until it all stopped. When the blue-grey smoke awoke his nostrils and the roar of gunfire still throbbed within his ears; when the blood screaming through his body slowed a little to release the machine. And sometimes he saw it all in minutiae, every detail burnt into his brain, measured and processed so every movement he made exacted the desired result.

Like this time. The flash on the wall illuminated the damp, floral wallpaper faded not by the sun, but by the dank oppression of rundown misery in a lost hotel. Of the cheap brass, 49 held by a screw to the splintered door as it swayed back and forth, slowing down but not yet stopped; the feel of the worn carpet beneath his shoes, slightly sticky like a carpet swollen with beer in a deserted pub the morning after; the tendons jutting from the back of Hill's neck, sweat beading from skin recently shaved with a barber's number 2; the acrid smell of cordite filling the room faster than the screams in his ears. Butler followed Hill into the room.

Bang!

Eject. Recoil.

Bang! Bang!

A man clambered over the back of a couch, firing aimlessly. A bullet burned past Butler's head. The bathroom door closed to his right but he was too busy firing at the man behind the couch. Hill's eyes bulged, his grin widened, and blood ballooned from the arm of the man behind the couch. The next bullet took the man in the chest, crashing him back

158

against the wall. His gun hand smashed the lamp from the table and the light bulb exploded. Hill leapt over the couch and fired once more. The two of them stood there in the calm and the smoke. Blood arced over the wall, smearing down to the body cooling on the floor.

'Has she passed? Yes? Okay we'll start from there . . . '

The guy they had been talking about on the way there was on the television. Butler turned it off. He wasn't even out of breath. Hill turned to him and nodded. He removed the earplugs and reloaded his gun as Hill searched the body.

A muffled sound, a hitch of breath or a barely suppressed whimper. Butler crouched, swinging the barrel to face the bathroom door. Hill crept along the wall until he stood poised next to the door. One finger. Hill raised his leg. Two fingers. And on the count of three Hill went to kick the door.

Then it started to go wrong.

A hole in the door exploded outwards taking Hill in the chest. He spun round, his eyes locking on Butler, mouth wide—*he's laughing as they high-five each other, Butler's getting blown while Hill takes her from behind on the stairs of the club; after they've finished the three of them finish off a bottle of bourbon*—and another bullet hit him in the back, erupting from his chest in a fountain of blood. Hill collapsed on the floor, the wind whistling through his lungs. Shot after shot ripped through the door, sending splinters flying across the room. Then the click of the hammer on an empty chamber. The sound of sobbing.

Without pausing to think, Butler hurled himself at the door. He rolled and kicked out. The door shattered. He was firing even before he focused clearly on the shape huddled against the toilet. Before he noticed the shape was a *her*, and the *her* held a baby in her arms.

Such a good baby, he thought, such a *quiet* baby.

And by the time he stopped it was too late.

☻

'Why didn't you come sooner?' his mother asked from her bed.

The room stank of roses and lilies, their perfume a weak mask for the dying flesh permeating the bedroom. Her flesh, hot and brittle, rested on his arm. The bones of her fingers bulged beneath skin drawn tight.

'You know,' Butler said.

'No, I don't. I thought maybe you had died instead of me.'

He tried to avoid her eyes; a thin film obscured the sharp blue that once shone from her face. A film Butler had seen glazed over the eyes of the freshly dead.

'Been busy at work.' It sounded pathetic, but he didn't know what else to say.

'Your work!' The words sounded harsh in her throat, like gravel thrown over broken concrete. She shook her head slowly. The cross on her necklace reflected soft light, drawing his eyes away from hers. 'You think I don't know?'

Butler held her hand tight in his own. 'I'm here, Mother. I'm here now.' He felt a squeeze, as gentle as her kiss on his brow as a child.

'You're a good boy, Robert,' she said. 'I brought you up with God on your side. You haven't forgotten that, have you?'

He couldn't help the snort of derision that puffed from his nose. A small sound, but in the silence of the deathroom it sounded like a gunshot.

'I worry about you, Robert. I can feel Him,' she squeezed his hand again, 'closer to me, every day. He brings comfort as my time approaches.'

He tightened his jaw, immovable. Silent.

'I'm ready to go to Him, Robert. But I can't leave until you promise me.'

'You'll pull through, Mother. Don't talk like that.'

She laughed, a papyrus rattle deep in her throat. 'You never could lie to me, my baby boy. Please, for your mother's sake, repent. Wash the blood from your hands.'

Their eyes locked, his hard and unyielding, hers milky, soft, forgiving.

'I know what you do,' she whispered. 'Grant a dying woman her final wish. Promise me. Don't be like Thomas the Doubter. Don't make me show you what is true.'

She's lying, he thought. The madness of approaching death. 'Mother, what are you talking about?'

'Sometimes, Robert, when my eyes hide behind sleep, He shows me things, of what will be and what can be. I've felt the demons come for me and He holds them at bay. Do you know why?'

Butler shook his head.

'For you, Robert. He wants me to save you.' Her hand clawed into his arm, the heat of her disease seeping into his skin. 'In your salvation shall be mine. Promise me!'

The second's silence hung like a shroud in the makeshift mausoleum her bedroom had become. Her eyes implored him, boring into his head.

The last words Butler said to his mother while she lived were a lie. 'I promise.'

He wondered if she knew.

The wheeze of a punctured lung, followed by a soft gurgling whistle.

Butler heard distant voices outside in the hallway. His gun still smoked, the barrel pointing where the last shot had been fired. At the chest of the woman on the bathroom floor. She slumped against the laminated wall. Tears ran down her cheeks, smearing the thick mascara into black trails. A thin trickle of bright, red blood from lip to chin, then the mess of brain and soft, yet-unformed skull splattering her chest.

She still clutched the empty gun tightly in her hand. Her fingernails were long and heavily painted—a red lacquer stronger and brighter than that dripping from her mouth. One had broken, the palm of her hand bleeding. Her gun clattered on the tiles as her fingers gave up. Small, mewling noises bubbled from her mouth and she clasped her arms around the baby in her lap. Her chest heaved again, another wet whistle, and the only scream came from her eyes.

Somewhere, a million miles away, something hissed his name.

Without air she couldn't speak, but her lips formed again and again. *My baby, my baby, my baby . . .*

When he closed his eyes he heard her, over and over. His mother's voice. Cracked and broken.

His name hissed again and Butler opened his eyes. The woman's sorrow burned up at him and he squeezed the trigger gently. The bathroom amplified the explosion and lent an echo to the cartridge as it bounced over the tiles.

'Buttssss . . . ' A slow hiss behind him. Hill on the floor, face down, a dark pool beneath him, soaking into the carpet as it spread.

'It's okay, it's okay. Don't move.' Butler knelt beside Hill. The blood had left Hill's face. Sirens howled in the distance.

'I'm . . . aahhhh . . . I'm . . . I'm . . . '

'You got to promise me, Hill.'

'I'm . . . I'm . . . '

'Like we said in the car. That guy on the TV. Promise me.'

Hill couldn't nod his head, but Butler thought he saw him move his eyes instead.

❧

'Sorry, mate.'

The last shot of the evening resonated in Butler's head longer than he'd have dreamed.

❧

The rain held session over his mother's funeral; a cold rain driven hard by the wind off the bay. They lowered her coffin into the grave—a hole full of nothing to be filled with even less. Butler worried his grip on the rope would slip, that in this, his mother's goodbye, he would fail her again. But the rope bit into his skin and the pain helped him concentrate on the task.

His sister dropped a single green lily on top of the coffin and retreated into the arms of her husband. Butler hardly knew him. In fact, he hardly knew his sister—she'd been no more than ten when he'd left home.

While the priest mumbled words about God and life, Butler watched his sister. Her face showed the same pain and emotions as the rest of the family, but it was to the bulge in her belly his eyes were drawn. He imagined he saw the bulge move beneath the stretched, black shirt, where a peak of white flesh showed between the seams and her skirt. A small kick of life urgent for the world, as the priest laid their mother, urgent for another. The passing of essence from one to the other.

162

I don't need this shit, Butler thought. He wished the priest would finish so he could get out of the rain.

They took turns throwing sodden clumps into the grave. The wind blew fresh, angry gusts as the funeral procession left for the warmth of the local pub. Something made Butler stay to watch the gravediggers fill the grave. He couldn't say what it was, but he thought perhaps he didn't want to be around his family. Didn't want to see their accusing eyes with knowledge of his 'life', and the disrespect he'd bought into theirs.

On the tombstone in gothic letters larger than her own name: In God We Trust. Butler stood there letting the rain whip his skin raw, with the chill barely settled in his bones. He could stand there for years.

He wondered what Hill's funeral would be like. Butler didn't know what the police did with unclaimed and unmourned bodies. And up until now, he'd never considered it.

❧

I don't care I don't care I don't care . . .

A mantra repeated, until the words lost all meaning and their form became a sound, a thought, in his head. A drone to coax Butler back into sleep. And when his eyes closed he felt the darkness draw around him, pressing tight against his face, squashing him beneath the covers of his bed. His skin crawled from the base of his feet to his groin, the sweat between his thighs clammy.

❧

The muted roar of the never-sleeping city, the lonely howl of interstate trucks tearing through the night on deserted freeways—a lullaby for the sleepless.

I don't care I don't CARE I DON'T CARE!

With every beat of his heart the hiss of his name pumped through his veins. He imagined his mother creeping across the ceiling when he slept. Leaning down over his face and whispering into his ear. *You promised me, Robert. Don't make me make you.*

The woman in the bathroom, clutching her baby. In his sleep it wailed as its mother rocked it slowly back and forth in her arms.

It's a boy, Butler thought, it's wearing blue.

Blood pooled on the tiles.

How can the baby make so much noise, he wondered. Such a *quiet* baby.

The mother lifted her head toward the light bulb and howled, the cry a horde of insects disturbed from their feast on the dead. The baby turned to Butler, the top half of its head splattered over its mother's chest. A tiny eyeball sat propped next to the mother's foot from where it had been torn from the impact of the bullet. The tongue flapped in the remains of the baby's shattered jaw, faster and faster, the intensity of sound increasing in pitch, higher, higher—

—the banshee screaming 'Promise me!'

The Devil calling.

❦

'I've been a psychic medium for over fifteen years,' said the man in the black suit. His voice purred confidence. 'Anything can happen during my readings.'

A soft murmur of expectation from the studio audience. Butler sat uncomfortably on the seat, his gut a twisted knot. If Hill could see him now. What shit would he have dealt Butler for being here? But Hill couldn't see him now. *Could he?*

The psychic wandered over to a section of the audience on the other side of the room. Eager faces, bodies straightened—a pregnant hush.

'I'm getting a Marge—a Margaret over here,' said the psychic. 'I don't know what this means. Marge could be someone who passed over, she could be someone here, she could be someone that you know. A Marge, Marga, Martha . . . '

'I had a Martha,' said a middle-aged woman.

'Okay. Has she passed?'

'Yes.'

'Okay. We'll start there. They're making me feel like there's some type of motherly vibration that has passed because there's an older female coming through and I feel like—'

'It's my aunty.'

'Okay, that explains it. She's telling me something to do with an *R* . . .'

Butler almost snorted. There *were* microphones in here. He'd heard the name 'Martha' mentioned when he'd arrived. He was wasting his time. This guy was a cold reader, another James Van Praagh, another John Edward. It was all a farce. Butler stood to leave and one of the lights exploded, showering sparks across the stage. The room temperature dropped and so did the man in the black suit—to his knees. The psychic's eyes rolled back, veins bulged from his temples and a trickle of urine formed beneath him.

The voice that hissed from his throat froze Butler where he stood. It sounded like the wind howling at his mother's funeral. The man in the black suit stared blindly with an arm raised, finger pointing straight at him.

Then the lights shone bright upon Butler and the voice began its howl anew.

❧

'What do you do with all your money?' Hill cranked the heating in the car up full. 'Get yourself a good set of wheels with a decent air-con system, for Christ's sake! It's freezing in here.'

'I like the cold,' said Butler. 'Keeps me awake.'

'You want your fingers to be working. How the hell you going to pull the trigger if they don't?'

'They'll work.'

They drove in silence for the next few minutes, content to watch the docklands passing by. Lonely neon and wide empty roads, the occasional semi-trailer for company. It wouldn't take long before they reached the hotel and business began.

'You're pretty quiet tonight,' said Hill.

'Yeah,' Butler said. He didn't like to talk before a job, and Hill never shut up until they were actually doing the job.

'I heard about your mother.' Hill stared straight ahead. They knew eye contact could be uncomfortable, too intimate. Easier to have sex with the same woman than talk, really talk, to each other. 'Sorry to hear about it, Buttsy Boy. How bad is it?'

'Doctor says three months. I haven't been to see her yet.' He hated it when Hill called him that name.

Hill didn't need to say what Butler was thinking. They'd both killed before and thought nothing more of it than an exchange for a healthy bank account transaction.

'If it's going to happen, it's going to happen. You know what they say, ain't nothing guaranteed except for birth, death and taxes . . . '

Hill laughed. 'I'm not paying any fucking taxes.' He turned the heater down a notch as the car finally began to warm. 'That reminds me. You seen that show on the TV? The one with that psychic guy who speaks to the dead?'

'Yeah. Pretty freaky.'

'Nah, it's a crock of shit. This girlfriend of mine is into that sort of thing and she was telling me all about it. He's what you call a cold reader. Just picks stuff up out of what you say. You know, starts off saying he's getting a John, anyone know a John.' Hill loaded his gun. 'Who the fuck doesn't know a John? And the sucker in the audience is just dishing up the clues, desperate to make contact. Yeah, yeah, my dad is a John they'll say. And then the guy will ask if they're dead or not. For fuck's sake! If he's talking to them from the other side then they must be dead! How come he doesn't already know?'

Butler laughed. 'You got a point there. I was thinking maybe he was picking it all up from the audience. Some sort of ESP thing.'

'They ain't that fucking flash, Buttsy Boy.' Hill loaded the other gun and put them both into the glovebox. 'Just another charlatan, my friend. You don't get to ask a thing of the dead in those shows. The guy asks you stuff, you confirm it, then he tells you it straight back like some revelation from heaven. Death is a part of life and if the dead are gathering in a television studio to talk crap with a TV show host, well, you just got to think about that, eh?'

Butler laughed again. 'Too right. I mean, if you were dead what would you be telling the living? That your Uncle Jimmy always loved the red chair in the hallway, and he wanted you to have it?'

'No way,' said Hill. 'I'd want to know if there's a God. Am I going to burn in Hell? And is Hell so bad I better mend my ways? You're Catholic, right? You can repent, can't you? Can I do that or do I have to convert?'

'I wouldn't know. I'm lapsed.' Butler turned off the lights and the engine and then coasted down the driveway of a dilapidated hotel in the back lots of Footscray, the industrial area by the river. There were only two room lights on, the rest slumped in darkness. Why the hell would you hide out here? It's too quiet, thought Butler. Guess the guy thought it'd be harder to find.

'You heard of Harry Houdini, eh? Greatest magician who ever lived. He spent years trying to talk to the other side and ended up becoming one of the greatest spiritual debunkers. Made a deal with his wife to use a secret code.' They got out of the car and Hill passed Butler his gun. 'I'll make you a deal, but we don't need a secret code. If you die, come back and tell me what I have to worry about. If I die, I'll tell you. Now, let's go wipe our conscience clean and earn our pay.'

☜

The man in the black suit's head shot back, his adam's apple huge and exposed, grinding up and down in his throat. Blood trickled from the corners of his mouth where he'd bitten into his lips.

'Did you know he was going to do this?' one of the minders nearby whispered to another.

'No, I wish he'd tell us about these stunts beforehand.'

'You know ratings. Looks better if we're surprised too.'

Butler stood transfixed, staring in horror at the psychic kneeling under the lights.

'Do you remember the promise?' the voice hissed. Someone in the audience started crying. 'Do you remember the promise you made?'

Butler sank into his seat. His head nodded slightly, while his lips worked soundlessly, his tongue dry and thick in the back of his mouth. A small, keening noise fluted from his throat. He'd made two promises, but the voice—it was all wrong, neither male or female—an inhuman sound.

'Who . . . who is this?' The sweat poured from his groin, his armpits. Bile threatened his mouth. An image of his mother coursed into his head, her face sweet in death, an ancient book bound with skin in her hands. His name written on the pages in the blood of those he'd killed. And the sweat poured and poured. Hill laughing and saying it's all bullshit, that it doesn't matter. There is no heaven and hell. Pull the fucking trigger, Buttsy Boy! It all adds to nothing.

The man in the black suit laughed, a hideous sound of splintered wood and twisted metal, of broken limbs and bleeding wounds. A hysterical wail teetering on salvation.

Say my name, please say my name. Butler, affectionately known as Robert, lapsed Catholic and devout atheist, wiped the sweat from his palms onto his trousers. Then I'll know. Come on, Hill. Call me Buttsy Boy.

SLICE OF LIFE

I felt like taking the paperweight and caving in the back of Carver's head. Discovering whether that brand of gel he smears could stem the flow of blood and brain before it soaked into the wool of a thousand-dollar suit bought in Chicago on a holiday. (What sort of wanker buys suits on their holiday?)

If Vogon was here I'd probably do it, but he rarely turns up at my work. He reckons nothing good ever happens there. No intensity. Vogon's pretty fucked up though; his good equals Bad.

'Sure thing, Mr. Carver. Be on your desk in the morning.' It doesn't have the satisfaction of crunching bone so, when no one is looking, I give my boss the finger instead.

Carver turns in his stride, his corporate cunt of a hairstyle still shining under the office fluorescence of another late evening. He nods serious professional attitude then retires to his office. From the window I watch his Merc depart the carpark less than ten minutes later.

'You want a future in this company, Haines?' Carver had said. He'd perched on the corner of my desk, manicured hands clasped between his thighs. 'I'm counting on you. I need it first thing tomorrow.'

Life and death, I'm sure. And because I'm not married and don't have kids, I get 'volunteered' for overtime. There's a reason why I'm not married, not that he'd give a fuck. How the hell will I meet anyone real, with pricks like him hoisting work on at me the end of the fucking day?

Still, there's no point bitching about it. I might as well just get stuck in and finish the bastard before 11:05pm. If I don't leave by then, the Belgrave-Lilydale train will be nigh on empty. And that would deprive me my main course of pleasure for the day.

Doesn't Carver realise I don't give a fuck about the promotion?

The reflections of my colleagues in the darkening windows form a firmer reality than does the city. Sometimes, when I'm the only one left, I switch off the lights and stare out onto the city, watching people flush through neon streets, the dead and alive, brains dulled in skull soupbowls, one stumbling foot in front of the other. Living empty lives until, eventually, even they see the decayed flesh wrapped in expensive wool and leather, sloughing from the bone of once-bright youth.

I'd switch off the lights now, but I'm sure Suzanne wouldn't appreciate it. The very model of corporate efficiency, long hours and hard work and usually my supervisor on the big projects. Craig is working back too, as usual. He's into it, the lucky bastard. Once, over a few beers at lunch, he'd expressed his desire to 'sleep' with Suzanne. I laughed—I'd never thought about it before. She was such a cold bitch socially. Craig reckoned he'd wait until she broke up with her boyfriend before he tried anything. I hardly speak to her now, not that it matters.

I copy responses from an old proposal and paste them into the RFI. Another Request-for-Fucking-Information where we forced 'No' into 'Yes' without legally lying. It wouldn't take too long to finish this. Same old shit pushed out somewhere else. Someone would buy. At the end of the month I'd be up for review and Carver and his cronies would offer one of us a 2.5% commission on any successful proposals.

'What time you working to, Craig?'

'Till about eight,' he says. Diligent bastard never took his eyes off his monitor. He doesn't look at me too much since I'd fucked Suzanne at the Christmas do. We haven't been out for a beer or lunch since. I got as big a kick out of the blood draining from his face as I did licking the sweat from the hollow Suzanne's back made as her spine curved into her arse. Sure sign she was about to cum, I had told Craig.

'Well, I might have a smoke. Anyone?' I offer a half-empty pack as I walk past their desks. Silence usually means no takers.

I waltz into the women's toilet—I don't smoke, but the less people really know about you the better—and slip into the cubicle Suzanne prefers. I unzip, spit into the palm of my hand and masturbate, remembering her reaction when I'd thrown the photo of the boyfriend down on her bed in front of her as I was taking her from behind. She'd clenched tight, rigid as, but she was too close to care. She'd wept afterwards as I'd dressed. I hadn't expected the tears and was pleasantly surprised, so I didn't tell her I had taken the condom off.

'This is risky, you realise,' says a voice behind me.

It's Vogon halfway through a transformation. I see my chin and nose forming on his misshapen visage. His body appears more in proportion to a humanoid now too—he's managed to elongate his limbs from the squat appendages he'd begun with.

'Not now, Vogon. Can't you see I'm busy?'

'She could come in at any moment. You could be fired instead of doing the firing.'

'That's the point.' I squeeze the last drops onto the seat and smear it where her flesh will contact. He's ruined the moment for me, though. 'What the hell are you doing here? This is not the norm.'

'Just making sure. It worries me I might lose my host through some preventable act of stupidity.'

'I'm touched.'

'Yes, you have been. Probably since birth.' His face ripples as he studies the cubicle door. 'It seems the female of the species does not adorn the toilet door with decorations from the nose. Why is this?'

'Because.' I push past Vogon into the washroom. I notice he's not reflecting in the mirrors. 'What are you doing here, seriously?'

'Are you going to be bad again? I think that you are.'

'What? You're out of your warped little mind, buddy.'

'And you're not?'

'Point taken.' I indicate the mirror. 'You'd better sort that out if you want to pass as human.'

I leave Vogon panicking in front of the mirror and make my way back to my desk. The cheek of the prick coming in here to check me out. What if someone walked in on *him*? Now that would be a little risky.

Suzanne lifts an eyebrow as I pass her, the eyes in her sockets professionally calculating, emotionless. I have to admit she's consistent. Cold before we fucked; cold after. I wish the bitch took the late train home with me —just to give her a fucking scare, snap her out of her reverie. Or better still, maybe I should let her know I told Craig. He is still head down, so I rub him on the shoulder as I hover over him.

'How's it going with the report, Craig?'

'Almost there, just got to tidy up the executive summary before I print it.'

'You applying for the position?'

'No.' His shoulders tense so I dig my fingers into the muscle.

'Same.'

'I'm finishing up in five, Craig,' says little miss ice. No capitals. 'Can I still get a lift?'

'Yeah, sure thing, Suze.' His lips worm into a smile. 'I can print this out first thing tomorrow.'

I clap him once more on the back, my hand now dry, note where he's saving the document and go back to my desk.

Copy. Paste.

Copy.

Her arse: two ovular haunches gliding seductively beneath red cotton, tight and sweet. The calves lean and defined, flexing muscle-toned power. A fine piece of meat, as they'd say. The click of high-heels over the floorboards as Craig shuffles after her. I imagine his tongue drooling from his mouth as he pants behind.

After they leave, I open Craig's document, delete several lines from each of the pages, type 'Fuck you, Carver' and run a utility to reset the date-timestamp to when Craig had saved it. Maybe I will go for that promotion.

❀

The late trains are always on time.

I think it's because they worry that the monsters come out late at night, and darkness provides the finest prey. I take the carriage that most of the people get into, knowing after a few stops it will be lucky if there are half a dozen of us left. Safety in numbers, they say.

Come Box Hill and the opportunities finally present themselves: a guy in a dark suit busies himself with the evening's MX; a couple of teenagers nurse their skateboards and tag the train with thick markers; a girl in her late teens, recently finished a shift at a David Jones cosmetic counter, sinks against the wall seeking refuge in her headphones; an old drunk shuffles between carriages bumming coins; a woman in her late twenties with heroin-eyes and a face drawn tight over her skull languishes on a three-seater, a battered wind-cheater draped over her dependant body. She hasn't been *here* since East Richmond.

Any of these will do. The end of the line.

'Don't.' Vogon appears beside me. He's managed to get the colour of my eyes right, but he's used the same blue for the nostril hairs. 'It's not worth it.'

'Keep it down, someone might hear,' I whisper. 'Why are you on the train? Are you following me?'

'I'm just making sure. I don't want you to jeopardise the mission.'

'What fucking mission, Vogon? You and your race conquering Earth sometime soon? I'm telling you you're wasting your time following me around. I can't help you.'

The suit is looking at me so I glare him back to his papers.

'As I was saying . . . Vogon?' He pisses me off when he ups and disappears like that, leaving me sitting here talking to myself. People might think I'm weird.

❀

The two skaters get off at Blackburn. One of them gives me the finger and shouts 'Crazy motherfucker.' They laugh, throw down their boards and skate off. I sense the suit sniggering but the vocal abuse is worth it—the cosmetic girl's eyes flutter briefly open and snap shut when she sees me staring. *That's twice now, girly. Three times and you're out.* The junkie moans softly and rustles in her skin. The drunk has moved further down the carriages looking for easy bucks, some food or booze, or fast-food wrappers to suck the grease from. Whatever gives, he's taking.

Vogon manages to slip into the seat behind the cosmetic girl. He has sprouted thick, black curls from his misshapen scalp, and his greyish skin pales in an imitation of hers. Blood red colours his lips. He turns to me and grins, his pouty lips peeling back from thick irregular teeth. He obviously notices my consternation and comes over to sit next to me.

'Not her,' he says. 'She still lives at home. Parents will be expecting her. I want you to really draw out the experience. Maybe for a day or two.'

'How presumptuous of you. Why do you think I'm going to do something?'

'I know you. Better than you know yourself.'

'I don't think so.'

'If it's her, I won't let you. It's too risky.'

'That's the point. My reasons for doing it are entirely different to yours.'

'I won't let you,' Vogon says. The adopted human features dissolve from his mass, leaving a grey bulk sulking beside me. He is serious.

'Now approaching Mitcham station,' pipes the inflectionless drone over the loudspeakers.

Cosmetic girl opens her eyes.

Strike three. You're out. I grin. She looks away, rises and makes her way to the doors. The suit is still absorbed in his paper, junkie still out, Vogon has disappeared again, and Mitcham really isn't too far away from my place.

I stand slowly, stretching my legs and arms, and languidly stroll to the doors, holding onto the rail above her head, near enough to smell the perfumes she's been trying at work. J'adore, I think. She moves closer to the doors. As the train lurches to a halt, I bump her and apologise, savouring in the brief warmth of contact, wishing I had managed to touch her skin. She'd moved at the last minute though, and I only got the tease of white cotton.

I'm close behind as she steps off the train, her knee-length skirt revealing calves a little thicker than I prefer, but still a most accommodating cut. Someone pushes me from behind.

'Sorry,' says the suit. He slips past and falls into step behind the scurrying cosmetics girl. Headlights flash in the carpark, and she waves and runs towards the car.

In the carriage Vogon mouths the words 'What did I say?'

The train utters its warning beeps; I jump back on and the carriage jerks its way towards Lilydale.

Vogon smiles; he's perfected the shit-eating grin of corporate smugness. I should smash him then, hard in the face, but I don't. Vogon can be very unpredictable. Every fibre of that alien, metamorphosed body of his cries out 'I told you so!' He sits awhile basking in it, too. Sometimes he embodies everything I fucking hate about the face I present to the world during the daylight hours. The gloating, conservative cunt knows this—he's imitated me for years now—and I wish I had the mental strength to kill him. And, in the end, I conform to the mouldings of others.

'It's the junkie then,' Vogon says. 'What do you think?'

'I don't know. Look at her.'

He peels back the wind-cheater, tugging gently at it where it has scabbed to her upper arms. 'Been picking at herself a little, but she's fine.'

'She's too skinny.'

'No, no, no, there's enough meat on her bones. I know you want to. It's why I'm here.'

'She's diseased, Vogon. Who know's what she's carrying?'

'Then cook it longer.' He shudders and laughs. 'Quick, your stop is coming up soon. Pry open the lips.'

'You do it.'

'You work with the flesh.'

'I'm not touching her.'

'Pry open the lips!'

I pinch her nose and her mouth pops open, strands of thickened saliva bridge raw, cracked lips. Her breath is damp and shallow.

Vogon quivers and moans. His form dissolves and he swarms over her body like a sea of black ants over jungle flesh, forcing his way into her mouth. Within seconds his amorphous mass has slid inside her, waiting.

His voice echoes inside my head. 'Do it.'

Reluctantly I touch her cheek, the elasticity of her skin burnt from abuse, now cold and dry against my fingertips. Not unlike newspaper thawing from the morning rounds. A world away from the living.

'The quota needs to be filled for the first phase of occupation.' Vogon's voice swims between my ears. 'You don't have much time. Do it!'

Her eyes flutter open, pinpoint pupils struggling in the bright lights of the carriage. She coughs and a splutter of blood-flecked phlegm sprays the seat.

'Ahhrrgg . . . ' she croaks. She pulls the windcheater tight as she struggles to sit. The stink of chemicals pours from her skin. 'Wha the fuck . . . who?'

I sit there, silent, trying to look blank, to stop my lips curling.

'Hey, we passed Nunawading yet? I gotta get off Nunawading.'

'You missed it. Croydon is the next stop.'

'Ah, shit. Hey, you got $2.60 for a ticket? Need a ticket to get back.' She scratches at her arms.

Vogon hisses. 'Do it!'

I leaf through my wallet, making sure she sees the wad of orange and red bills. 'Sorry, lady. Got no coins on me.'

'Some notes then maybe, just a fiver. Please.'

'I've got nothing that small.'

'Look, mister. C'mon. Anything.' She edges towards me. 'I'll suck your cock.'

'Maybe I could give you some cash for a cab at the next stop. I'm getting off there. If you know what I mean.'

Vogon laughs at the pun, though her mouth doesn't move. 'Very good.'

She wipes her lips and forces a smile. 'The ride'll cost at least a twenty.'

As the train brakes into the Croydon stop, I follow her to the doors. Vogon keens in anticipation within her body as we step from the train and move into the shadows outside the station. Where the lights and cameras are blind to my slice of life.

❦

Vogon is home before me. He glares at me from the couch. He still wears the cracked lips of the junkie and blends the cut of my suit with the fabric of the wind-cheater.

'You cheated me,' he says sullenly.

'You sucked my cock.' I laughed. 'How'd my cum taste?'

'You cheated me! You let her go!'

'You don't decide who I choose. Since when did you think you had the right to make my decisions?'

'I keep you safe!'

'You're not my fucking moral conscience, Vogon. I will not let you decide who I take just because you've developed a taste for it. Anyway, she was a junkie.'

'There's hundreds of them. They teem in this city. Why won't you let me try them?'

I sigh. 'They are unhealthy.'

'Whatever happened to "too risky" being the point?'

'You wouldn't understand.'

It is a quarter after midnight and the evening has left me with an appetite. I put on a Sisters Of Mercy bootleg and busy myself in the kitchen. I slice a spanish onion and sliver two cloves of garlic as Vogon sulks in silence, slowly metamorphosing into a rough semblance of his host—me. I dash some olive oil into a deep saucepan and place it over the gas flame.

'You want some?'

'You know I don't eat.' His form shifts again, his face narrowing into the pout of the gay boy from last year.

'That's my point. It's like drinking wine. You start off with the sweet moselles of this world, and you work your way up the ladder until only the shiraz and cab sav's will do. Like cheese, from your shrink-wrap plastic to the finest French blues. The well-done steak to the lump of meat still warm from its own blood. Taste is so delicate, Vogon, and she'd been tainting hers for too long.'

As the oil heats, I remove two fresh kidneys from the fridge. I slit the round side of the kidney and peel the membrane back towards the fatty core. I prefer to leave the core intact as it moistens and bastes the kidneys as they cook. I sauté the onions and garlic, and when browned, place the kidneys into the pan, the sizzle of searing flesh salivating. After one-and-a-half minutes—I like them pink in the middle—I turn the kidneys, adding a dash of mustard and Worcestershire sauce. The frying aromas tantalise my tastebuds, and that last minute waiting for the kidneys to brown seems as long as the train ride home from work.

'You know,' I say to Vogon as I serve the meal, 'I'm thinking of going for that promotion at work. Get me closer to Carver. I think I'm ready for that next slice of life. What do you think?'

But Vogon has already disappeared.

THE SKIN POLIS

A barefoot boy slips me a note as he weaves through the crowd, his foot-falls disturbing the dust layered over the cracked cement cooking in the morning sun. I search for faces, find no-one, and retire to the room at the back of my shop. The note is a grey and creased, stained with months of sweat from dissident fingers and, as I unfold it, insect wings flutter in my stomach. The message is written in a soft, thick graphite:

You're next.

After I read it, I smear my thumb across the words on the paper. Another boy will return before twilight to collect, to return it for reuse; purchasing paper involves too many questions these days, let alone the cost. DNA testing is outlawed, though we all suspect they'll use it if they find this piece.

Simple words: *You're next.*

It's that time again and I wonder how much I have left before they come. Perhaps a day, not less, but no more than three. I don't have much to do though, I've been careful since my brother. You learn lessons quick these days. You have to. I have a photo of him and me up on the false wall and I should take it down. Some of the others say it draws unnecessary attention; you're allowed family, but no icons, nothing religious unless prescribed, no political activists, no criminals, no martyrs. It's too big to fit into my wallet, and though I have the equipment to make a reduced copy, I dare not take the risk. That stuff is too easy to test for authenticity.

I admire the photo for one brief moment—the last record of anyone in my family, discounting the stoning of my brother, which can be found in 'educational' texts—how young we looked, for I am still young though I look much older than I am, and the clothes we were allowed to wear. I remember him bragging about that shirt, a $10 ill-fitting bargain in garish fluorescents depicting Polynesian women gathering fruit and vegetables. So ugly it guaranteed him getting laid.

Chimes tinkle softly as someone enters my shop, and my hand freezes as it reaches out to take the photograph. The wings no longer flutter; they beat.

'Hey, Richie,' a familiar voice calls. 'You in?'

'Christ, you scared the hell out of me, Max.' I say, coming out into the shop.

'Careful, they might hear.' Max—his real name is Ahmed, after his migrant grandfather, but he hates it—pretends to look around nervously. 'Wouldn't want them to think you're a sympathiser.' He dumps a pile of laminate-composite posters on the counter.

I try to smile but my lips have worked themselves still. For a second that could be an hour I stare at him and wonder. In an age of religious and spiritual enlightenment, is this man my Judas? I have known him too long, but then so did Jesus.

'Take it easy, Richie. I know, already.' He looks behind him, through the dirty, glass windows, past the fruit and vegetables, into the street and the riverbank beyond. 'You're not the first. Thommo and Vinnie already been seen.'

Max stares at me, through me, into me. He nods slightly, and even though it's in the mid-30s, I'd swear he's not sweating solely from the heat. Then again, maybe he is; it's just a different heat he's burning under.

'You need to move, man? I'm here for you,' he says.

'Sorry, Max. Losing it a bit, eh? Yeah, I need to move.' I indicate the display of produce in the window. 'I've also got about three dozen boxes in the back of the store.'

'We'll have to wait 'til after curfew. The Yarra's crawling with the Skin Polis at the mo'. Say ten o'clock.' He glances behind him again and whispers under his breath, 'I hate elections.'

'Who you gonna vote for you?'

'Who do you think?' He looks at the boxes of vegetables. 'Can I take any now. They won't suspect one or two.'

'Take the bananas near the window. It's the latest from Europe. Break me off one before you go.'

'You haven't even checked it out yet?' He plucks a banana from its bunch and tosses it to me. 'It better be good.'

'Like I said, Max. It's the latest from Europe, I just wish it was from Prague not Dusseldorf.'

'You must be getting old.' As Max walks out the door he yells, 'When you going to wash those windows?'

'When you do,' I laugh.

I watch him walk down Southgate balancing the fruit boxes, where he gets into a dinghy, and the man waiting for him there pushes the boat with long, wooden poles out into the turgid, brown slew of mud the Yarra has dried to.

The dirt on the window casts brown shadows on the skin of apples as the sun beats down in earnest. When I first took over the store I had kept the fruit out in the open, but within hours dust caked what hadn't begun to wither. I press my fingers to the glass, already cool as it counters the heat of the morning—hypocrisy abounds in what the government deems 'proper' use of technology—and I remember my brother telling me when our father was young they could wash windows any day they wanted to.

❀

I was too engaged in hating the thin, elderly man I had hung in my shop so I missed the warning sounds: the pebbles flung against the window; scurrying feet on concrete; startled voices. Too engaged with the hooked nose and smooth face, staring down from the posters with steel eyes and a smile that curved like a blade that parted and spoke small mercies while it revoked all that did not make us his. Too engaged to hear anything until the chimes chimed and the slow tapping of metal upon metal finally sank home

'Mr Hao. It is a pleasure to finally meet you.' A voice like oiled machinery humming with an accent betraying treacherous hints. 'We studied your brother in training, you know.'

He is dressed in a royal blue uniform, neatly pressed, and his boots shining bright and black, even the dust too scared to settle there. He taps the metallic rod against the door frame once more, adjusts something in its handle—I presume he's taking a reading—steps closer and removes his government sunglasses. His eyes lack the blood flecks and the yellow mottling that grow in ours; his are healthy, protected from the disease in our daylight by banned technology obviously in use. A badge with 'Polis' engraved in gold adorns one sleeve. I think he has Turkish ancestry.

'How can I help you, Officer?'

'Just finished hanging these, have you?' He indicates the campaign posters on the walls with his rod. 'I know these were not here last week. A man in your position should be careful. You know how rumours can start.' The other hand caresses the holster bulging at his waist.

'It's true,' I shrug, butterflies twisting, as foul words slide from my tongue. 'I have put more up for the election. I love the President as much as you. I am proud to support the Party. I will do what I can to make our society successful.'

He steps close to me so his breath, fresh with mint, cools my face. I hear his rod whirring as it retracts and he slides it under my chin, pushing my head up and back.

'You fucken technologist! Your father a technologist. Your brother a technologist. You lie to me. Fucken technologist!' He thrusts the rod harder than he has to to take the DNA sample and shoves me hard in the chest. I stagger back into the counter, knocking the scales to the floor, and my elbow crushes the banana Max had thrown to me earlier.

The Skin Polis laughs. 'You farking fuck. I know about you.' He picks up the split banana and wipes the ooze on my sleeve. 'This is GM. The skin is too clean for this time of year.'

I pray—though I don't believe—he looks no closer at the pulp smeared over the counter or my arm. I pray he doesn't peel what's in his hand. 'It's not GM, that'd be an illegal and unauthorised use of technology . . . '

'Don't spout law books at me, Hao. If it's not modified, how do you explain the skin? Are you using water to clean?'

'That'd be an illegal and . . . '

He peels what is left of the banana. 'I have heard there may be another political party this election. Have you?'

'There's always been the opposition,' I say, not looking at the banana as it moves towards his mouth. The insect inside me is beating frantically to escape, if it had antennae they'd be probing my lungs.

'Not that one. A real one,' he says, taking a bite. He chews slowly. 'Like your brother's.'

'My brother was a traitor to my country.' I'm drinking poison and it burns in me with every word, but right now I'll say anything to keep him occupied.

He smiles and then screws up his face 'Phhha! This banana is not ripe. The seeds are still hard! How you even sell this Queensland shit is beyond me.'

He throws the banana at me as I wipe the spit from my face. Inside, I'm thanking his God for lowering the IQ to enter the Polis force. He grabs me and pulls me close to his face and hisses into my ear 'Electronics. Music. Books. I know about you.'

He pushes me away, extends his rod and takes a sample of the banana from my cheek, checks the reading, nods and smiles. He struts into the storeroom, stares at my brother's photo still on the wall, laughs, takes a box of tomatoes—my mind fills with hot noise and the insect wants to crawl from my throat—and walks out of my shop. He turns to face me, shakes his head while he mouths something silently, and steps into the street.

'We're onto you,' he shouts.

I watch him make his way down to the river, laughing and jostling with other Skin Polis, handing out tomatoes as they board the Polis Cruiser, the only petrol-driven vehicle in Southgate these days.

As I pick up the 'seeds' from the remains of the banana, I think about fleeing. Australian State border security will be too heavy with the upcoming election. Refugees had been shot last time, trying to make it to the inland Koori Reserves. At this short notice I wouldn't be able to purchase enough water for the journey without raising suspicions anyway. Let alone carry the water. If the Reserves existed.

The Skin Polis had mouthed the words 'Not Dusseldorf. Warsaw.'

He meant: *You're next.*

I am as good as dead.

A small girl with scabbed knees takes my note late that afternoon and skips up the decaying stairways to St Kilda Road, Melbourne's once-famous boulevard. From there she'll take a series of trams—she won't have any money to pay the ticket collector, she'll cling to the outside like the others—until she ends up in the parts of Middle Park that suffered the heaviest shelling. Amongst the slums there, she'll pass my note to a man who will read it and hopefully give one back to her.

It is near twilight as the sun singes the haze that hangs low over the city when a piece of paper is slipped to me. I pull the shutters down over the windows as two Polis stroll by to enforce curfew and I lock the door. It's the same piece of paper that had been handed to me early that morning.

Don't panic. Sale on. Everything must go.

I wonder if that includes me. If I was more like my brother, perhaps I'd revel in this moment. Death or glory. I want my life; they want the contraband. My brother died for more than this—a Mandela, an Arafat, a Kennedy.

I'll die for less. A smuggler.

The false wall slides back on a series of pulleys and levers—nothing electronic, too easy for Polis sweepers to detect, and, of course, a direct violation of technology usage—and opens into a small storage area containing crates of fruit and vegetables. The air in the room welcomes my skin with cool kisses. I think of this room as a refrigerator; I've had an air conditioning unit rigged that diverts water—another violation in these times of water restriction—from the Yarra to keep it temperate in here.

I transfer several boxes of produce on display into the back room. Outside the street is too quiet and I can faintly hear patrolling government boots on concrete. I don't have much time; my contacts will be waiting. I kill the lights in the shop, close the false wall behind me and stand in the fridge breathing in the fragrance of apples, oranges, the hard earth of potatoes and turnips, the scent of strawberry and tomato—amongst crates of genetically modified vegetables impregnated with miniaturised chips—and wonder where this night will end.

A tapping on the wall at the end of the fridge rouses me from my reverie. I open a recessed door and Max and a burly Anglo I don't know step in from the shadows of the tunnel beyond.

Max nods, indicating the Anglo. 'This is Cherry. He can lift heavy stuff.'

'The Skin Polis know what's happening, Max. They've got me . . . '

'Take it easy, Richie. They can't know. They don't know anything. Cherry, start taking the boxes down to the boat.'

Cherry grunts, takes four of the boxes and disappears into the tunnel leading to the river. Max stares at me for an uncomfortable second, his eyes flicking back and forth, and bends down to pick up some boxes.

'Come on,' he says. 'We don't have much time, the cruiser will be back in twenty minutes. Let's get this loaded.'

'Listen to me, Max. One of the Skin Polis came round after you left. He knew, Max. He fucking knew! He even knew the music came from Dusseldorf.'

'That's just paranoia, mate,' Max says, hefting some boxes. 'How the hell would he know that?'

'He . . . wouldn't . . . ' and the insect wings are scraping the backs of my eyes, beating, pounding. The only person besides myself who knows the chips contain the latest from Dusseldorf is the person I'd told this morning.

Max.

My Judas.

And the fear inside finally hatches and carries me along, helpless.

Max slips into the tunnel, laden with boxes. 'Hurry up, man.'

I think of running, but where can I go? Southgate crawls with the Skin Polis at night-time and I'm sure boots are lurking outside my store. Waiting with shock-sticks in hand. So instead I slip a fruit-paring knife from one of the tables into my pocket, grab some of the boxes and follow Max into the earthen tunnels winding down to the riverbanks of the sluggish Yarra. Cherry is making his way back up to the store and he shoulders me as he passes. He scowls with cold eyes, grunts an apology and is gone. Max keeps walking ahead of me.

'Who you voting for, Max?'

He ignores me, the dirt beneath out feet squelching as it meets the water seeping in from the river.

'Max?'

Mud slurping at feet, the sound of water lapping the riverbank. We are close now. I think I can hear the purr of an engine out on the river.

'How much, Max?'

Squelch. Silence. Squelch.

'To sell me out, Max? Thirty pieces?'

He stops at the tunnel's mouth, next to the concrete, mud-encrusted plug that conceals the entrance from the outside. He turns to me, jaw set and eyes mean. 'Shut up, Richie. Just load the fucking boxes, will you.' He nods his head sideways towards the entrance. 'Move it.'

I don't. 'Who's out there?'

'Just our people, Richie. Move!'

'You sold me out.'

'Fuck you.' Max steps out into the darkness.

I stand in a clammy, dimly lit tunnel made of mud, the river before me, a thug called Cherry trudging back down towards me with his arms full and I'm lost in a moment, too scared to move forward, unable to step back. I put down my boxes and hide the knife in the palm of my hand.

Max strides back into the tunnel, followed by the Polis officer who had been in my store earlier.

'This is Keffin Mustafah. I believe you've met,' says Max.

Keffin steps forward, hand outstretched. 'This time, Mr Hao, it is a pleasure to meet you.'

I try to back away, but Cherry pushes me forward, past us, and out into the river. The knife falls from my hand into the mud. The three of us stare at it and Keffin breaks the moment, offering his hand again.

'He's with us,' says Max.

I reach out and take his hand. His grip is firm and dry; strong, sure.

'I'm sorry about today,' says Keffin. 'We've, the Polis that is, have organics planted around the front of your store. You won't find them with an electronic sweep. You've been targeted this election as a possible dissident. Usual shit, what with your brother's record and that.'

'What is this?'

'Nothing,' Max says, pushing past me on his way back to the fridge. 'We have to move this stuff. Keffin says the Polis are raiding Southgate this week. You're definitely going to be hit.'

'He's part of the movement?'

'Things are changing, just slowly is all,' Keffin says with a wink. 'We can't get it in the country like you can—still too many hardliners—but we can sure move it faster once it's here.'

He picks up the boxes at my feet and loads them onto the Polis cruiser outside. I help him.

'I've got a cousin living in Germany,' he says, as I hand him a crate of tomatoes. 'Loves his music. I have access to the Net—not approved, you know our government—but it is forgiven. I can put you in touch.' Keffin plucks a ripe tomato from the crate and shines it on his shirt. 'I will require some small compensation however.'

'You bastards are all the same.'

He smiles. 'These days a corrupt cop is a good cop.'

For a moment I'm speechless and then I realise he's right. 'Sure. Come by Monday evenings. I'll give you an apple and you show me round your office. '

We load the boat in darkness, the night silent for the chugging of the engine and the thick buzzing of mosquito hordes lifting from the tepid river.

☬

The following morning, Max and I queue in the Voting House, or as we like to remember it, the Old Casino. The crowds shuffle dispiritedly amongst the unused flame towers that stand sentinel along this part of the river, and it seems nature has granted us a reprieve from the heat as the sun hides above the smog where the clouds play.

One of the Skin Polis prods Max in the back. 'Go to Booth 14. Move.'

I risk a glance at the officer only to incur a snarl and a rod whips against the back of my legs.

'You're next,' he grunts. As he moves off amongst the other voters, he whispers some hatred of my brother.

The booth next to Max's comes free and I sit down to study the forms. As usual, there is a lot of small print tucked underneath a large warning across the top of the page. The fines for not voting or for voting incorrectly have increased this year.

Max is already waiting for me to finish, there's no need to read any of it. It's best to be safe, I can't risk losing my trading and water rights this early into summer. I strike a dash through the President's box and stroll back along Southgate to resume business.

'Who'd you vote for?' Max asks.

I put an arm around his shoulders as we walk. 'Does it really matter?'

DOOF DOOF DOOF

'Please don't take this the wrong way,' she murmured, pretending to pick a piece of fluff from off his coat, 'but I think I'm falling in love with you.'

She left her hand upon his arm after she finished speaking, stroking him with short, delicate movements.

'You have no idea how long I've waited to hear those words,' he said, as blood soared throughout his veins. He swam deep into the green grass of her eyes. The scent of her body; her perfume strong and seductive; her lips soft, red and full; her hair gold and shining in this perfect summer afternoon.

She moved closer, pressing against him, her bosom firm but yielding against his chest. He fought to control and hide his instant reaction.

She smiled shyly, moving her mouth inches from his own and whispered 'Would it be to much to ask for a kiss?'

An orchestra of a thousand fluting birds piped into his brain, almost dizzy, blood rushing behind his eyes.

'Of course, my beloved Little Red Riding Hood,' he replied, bending towards her, preparing finally to taste her tongue, to drink the sweet nectar from her lips.

'Oh, but wait.' She stepped back from his arms. 'Listen. Can you hear it?'

A low doof-doof-doof grew louder and louder, until the sound surrounded them, overwhelmingly powerful and deafening. Little Red Riding Hood began to dance wildly, throwing her arms and legs around manically, pumping her body to the beat.

Doof-Doof-Doof!

'I love this song!' She jerked her head up and down. 'Sorry Wolfie, gotta dance, Ciao!'

'Nnnooooo!!!!' screamed the Wolf. 'Wait, wait! I'm so close, she loves me, she finally loves—'

◉

Wolf awoke to the ceiling fan above him shuddering to the doof-doof heavy bass of music thudding through the walls of his apartment, the ecstasy of his dream ripped quickly from his head.

His raging hard-on rapidly failed as he glanced despondently towards his alarm clock.

'It's three in the fuckin' mornin',' he growled, climbing out of bed and throwing on a beaten, old, yellow bathrobe he'd stolen from Papa Bear's place a few months ago. And in case he had to venture out, he whipped on his *kippar*, and had to adjust the skullcap slightly as it slid upon his bald patch.

He bleared his way towards the kitchen, flicked on the light, grabbed a broom and beat futilely on the ceiling against the bubblegum squeak, chanting soullessly to the thudding beats.

Ooh Baby, boogie baby, yeah yeah yeah,

Everybody, everyone, yeah yeah yeah.

'Turn that shit down!' he screamed, bashing the ceiling with the broom again, this time punching little round holes into the plaster.

Ooh baby, yeah baby, yeah yeah yeah.

Wolf shook his head in despair, eyeing the half-eaten chickens strewn around his lounge floor, the beard of mould that grew stubbornly and silently across his kitchen bench, and his grubby, dishevelled, barely rooted-on, double-bed. This wasn't the best place in the world, hell all it needed was some new wallpaper really and maybe a bit of a clean, but this was where he called home. His fucking home for Christ's sake! And worse, all he could afford if he wanted to live anywhere near Little Red Riding Hood, who had the penthouse suite in the very same building.

'But I can't fuckin' stalk her if I can't get any fuckin' sleep!' he yelled, pounding the ceiling.

Doof doof doof.

Yeah baby yeah baby

'Fuck you!' he howled, swinging the broom into the cordless phone set on the wall next to Miss December. It splintered into little, black pieces of plastic scattering across the brown and orange chequered lino, as useless in pieces as it was whole. He'd been disconnected last week for not paying his bill.

Not much satisfaction though.

Doof doof doof.

Not much at all.

He opened the cupboard beneath the sink. Shoving aside some old plates caked in grime, he found a fried egg sporting greenish veins over the yolk. Pleasantly surprised, he peeled it from the congealed fat in the roasting dish and popped it into his mouth and then pulled out his trusty crowbar from behind garbage bags he'd filled and discarded some weeks back.

He felt reassured with the cold weight in his hand. Made of tungsten too. Heavy duty, twice the cost and worth every cent. He knew where that beat was coming from.

Wolf stormed out of his apartment, slamming the door behind him. He marched up the stairs to the third floor, nostrils flaring, a mistake he soon realised because the stairwell stunk of stale dwarf vomit and piss. Those little bastards must have snuck in through the fire escape door again.

He threw open the third-floor entry door and stomped down the hallway towards the noise. People in this building would appreciate this. For sure, this time *he* would be the hero.

Doof doof doof.

This sort of carry-on was unacceptable, especially mid-week. Good God, this racket would even wake Little Red Riding Hood, asleep in her penthouse suite. Maybe she'd thank him for this later, this heroic deed of his. Yeah, maybe she would.

Christ, he'd almost kissed her. And then that bloody music had woken him up just as he—just as—it was just too much.

Wolf watched the walls vibrating as he stood outside the guilty apartment. On the wooden door a gold plaque proclaimed to the world '412'. Big, gold lock. Tiny, silver peephole.

He thumped on the door.

Doof doof doof.

He thumped again trying to thump his thumps between the drumbeat, but the bpms were too fast for him.

'Little Pig, Little Pig,' Wolf yelled, cracking the crowbar against the door, 'Let me come in!'

The music grew louder.

'Right then,' he muttered under his breath, and swung the crowbar into the door. This baby would even rip through brick. Special designs for special purposes. He grinned, and swung again.

The door splintered and Wolf laughed, ripping away large strips of wood with the crowbar, his energy high, his blood boiling.

And behind the wooden door stood another, a door of thick, solid steel. Cold, hard, unrelenting steel. Impenetrable.

Wolf stood there stunned, as defeat rose in his mind, eroding the anger infused in his limbs. He howled and beat upon the steel door with the last of his strength, steel on steel clanging, bouncing from wall to wall down the hallway, staccato with his sobbing.

Broken, Wolf ceased his hammering and faced the distant stairwell. It's what's always happened, he thought bitterly. To his father, to his grandfather, and to his father before him. An endless cycle of losers, eventually beaten down and whipped.

Suddenly the volume went down. He heard bolts being drawn from behind thick inches of steel. It opened silently, ominously and a high-pitched voice squealed from behind it.

'Hey guys, I think the pizzas are here.'

A savage grin crept across Wolf's visage.

A pig wearing a bright, blue shirt thrust his head out the door. His eyes were unfocused, the pupils dilated.

'Hey, you ain't the pizza guy!' said Stupid. Flecks of white powder had crystallized in the snot dripping from Stupid Pig's nostrils.

Wolf remembered smashing down Stupid Pig's wire-mesh fly-screen door last year and beating the shit out of him for late-night drug parties. Thought he'd fucked off since then.

'Nope, I'm not the pizza guy, but I got something for you anyway,' Wolf growled, pushing Stupid Pig back through the doorway and clubbing him around the head with the crowbar.

Stupid Pig fell to the floor, already unconscious, and Wolf put in the boot until blood leaked from Stupid Pig's ears.

Feeling invincible, Wolf strode into the room and stopped speechless, his heart frozen, the scene in the room burned in his brain. His first instinct was to tear them limb from limb, but he knew he couldn't. It wasn't allowed according to the scriptures.

Little Pig lay grinning, sprawled naked on the rotating, king-size, four-poster bed. He was handcuffed to the headposts. Little Red Riding Hood, clad only in her satin red cloak, kneeled over him, her head bobbing up and down over Little Pig's groin. Little Pig squealed in delight thrusting upwards, ever upwards.

Fat Pig grunted frantically, thrusting his fat little hips against Little Red Riding Hood's arse as he fucked her from behind. His body was slick with sweat, he looked like he had been at it for a long time. Little Red Riding Hood moaned with every thrust, as Fat Pig porked her, and Wolf threw up over himself and began choking.

'What the fuck?' said Little Pig, noticing Wolf for the first time.

Fat Pig kept pumping.

'Oh sweet Jesus,' wept Wolf, as he attempted to wipe the spew matting his chest fur. This couldn't be happening, he must still be dreaming. The vomit burning in his nose assured him that he was in fact, wide and horribly awake.

'What you doon here?' slurred Little Pig. 'You want some this?'

'Hey, no weird shit,' said Little Red Riding Hood, unhinging her jaw from Little Pig's loins. 'No inter-racial stuff. That costs extra. And turn that music back up, I love that song.'

Wolf watched in horror as his own fingers turned the dial on the stereo back up.

Doof doof doof.

Fat Pig kept pumping, pumping, pumping . . .

❧

Wolf wandered dejectedly back towards his room. His mind was closing down. Blotting out everything, everyone, his emotions, his feelings, his love, his hatred. There was no point, none at all. She had been his reason to live. Fuck this. He'd save them the trouble. He'd go the same way as his old man. Christ, if only pork was *kosher*!

He staggered into his bathroom and filled the cauldron he'd pinched off the witch in the forest with cold water. He hadn't paid the bills. He found a match and lit the coals beneath the cauldron and climbed on in and waited for it to boil.

It was a stupid way to die he realised, watching the surface of the water ripple with every doof-doof beat.

MNEMOPHONIC

The man in front of me studies my fingers, memorizing every deft movement, as they expertly and instinctively tie the knot in the silky, black, bow
tie. His fingertips are raw, gnawed and chewed to the quick. Not the hands
of a professional.

I look up at him and he stares back, his eyes narrowing, brow wrinkling
in a series of fine lines, trying to understand who he sees. Who is that man?
Do I know him? He looks familiar, I see his unchanging face every day but
I never speak to him. I watch him straighten his tie and we turn and reach
for the only garment on the clothes rack, a black tuxedo jacket, always
clean and neatly pressed. It strikes me that I do not know who presses it. I
don't do it. At least, I don't think I do it.

I put the jacket on, shrugging my shoulders up and down, watching
myself in the mirror as it nestles comfortably like a cat against my frame. It
fits well, it fits perfectly. Of course it does.

I glance at my watch, 5:15pm, as it always says at this time of day, and
take a quick glance around the apartment to see if everything is in order
before I leave for work. The bed is made, the chair is empty but for my
favourite white cushion positioned proud and correct, (it has some
embroidery on it, I think my mother did it), the dishes are done—they're
always done—and so I go to leave, but as I reach for the door handle, my
stomach flutters uneasily. I don't know why. It's a plain and inconspicuous

door, the same pale, yellow colour as the walls, and the handle; tarnished brass, the lever kind. My nervousness quickly passes, so I open the door and leave the room, wondering who uses those dishes. They're not mine.

�◉

Jenny inspected herself in the mirror, staring past the spires of imported whiskies and liqueurs that lined the bar. She wasn't sure if her new haircut, short and straight like the woman who was in all the movies at the moment, made her look any younger. Or slimmer. Or prettier. She teased it again, cocking her head to get a different perspective on how she looked. She was getting old. She should get married again, she thought and almost laughed out loud. Again? Why did she think that? She'd never been married before. Jenny shook her head, perturbed. She'd been having lots of weird thoughts like that lately.

She self-consciously smoothed her hips with her hands, picked up her lemonade from the bar and took a reflexive sip. She wasn't thirsty, just bored. Her shift had only just started and most of the evening's clientele had not yet arrived. Give them another fifteen minutes, she thought, glancing at her watch.

A middle-aged man in a dark-grey suit sat at one end of the bar nursing a whiskey. Folds of fat rolled over the tight, white collar of his shirt. He looked uncomfortable, his bulk too large for the barstool. She knew he would sit down at one of the tables soon, still alone, still staring morosely at the drink he held in his hand, his one and only companion. No-one ever spoke to the man and he never spoke to anyone one either.

Two women sat smoking and talking at one of the tables by the window near the fountain. They wore tight-fitting, immaculate business-cut clothing, one in red, one in blue, lipstick stained cigarettes smouldering between long, thin fingers on outstretched hands, lipstick-smeared glasses half full of chardonnay occasionally quaffed. They were talking animatedly about someone.

'And darling,' they would say, heads upturned, eyes rolling in exaggerated disbelief, 'you just won't believe . . . '

Oh, to have a life outside of this bar . . .

A young man, wearing a red and yellow patterned tie fixed in a fabulously large knot, ordered one of the expensive designer beers. His hair was cut short in the style of the well-to-do, middle-class corporate career, with just enough glistening gel to separate him from the older suits. Jenny gave him his beer and took his money, briefly eyeing him up. He knew the etiquette. You did not order from the tap in here. That was a lower socio-economic habit, and not looked on favourably in this establishment. She wondered why they even had beer on tap here.

And speaking of the other side of the tracks, how did that guy get in here? He slouched at a table near the corner by the restrooms wearing a beat-up leather jacket, probably taking that position so he could peer easily into the ladies toilets when the doors opened. His hair was black and unruly, stiff with oil or dirt; his eyes intense, encased above dark hollows that joined his gaunt, unshaven cheeks. Those who inadvertently caught his eye were briefly subject to a burning gaze before quickly looking away. He didn't look like the typical customer for this place, and he certainly wasn't a regular. She looked away just before his eyes turned on her. As it got busier in here, security would politely and firmly persuade the man to leave. None of his types in here, thank you.

The doors opened and a tall, thin man wearing an expressionless face and an immaculate tuxedo entered, stopped, momentarily taken aback by his surroundings, and then strode towards the bar. Towards Jenny.

He was the piano player wasn't he? What was his name? Oh yeah, Simon, she read off the employee list taped to the wall. That's it, Simon; he's new here.

'Hi Simon,' she smiled.

'Hello,' he replied, recognition, perhaps confusion, darting over his face.

'Can I get you anything?' she asked, her eyes suggesting something else.

'Just a water thanks,' he said studying the cigarette butts on the floor.

'Here you go. You start in fifteen minutes.'

'Yes. Thank you.'

He took the water and sat down at the piano. A shy boy Jenny thought. He'd be gorgeous if he smiled.

Fifteen minutes later, as more people entered the warmth of the bar, Jenny heard the piano player begin to play. It was something familiar, something popular transformed into banal background night music. She couldn't quite name the song.

❧

Mike looked up expectantly with the whoosh of the doors from the local paper he was pretending to read. An elderly man wearing a dark-blue, pinstriped suit limped in from the cold and made his way to a vacant table. Mike returned to his paper, wondering how much longer he would have to wait for Grant to show up. He picked absently at the dirt caked onto the sleeve of his leather jacket as he read.

He turned a page, his eyes flicking uninterestedly over the articles, his mind elsewhere. Premier Fashions Launches New Range. The other page advertised a multitude of mobile phones with colourful, programmable, detachable features he'd never need. There didn't seem to be anything in this paper he could relate to. Sell. Free. Win. Offer Valued At . . . Buy Buy BUY! Nothing he wanted to relate to.

He knew who he was.

The door whooshed again, a quick glance, no recognition, turn another page.

His eyes felt sore and grainy, like someone had rubbed sandpaper over the surface of his eyeballs. The lack of sleep and sustenance was starting to wear him down. The white noise in his head had been growing louder and louder over the last week, an ever-nearer, relentless machine grinding away inside his skull. It made it harder and harder to focus, to remember, and he struggled desperately to concentrate, to keep the spark burning in his memory.

He had to tell Grant what he had discovered at the clinic. It was definitely biological, a genetically modified organism, but he still had no idea how it could be transmitted and assimilated over such a wide area. Together, hopefully, they could figure out what to do.

He caught the barmaid staring at him again and she quickly studied the glass in front of her, wipe, wipe, up to the light, one more wipe. He could see by slightly screwed-up nose and the faint downturn at the corners of her mouth that she didn't want him in here.

She had a haircut like that popstar had. Or was it the woman from the TV? He wasn't sure anymore. She wore one of those chokers that had been all the rage a couple of months ago, and continually toyed with it when she flirted with the men at the bar. She had a pretty good body for someone her age, using all she had left, predatory, hunting for what her society dictated she should have. She thought she was too good for him.

He needed a drink, something hard, but was too scared to go to the bar. She might ask him to leave, or even worse, serve him one. And then he might forget.

He ran his fingers through his hair, the grease shining thinly on them in the pale light of the bar. He stared at them, fascinated by the black dirt growing beneath his fingernails. Mike could smell himself too. He hadn't showered for days, too scared to go back home. He might lose it if he did.

'I know who I am,' he said quietly to himself, looking around to make sure nobody noticed. Nobody did.

Mike caught the conversation of two women, red and blue suits, posturing and posing.

'. . . corrugated they say. Apparently it's going to be *the* new line.' Puff. Exhale.

'But how does that improve on the existing product then?' Puff. Exhale.

'Well darling,' red-suit implored, her eyes rolling exaggeratedly, ' you just won't believe this, but . . . '

Another table; a young man and woman, good-looking, trendy, hair-styles and cut, clothing latest fashion.

'So how's things?'

'Good, good. And you?'

'Yeah good . . . how's work going?'

'Not bad, really busy at the moment, you know how it is.'

'Yeah.'

They laugh. Sip tentatively at drinks.

'So, been keeping busy?'

Mike stared back at the paper, the conversation around him similar to the content within. Nothing seemed to matter anyway, why should he care? He looked at his watch but it wasn't there so he tried to read the time from the young man's watch. It was flash looking with a thick band of gold for the strap. It had stopped.

Where the hell was Grant? He didn't have much time left.

The door whooshed open again but it was someone he didn't know.

My hands move lithely, intuitively over the keys, the music soothing and bland, white comes up, black goes down, then up and white down. Sometimes I find myself watching my hands in amazement. I don't know how they do this, they are an entity unto themselves, a subconscious extension of my body. I don't even know the song I'm playing, it sounds vaguely familiar, but that's all.

Every now and then I seamlessly turn the page in front of me, the music continuing uninterrupted. I wonder why I turn the pages. I don't need to. I can't read music. I see only squiggles of black on white, a delicate, undecipherable pattern. It's not a problem. I don't mind.

I do this every night. I can't remember a time when I didn't. No-one notices me, no-one applauds when I finish, no-one talks to me. I don't mind, it's my job.

A man with dirty, black hair in the corner of the room keeps staring at me. I wish he wouldn't, he's making me nervous. There's something about him that I don't like. I don't know what it is, but I wish he would leave; he doesn't belong here.

Jenny tried sparking up conversation with the piano player in one of his breaks, but his responses were shy and closed. She flirted with a few of the richer, good-looking men at the bar but she was getting very little response or interest.

She adjusted her low-cut top, reassured by the firmness there. Still in good shape, still had the curves, maybe it just wasn't her night. An off night. The other barmaid, the new one, seemed to be getting all the attention. She always did, being a lot younger then Jenny. The list offered the name Lucy. From the expression on Lucy's face it looked like it was mainly unwanted attention. How long had Lucy been working here now? It must have only been a couple of weeks but it seemed like forever. Jenny didn't really know anything about her at all, not because she was jealous of Lucy, she just didn't seem to have the time to get to know her.

The strange guy in the corner was still there. There was something familiar about him, but she couldn't place it. She had caught him staring at her a few times, but he now seemed to be perversely focused on Simon. Jenny wondered why he hadn't been removed yet. He didn't have the right dress standard for a start. Looks like security is also having an off night too, she thought idly, drying a long-stemmed wine glass.

The piano started up again, something bouncy and tinkling, a tune she knew, teasingly on the tip of her tongue, but it remained elusive. She hummed along contentedly.

☮

Sometimes I get the urge to talk to someone, there are lots of people in here, surely someone would like to talk to me. The urge doesn't last long though.

In my break I sit at the bar with a water. I stare at it. The woman behind the bar, I think her name is Jenny, keeps trying to talk to me, but I don't feel like talking anymore. I think she's coming on to me, I should be flattered, I can't remember the last time I was with a woman. I've got a funny feeling that maybe it was her, back when I was drinking, but surely I'd remember more than just that.

She asks me about the piano, but I pretend I don't hear her, and then someone orders a drink and she leaves.

I take a luke-warm sip, it's bland and tasteless. The lemonade here tastes the same, except the bubbles in it hurt my throat; I don't drink lemonade anymore.

Someone taps my shoulder, and my body jerks convulsively, a cold shudder passing through me. A touch from another life. I turn around and it's the man with the dirty hair who's been staring at me all night. My insides squirm and sweat breaks out under my arms. On my back. I want to run away. I can smell his stink, thick and warm, a fetid cloud enveloping me and he opens his mouth and speaks, his voice thrusting shards of coiled steel into my head.

'Grant, it's me, Mike . . . '

Chris noticed Jenny waving frantically from the bar, pointing towards some rough-looking guy who seemed to be hassling the piano player.

'Back in a sec,' he said to the other guy working security tonight. Chris didn't know his name for sure, it was something ending in 'ee', like Tunney or Whitey or something. 'Some trouble at the bar.'

'Need a hand?' Tunney-or-Whitey grunted, not looking around.

'Nah,' Chris said, weaving his way through the crowd, his bulk magically parting the sea of people.

Nearer to the bar, Chris saw the guy in the leather grab the piano player's shoulders and shake him, his voice rising over the noise of the crowd.

'For Christ's sake Grant, it's me, Mike!'

The piano player's face was pale and his body trembled. 'My name is Simon,' he said, colour spreading back to his cheeks, 'I don't know who you're talking about. I don't know any Grant. I've never seen you before.' The veins in the piano player's head throbbed, pulsing with blood. They looked like they were going to burst.

Mike continued, his face reddening, spittle flying from his mouth 'I know what's going on Grant, at least some of it, and so do you! You were with it last week man, what the fuck's happened! You got to remember! Can you remember?'

He shook the piano player again and raised his hand to slap him across the face.

'Hey mate,' Chris called out, almost at the bar now. 'I wouldn't do that if I were you!'

Before Mike could react, Simon had him by the throat. The piano player's face was scarlet, and the white of his knuckles shone in the pale bar-light as his fingers sank into the other man's neck.

'I . . . don't . . . know . . . you,' Simon spat. 'Leave . . . me . . . alone.'

Chris grabbed Mike, carefully prising the Simon's hand away. 'It's okay, it's okay,' he reassured them both, twisting the offender's arm up behind his back and forcing him towards the door. 'You're out mate, come on, let's go.'

Mike twisted his head back, 'It's not too late Grant, you just got to remember, we can still fight it, we can still . . . ooomph'

Tunney-or-Whitey silenced him with a punch to the stomach, and they threw him out into the cold and dark of the night. They watched Mike tumble down the stairs onto the sidewalk. He didn't get up.

Tunney-or-Whitey laughed and said something Chris didn't catch. He said 'Yeah,' back and laughed. Back at the bar, the piano player sat crying, his face bewildered. The barmaid was trying to comfort him.

A few minutes later, the piano started up, a tune Chris used to know when he was younger. He couldn't remember what it was called anymore.

❧

No-one noticed the fat man sitting alone at the table with his whiskey; no-one ever did. It was times like these the fat man knew who he was, what he was supposed to do. He discreetly attached his phone, pressing in his earpiece and prudently made the call.

After the line went dead, the fat man left the bar and waited outside in the shadows for the government vehicle to arrive. He saw blood trickling out of the man's nose, coagulating slowly in the cool night air, the neon light shining on its wetness. The rasping of breath, loud and ragged, amplified the silence of the city. They would do something to make him more comfortable. About who he should be.

When the man was taken away, the fat man went back into the bar, his memory of the evening blurring with some other life he sleepwalked through.

❧

Mike groaned and opened his eyes, matted blood breaking in his eyelashes. The pain in his skull pounded incessantly, it was hard to breathe, and he couldn't move.

'He's regaining consciousness,' someone said.

He was strapped to a table in what appeared to be an ambulance, although there were no windows and the walls were padded. He knew they were moving as the vehicle they were in slowed and turned, accelerating quickly again.

A man sat next to him smiling. He looked 'nice', the family man in a commercial selling house insurance, a dark-grey immaculate suit, expensive cut.

'Where am I?' Mike asked. 'Who are you?'

Another man, identical to the first, moved from the back of the van towards them.

'Here.' He passed a syringe to the sitting man.

Sitting Man depressed the plunger slightly, studying the liquid as it arced from the end of the needle onto Mike's chest.

'What are you doing?'

'Don't worry,' said Sitting Man. His fingers slicing through the sleeve of the leather jacket, paring back the folds to reveal the skin. 'You're not who you think you are.'

The fluid injected into his veins was almost as cold as the touch of the man's fingers upon his arm.

Underground . . . fluoro, being carried somewhere, want to be sick, can't move . . .

' . . . blood tests? He's waking . . . '

Voices, blurred, fading louder . . .

' . . . strong metabolism, he should still be under.'

'It fits the pattern for those who don't take to it.'

The air is warm and unnatural, air conditioned, and tasteless, clinical . . .

'Who is he?'

'Nobody.'

'He's awake again.'

'Increase the dosage. If he doesn't react to it this time, begin the tests.'

Mike tried to kick and struggle but his nerves were no longer his own and the substance slowly filling his body overwhelmed him, pushing him back into a muddy void of someone else's memories.

◉

I don't remember leaving last night, maybe I started drinking towards the end of the evening again. Every time I hit the booze these days I seem to black out. Think I must have pushed it too hard in my early days. Don't remember even having a drink last night though.

The house is quiet and I'm awake so I get up. The apartment doesn't have many windows, just one, and I wander over to it to stare out at the empty, concrete parking lots and the abandoned buildings my view commands. Maybe no-one comes to this part of town anymore: I never have any visitors.

The sun is already disappearing behind the skyline, the warmth in its colours barely penetrating the oncoming grey. A smudge of orange, flecked with red, the occasional streak of yellow and then it's gone. A few street lamps sputter on, feebly lighting a deserted footpath; most of the lights don't come on at all.

I don't know anyone in this city.

I'd better start getting ready for work soon. I think about getting something to eat first, but decide not to before I reach the fridge. I look at it blankly for a second, an exterior devoid of stickers or magnets, wondering if there is anything inside it. I don't really want to know. I used to stick my bills on it once but I don't think I get them anymore. I've got a pile of envelopes for someone called Grant. I think I know him, maybe he used to live here with me, but I'm not really too sure. It doesn't matter though, they're not mine.

I shower and dress, fixing my tie and slipping into my jacket. The man in the mirror smiles at me. We look good, we look smart. Before I leave the apartment I check the room, the dishes are done, and the bed is made.

There is a choker on the floor next to my bed. I wonder whose it is, I've never seen it before. I pick it up and put it in the bin. It's the only thing in there.

As I reach for the door handle something tugs at my mind, something to remember, to be careful, but . . .

I open the door and leave for work.

SLICE OF LIFE:
COOKING FOR THE HEART

It's hard to find good recipes for the heart these days. Look in any cookbook: your Stephanie Alexander, your once-naked Jamie Oliver, your bountiful Nigella—you won't find them. Social trends are pathetic, but we go along with them, swept up in their short-lived bursts. What's wrong with organs, people? Cardiovascular disease and stroke are the number one killers of Western society. You want a healthy heart? Then fucking eat one!

I crank up the Fields Of The Nephilim—normally night music—to drown out the doof-doof doofing from the upstairs apartment. They must have just got back from the East 93 club in Ringwood. This morning I don't mind—it takes time to prepare this meal and I've a busy day planned. The slow, dark guitar of *Endemoniada* razor-blades from the speakers.

I finely slice a red onion—they're sweeter—then wipe two, large flat mushrooms with a damp cloth. I prefer the fully mature flavour of these babies as they're the closest to field mushrooms in taste I've come across in the city.

'Who's this?' Vogon hovers near the kitchen bench, his amorphous body rippling as he adjusts his form. As always this early in the day, he is faceless.

'Did you know only the Pharaohs were served these?' I brandish a mushroom where his mouth should be knowing he can't appreciate it. 'Food for the gods.'

Vogon nods thoughtfully. 'Yes, I remember them. Stupid lot really, but eager to please. The Pharaohs, that is. Not the gods. Haven't met any of them yet. '

'I thought I was your first assignment?' I slice two lean rashers of bacon while I wait for him to reply.

He doesn't take long. 'I had to pass the examinations before I was accepted. They don't allow just any field operatives.' But probably a little *too* long. I'm starting to suspect Vogon is a bit of a bullshit artist. He's one of those 'I did this and I did that' sort of blokes. Well, if aliens can be blokes.

The oil in the pan spits so I sauté the onions, bacon and the mushrooms, until the onions are golden. I take the fist-sized heart soaking in the sink—the pink water indicates most of the excess blood has washed away—and cut away the tough, fatty aorta, the main and pulmonary arteries. Too hard on the teeth.

'You didn't answer my question,' Vogon says.

'You going to try some?' I stuff the fried mixture into the atria and ventricles. 'You know the rules.'

'You always have to be such a difficult bastard, Haines. You know I can't eat. Why do I have to go through this charade?'

'You know the rules,' I repeat. I don't look at him yet, intent on sewing the heart closed so the stuffing won't spill.

'Him?' His face transforms into the young gay's pout, though he's got the colour of the eyes wrong. 'No? How about this?' Coarse hair sprouts from his widening chin as a large, pock-marked nose burgeons from the centre of his face.

Bang! Bang! Bang! on the door. *Who the fuck would come calling on me?* Vogon disappears. I glance around the kitchen, then the lounge. Nothing seems out of place. At least nothing to me. The smell of the cooking should mask anything else. The sound of the fist on the door bangs again, louder, angrier. It's times like these I wish I had a frosted-glass door so I can make out the shape(s) on the other side. Even better, one of those TV security systems, but fat chance of that happening with my land-lord.

Bang! Bang!

'Who is it?' I edge the door open, the chain still in place.

'From number four.' It's the wizened Italian couple two doors down.

'It's seven in the morning. What do you want?'

'We come a complain. Your music is a too loud,' says the hairier one.

Her husband, a swarthy man with fat lips, nods furiously in agreement.

'Yeah, well blame upstairs. I've only got it loud enough to drown out theirs.'

'We a complain to them too,' Hairy says. 'We sick of complaining. Every weekend. Every night. You no listen. You have no respect!'

'And strange noises.' Fatlips stabs a fat finger to emphasise his point.

'Listen. It's not me. It's upstairs. *Comprendere?*'

'You no *comprendere*. We have petition.' Hairy throws her hands in the air.

'And strange smells.' Fatlips stabs another finger. 'We call police.'

I throw back the chain and open the door. 'Don't do that, old man.' I thrust *my* fingers at his face. 'We can come to—'

Fatlips' swarthy face pales, then Hairy screams.

The chef's knife is in my outthrust hand, the blade pink with artery. *Fuck.*

'He try kill us!' Hairy screams again.

'No, hold on,' I try to explain as I chase them down the hall. 'I'm only cooking. I didn't mean to—' And their door slams in my face.

Jesus fucking Christ. The stupid old cunts. People watch me from their doorways. I don't need attention, especially not now. The prostitute from number eight smirks and shuts her door quickly.

Vogon's returned, lounging on the sofa. His lips are bulbous and hairy—he forgets where the moustache goes. 'Can we handle the police?'

'Not if they come in.' And if they decide to search I'm fucked. No point stressing about it. 'Those old diddy fucks have called them before. I'd be surprised if they even turn up.'

'You chased them with a knife.'

'I'm cooking, for fuck's sake.' I pop the stuffed heart in a casserole dish and put it into the oven. On real low. By the time I get back this afternoon it'll melt in my mouth.

'You should consider looking into purchasing some Earth, Haines. Invest that extra income from your promotion.'

Vogon tries to form a wise face as he tells me this. He uses a newsreader from Channel Ten.

'Use a male, Vogon. I don't beat off over them.' For an alien bent on colonising the planet, he can be a real thick bastard. I indicate the auction brochures on the coffee table. 'And what do you think those are?'

I turn up the stereo as *Chord Of Souls* hits its depths and wait for the cops not to arrive, as the smell of slowly roasting heart in a wine and garlic sauce suffuses my apartment.

❧

The prick with the slicked-back hair in the smarmy suit saunters back into the house. I feel surprisingly calm—I think I'm in. What was all that shit everybody spouts about getting someone else to bid for you? Takes the pressure off? Removes the emotion? It's only a fucking house for Christ's sake!

The other bidders have backed off and the smarmy prick's walked in with the last offer—mine. *'We're here to sell today, folks.'* No shit, Sherlock. We're here to buy. There's a few Asians loitering at the back, they threw in a couple of bids early on but I soon shut them out. Good thing too, they're buying up everything. An old fat, couple in the shade of the gum tree passed in a few rounds ago. Probably investment property arseholes. Too many of them round these parts too. There are very few want-to-be home-owners at auctions actually putting bids in. Most people seem to be looking.

I should've bought in some intimidators. Problem being there's very few people I can trust. I thought Vogon would've turned up but then again, this isn't really his scene. Not enough action going down.

Smarmy re-emerges, a slimy grin spread over his solarium face. He whacks the rolled-up real estate magazine in his meaty palm for effect. 'Right, folks.' He doesn't need to use a microphone. He's good. 'The owners have instructed us to sell and that's what we're going to do. The bid is currently at $210,000. I don't need to remind you, folks, but this is a prime piece of real estate. Close to the shops and public transport. Are there any other offers?'

What? We're still going? I thought my bid was in. What's this prick playing at? I glance at the crowd. A few people are staring at me, including the old couple.

'215,' says a timid female voice.

Smarmy's grin broadens. His tongue licks the front of his whitened teeth. His watchers have already signalled out the new bidder. Some frumpy, mousy-looking woman with black-rimmed glasses.

I raise my hand. '217.'

'220,' she says instantly. Smarmy throws a sage nod and a wink her way.

Where the fuck did she come from? She wasn't even here when the auction started. Probably too busy flicking herself off before she got here.

'221,' I respond. I'm getting close to my limit and this place isn't worth that amount of money.

'225.'

Fucking bitch. That *is* my limit. Smarmy looks at me, his body leaning towards my anticipated answer. Little beads of sweat are forming at the base of his scalp, or perhaps it's the gel melting in the sun. Silence hangs in the air.

'It's not fair. He had it first,' whispers the old fat woman to her husband.

I give the old couple an appreciative nod. Good on 'em, the battlers. Probably here trying to secure their grandchildren's future. '230.' I say.

'235.' Frumpy wears a stone mask, eyes never straying from Smarmy.

Vogon slinks from behind one the parked cars. His face metamorphoses into mine, though he keeps his body grey and formless. He motions with his fingers, indicating higher, higher. 'She wants this place bad,' he mouths.

'240.'

'245.' Her voice isn't so timid. It's actually sharp and nasal. She's determined to win.

A horrible feeling sneaks into my stomach. What if Vogon is trying to get me back for making him suck my cock? He's standing with the old couple, inflating his chest. He's imitating the old woman's boobs, not paying attention anymore. Vogon wouldn't screw me, would he? I could expose him. He wouldn't dare. Vogon grins. His fingers urge higher.

'250.'

'255,' Frumpy honks.

Vogon shakes his head so I shake mine at Smarmy.

'Going once, going twice . . . '

Smarmy can hardly believe his luck. Frumpy stands there with her little, lesbian arms folded defensively, a self-satisfied smirk playing over her lips.

'Sold!'

She breaks into a smile and shakes her hands excitedly. Stupid bitch. She just paid forty grand too much for this dump. And she thinks she won. Frumpy turns to a tall, muscly guy and they kiss on the lips. He keeps an arm around her waist as Smarmy guides them into the house to seal the contract. The old couple give me a sympathetic nod and shuffle up the street as the crowd disperses.

One of the watchers pounces on me, his clipboard and pen at the ready. A badge states his name as Gary. 'Sorry about that. Mr . . . uh . . . '

'Haines.'

'Sorry, Mr Haines.' His pen scrawls on the clipboard. 'You're interested in three-bedroom brick veneers in this area? Yes, of course you are.' Gary grins weakly. 'Do you have a contact number?'

'Yeah, I've given my details before to your mate who sold the house.'

'To Mark? Of course, Mr Haines. It's just that . . . '

'You didn't think I was serious before?'

'Ha ha.' The laugh piddles from his mouth. 'No, it's just . . . '

'Look, I don't care so much about the exterior, or whether it's two or three bedrooms. Garage and cellar potential and must be close to the train station.'

His pen scribbles furiously. 'Yes, yes. Bit of a wine buff are we?'

'Eh?'

'The cellar. I've got about three hundred bottles in mine.' Gary tries on a smile that drips bonding.

'Yeah. That's a lot of wine.' Not for bottles, Gazza, old chap. But stick around and you might find out.

Vogon leans on a dark blue BMW parked near the driveway. All the other cars on the street are Fords or Holdens. 'Come on,' he mouths.

'Listen, Gary I've got to make a move. Is that your BMW there?'

'No, it's Mark's. I've got an older model.'

'Beautiful car. Get Mark to give us a call.'

I pause near Smarmy's BMW as I leave the property. 'Is anyone watching?'

'No,' says Vogon.

I take a small paring knife—a Furi, Japanese, the best steel, particularly for slicing into gut—from my jacket pocket and scrape the driver's side of the car. After a quick glance to make sure Vogon isn't lying, I punch the blade into the front tyre. The hissing relieves some of the day's frustration before I make my way to the train station.

I'm getting hungry.

❧

I finish off the last of a sweet red-bean bun I bought at the Chinese bakery on the way here. A very short Chinese girl, slender and pretty, served me—with a gorgeous smile too. They say Asians have one of the lowest rates of heart disease in the world.

The location isn't bad. It's about a ten-minute walk from Blackburn station, nestled between a Seventh Day Adventist Camp, a retirement home, the deaf society and a big fucking marsh posing as a lake. Good access, few neighbours and discreet.

'Lovely to see you again, Mr Haines.' Smarmy smacks his meaty palm into mine and shakes vigorously. So do his melanin jowls. He's a bit fatter than I remembered. 'Mark Creasemore at your service. It might have seemed like bad luck missing out last week, but as they say: One Man's Loss!' He sweeps his arm back majestically at the house.

It's square, squat and brutish. Your stock-standard, soulless 1960s brick veneer stranded in a yard of sprawling weeds. Smarmy leads me up the garden path and into the house, all the while wittering on about bullshit. A musty smell pervades the drab interior, as we move from room to room.

'Needs a little work.' Smarmy smiles after every sentence. I think he thinks it makes him human. 'Deceased estate, you know.' He laughs as if that explains everything.

I nod uninterestedly, calculating room size, potential storage, cooling facilities, window access to rooms. It's looking good.

'You'll love this, Mr Haines.' A small set of stairs leads down off the side of the hallway to a wooden door. 'Fantastic cellaring potential here. Gary told me you were a bit of a wine buff.'

Smarmy pushes hard at the door—it appears swollen in its frame—then it swings open, the hinges screeching. The cold, damp air seeps over us and we enter the cellar. Smarmy pulls on a cord and dim bulbs light the room. It's massive; it must be almost the size of the entire house down here.

'Ow, fuck!' In my excitement I press too hard on the blade in my pocket and skin slices open.

'Sorry?' says Smarmy.

'How much?' I attempt a grin, something friendly.

'220.' Smarmy doesn't miss a beat. Something slides in the shadows in the corner of the room behind him.

'Oh, look, I dunno . . . '

'It's worth more. It's . . . uh . . . been on the market a while, and uh . . . the family are keen to settle quickly, you understand.'

Vogon slips from the shadows, sidling up behind Smarmy, nodding enthusiastically. Not about the house though. The knife in my pocket is slick with my blood. Vogon's mouthing 'Do him. Do him.'

Smarmy has stopped smiling. 'You interested?'

'Very.' I take my hand from the pocket and reach to shake his hand.

☜

The blonde leans back on her haunches, legs wider, then spreads her lips wider still with a manicured finger. Her tits stay rigid as she sways to some shit mid-80s commercial rock.

'See that? Aw, fucken great pussy. See that? Did ya?' Gino slurps at his beer, his eyes never straying from the feast on display until my silence distracts him. He peers at me from the corner of his eyes. 'You ain't queer are you, Haines?'

'No way, Gino. Too busy thinking about eating her out to fucking answer you.'

Gino laughs, relieved I won't try to punch his date a little later on when he's too pissed. 'Thanks, love,' he says to a topless waitress with chocolate areolae as she places a plate of deep-fried chips on our table. He wipes his hands on his oily overalls and grabs a fistful.

'You still shifting?' I ask.

'Yeah.' Gino stuffs chips into his mouth as the dancer stuffs fingers into her vagina. 'What you got?'

'BMW 3 Series. Maybe two years old.'

'Give you twenty.'

'It's worth at least three times that. That's fucking highway robbery.'

'That's right, ya cunt.' Gino guffaws, spraying half-chewed chips over the table. 'It *is* fucken highway robbery.'

'Twenty five.'

'Done. Look at that fucken pussy, mate. Bewdiful!'

Great, that's my deposit for the house covered. 'I'll have the car for you in a couple of weeks. Catch you later.'

'You off?' Gino stares in disbelief. 'The next sheila is pierced to all buggery, mate. You can't fucken miss her!'

'Only got an hour for lunch. And I'm not eating that shit.' I point at the chips shining in their grease. 'You should think of your heart a little more and not your cock.'

Gino laughs and gives me the finger. The dancer has her legs over her shoulders and is using her hands to paddle herself around in a circle on the dance floor.

I take a taxi back to the city and charge it to the company. Fuck 'em, I deserve it.

❧

'What shall I play?' I ask.

'Something loud, I suppose,' says Vogon. He leans against the cellar wall alternating his skin colour.

I pop Killing Joke's *Revelations* into the cd-player and skip to *Chop-Chop*. The drums soon kick in and the guitars rasp through the cellar—the acoustics are fanfuckingtastic down here! I turn it up to the point it's painful and leave, closing the door behind me.

'Well?' I ask Vogon when we're in the living room.

'It's very solid. I can hardly hear a thing.'

I nod, trying not to smirk. 'Let's check outside.'

We stand together amongst the weeds dying in the parched front yard. The roar of distant traffic thundering along the Maroondah Highway is as reassuring as not blowing your load in the first ten thrusts. I can't hear the music at all.

'Perfect,' we say.

I call Smarmy on a mobile I've borrowed off Craig from work—though he doesn't know I've got it—and arrange a time to meet this evening concerning an investment property recently advertised. Vogon chuckles and tans his face, broadening his belly and shoulders, taking on a close approximation of Smarmy.

'I haven't been here long enough, so don't consider me an expert, but you're on this eating for a healthy heart trip at the moment and, well . . .' Vogon says.

'I know, I know,' I say. 'I get the hint. I'm planning on slimming the bastard down a little.'

'Ooohhhh,' Vogon moans between pursed fat lips. He's managed to get the mo above the lips this time. Vogon's eyes widen and he leers at me expectantly.

My stomach grumbles. 'But right now I feel like a little Chinese.'

THE LIGHT IN AUTUMN'S LEAVES

She lay upstairs in darkness, alone in her bed, listening to the rapping on the front door. Each sharp rap sank deeper into her bones and she pulled the blanket up tight around her chin, willing the sound away. Soon all she heard was breath in her ears, rising and falling with the rustle of sheets, in time with the racing beat of her heart. Her fingers slowly released their grip on the blanket.

She could creep to the window and pull back the heavy drapes. She could call the police. She could turn on the lights and answer the door. She could scream for help. And if she peered past the drapes down to the front doorstep and there was no-one there? And if the police arrived, could she be sure it was them knocking on the door?

She could hear their voices now, spinning and echoing, as they laughed and pointed and whispered behind each other's hands.

'She's never been the same since Frank left . . . '

'How healthy can it be to stay cooped up in that house . . . '

'My, how she's aged . . . '

'My, hasn't she let herself go . . . '

And if she opened that door, and whoever—whatever—had stood there knocking patiently for so long, night after night, had given up and gone, what would she do?

She held her breath, straining to hear the creak of weight upon the veranda, the assurance of footfalls retreating on asphalt, the humming engine of a car passing by in the street, hoping to hear anything but the words that followed the silence.

'*I know you are in there.*'

And she pulled the blankets over her head and hid beneath her pillows, sure that there was no-one at her front door, the words spoken only inside her head. She drifted then, as she always did, in a shallow slumber from which even the dead could wake, and when dawn finally beat against the house and crept through the chinks between wall and window and drape, her eyes fluttered wide open in surprise, her lips dry and cracked, the stale saliva caught in the wrinkles at the corner of her mouth, and she rose cautiously and pulled back the drapes to let the light enter her world once more.

☻

She sat in her chair in the sitting room sipping a cup of tea. Early-morning television filled the room, though she wasn't watching. The volume was too loud, she knew, but it gave her comfort, provided voices for any room in the house. As she sipped, the photo on the television of her husband, Frank, bulged and his mouth and lips formed the words the newsreader used. Frank smiled and laughed as he told her about the boats pulled up off the north-west coast, warned her sternly not to trust any foreigners, and suggested that with interest rates at a thirty-year low, property was a good investment.

'Oh, Frank,' she laughed, rocking back in her chair, as her two children smiled mutely from their mounted positions around the room, around the house. 'We've all we need right here. Why would we need another house?'

Frank looked at her stonily and disappeared back into the photo. He didn't like to talk when the woman who read the weather spoke, but he mouthed something sullenly before he left.

'Sorry,' she said, leaning forward and turning up the television. 'I didn't quite catch that, Frank.'

Frank sat silently, staring blankly outwards circa 1984.

She turned the television up a little more hoping to coax him. 'What was that, Frank?'

Underneath the sounds from the television she thought she heard him speak.

'*It would be best if you left.*'

But she couldn't be sure if it was Frank's voice or the one that came from the front door in the dark, dark hours of the morning.

❧

That night, huddled in darkness, swaddled in blankets, she almost called out to the person—the thing—knocking on her door. Almost, for her tongue stuck in her mouth, the words unformed lodged in her throat. The knocking ceased momentarily in anticipation, the unseen hand hovering over the peeling painted wood for one more rap, hungry for the words it wanted to hear.

She waited with breath held tight in her chest for the hand to fall. She feared what lay unbidden in her heart. Was it a plea to leave her in peace, or was it an invitation?

❧

She spent the afternoon staring at the autumn trees lining the street from the safety of the bay windows in the sitting room. The wind rustled through the branches, tugging at them, urging them gently onto its breeze. She followed a leaf, flickering between brown and gold in the pale sunlight, as it drifted free over fences and roads until she fancied she followed its flight.

The phone rang, startling her.

'Hello? Who is this?'

'Mum? It's me,' said a male voice.

'Who is it?' she asked again, her gaze flitting around, seeking solace in the photographs on the shelves, sills, and walls.

'Mum, it's Daniel.'

'Daniel?'

'Are you okay? Jesus, Mum. It's your son, remember?'

'Daniel! Oh, it's so lovely to hear from you. How are you? You haven't written or called in so long. I was getting worried about you. Have you . . . '

'Mum, look I don't mean to cut you off, but the money is going to run out soon and I don't have any more coins. I want to tell . . . '

'Then I'll call you, Daniel. You'll have to give me your number though. You know I could call you if I had your number.'

'I don't have time for this right now, Mum. I need a place to stay for a while, okay? I'm catching a train tonight. I'll be there by about lunchtime tomorrow.'

'Is everything all right? You're not in trouble are you? Daniel? Daniel?'

The line was already dead. Outside, she could see a man mulching the fallen leaves, the angry buzz of the machine chewing up and spitting out the leaves into a caged trailer that would be later carted away.

She moved quickly around the house, sweeping up any photos of her husband while he complained bitterly as she did so. She hid them beneath the tea-towels in one of the drawers in the kitchen, piling heavy cookbooks on top hoping to muffle her husband's cries.

She planted herself in front of the television and turned it up loud, this time to drown Frank out rather than encourage him.

'*You're only fooling yourself,*' he called from his cell in the kitchen.

She refused to acknowledge him, burying herself in the sounds and images emanating from the screen. Her mouth betrayed her though, and her lips were willing conspirators.

'I can't hear you, Frank,' they whispered.

☉

She lay in wait for the knocking that night, but it never came. Instead her mind raced with Daniel's face ageing through his childhood and the soft timbre of his voice and creamy skin and fine, blond hair; the warmth of his touch and smell of his young body cleaned and dried and powdered; the birthdays and cuddles and kisses and crayon drawings taped to fridge doors and tears wiped from eyes and blood cleaned from scabbed knees; her son; her baby.

She wondered what he looked like now, whether time had been kind, whether the world had replaced his anger and fears with wisdom and temperance. Whether she would recognise him. It had been more than ten years.

As she drifted into the land between the living and the dead, she dreamt that they had forgiven each other, and maybe, just maybe, she had forgiven Frank.

❧

By noon a thick minestrone simmered on the stove, filling the house with warm, earthy smells. She rang the station to check arrival times, and a woman reassured her that the train from Melbourne would be in by half twelve.

She popped cheese and onion scones into the oven at half past twelve, knowing that in fifteen minutes or so they'd be ready for her son when he walked in the door. She sat in her chair, pretending to read a book, and waited. Frank said nothing from the kitchen.

At one o'clock she called the station again, and was informed that yes, madam, the train had arrived half an hour ago. By two that afternoon, she nibbled listlessly on a cold scone, occasionally dipping it into the minestrone, though her appetite had disappeared with her son.

'*What were you thinking, woman?*' Frank called, the spite sliding from beneath the towels. '*Did you think he'd come home?*'

She chewed, swallowed, ignored. Leaves swept past the window, laughing, screaming, as they danced to Frank's words, battering up against the pane.

'*When I left you, woman, you tried to turn my son against me. So he left too, woman, see he hates . . .*'

'Be quiet!' she yelled, dropping the scone into the soup bowl. Little brown splashes stained her frock, but she didn't notice.

Frank's low chuckle emanated from the drawer. '*You don't think you actually spoke to Daniel, do you?*'

'You're dead! You can't hurt me anymore.'

'*I'm not dead, woman,*' said a dozen Franks. '*And I'll never stop hurting you.*'

Stifled giggling from a young Daniel on the mantelpiece. Sniggering from the teenage Daniel on the bookshelf, and soon all the Daniels in the room were laughing at her, laughing with the Franks hidden in the kitchen.

In the pitch black of night she woke to the sound of knocking on the door. She lay frozen, as the pounding increased, hammering into her heart. And for the first time in years her throat coughed up an anxious plea, though it drowned in the darkness.

'Go away, Frank.'

The pounding on the door resumed, each thud on the wood resonating through the house, climbing stealthily up the stairs and creeping into her bed to swallow her bones. She lay in silence, the blanket tightening around her chin, drawing it around her head like a hood, a deep shroud to hide within.

'Go away, Frank,' she whispered once more. 'Just go away.'

'Let me in! I know you're in there,' a thick voice slurred, heavy with the night.

The blood in her veins iced, the hair on her body stretching away from her skin, eager to flee with her thoughts and her mind to somewhere safe, some place still innocent and untouched. It—he—had never, ever, spoken from behind the door in all these long years.

'Frank?' she croaked, though the sound barely passed her lips. 'Is that you?'

'I'm sorry,' the voice called. 'It's me. It's late . . . I've come home . . .'

She heard him start to cry, small, snuffling sobs, and she slowly, cautiously crept from her bed, tiptoeing to the bedroom door. The door hammered again and she froze halfway between the landing and the safety of her bedroom.

'Let me in!' he roared.

She slid to the floor, trembling, burying her face in the sleeves of her nightgown. It wasn't meant to be like this. She had hoped and dreamed and prayed he would return, waking every night for years, thinking she heard him approach the door. But it had been too long, far too long, and she was unsure of herself. If she were to answer that door and find no-one, what then? She feared that behind the door lay nothing but the workings of her mind, and if her last hope shattered, then the descent into her final days would be swift.

She heard Frank, the other Franks, rattling in the kitchen, banging against the drawer.

'*Let me out,*' those Franks pleaded. 'Let me go.'

'No, I can't . . . ' she cried.

Other voices sprung from the photos on the walls, as one Daniel and then another called out to her. '*Let him go, Mum.*' Deborah—her daughter long dead in a twisted car wreck on a country road—smiled and reached out. '*Open the door, Mother. Let him go. Let us go.*'

'I'll have nothing,' she wept into her hands, tearing at her hair. 'I'll have no-one.'

The voices rose and spiralled into a noise that smothered her and filled her ears. The hammering on the door stopped and the room fell silent.

'Mum? It's me, Daniel . . . ' said the voice behind the door, faltering and hitching.

'Daniel?' She scrambled to her feet, urgency lending her strength. 'Daniel,' her throat too dry to sound the words, 'I'm coming.'

She slipped and staggered down the stairway in the dark, fumbling against the banister, fearful of the photographs' silence, terrified that their voices would return and drain her of all strength.

'Daniel?' she rasped, though her throat lent her no mercy, the words barely a whisper. Her hand closed upon the latch of the door and drew back the lock and chain. Sweat, cold as winter chill, streaked across her palms and she drew down the handle and pulled the door open.

The night swept howling into her house, past the empty front porch, pouring down her throat to still any cry she might have made against it, flowing despair through her veins, and pulling the final blanket down and around her.

Like a drowning woman granted one more breath, she thought she heard her son's footsteps shuffling away through the fallen leaves, fading into the night, but before she could be sure, the whispering from the walls inside the house pulled her back under.

THE SKY IS TURNING BLACK

People haven't got a fucken clue. They're walking round with their eyes closed. They can't see the big picture, can't see past themselves and their insignificant, inconsequential lives. Most people aren't important. It's the truth. No one gives a fuck unless it's happening to them.

I know this. It's my job.

I have to know what's going on, the big picture, but I still have to know what everyone else thinks, and the way they'll react. Especially the people who think they *are* part of the big picture when they're not. That's where the crazies come from. They're easy to spot most of the time, so they aren't the hard part of the job.

Like this clown. What the hell is he doing setting up outside the hotel doors?

'Excuse me sir,' I say politely, and you have to be, it's part of the job, 'but you'll have to move along.'

'What?' he says, his face screwing up in indignation. 'I gotta permit. The council says I can sell these here.'

He indicates the armful of homeless bum magazines he's hawking. The Big Issue they say. The Big Fucken Issue. This junkie cunt wouldn't know the big fucken issues if he shot them into his veins.

'I'm sorry sir,' I smile sympathetically as I flash him the badge. 'Government business here today. You'll have to move along. Perhaps you could try the corner of Swanston and Flinders?'

He grumbles something and begins to shuffle away.

Fucken cunt, he won't get away with that. I remove my earpiece in case someone picks up on what I'm about to do.

I grab his shoulder and dig my fingers into his flesh, spinning him around to face me. There's not much meat on his bones. 'What did you call me?'

His eyes widen and his mouth pops open. He starts to stammer something and I can feel his saliva spray my cheek. I can't understand him now, he's too scared, just stuttering bullshit. His breath stinks and I'm standing in the warmth of his BO.

'What did you call me, sir?' I make sure he sees my free hand reach underneath my jacket for the inside pocket. 'What did you say?' I shake him hard. He drops some of his homeless bum magazines.

'I d.d.didn't say nothing.' His limp, dank hair glistens in the late morning sunlight like weeds wet with piss.

'You better fucken not have mate. Move along.' The cheek of the prick. He picks up his magazines and shuffles off.

I put my earpiece back in, no longer incommunicado, back with my team. I tap it lightly to make sure it's still receiving and look around to see if anybody noticed the incident. No one did.

Yeah, it's not the crazies you have to worry about. No one much cares if you have to pop one of those fuckers, maybe their immediate family or something, but after a week or so of headlines the rest of the world moves on. Something else comes along, something more tragic or important like one of those sluts leaving that bimbo band where they all mime shit and don't write any of the music anyway. Talentless fucks.

One of our cars has pulled up near the corner of Elizabeth and Collins Street. I can see the guy inside the cab and I give him a nod. He's an undercover. He nods back, pulls the 'Not For Hire' sign down on the sunvisor and pretends to read a paper. He's right on time. Can't remember the bloke's name but he's dependable. What you'd call a good cunt.

Not many people know we use taxis—great cars for cover, eh? We use lots of things people wouldn't suspect. Couple of the fruit stalls around here for instance. The owners don't mind, we make it worth their while. The government has a lot of money, my friends.

Don't get me wrong, I'm not a cop or anything, that ain't my job. I'm further up the ladder than that, past that shit. The cops clean up after us. I'm what you'd call a regular. We dress a certain way, look a certain way, so Joe Public can recognise us. Good suits too, fucken good suits. Couldn't buy this sort of material if I was in your average suit job, fuck no, I'd be lumbered with some shitty, four-hundred-dollar piece that after a few dry cleans looks shiny and worn.

Yeah, nah, it's a bonus with this job, you have to look smart, tailor-fucking-made, mate. The public expect it. They don't want a shabby, two-bit loser looking out for the winners, do they? No.

You need to stay clean. Mind and soul, mate.

Some smarmy prick across the road is staring at me. I think he's one of the local politicians, nothing big, just local council. Munching on a muffin, chewing away on the taxpayer's dollar. I've seen his face around before, thinks he's a fucken bigshot. Well he's in the fucken way. Here he follows my rules. I start to cross the street but he sees me coming and hurries off.

Fucken politicians. Mostly wet cunts, all weak at the knees. Never trust a thing they tell you, lying bastards using someone else's beliefs.

And you don't want politics fucken with your head in a high-pressure job like this either. No way. We're expecting the Foreign Affairs Minister of some war-mongering country at this hotel at midday. She's meeting with the P.M., and there's a whole lot of sensitive shit to sort out. Human rights issues, economic sanctions, you know the story. The problem is this Minister has a President with a fucken big army and they're only a little way away from our shores so we want to keep this woman happy, but not to the point of pissing the UN off. Then we'd be one of the bad guys too. If things don't get sorted out today we could have a real war on our hands.

Almost noon. Fifteen minutes. Should've eaten before I started, who knows when this shift will finish. And that cunt with his muffin hasn't helped. Fucken politicians, fucken council members. Useless bastards really.

Not like me. I'm fucken good at my job.

I'm smart, I'm strong, I'm tall, I'm handsome. I'm good with guns. Shoulda been an actor.

I use a Colt .45, a classic piece, and non-issue for police. You want something fast and meaty in this line of work and the government makes sure we get the right tools for the job. I've heard say that there are men who substitute their gun for their cock, and I reckon some of that say is bang on. Not saying it's me mind, but I know what they're saying.

I'd feel naked out here without my piece. I've got to carry it off duty these days. People eventually get to know who you are if you're good at what you do. And I'm good. And I'm ready. I'm always ready.

Things are starting to heat up now. The church bell is tolling midday. The time is getting closer. The lunch crowds are starting to spill from their office prisons into the street, all noise and mouths and feet and bodies, making things harder for guys like us. Why the fuck did the government choose lunchtime for the meeting? And in the middle of town for Christ's sake?

Stupid fucken question. I know why.

It's for the cameras and crowds. High-profile people, let's make it big. Let's make it look like we love each other, we're the best of friends. I hate that shit, all that insincerity, it's just fucken showmanship. PR. Cocksucking.

About twenty metres away two of my men are stationed, one on either side of the street, dark suits, dark glasses, closely cropped hair. Good.

There are two taxis at the corner now, and one of the drivers has got out the cab and into position. He's one of the Greek boys. Fuck he's got fat, I'll have to have a word to his boss. No room for slouches in this job.

I'm surprised there's so few protesters here. I thought there would be dozens of the moaning cunts by now but there's just a handful of gooks up near the taxis. They're not waving their placards and signs yet, but as soon as that Minister shows up I'll bet you my niece's virginity they'll start making noise.

A couple of boys in blue have just walked out of the coffee shop over the road and up a bit. Good to see the local force involved in this operation, always reassuring for backup. They've got take-away cappuccinos or something and are too busy to notice me acknowledging them. Fucken pricks, who do they think they are? And what sort of cop buys coffee from a fucken café? If you're a cop on the beat, you go to places like Maccas. It's cheap, and more importantly it's fast. You just don't have the time to fuck around while some trendy homo bubbles your cup for you. Not that I got anything against homos, but you know what I mean.

These cops are a bit fucken suss if you ask me. It's things like this you have to watch out for. These are the guys who'll most likely surprise you—the hired hands, the assassins. I'll have one of the boys move a bit closer to them.

'Roy, you on?' I murmur into the mike attached to my jacket's lapel.

Nothing comes back, so I press my finger against the earpiece hoping to hear better.

'Roy, can you hear me? Got a couple of suspects in uniform outside the coffee shop. Over.'

Still nothing.

'Roy, you there?'

I look down towards the corner of Queen and Collins where Roy is positioned. The prick has his back to me and is talking into a mobile. Jesus, what the hell's going on here? I'll be having a quiet word to him after this, the daft prick. You can't afford to have an unreliable member of the team. It could cost you dearly. Looks like I'll have to keep an eye on the cops as well.

I'm getting a bit nervous now too, I can feel it worming its way through my guts. This is a good sign, it means I'm up, I'm on. Complacency will kill you in any profession, and just like emotion and politics, you can't afford it.

Ten past midday. A car pulls up near the curb. It's a late-model BMW and three people get out, two men and a woman. It's her, the Minister, and she's bang on time.

She's quite attractive, something I wasn't expecting. Wonder what it'd be like to fuck her? She looks like one of those cold, hard bitches. Fuck her and break her defenses down, open the emotional flood-gates lurking beneath that pristine visage, inside that tight, little cunt a hers.

I check out her two bodyguards as they walk with her to the hotel entrance. Seem like regulars although something doesn't sit right with one of them. He keeps looking at the Minister and he's too old—maybe early forties—and he's too fat. I don't remember him in any briefings.

Things are starting to move more slowly around me now. I think faster, sharper, my reflexes honed and keen. Time is slowing down for me. The gooks up near the corner have started to move towards us. One of them is shouting something at my man in the taxi who's giving them the finger. Their feet move in slow motion.

I glance quickly back towards Roy. He's moved closer to the cops. The cops aren't doing anything strange yet. Jim's also in position.

I keep my body between the Minister and the curb, between trouble, and I can see clearly now, so clearly. Everything is moving so slow. Traffic drifts by at half speed, the noise slurred and muted. The world is suspending in ice and I am fire through it.

The Minister approaches the hotel doors and she pauses. She stares at me, looking like she's about to say something, but the man behind her, the fat one, looks at me. I can see it in his eyes. He knows. He looks back at the Minister as one of his pudgy hands moves to touch her. The other hand reaches inside his jacket.

Jesus Christ, it's happening. They're going to take her out.

'David? Is that you . . . ' the Minister is saying but I'm already moving, the gun in hand, aiming at the fat man.

'Get down!' I yell, throwing myself between her and the assassin. She's screaming as I push her down onto the ground. My gun barks loudly and the bullet takes the assassin in the forehead. Blood sprays from the back of his head and his knees buckle. I put another bullet into his throat as he falls. To make sure.

The other bodyguard makes his move but I fire into his stomach. He's so close his blood spurts over my hands ruining my suit. Then I'm shielding the Minister, her body safe beneath me. She's screaming hysterically. Someone is yelling, I don't know at who, and the gooks are running away screaming.

Where the fuck are Roy and Jim?

The yelling voice is getting louder as things start to speed up again. Things burst back into real-time. My ears pop and the traffic noise is suddenly deafening. The Minister is screaming and crying. Her body shudders through mine. There's a moment of intimacy here, something she'll never have again with anyone. I can feel her heart beating inside me.

'It's okay, it's okay.' I try to soothe her. 'It's over now, you're okay.'

'David!' she screams beneath sobs, 'What have you done? What have you . . . '

She knows my name. I get slowly to my feet, looking warily around.

' . . . the gun!' the voice yells clearly now. 'Drop it now! Drop the gun or we'll shoot!'

It's those fucken cops! They're in on this too.

Where the fuck is Roy?

I can't see him anywhere. I can't see anybody anywhere, the taxis are empty, what the fuck is going on? They've all fucken deserted me! I'm going to have to take these bastards too. This will be tricky.

'It's okay, officer.' I raise my hands. 'It's under control now.'

'Drop the fucken gun!'

The eye of the storm descends and now is my time. I move languidly, taking both the cops out, a bullet to the head for one, a bullet through the eye for the other, but before I can move, something smacks into my chest throwing me backwards onto the concrete.

They shot me, they fucken shot me! I didn't see them move, it was too fast, it was . . . fuck, my chest, oh fuck, I'm hit. I'm hot, far too hot. Something inside me is ripped and I can feel it bubble with every breath.

The buildings tower up above me on either side of the street to a clear, blue sky. There are no clouds.

The woman next to me, the Minister, is crying. Her face is a strange

231

mixture of pity and hate. 'You fucken crazy bastard, David!' she screams at me. 'Look what you've done!' She is covered in the blood of different men.

How does she know my name?

The man I shot in the stomach is writhing around somewhere near my head and moaning loudly. He was screaming but his throat isn't working too well now. I wish the cunt would shut up, I need to concentrate. His blood is pooling around my head and matting in my hair.

My chest is on fire and every breath I take burns.

'What have you done?' she whispers. She's not the Minister.

'Sarah?' I choke. What the hell is she doing here? I try to say more but blood is thick in my throat. The pain is fading. This is the first time she's talked to me, really talked to me since she . . .

One of the cops is above me. He's kicked away my gun.

'What's in his ear?' one of them says.

'It looks like a hands free for a mobile,' the other says. 'It's not attached to anything.'

'Ma'am,' one of the cops says gently as he puts his filthy fucken hands on my woman and pulls her away from me.

'I know him, I know him,' she says sobbing into the cop's shoulder, one of her hands pointing back towards me. The ring on her finger sparkles in the sunlight, singling me out, accusing me. It's someone else's, not mine. 'I used to work with him at the city council. In accounts. His name is David Strathwick, he . . . '

I knew her once.

Her voice drains away into meaninglessness. It's getting harder to breathe and I can hear sirens wailing.

Above me the sky is turning black.

WARCHALKING

(co-written with Claire McKenna)

The war drivers were out in force that night, cruising the perimeter of the refugee camp like satellites in an erratic orbit. Tom clutched the sacking of the makeshift pillow around his head, and heeled the rough fabric into his eyes. No mistaking the pirate gangs of the wireless, not by shadow or sound, not with their stumbler-cars so ragged with gain antennas and their engines so huge that the subsonic frequencies growled over the distance and through the shack walls. Even the rats behind the newspaper walls squealed in alarm.

Behind his pressing hands, his cruel eyes betrayed him. An image had phosphor-burned into his memory years ago. Eyes shut, he could still see it. A vision in fragmented light across a spectrum never meant to be seen with organic eyes. High crystalline spires, verticals of blue, geodesics of red, planes of aching iridescence, all populated by free souls of unearthly light. To be immersed in this place, to shed your foul skin and *immerse* yourself, to be free . . .

A voice whispered, 'I see it, the City . . . '

Alarmed, Tom released the sacking. He returned to reality like a diver surfacing. The afterimage shimmered and was gone. The synapse contacts at the back of his neck ached with phantom pain.

'My port . . . don't . . . unplug,' said El-lat, amid a stream of modulated whines. 'I see it, I see it, the City . . . '

'Sshh, baby,' whispered another voice. 'It's okay, sshh.'

Tom lay on his bug-infested mattresses, pressed in amongst the other immersant refugees, watching the war driver headlights sweep through the cracks in the cement-fibre panels. Several bodies away, El-lat continued to mumble in assembler patois, a machine dialect. He listened to her, concerned. Unplugged too long, unable to exist like this. She would die soon. But if the war drivers heard her and came to investigate . . .

'Keep her quiet, Palouse,' said Tom. 'Whatever it takes.'

No answer from the older immersant, but El-lat's cries were soon muffled.

Tom felt Magdalen stir next to him. The girl's restless limbs chafed against his own. Her partner D-Cay, one body over, murmured from disturbed sleep, and wrapped his arm around her waist. For a brief, atavistic moment Tom desired her like the rats in the walls desired one another. He had listened to Magdalen and D-Cay grunt through a minute of pointless fucking about an hour ago. Her body had kept bumping against his as D-Cay took her from behind. Tom had tried not to look, but when he did, he had found Magdalen staring at him.

At him. Or through him. Sometimes it was hard to tell.

He looked at her now, in the half-light of prowling headlights, asleep, her young face twitching in disturbed dreaming. Her dark hair had started to mat and dread, and the dirt couldn't hide the beauty beneath. Tom wanted to run his fingers over her skin, to touch her throat and feel the pulse there warm and alive. She opened her eyes. Tom smiled and looked away.

'Why do they drive so slow, Tom?' asked Magdalen.

'They're searching.'

'For what?'

Tom looked up to where the camp floodlight bled under the shack roof, painting cold white stripes into each ridge of the corrugated iron. An old sadness gripped him, homesickness for a life that had long ago been taken away. The combined breathing of the other occupants synchronised for a few seconds, before each fell into their own desperate rhythms.

'For what we all look for. An access point. A way back into the City.'

Magdalen let out a noise halfway between a murmur and a sob. 'The *City*.'

She reached up a pale arm high, her fingers spread. The floodlight caught the tips. He knew the sign, that hope of all immersants that perhaps they could catch the wireless layer by mere touch, to establish connectivity through the skin, and to melt, if only for a second, back into the heaven they had fallen from.

Her sleeve fell. Black veins were visible beneath her waxy skin—runnels of nervous system analogue. Tom knew what the blackening of the wire meant. Necrosis of the cable's outer biological layer. Magdalen had been offline for so long the wetware infrastructure was beginning to decay and be absorbed back into her body. Soon she would become sick, and if the necrosis was too quick, too toxic for her weakened liver to handle, she would die.

Tom absently stroked his own arm with his gloved right hand, just feeling the wires within his own skin. His secret. Nobody knew his wires hadn't necrotised, hadn't been absorbed into his body like a contamination. The prison barcode on his wrist, although in many respects a stigma, did have some unknown benefits. His wires were still whole.

'They won't find anything,' he said. His fingers still ached to touch her. 'Hunnypots and WEP-nodes so solid you'd starve to death waiting for the password. Nobody in this camp will ever access the City broadband here.' For Magdalen's benefit he added, 'We still have to keep searching. There has to be a node out there that will get us back in.'

He struggled to keep the sceptical tone from his voice.

'But maybe the war drivers know something we don't, maybe they *know*.' Magdalen's voice was strident.

Tom patted her shoulder awkwardly, feeling her bones through the rough polyester of her shirt. She was unnaturally modest for an immersant. Even with D-Cay she remained fully clothed. Her bathing was infrequent and furtive. The fabric felt stiff and grimy with dirt.

Tom could not feel altogether fearful of their late-night visitors. Where there were war drivers there were bound to be Access Points into the old internet, the network that had existed before the City. Where the points were, credits and food were sure to follow.

In the far corner of the shack, El-lat moaned again.

'We'll find out tomorrow, Magdalen. Please, get some sleep.'

Tom lay awake until morning's grey light, listening as her breathing took on the rhythmic depths of sleep. His memories were restless with blue water, white sand, and a vision of a City worked in crystal, glowing with a diamond's deep fire.

☻

'El-lat? Wake up.' Palouse knelt over her body, gently shaking the woman's shoulders.

Tom had heard her breathing stop during first light. There was nothing he could do to save her. What would be the use of waking everyone when she had already gone?

So now she was dead.

'El-lat?' Palouse's voice trembled. 'Please.'

Tom left the shack, emerging into a rubbish dump where a dozen hastily built huts had been erected. The shacks leaned together in a piece-meal craze of corrugated iron and prefab. A good storm would bring it down before the thunder could even clap. Not more than fifty paces away a larger, more permanent camp worked itself into the shelter of the rotting mountain. The plague ghetto. A lone resident was stoking the remains of an acrid fire in a chemical drum. A yellow bio-hazard patch was sewn onto his jacket.

He glared at Tom for a second before returning to his task. Tom turned away, despairing for his kind again. At least the plague ghetto knew how to survive in this world.

The only thing El-Lat had managed to do right was time her death well. The sun was not yet high enough to bring the legions of biting insects from the garbage mountains surrounding the camp. They had at least half an hour to bury her before the swarm descended.

He heard a footstep behind him. It was Angeles Del Mer, the preacher. Del Mer was an old man, parchment skin over puppet hinges and animated bone. What made Del Mer so different from the rest of the refugees was the age of his wire-scars. He had clearly been unplugged for a long time. Longer than those taken during the first great pogroms against immersants. Even his port scars had disappeared. A pair of fingertip-like nodes gummed to the back of his neck, the remains of the wetwire incursions into his central nervous system. Certainly, he'd been walking the real earth a lot longer than Tom.

What are you doing with us, Del Mer? You can pass as a real-lifer now, Tom thought, unable to conceal his bitterness.

'Tom DeLamb.'

'Father. You shouldn't call me that. I don't have a handle any more. I'm just Tom now.'

Del Mer shrugged, as if Tom has said something of little importance. 'You know about El-lat?'

'I could say she has gone to a better place,' said Del Mer.

'Rather than that she came from one?'

Del Mer looked pained. 'We are all going to a better place, Tom. One day we will be released from this world. We shall return to the heaven that was taken from us. Once we upload into the new City of Light everything will be as it was before.'

Tom spat on the ground. 'Spare me the dogma, Del Mer. The younger ones might still believe there's a City waiting to take us back in, but it's all bullshit. The City of Light is dead and the data erased. It's just text-internet now. We're all trapped in our own stinking flesh.'

'Be quiet, Tom.' Del Mer lowered his voice. 'Don't let *your* lack of faith poison the hope in others.'

'Hope? That's not a word to be spoken here, old man.'

'Think, Tom. You used to be a programmer for the City. The City always had an echo archive of itself somewhere, an off-line archive that was never part of the other physical networks. On the other side of this continent there is an independent network where the City saved a copy of itself. You know this to be true.'

Tom laughed, a bitter sound that caught in his throat. 'Give me a break, old man. There's a fucking desert between us and the so-called City archive. You notice our neighbours with their bio-hazard patches lately? The border towns have been quarantined. We're stuck living off the plague towns. It's all fucking infected. How do we get past that, eh?'

'Unless we try, Tom, what life is left to us? Without the City, without our connection to each other, we will all die.'

'That's what the real-lifers all wish we'd do, isn't it?'

Del Mer pushed past him. 'Now let me do my job.'

Palouse's shouts rang out in the morning. 'Lift her! Careful! Careful.'

El-Lat's body emerged from the shack, wrapped in foil and tied down with copper-core wire. Palouse and another man from the camp, Basic, carried her to the oldest of the sanitary pits, the one due to be filled in this morning. The short-time immersants regarded the corpse with disgust, while the long-timers only stared. Death was still an unknown to them.

Once, Tom had come across a refugee shack reeking of rot and gas. Inside were an immersant family living with the decaying bodies of previous occupants. They didn't even know what the dead people meant. To them, all bodies were lifeless, all bodies stank, even the ones that moved around and spoke to them.

The stench had been so overpowering that Tom had vomited. The children had stumbled forward on crooked limbs and scooped the vomit into their mouths. Tom had fled.

They had fallen, all of them, fallen from their virtual heaven to the rank earth.

'Slowly!' Palouse staggered backwards with his end of El-lat's body. 'Careful, Basic!'

Magdalen stood at the shack entrance, her hands clenching the shirt collar at her neck. Tears streaked through the grime on her cheeks. Half-crippled Justice, his limbs weakened from half a life suspended in an immersant's gel chamber, stood a little distance away, his expression the same as those refugees who'd lived with the corpses.

Only D-Cay was restless. 'Come on!' he shouted. 'We have to get on the road before the media-text network fills up.'

'You maleficent boy! Have some respect for the dead,' said Del Mer.

D-Cay stuck his lower lip out petulantly. The darkening wire-lines on his arms stood out on his milk-pale skin. He brushed his still-dark hair back from his sharp, impatient face. Like Magdalen and Palouse, his body was still producing melanin, a trait that set him apart as a short-timer. A new immersant. Going online permanently leached the corporeal body of all its hue.

'She was always weak.' D-Cay shrugged.

Justice tried to stand straight. His fragile body trembled. 'El-lat was born online. Taking her from the City was like waking into hell.'

'Okay, man,' said D-Cay. 'No need to go spiked on me. She was home-sick for the City of Light. I can understand that.'

'How can you even begin to understand how it was for her? How long were you online? A year? Two?' Justice clenched his fists. 'And only in blinks as you played stupid games with witches and unicorns while eating and shitting in the real world!'

'Fuck you, Justice,' said D-Cay. 'What right do–'

'Enough,' said Del Mer. 'Justice is right. So is D-Cay. El-lat suffered, we all do ... but now's not the time to mourn the dead. The wake will be held tonight.' Del Mer glanced at Tom. 'The bus is coming soon.'

'Ten minutes, people,' said Tom. 'Those of you strong enough to war walk, grab your gear.'

The camp members murmured and nodded to themselves, ducking back into the shacks for their equipment.

Magdalen froze. Her tears stopped. Her face became grey.

'Look,' she said to Tom. 'A closed node.'

She pointed to a large chalk circle drawn on the road at the entrance to the camp.

'War drivers,' said Palouse with a grunt. 'What do they think? That there's a network here among the ghosts and lepers?'

He turned away to join the others, but Magdalen did not move for a long time.

Despite the war drivers of the previous night claiming they had found a closed node near the refugee camp, there was little to be gained from trying to crack it open. Nobody had access to the kind of encryption software the war drivers had, and if the boys in their black cars couldn't crack a node, neither would anyone else.

Nobody was going online here.

The garbage mountains steamed as the sun rose. The ripe stench attracted swirling clouds of birds—crows, gulls, pelicans, mynahs. The refugees who had enough strength left to brave the streets shuffled to the rendezvous point.

An ancient bus choked to a standstill at the intersection nearest to the camp entrance. It looked like a block of tin-foil on wheels, belching smoke and burning brake fluid.

'Jesus, we're going to get killed in that,' said Palouse.

The bus doors wheezed open and the driver peered down at the ragged group. His mouth fell open and he recoiled in his seat.

'You never told me what youse were.' His moustache trembled over his top lip.

'Didn't know credits needed an ID. You've been paid already,' said Tom. 'Over the net. Yesterday.'

'Freakin' immersants!'

'What? So you'd rather be picking up plague inmates?' asked Tom, jerking his thumb back towards the larger camp.

The driver noticed the quarantine placard still perched on his dash and snatched it away.

'I gotta make a livin' with them. But youse—'

'Have to make a living as well. Just looking for a way to score some honest work.'

The driver squinted, peering at their ports and black veins, clearly not trusting the work they were capable of. At last he nodded in surrender, and opened his rear doors for the group. They crept on board, clutching satchels and carrybags to their chests like one would children. The driver frowned into the mirror. The bus ground into gear and lurched away from the verge. Tom sat near him.

The driver was still wary. 'You don't look like they do,' he said over the rattle of the diesel engine. 'Have a tan and all.'

Tom paused, then flashed the prison barcode on his wrist. The driver had one as well, an angry red pattern not quite hidden under the wristband of his watch. He gave Tom a wry smile. They were brothers of a sort.

'Been inside for a couple of years,' said Tom. 'When I came out, there was nothing to go back to. All the immersants had been kicked offline.'

'Oh.' The driver didn't pretend to be sympathetic. 'Why don't you pretend to be a normal person? You could pass.'

'They're my people.'

'Body-snatchers,' mumbled the driver. 'Memory stealers.'

'Only very few immersants were like that. We've all suffered for what they've done.'

The bus driver didn't reply, but Tom could hear the unspoken, *not suffered enough.*

'Do you get many of us coming through?' Tom asked.

'Been a few waves,' he replied. 'You'd be the biggest bunch I've seen so far.'

So the meme of the still-alive City was widespread. The refugees still came, still flowing westwards.

Soon the bus trundled into the suburbs. Rows of houses that had seen better days, gardens on the point of overgrowing, uneven picket fences. The refugees gaped openly through the grimy windows, many of them remembering former lives. Lives they had disavowed for a dream.

'Is this place immersant-friendly?'

'Friendly?' The driver laughed. 'You gotta understand a small regional network can't accept the kind of bandwidth infestation you people had. I mean, skin, senses, the whole fucking thing immersed into artificial shit twenty-four-seven, even having goddamn *babies* moved into the network—most folks just can't accept that kind of denial of life.'

The driver laughed again, this time shaking his head. 'And the stories. About you guys stealing memories like a fucking vampire stealing souls. Can you blame us for hating you?'

Tom bit his tongue. The fear of stealing souls was not urban myth. The programming meta-language Tom had worked on codified brain functions into digital 'qualia'. In turn, that sensory experience created the body-computer parallel that was the City of Light.

He'd known of the maleficents, the immersants who had subverted the meta-language for their own appetites. Working with black-market traders, the sense-hungry maleficent would lure an unlucky victim online, snarf out a feast of memories and feelings and give the drained shell to the real-life body-snatchers.

Very few immersants were maleficents, but enough existed for the tide to have turned against them all.

'What about you, man? Was you one of *them*?'

Tom touched the plugged interface on the back of his neck. A brief flash of phantom pain—vertigo, diamond light—assailed him.

'No, I was just a programmer for the network as it used to be.' Tom didn't bother telling the driver the secret of the City. How could a real-lifer understand? But only in memory would the City live.

'Didn't need to be wired up for that, did you?'

Tom sighed. 'I spent most of my time immersed because, well, for that level of coding you need to know what you're doing. And the life is addictive. It's so much better than this one. It's like heaven.'

'Must have been a bummer when they yanked you out, huh?'

'I came out of my own accord.'

He adjusted the glove on his hand over his fading prison barcode, and waited for the bus driver to ask him what the charge had been.

The driver only turned to face the road, his thumb to his inked wrist, his teeth gnawing the inside of his cheek.

◉

Once in the city the group disbanded, and went war walking. Despite a spread-pattern being more successful in discovering nodes, Tom stayed

242

with Palouse and Magdalen. The two former immersants were quiet and withdrawn, alone in their grief. Tom grieved, too, but knew how to cordon off that place in his mind. An immersant programmer's legacy, to be able to strip the emotions away and work logically.

D-Cay took out his laptop, glared at them, and stomped off towards the business district. His balance was not good. He weaved about the path like a young drunk.

'Will he be all right on his own?' asked Magdalen. 'He's not recovered quite so well.'

'When was the last time you saw D-Cay join in group physio sessions?' said Palouse. 'Never, girl. His own fault if he falls over 'cause his muscles are still weak.'

The town was quiet this morning. A few supply trucks in the main roads and some commuters were hurrying to their destination, but they saw nothing that could be called a crowd. Most people telecommuted, filling the media-text networks with business.

But only with eyes and ears. Never immersed. Never given over completely.

Tom opened his satchel and brought out his terrapin—the warwalker's weapon of choice. A military-grade, sixty-four-q-bit, quantum-processor laptop encased between two halves of super-light armour plating. The unit was constructed to survive a drop from an aircraft without suffering major damage. He rubbed his fingers over the security plating and the yearning for immersion came over him again.

'Are we booted up? Let's go,' said Tom.

After a few minutes of walking, Palouse pointed out a chalked sign on the corner of a shopfront. Two half-hemispheres, facing outwards. The warchalk had been refreshed a number of times, to suggest the wireless network was always open, and had been for a long time.

'Open node warchalk, no encryption,' said Palouse.

'What's the bandwidth like?'

Palouse checked his own terrapin. 'A few hundred megs.'

'It's just a retail connection. Some text and graphic work maybe. You take it, Palouse. Magdalen and I'll move on.'

Palouse tucked himself into a doorway, his fingers already tapping on the keyboard.

Tom and Magdalen moved further down the mall, past cafes serving people mock-coffee and tofu and juice. His stomach grumbled, a memory of a past life where he too could be sitting there eating and drinking. Talking. Working. Ignoring the homeless shuffling by on the street. *Fuck them.* He bluejacked their personal data pads as he walked past, and snarfed the contents into his own machine. The terrapin's cooler whirred as the machine began to sort for decent intel. There had to be something useable amidst the address lists and calendar dates. Someone had to have a programming contract he could spoof.

'Find anything?' asked Magdalen.

'Not yet? How about you?'

Magdalen shook her head as she visually scanned for more warchalks—the sigils suggesting food, dangers, open nodes, or even short-termers segued back into the real world that could still be relied on for help. He watched her kneel on the pavement, her calves too thin and smeared in grime. Her delicate fingers traced a faded chalk outline. Tom saw again D-Cay's fingers intertwined with hers. Pulling her body away from Tom's. He shouldn't care, but he couldn't help it.

'Why do you stay with him?' Tom asked.

'He's good to me,' said Magdalen, without taking her eyes from the pavement. 'Why do you care?'

'I care about you.' Tom didn't mention he'd seen D-Cay fucking El-lat, poor stupid El-lat who could barely stand upright, behind the sanitary sheds at the last camp. He didn't need to see that on her face.

'So does D-Cay. He believes in the City.' Magdelan stood and looked Tom in the eyes. 'Do you?'

'The City.' Tom snorted. Her face was still so young, her eyes innocent, ready to be hurt. He wanted to tell her the City was a pile of shit, some stupid dream society had built for them so they would move from town to town, network to network, never staying, never settling. Tom wanted to shake her until she knew what he knew. She was too young to be with him. He wanted to kiss her.

'I know what you're thinking,' she said. 'But you're wrong. The City does exist, Tom, just not as you knew it.'

When she looked away, he studied the data on the terrapin's screen, but his mind was elsewhere. They moved through the city streets in silence, heading towards the business precinct. A street-sweeper drove past them, pushing fast-food wrappers and torn newspapers through the air.

Magdalen eventually broke the silence. 'They drew a node at the camp entrance. The war drivers.'

'A closed node.' Tom made the sign with both thumbs and forefingers to indicate a circle. 'There's no way into one of those.'

'But it means they know something's there,' she said.

'There's no network operating out of the camps. We'd have found it already. And we wouldn't be out here looking for a node to work on.'

They crossed the road into the business district. This side of town was always clean, and several cars were parked along the sides of the street. People still worked here, came here, used here.

'Tom, what's D-Cay doing down there?' Magdalen pointed down a sloping alley.

D-Cay was leaning into a car window, exhorting with the unseen occupants. The car was black. High-gain directional antennas and feed-horns rotated on the roof.

Tom pulled Magdalen into a doorwell.

'War drivers!' he said. 'D-Cay's talking to them!'

Magdalen pulled herself out of his grip. 'What's wrong with war drivers? Aren't they doing the same thing as us, looking for a place to log on?'

Tom shook his head. 'We weren't the only ones to be kicked off the network. Crackers and maleficents came off as well. They're only looking for a place to do the most damage.'

'Maleficent.' Magdalen's mouth tightened. 'That's what Del Mer called D-Cay.'

'They were the worst. Immersants who stole the memories of the living and sold the shells to body-snatchers or kept them for themselves.'

Magdalen studied her black-veined forearms and frowned. She peered around the doorwell.

'Well, he's not there now. Just the car and it's not coming this way.'

'Let's get out of here,' said Tom. 'War drivers don't like other people using their nodes.'

'Perhaps he was only asking them for intel? D-Cay is very good with people.'

Tom gritted his teeth. He grabbed her by the arm and they fled down nearby stairs into the dank safety of a decommissioned subway.

❂

Magdalen found a chalked open-node sigil on one of the subway platforms. She held out her arms and wandered slowly around the immediate area.

'Come to me,' she whispered to herself. 'Signals, come to me.'

She smiled and headed towards an old switchboard. Tom followed her.

'The signal's strong here.' She stroked the black veins in her arms. 'It's open.'

'Keep a good lookout for me,' Tom said.

She nodded, while he gloved and goggled up, as he prepared to go sub-virtual. *Gloves and fucking goggles.* Here he was reduced to a half-person in a land where once he had been whole. He removed a cable from his carrycase and inserted one end into the jack in his terrapin. He removed the plug from the CNS-port in the back of his neck, wiped it, and put it away in the case.

'Where did you get the plug?' asked Magdalen. Her fingers were behind her neck, no doubt teasing the scar tissue trying to form over her CNS-port.

'Prison,' he said. 'I went in before the City of Light was decommissioned. You don't get them anymore.'

'I know,' she said. 'We need them to keep our ports open.' She paused, watching him. 'Why do you wear a glove? Your black glove, not the gloves you connect with?'

246

Tom ignored her and connected the other end of the cable into his CNS-port.

The subway shifted.

He found himself in a half-rendered simulacra of the City's index network, close to the core. If once the City had been rendered in crystal, he was in a forest of black glass. The apocalypse had come and gone. The City of Light was dead. An overlay grid had been imposed that verified his signature and re-routed him to his allocation. The first thing he did was send a salvo of pings to known Western servers. He didn't think he'd get a reply—he *knew* he wouldn't, he never did—but he sent them anyway. *Honour bound and a fucking waste of time.* Deep down though, Tom hoped that one day a message would return. That if not *the* City, then at least *a* city existed on the western side of the continent and they weren't heading into the void.

After Tom had finished with immersant duty, he brought up the bluejacked data. It detailed a programming contract requiring bridge patches for an insurance company's network. Tom hacked the identity of the contractor and within seconds he acquired the contractor's allocation. Under the alias of the original programmer, he spent the next few hours modifying the existing code and submitted the patch. Tom then applied algorithms to intercept the payments and re-route them to his account. He was glad when Magdalen finally pulled him out. He felt like an outcast lurking at the gates of heaven.

'It's getting dark. Did you get anything?' she asked.

'Yeah, enough to move on to the next place. Let's hope the others were lucky, too.'

She held out an arm to help him stand. The black veins stood out beneath the skin. The necrosis was entering its mid-phase. Soon the toxins would break down and be released into her system.

'You've got about six weeks left, you know,' Tom said.

'Before I'm no longer any use as an antenna?' Magdalen pulled Tom to his feet. 'I do have other uses.'

❧

The refugees stood in a semi-circle around El-lat's grave. The security floodlights cast a harsh glare over the campsite, making their skin look more ghostly than usual. Tom stood next to Palouse. On the other side of the group, D-Cay had his arm wrapped around Magdalen's waist. She had started to cry again.

'You hear the cops got Basic?' whispered Palouse. 'Picked him up on a node near the old town hall. Warchalk said it was open and safe.'

'I heard,' said Tom. The mood in the camp was the lowest he'd seen since joining it three months ago.

'He ain't coming back now,' said Palouse. 'Bet it was a spikin' trap. I'm gonna go chalk it proper tomorrow.'

'Then be careful.'

D-Cay was saying something into Magdalen's ear. She shook her head. He grabbed her arm but she shook him off.

The conversation hushed.

Del Mer appeared transformed under the harsh illumination of the security floodlights as he approached the grave. His face became bone-white, with deep crevices forming in the folds of his skin. The old man radiated an energy that swept across the refugees and gathered them in.

In one hand he held a tatty Bible. The other he held up, half to bless, half to acknowledge them all:

'I saw the Holy City, coming down out of heaven from God. The City does not need the sun or the moon to shine on it, for the glory of God gives it light. The nations will walk by its light, and the kings of the earth will bring their splendour into it. On no day will its gates ever be shut, for there will be no night there. The glory and honour of the nations will be brought into it.'

Headlights flickered near the edge of the garbage mountains. Tom frowned. *It's just gone nightfall. Too early for war drivers.* Solemn faces surrounded him, concentrating only on Del Mer.

The preacher tossed a handful of broken glass chips onto the grave, the glass symbolic of the place they had left behind. Tom saw D-Cay and

Magdalen slip away from the gathered group. They slid down the hillside, towards the fence line.

Not wanting to spoil the solemnity of the funeral, Tom crept from the crowd and followed them around the still-smoking incinerator pits. They made a dogged bee-line towards the sanitary station, the truck bay that faced the leading edge of the garbage mountain. D-Cay was slow. After a year immersed, one had to learn how to walk again. Flat streets D-Cay could handle, but he was unsteady on his feet over rough terrain. He tripped several times and Magdalen helped him up. Tom moved in close in the shadows. D-Cay clutched a carrycase to his chest.

'What is it, D-Cay?' Magdalen asked. 'What's wrong?'

'Just come with me,' he said. 'We need to hurry.'

'But El-lat's funeral. You promised!'

Bright headlights flashed over the garbage mounds behind them, back towards the camp.

'There's fuck-all time left,' said D-Cay. 'Do you want to get to the City or not?'

They staggered down into the bay where a vehicle was waiting. An old ambulance, painted blacker than the night sky, its engine growling, the headlights dimmed. The antennae on the roof whirled slowly.

Tom gritted his teeth. *War drivers, here!*

Over the fetid moraine of the garbage mound behind him, more bright lights clustered. The hairs on the back of Tom's neck prickled. His cut nodes pained him. War drivers rarely had headlights so bright.

But the cops did.

'D-Cay.' he hollered. 'D-Cay, you bastard!'

D-Cay grabbed Magdalen and pulled her along as he tried to run towards the black ambulance, his immersant limbs crooked and bent.

Tom sprinted towards D-Cay, his feet splashing in the mud. The ambulance headlights flicked on.

'Tom!' Magdalen tried to shake D-Cay's arm.

D-Cay turned to strike her and Tom tackled him around the waist, sending the three of them sprawling across the broken bitumen.

Over the ridge the screech-alarm sirens were already sounding. Spotlights swept across the camp in long, sharp lines of white. Screams undercut the sirens.

Tom clambered onto D-Cay. He smacked D-Cay's head onto the ground. D-Cay grunted. The ambulance revved and slowly rolled towards them, bathing them in the headlights, its antennae whirling. Magdalen crawled away.

'It's a camp round-up! You knew the cops were coming, you little fucker!' shouted Tom.

'Get the fuck off me!' D-Cay wriggled, bucking his chest, trying to dislodge Tom.

Tom wedged his hand beneath D-Cay's head. His fingers probed for D-Cay's CNS-port.

D-Cay smashed the carrycase against Tom's head. Tom toppled sideways. D-Cay clambered to his feet and swung the case again as Tom tried to rise. It connected with a crack and Tom's nose burst. Blood fountained through the floodlit air. Tom went down.

Magdalen knelt beside him. 'D-Cay, look what you've done to him.'

'Spike both of you,' said D-Cay.

The ambulance stopped next to Tom's head. The doors opened and two figures emerged, their outlines ragged from their body-armour and equipment. *War drivers.* Tom managed to get to his knees.

'Who are these people, D-Cay?' asked Magdalen. She stood and backed a step away.

D-Cay leaned over Tom, leering in his face. 'You're fucking dead!'

'Ah, brother,' said a coarse voice, one of the war drivers with a thick mane of white hair. 'You have the price of passage?'

'Yes.' D-Cay opened the carrycase and pulled out Tom's terrapin. 'Military tech!'

'Good,' said White Hair. 'But that buys passage for one only. Although we can use the girl.'

'Don't you touch me,' said Magdalen, her hands gripping her collar so tightly the fabric stretched across her thin shoulders.

The other war driver, an Asian woman, laughed. 'It's not your body we're after, baby. It's your mind.'

'Don't hurt her,' said D-Cay. 'You don't understand what she—'

Tom punched hard into the back of D-Cay's knees. D-Cay buckled, his weakened legs collapsing. Tom seized a handful of D-Cay's hair and yanked him down. He wrapped his arm around D-Cay's throat. Tom used his teeth to peel back his black glove. He stuck his forefinger deep into the tender part of D-Cay's CNS-port, in that place where the wires and central nervous system met.

D-Cay spasmed, a yelp of pain burst from his mouth.

'Don't come any closer. I can kill him in a second.' Tom held D-Cay with his finger and reached for the terrapin. 'This machine is signature coded. It won't work if anyone but me tries to use it.'

The two war drivers stopped, exchanged glances.

'Fuck . . . you . . . ' D-Cay grunted through a paralysed jaw.

Tom directed D-Cay to his feet, using the nervous system to guide him up.

White Hair stepped forward. The dongles in his dreadlocks clinked together and the LEDs flashed star-sparks. A machete and a steel spike hung from his belt. 'Easy, friend. There's no need to kill our brother just because he wants to save himself. You're way out of the loop, friend. Sig-tech is way obsolete.'

Tom dug his finger in a fraction deeper and D-Cay's curses stopped.

'You call the police? Tell them what we were?'

'No, man.' White Hair smiled, black, carbon-fibre teeth hideous in his mouth. 'They already knew. We can dive the networks, my brothers and me. Hack the channels as natural as breathing. The good citizens out there were all just waiting for the next bunch of freaks to arrive. They've heard your legend, too.'

Tom squinted his eyes. 'The legend?'

The black grin became wider. 'The one where you're all heading west. West to where the spikin' sun sets. To where the rest of the archived City of Light network is supposed to be.'

'You know that's all bullshit,' said Tom.

The war driver laughed. 'You think so, do you? It's just a lure, man, and we're using it to reel you in. At least, when the cops don't get you first. Yeah, man, they say the City is *so* beautiful. The Big Rock Candy Mountain. The other half of the City that existed before people became so 'fraid of our soul-stealin' ways and cut the network connections, made us become like ghosts, haunting the spikin' wireless.'

'You fucking maleficent!'

The war driver shrugged. 'None of my memories are my own, brother. Why should your words harm me? Now, just give me the terrapin, then you and the girl can go.'

'No,' said D-Cay, shrill with panic. 'We *need* her.'

Tom pushed his finger deep into the bundle of nerves and uploaded a burst of code into D-Cay's core. D-Cay trembled. He tried to speak, and could not.

Back at the camp, the systematic crack of gunshots could be heard. Tom knew what an execution sounded like.

'Magdalen? You still there?' asked Tom.

'Yes.' Her voice sounded distant, afraid.

'Come, brother,' said White Hair. 'You have my word. Give me the terrapin and the boy. You and the girl can go.'

Tom threw the terrapin at White Hair and pushed D-Cay towards the war drivers. D-Cay staggered towards them and fell. The war drivers laughed and Asia scooped him up and dragged him along.

'Come on, little man. I bet you got a server full of secrets we can use. You gone all quiet on me?'

Tom watched numbly as Asia helped D-Cay into the ambulance. White Hair climbed into the driver seat and shut the door. The gunshots and screaming had ceased, and the floodlights had stopped sweeping the camp. The work here was done. The war drivers pulled out, their taillights fading into the night.

Tom sank to his knees. Without his terrapin he was fucked—no more work and no more credit. He was as good as dead.

Magdalen knelt beside him, touching his shoulder. 'You okay?' she asked.

Tom didn't know. He felt hollow inside. Missing. He hunched over and buried his head in his knees. Magdalen sat in behind him and wrapped her arms around his chest, laying her head on his back. They sat that way until sleep claimed them.

☙

'Tom DeLamb?'

He stirred at the woman's voice, the one speaking his name so softly. When he opened his eyes, he opened them to crystal fire, pink and blue light, prisming spectra.

'Not my name anymore . . . '

He drew in a breath, and the vision was gone. He could smell smoke and rot. A crow cawed nearby, mournful ahh-ahhs.

Magdalen knelt next to him in the mud, her features grey in the pre-dawn. She held El-lat's terrapin in her lap. A cable connected to the terrapin had been roughly spliced into her veins.

Tom rolled onto his knees and crouched with her, feeling small and stripped and without hope.

'El-lat willed me this.' She stroked the laptop. 'They're all gone, the whole camp.'

The memory of the night crowded in.

'Tom, you never told me why you went to prison.'

Such an odd question, sitting here in the cold light, with only carrion birds and the smell of their lives burning.

'Why do you want to know? It doesn't matter anymore. Nothing matters.'

'You matter to me.'

He was too ruined to deny her. 'I stole a program. I'd been working on it for the government. I was unplugged, charged with grand theft, and did my time.' He exhaled. 'When I was released, there was no City to come back to.'

Magdalen tilted her head up. 'What language was the program in?'

253

'The meta-language that gave us our sensory immersion. The same language that allowed the computers to talk with our own minds. And for the maleficents to steal memories.'

'What did the program do?'

'It was designed to eject immersants from the system. Ha! A safety precaution they said. A neural fucking stun-gun. So I stole it. I still hold it.' Tom touched his temple. 'In here.'

'You hid the program in your mind.'

'Yes. The human mind can hold unimaginable amounts of data.'

Her tapping became more agitated.

Tom showed her his forefinger, the one on the hand he kept gloved. The tip of the finger was cybernetic. 'I used it on D-Cay. To shut him up.'

She touched it tentatively and withdrew her finger quickly as she made contact. Magdalen took a deep breath.

'Tom, there's something I need to tell you. About the City of Light.'

Tom looked over the rotting mountain. A stone had fallen into his stomach. 'Magdalen, I already know. It doesn't exist any more. This legend, it's just a lie. We move westwards into emptiness and death.'

Magdalen bowed her head. 'No, Tom, it's not true.'

'Yes it is. We're trapped here in real life. All of us.'

The crow cawed again. Magdalen's fingers tapped on the terrapin's case nervously.

'I stole something, too,' she said.

The crow stopped squawking and flew away. In the near distance a car made its way along the hot-zone road.

Tom shook his head. 'Magdalen, we don't have the time to sit here and talk like this. The cops might come back—'

'No, Tom, I need to tell you this. I was never an immersant for long. I followed D-Cay because he asked me to, and I didn't want to go. I didn't. I was so afraid. D-Cay made me take these plugs, forced them onto me.'

Tom closed his eyes and averted his head, not wanting to hear of Magdalen's neural rape.

'I was forced into the City, I drowned in it. All that light. Those colours. All that information. Like going insane.'

Slowly, Magdalen unbuttoned the top of her shift, revealing the slats of her chest. Tom knew he should not look. Not when Magdalen had been so protective of her body, so modest. This was even more intimate than her furtive couplings with D-Cay.

'A man came to me. A most beautiful man. He said to me, "Don't be sad girl, don't cry. There's no place for tears here." He touched me, the way D-Cay never did. Gave me something that was not his to give.'

Magdalen took Tom's hand and drew it to her. Made his fingers trace a scar that had been knifed on her chest. Two uneven Cs, each facing outwards.

The warchalk sigil for an open node.

'He wasn't a man. He was ... he was the City. He said he was the an .. anth ... *anthropic permutation*, the City made into a person. Because if the data could be fashioned into a City, equally it could be fashioned into a man.'

'A goddamned AI!' Horrors ran through his mind. Synaptic worms, neural trojans, memory bombs. A wild AI was a hundred times worse than any maleficent.

'What did this person give you?'

'The City.'

Tom jerked back. 'What?'

'He gave me the City. I carry it in me. In my memory, hidden, like you carry your program.'

Tom fell to his knees, his head reeling with the confession she had just made.

'I can't believe it. I can't. The City's AI was never permitted that level of sentience.'

'How could he not be sentient, when so many people uploaded into the City? All the volunteer immersants, all the memories stolen by maleficents?'

'Magdalen, there is no City ... you're talking crazy talk.'

'Feel your neck, and close your eyes.'

Trembling, Tom reached up to the ports at his neck and felt the cables that had been clipped there. They ran to the terrapin. She had connected them to the wires in her body.

When he closed his eyes he saw the City of Light, the crystal turrets and cathedrals rising into a sky as blue as the clear water surrounding. Rainbows and auroras in the sky, a honey warmth sinking into his disembodied soul.

When he opened his eyes again, she was smiling. 'This is what I was given. See, I'm an open node.' She touched her scars. 'I was warchalked, open to all. When we make it to the other side of the network, there will be a City. I promise.'

DOORWAYS FOR THE
DISPOSSESSED

For a long time I used to go to bed early. I relished any chance I had to practise. But not now. Caffeine, sugar, speed: anything to keep me from going back there. Exhaustion is here living with me though it goes by name, creeping behind my eyes, and pulling me down.

Sleep, Richard.

I know I'll have to go back soon and I don't want to. I can hear it whispering. There are too many doors still open . . .

I'd met her when travelling through India. Her name was Monika; she was in her late 20s, green-eyed, tall, lean and tanned, her English blurred with Italian and something Eastern European. She was searching for spirituality. I was looking for drugs and sex. In particular, sex with her.

We sat side by side on the walls of the fort in Amritsar, smoking hash and talking, as the sun slowly burnt off the horizon. Her skin was warm upon mine as our arms brushed when she leant closer to pass the joint. The smoke curled off into the twilight, and the first stars peeked tentatively above. I dragged deep. Tonight could be the night.

'Have you travelled far?' Monika asked.

'I've seen a bit. About a third, maybe. Still got two continents to go.'

'You've seen a lot then.'

'Not really, the world is a huge place. I don't have enough money or time to see it all.' I passed the joint back, trying to get some eye contact. 'I'd love to though.'

'Yes.' She stared out over the village below. 'Time and money. It all comes back to that, doesn't it?'

We sat in silence for the next few minutes as the night rushed down to meet the desert.

'Do you remember your dreams, Richard?' she asked.

'Sure. Most of them.'

'I met a man, a *sadhu*, when I was in Varanasi. He claimed to be able to travel in dreams.'

'Yeah?' Now I did have eye contact. She was looking for something; sarcasm, cynicism, or maybe something simpler—belief. Back then I'd say anything to get a root. 'Tell me more.'

'He began to teach me. The first step is to realise you are dreaming and not wake up. Once you know this, then it's all about control. You must hold your left hand up to your face in your dream. It must be your hand.'

'Your hand? Why your hand?'

'The *sadhu* said it was because you never look at your hands in dreams. It is a detail you would never remember, never think of. He said you need to be able to master the smallest detail before you can journey. Once you have your left hand, you must bring up your right, and when you have mastered this task, you are ready for the next step.'

'And you can do this can you, Monika?'

She nodded and smiled, her teeth straight and white. 'It took me many months, but I can do it. It's very difficult to stay in a dream once you know it is one.'

'I know what you mean.' All those dreams, all of them; I'm surrounded by gorgeous women and I'm about to come, lots of those; it's the rare double album of my favourite band, cheap and in mint condition and I don't know any of the songs; my life is how it should be, happy, content, my furtive male hungers satisfied; and then I recognise them for what they are—dreams and I wake, never climaxing, never fulfilled. I don't tell

Monika any of this though. She's searching for something much deeper than what can be found in my shallow life.

'It's the next step I'm working on now,' she said. 'When you take your hands away from your face there will be a door. And if you can open it, behind it lies your destination. You can step through and you will be there.'

I tried to keep the scorn out of my voice—after all, tonight could be the night. 'Like what? As a ghost? Can other people see you? Are you real?'

Monika shrugged. 'I don't know, Richard. The *sadhu* did not tell me what I would be like. He said the place would be real; it would be as it is now. He stressed that you must close the door when you leave, that they shouldn't be left open.'

'Why?'

'I don't know. I didn't ask. He just said you must close it. Why are you looking at me like that? Don't you believe me?'

'I didn't say that.' There were a lot of people travelling the East who believed in all that mystical shit. Looking for the inner 'soul', who they are, what they are, where they fit in the cosmos, one with God, whichever one it was; all that unattainable, born-again shit. I just wanted to fuck her.

I took a battered photo out of my wallet and gave it to Monika. It showed a younger me, lying back on a recliner next to a pool. Behind me, a gum tree towered over ferns banking a small creek.

'If you want to see where I live, then check this out. There's something to the right of me, just out of the photo. When you get there, tell me what it is.'

Monika laughed. 'Look how young you were. You must be only, what, eighteen then? You are funny. Now I must go to bed and practise.'

At first I thought she meant with me, but she put the photo in her pocket, kissed me gently on the cheek and walked back to the hostel. I lit up another joint. Tonight would not be the night, but at least she would have something to remember me by, even if it was ten years out of date.

❧

We travelled together for the next few weeks, making our way down to Bombay. She would ask me how my dreams were going, and I would tell her I was still trying to bring my left hand up. The craziest thing was that it was true. I could picture my hand in the dream, yet I would get too excited when I understood what was happening and wake up. My nails, bitten and uneven, my lifelines, even the silver Celtic ring I wore. And Monika? She was still trying to form a door. It could have been great between us, but the lust of the beast was too strong in my blood. For all my efforts, I still hadn't managed to get any more intimate than a kiss goodnight; she was infectious and unattainable, and eventually frustrating. I needed more than friendship.

Monika and I parted ways when I headed off to Goa with a young, blonde, German girl, who had found what I was looking for. In the weeks that followed I lost myself in ecstasy-fuelled nights and bhang-lassi days, loving all and being loved. This part of the world catered for all of my worldly desires and I soon forgot about Monika and hands and doors. I lived for the me in the now. There was no time for dreams; I was living them.

❧

My eyes are full of sand. Grain after grain scrapes raw against flesh as my eyelid closes, briefly, only briefly. I am not ready. Sleep calls me. What happened to you, Monika? Did you forget to close them, too? Dragging me down . . .

❧

London had reality strip me back to my bones and leech the sun from my face. Grinding away at low-paid bar work or dull, well-paid bookkeeping tasks kept me going, and for all the urgency that surrounded me, I felt myself worn-down and slowly bludgeoned into a corporate slavery. I'd arrived broke from India, and seemed to be barely keeping my head above water.

I shared a room with too many people, I owned nothing in a city that boasts of wealth, and it was always cold and wet and dark and crowded. Most people I knew were scrounging to earn enough for their next trip away, somewhere magical and ancient, primitive and spiritual, and I think I was finally beginning to realise what they were looking for. I'd been there, I'd almost had it, and with a Western indignity I had abused it and myself, losing sight of what was within reach. Karma, finally, for me was real and believable, a tangible essence reaching out and making me pay for my highs.

At my lowest ebb, and a year and a half after I had last seen her, I received an email from Monika. Her message was short:

> Hi Richard, Long time no hear. The gum tree has been cut down, there's only a stump now. It's a gazebo, and it overlooks a small pond that is fed by the creek. It's real and you can do it. Open your mind. Believe. Thinking of you, Monika xx

I read it three times. Dad had cut the tree down a few years ago because its leaves choked the garden and filled the pool. He had built the gazebo and dug out the pond before he'd even planted the tree. My first instinct was that she had called my parents. She hadn't. She'd been there, had seen my parents, she described them to me, she'd heard them talking, and they had never seen or spoken to her. It was real.

Monika sent me another message with an attachment. It was a recent picture of her standing in front of an apartment block, stone and ivy, shuttered windows. 'Start with what you can see. Come and visit.' It read. There was no address.

I believed. I wish to God I never had.

❧

Sleep now. You owe me.

I can hear it—the one who calls itself Zaehner, I don't know what it is—whispering, clawing at the inside of my head, persuasive, insistent, insidious. It wants to be me. I can't find all the doors I've left open and I'm scared to go back in. I might not come out as me, but then, that is the deal . . .

❧

I took every opportunity to practise in those days. I stuck to bar work in the evenings, it afforded the best REM moments, late morning, late afternoon, eyes bulging under closed lids, a little booze, a touch of hash, and I became a regular entrant into the world of dreams. It took me a month before I could bring one of my hands back into my dreams, another two before my right hand materialised. It wasn't easy, sleep was often interrupted, a factor, from sharing a flat with seven others, that gradually became intolerable. I worked fewer hours and went out less. While those around me partied and drank and fucked and travelled to Amsterdam and Morocco and Spain and Greece, I slept and dreamt.

By the time the weak English summer tiptoed back, I had managed to form a door. A simple white door, wooden, with a copper latch, standing solitary in a field of grass. I opened it and stepped through into Monika's world.

It was as her photograph showed. A two-storey, stone-block apartment building, not built in this century, with vines creeping over and across the walls. A narrow cobblestone path led between similar buildings, down to what appeared to be a market. Old women called 'Hola' to each other from balconies and I realised she didn't live in Italy at all. On a nearby wall a matador danced with a bull, poster declaring to all the bullfight this weekend in Sevilla. People passed me by, oblivious. I could smell the heat in the air, hear fragmented Spanish conversations as people walked past, I could almost taste their cologne and yet I couldn't touch them. My hand passed through them as they lived their lives, oblivious to me. I was here, I was real, and yet I wasn't.

Behind me stood my door, and people passed through it as if it didn't exist. Never once did it occur to me I was dreaming. This was real for me, why would I think to wake up? Monika. She would be here, too. I looked for her door, a door of this world, a door on the apartment, and knocked. I knocked again, this time louder. Either nobody was home, or they couldn't hear me. I suspected the latter. I tried to open the door, but my fingers slid around the handle, refusing to find purchase.

I stepped back and looked up at the building, trying in vain to peer into the windows. As I was about to give up a window near the top opened and Monika looked out. The photograph had been recent, she looked the same. Beautiful, restless.

'Monika!' I called waving my hands up at her. 'I'm here. I've made it!'
She looked past me, through me, down the cobbled street.

'Hola,' she waved, and a woman from a balcony across the street called back. The rest was lost on me as they conversed in Spanish. Monika didn't know I was there, she couldn't hear me or see me. I was a passive observer here, unable to affect those around me. I watched her as she spoke and when she closed the window and didn't come out I wandered down to the markets and immersed myself in smells and colours, food, textiles, people and eventually found myself being drawn back to my door. It started as a niggling feeling and quickly became too insistent an urge to ignore. My feet moved quickly over the cobblestones, almost floating, and the door came rushing up to meet me. I stepped through, closed it behind me, and woke up. I had been asleep for no more than an hour and I had spent half a day in Spain.

I wrote to Monika, describing what I had seen. She told me of the places she had been and the people she had met, most of the destinations from an image she had focused on before sleeping. I didn't tell the people I shared the house with what had happened; they had begun to think of me as reclusive and eccentric. 'Weirdo' was a term I heard used on more than one occasion when they thought I wasn't there.

I travelled more often; safe places to begin with, the Spanish Steps, the Vatican, Berlin, and the pyramids. I went to shows at the Edinburgh festival and even followed my flatmates on their regular excursions. Sometimes I felt that I was not alone, that there were people with me, doing the same thing, but I could have been projecting what I was missing: food, drink, and sex, the purely physical pleasures. My sexual appetite had not been diminished, of course, God forbid the day. My job as a barman kept me in bed with numerous women, most of them young Aussie and Kiwi backpackers out for a good time. I wanted more though. I was lonely travelling by myself.

I decided to move back home. There was nothing in London keeping me and I was definitely not taking advantage of living there. Back home things would be cheaper; I could go on the dole and do some bar work while I figured out what to do next. I didn't travel for the first few months back in Melbourne, content instead to find some sort of routine, some normality.

I thought about writing down some of my experiences and began going through the email correspondence I had saved. One of the first I read got me thinking about travelling again. It was an early one from Monika. In it she talked of 'the people she had met'.

How? I had never been able to communicate with anybody. I had to ask her.

She sent me a photo of the Taj Mahal. The message said:

Hi Richard, I thought you would never ask. Sometimes you don't see what is in front of you. Sometimes you just don't listen. I know we've both been here before, but a familiar place is good for a first time. You never know, maybe this time we'll get a proper sunrise. Meet me here. Your time 7pm. Love, Monika xx

I arrived half an hour before dawn. People were already pouring in, cameras ready, sketchpads raised. Indians took rupees from tourists and herded them into lines for the perfect photograph. Last time I had been here the smog and cloud had hidden the sun until it was well overhead, denying me the pink-and-rose marbled marvel vista that greeted the dawn for the deceased and beloved *Mumtaz Mahal*.

I wandered around looking for Monika but she found me.

Something whispered in my ear. It sounded much like the voices of the dead that are rumoured to be echoing in the dome of the Taj's tomb: faint and echoey. It whispered again and this time I could understand it. It was my name.

'Monika?'

'I'm right here.' The hairs on my neck tingled. 'Can you feel that?'

'Yes.'

'That's me. It's my hand.'

'Can you see me? I can't see you.'

'Be patient, Richard. It will come. You were always in too much of a hurry.'

Something light brushed against my lips. She closed my eyelids. I could feel her breath on my face. It smelt fresh and minty. My scalp tickled.

'What are you doing?'

'Helping you. Don't open your eyes yet.'

'Why?'

'You ask too many questions. Because.'

We waited for what must have been only a minute, and a pin-prick of intense light shot through my head.

'What the fuck was that?' I tried to open my eyes.

'Not yet,' she said. 'That's just me. I'm giving you something, from me to you. I'm helping you open the eyes inside your mind.'

The tickling moved inside my head, and the blood behind my eyes danced, thick and alive. I gradually felt her body firm next to mine, and my hand reached out, groping her arm, until her fingers entwined with my own.

'Now,' Monika said.

I opened my eyes as the sunrise crept across the marbled surface of the Taj Mahal, infusing the stone with glowing pinks and reds. I stood next to Monika, hand in hand, and saw what I had been denied.

Monika turned my cheek gently with her hand, soft skin, warm, and kissed me gently on the mouth. She kissed me again, and our lips parted slightly, wet, searching, and I kissed her back, her taste intense. My lips burned as we pulled apart.

'Wow. That's like when I was fifteen.'

'Fifteen?' Monika grinned. 'You were slow, weren't you?' I pulled her closer and as we kissed, her hand slid down my pants, and curled around my erection. I hoisted her skirt, rubbing my hand against her, hot and yielding, moist. She moaned gently as my fingers kneaded her, at first slowly, and then with more urgency. She pulled down my pants and as I kicked my way out of them, she thrust her hips against mine. I pushed back, feeling her groove, sliding, hot and wet. I cupped one of her breasts, small and firm, the nipple long and hard, fingers squeezing harder, harder.

'Fuck me,' Monika whispered, dragging us down, kissing, stroking. 'Here. Now.'

Her thighs wrapped around my waist and I slid into her, soft, hot, wet, her hands gripped my buttocks, trying to push me in deeper and deeper. I was a virgin again.

We made love in front of timed exposures and popping flashes, in the water gardens amongst the fountains that led to the monument.

We met once a week thereafter. We'd swap photos of places we'd never been; the ruined rock city of Petra, the stucco mosques of Timbuktu, the ancient Persian mud city of Bam, Babylon, Kakadu, Mecca, Kathmandu. We visited them all. I even walked on the moon.

I gradually became aware of other travellers, at first indistinct and distant; eventually shapes became people and people became faces and the faces became familiar: Asians, Indians, Africans, Europeans. I formed friendships and took lovers, I assumed Monika did the same, though I never mentioned it.

I never got sick from the food or water, no diseases, no malaria or yellow fever, no herpes, crabs, warts, no AIDS. My life, as shallow as it may seem, was fantastic. I felt complete, I wanted nothing more than I had. I would have happily stayed there in the dream world if my subconscious had allowed me to. But the door, ever the door, always came rushing to meet me, swallowing me and shutting me off from where I'd been. I would awake almost instantly, in a sleeping bag on an old mattress I'd picked up outside the Salvo's, in a room devoid of possessions and decoration. My flatmates didn't mind; Dave was a junkie, and I didn't know what Stacey did. The place was cheap and I didn't need much besides food and water. Like I said, my life was complete.

◉

Halcyon days, where confidence can turn easily into arrogance, and you don't realise until you've stepped from one to the other. I took that step. I took many of them.

Karma comes back. It's what karma is. I have to sleep soon, I must sleep.

Richard? Are you ready?

I think I'm about to pay the price for those steps . . .

❧

It started, as always, with Monika. By telephone. It was generally faster and more immediate than setting up a sleep time convenient to us both.

'Do you ever think of other places to go, Richard?'

'Yeah, sure, all the time. I'm thinking about seeing some of my own country again, maybe Fiordland, or the Sounds . . . '

'No, that's not what I mean. *Other* places.'

'What do you mean?'

'Turn on your computer.'

She sent through a picture of Tolkien's Middle-Earth, a terraformed Mars, a lost world teeming with dinosaurs. It had never occurred to me.

'These places aren't real,' I said.

'Aren't they?' She also had the Koran, the Ramayana, and the Bible. 'There's more. Confucianism, Taoism, Buddhism. What if we can find them?' I realised then that Monika had never stopped searching.

'They're stories, Monika. Stories, that at their best explain away our fears and tell us how to live our life. Give meaning to our world.'

'How can you think that? What have you been doing for the past couple of years, Richard? Was it just a story the *sadhu* told me? That I told you? You of all people should realise that there is more to believe in. Has everything that mankind has lived by for thousands of years been just stories? I don't think so.'

'Do you know anybody who's done this sort of thing?'

'No, but I've heard of people who have. We can arrange a meeting with one of them. His name is Dariq.'

It wouldn't have surprised me if Monika had already had contact with Dariq. Her accent got stronger the more she became excited. She knew I would follow.

'How do we get hold of him? Do you have his number?'

'We can only meet him in the dream,' she said quickly. 'He's funny like that.'

'Fine. When do we do it?' I asked. I should have done some asking around of my own, but I didn't.

☉

We were told to meet Dariq in the rock-cut houses in Göreme, somewhere neutral he had suggested. Neutral? I'd never been there before; I'd thought it was the name of a pizza shop back home. We sat huddled in the darkness of what appeared to be a cave, overlooking a valley. My door shone behind me, casting no light upon the cave's interior. I couldn't see Monika's but then she couldn't see mine.

'Where is this?' I asked. 'Cappadocia,' Monika replied. 'I think Dariq may be Turkish and that's why he chose here. He's supposed to be very old.'

As if that made any difference. He was late. We sat here for almost half an hour. Monika had initially been excited and talked of the places she had in mind, particular versions of what she thought were true, as far as heaven or hell was concerned. I felt uneasy, and didn't talk much. Occasionally something hairy crawled over my skin and I'd brush at it frantically only to find nothing there. Eventually Monika also sat in silence. Every now and then I saw her brush her arms, or shake her leg.

'It's almost like when you first feel the contact of another traveller, before you're made aware,' I said. 'Though this isn't pleasant, is it? It's not like tickling or a light caress. It's like . . . '

'Something's in here with us,' Monika whispered.

Her hand fumbled for mine, finding my fingers and grasping hard. Her fingers were icy. I reached out and touched her face. She flinched away, but not before I felt cold, clammy skin.

'Monika, what's . . . ' And then something damp and freezing wafted against my face, the last expulsion of breath from the lungs of something long dead. I reeled, my stomach turned, and the world around me wavered.

'Oh, Jesus,' Monika sobbed quietly. 'Oh, Jesus.' Her body trembled against mine.

In the dream world you can see things, hear things and smell things. The only thing I had ever physically felt here were other travellers. Something in this cave, hidden in the darkness, thrust ice into my veins and muddied my insides. I could hear laughter echoing in the back of my skull, coarse and venomous.

'Begone!' A rasping voice commanded and the cave flooded with light and warmth, and then back to darkness.

Candles flickered alight around the perimeter and a soft glow spread over the cave. Ancient crosses had been carved into the ceiling and walls. In the shadows before us sat a dark-skinned man clothed in grey robes. His hair was thick and dreaded, and woven into his long beard. Candlelight glinted off his pitch-black eyes and his lips peeled back from long, yellow teeth as he smiled at us.

'I am Dariq. I have been searching for you.' A voice of sandpaper, coarse with disuse. He stared alternately between us, and finally his gaze lingered on Monika. 'You seek guidance, yes?' He hissed his esses.

'Yes,' said Monika. She unfolded her hand from mine, and shifted her body, minutely, away from me. Her hand was warm again.

Dariq nodded and drew a circular symbol in the dirt on the ground.

'This is a mandala,' he said, swallowing her with those dark eyes of his. He leaned forward and smiled. 'I will help you focus on it. It will become your doorway to many doorways.'

'Yes,' said Monika. 'But we haven't chosen where we want to go,' I interrupted.

'You choose after you step through this doorway,' Dariq said, dismissing me.

He swirled his finger through the dirt in the circle and it turned opaque.

'Oh my God, it's beautiful . . . '

'What is, Monika? I can't see anything.'

Her body spasmed and her head lolled back on her shoulders, her throat upturned, artery pulsing. Monika swayed forward, her head swinging toward the circle, her eyes rolled over, white. She moaned low and her body shuddered. I had felt her beneath me when she moved like that. I had been inside her. She was orgasming. Dariq leaned closer, and his tongue flicked once over his thin lips.

'Yeesss,' he urged.

I still couldn't see anything in the circle. Monika began to keen and I reached out to touch her. Dariq's hand closed around my wrist, shooting pain up my arm, wrenching my body by the shoulder, twisting me off my feet.

'No,' he said without taking his eyes off her. Something moved beneath the skin of his face, another skull, another being. 'I do not need you yet.'

Monika's body began to twist and screw, as if giant unseen hands wrung her like a dishcloth, and her image wavered, flickered, and began to flow into the circle inscribed upon the floor of the ancient cave. The laughing in my skull intensified, and hundreds of whispering voices chattered unintelligibly beneath that laughter.

I writhed in the dirt, my free arm clawing toward the circle on the floor. 'Monika! Monika!' I wanted to scream, to cry, to break Dariq apart, but I couldn't move. I lay helpless, my stomach roiling and watched Monika disappear.

Dariq still held me in his grip and he turned to stare at me. He laughed and it was the same laughter in my head. Wet tendrils sprouted from his hand wrapping themselves around my arm, creeping up toward my neck. Their touch burnt.

'Your doorway is closing,' he rasped.

One of the whispers in my head called to me. 'Wake up.'

'I will keep you here in case. Look,' Dariq said pointing toward my doorway. 'It begins to close.'

I struggled to turn my head. The door began to fade.

'No! You can't . . . '

'Wake up.' Whispers. Louder. 'Richard.'

My feet swung toward the doorway but Dariq kept me pinned to the ground.

'Not for you,' he said. His eyes were yellow, each slashed with black.

'Wake up, Richard.'

My body shook. I had to get to the door.

'WAKE UP, RICHARD!' my flatmate Stacey screamed as she shook me.

I shot up off the bed, staggered around the room, arms flailing, and crashed into the door.

Stacey grabbed me again, still screaming, her eyes red, her face wet with tears. 'He's fucking dying!' She beat her fists on my chest. 'Fucking help me!'

At first I thought she meant Dariq, but I couldn't see him in my room. I was back, here in my room, my world, so he couldn't be there. My mind slowly came back to be my own.

'Calm down, Stacey,' I said taking hold of her arms. 'What's happened?' She pulled me down the hallway into Dave's room. He lay sprawled on the floor amongst his gear.

'Shit, shit, shit. Have you called an ambulance?'

'Of course I fucking haven't,' she cried. 'Do you think I'm fucking stupid? Do something, Richard.'

Stacey helped me drag Dave out onto the road where we left him, hoping someone would stop and phone the cops. That day I found out that Dave wasn't just a junkie, he was a dealer, too, and Stacey and her friends who worked the streets got their hits from him. Dave's habit probably saved my life—it definitely changed it. It was the day I left my first door open.

And the last time I ever heard from Monika.

❧

It took until the early hours of the morning before sleep finally overcame my fears, and I fell into a broken, haunted slumber, where things unbidden crept into my normal, everyday dreams. Things whose faces melted, and insidious whispering frayed the mind, where talons clawed faces, and shifting shapes fought for control. Creatures, like Dariq, who could maintain physical contact with the dream world, who could see others' doorways, and enter them. Curious creatures, hungry, envious.

❧

You can achieve many things when you are driven, focused, searching. I phoned Monika, I emailed, I wrote to her, I visited her house in dreams. I managed to contact the landlord and discovered that Monika was behind on her rent. The landlord discovered the apartment empty save for most of Monika's possessions. Dishes had grown mould and fused themselves with the dishwasher. Clothes sat damp and musty in the washing basket. No one had been there in weeks. I left the landlord my contact details in case Monika returned.

Reluctant travels took me back into the dream world, searching for Monika. I formed doors within doors, frantically jumping from place to place, hoping to find her. Many times I woke prematurely, soaked in sweat, still shaking from things I couldn't remember, leaving door after door open behind me. Monika had not been seen or heard from. Dariq was a subject of myth, everyone knew of him, but no one knew him and no one wanted to. Monika had described him as 'very old.' He wasn't; he was ancient. Dariq was one of the Dispossessed. A man who had been to heaven and hell, or at least somewhere not of this world. Two rumours abounded. The first was that on his return, he had found his body possessed by someone else. The second was that he had consumed his body in the real world. The result was the same; Dariq preyed upon those in the dream world, burning lives out as he lived in them, passing from one to another as he needed, doing as he pleased.

I discovered that there were many of these so-called Dispossessed, travelling the world of dreams, taking what they wanted, being who they wanted, experiencing the real world through the bodies of the unsuspecting and vulnerable. And finally one who could teach me what I needed crawled into my mind through one of the many doors I had left open. Zaehner.

❧

I visited Monika a month ago. The landlord notified me that she had been deported back to Romania, her home, after the Spanish authorities realised they didn't need to foot the bill. A dirty shell of a building housing empty husks that resembled people. A thick-set orderly, who spoke little English, escorted me to a room with large windows that several people sat staring out of. One of them was Monika. Her skin was pale and what was left of her hair was thin and greasy. Her face was pulled tight over her skull, any excess flesh burnt away.

I sat next to her holding her hand like we used to. I could barely feel the beat of her pulse in the small bundle of bones that built her wrist. Her eyes stared vacantly, nowhere outwards, and when I spoke she appeared not to hear me. Her eyes were empty; vacant, oily, black pools. Once they had been the green of the ocean in sunlight. Now they were like Dariq's. He had taken what he needed.

Across her cheeks, the blood vessels had burst into myriad tiny, red stars. The universe had made its mark on her. There was nothing here for me. Maybe she didn't want to return to her body, to this world. Maybe she couldn't. I hoped she had found what she was looking for. I made the deal shortly after.

Courage can be hard to find. I've used up my pills, my amphetamines, the speed. Zaehner is insistent now, demanding I relinquish. I can hear it inside my skull, every second of every day, excited, urgent, insane. It's managed to destroy the others that were competing for me.

Now. The time is now. You must sleep.

Its voice is clear now, thick and heavy with lust.

The pact has been made. You would not cheat me, would you?

I don't think I can. I'm not strong enough yet. But I will be. Zaehner has taught me much. I now have the ability to manipulate the matter that exists within the dream world. I can do what Dariq did, I can move objects, I can draw in the dirt, I can summon candles and demons and light. I can see others' doorways, and step through those left open.

I can cause pain. I can kill. I don't need my body to do this.

Zaehner told me of a room, a hallway, with a hundred doors. A hundred heaven and hells to choose from. One of these doors leads to Zaehner's world, its plane of existence. It tells me that this hallway is the starting point for those called the Dispossessed.

She will be there. You will find her. It must be now, Richard, I will wait no longer.

It claws at the back of my eyes, pulling me under.

Sleep.

I lie on my stomach on the mattress, exhaustion rolling over me. This is the last time I'll see this world with my eyes. The paint is yellow and peeling. Ants make their way across the wall from the ceiling duct to the window to the rubbish bin outside. From where I lie I can see blood seeping into the stained mattress. It trickles from my ear lobe where fishing wire has been freshly threaded. When Zaehner awakes in my body it will want to turn its head away from the wall. It will want to see my world. The last thing it will hear is the roar of the shotgun suspended above the bed as the fishing wire pulls the trigger. I hope it feels my body shredding.

This is not a suicide note. I'm going to close them all.

Sleep, Richard, sleep and dream.

YUM CHA

They say it comes in threes.

The first is my marriage—'You don't listen to me, you don't understand me, you don't love me'—and that's not true. I love my wife so bad I'd do anything for her. Maybe I don't understand her. I thought that would be the worst. It's not.

I've given up smoking. Haven't had one for six weeks and still counting. It's making me irritable and miserable to be around. I now have to pop a pill the size of a football with every meal; this one's supposed to be side-effect free. And I'm doing it for her!

The third is the worst; I thought I was going mad, but I'm not. I'm just hearing voices.

Mr Wong ushers me to a table in a tiny, crowded room hidden at the back of his restaurant.

Back again so soon? He leans forward and asks discreetly 'The same as Wednesday's, sir?'

'No. It must be a woman this time.'

'Certainly, sir.' Mr Wong bows as he accepts the money I slip him.

I ignore the gluttonous thoughts of the men and the hungry faces of the women around me as I wait for him to return. I place the pill carefully next to my cutlery and begin to read *Men Are From Mars, Women Are From Venus.* I'm here for different reasons. Men and women *are* different species, after all.

This all started when the stray cat that adopted our house alerted me to the voices about three weeks ago. The wife and I were retreating to another cold bed so I asked him if he wanted to join us. You know, stupid cat talk. He shot me a yellow-eyed glare and flicked his tail once.

Not fucking likely, pal. As soon as you leave I'm on the bench for those leftovers.

'What?' I stared at the cat and then at the bench scattered with Chinese takeaway and then back at the cat.

He just sat there, scowling and swishing his tail. I put the takeaway into the fridge.

You fucking bastard.

I heard the cat-flap bang shut before I reached the bedroom.

The following morning I heard voices from every cat in the neighbourhood. Not dogs, not birds, just cats. They didn't like me much and I didn't say anything about it to anyone. I put it down to stress; the strife with the wife and the nicotine withdrawal.

I spent most of that night shitting out the Vietnamese the wife brought home for tea. She was pissed off I'd kept her awake—'It's not the food, I ate the same as you'—and stormed off to work in the morning. I called in sick, got up late, had breakfast and went outside to throw out the leftovers.

The Doberman next door leapt up onto the fence, all slavering tongue and dripping froth.

You didn't eat that, did you?'

I locked the door and stayed inside. Over the next two days, I edged towards madness. I locked the cat-flap and shut the curtains. I could hear the cat outside, incessant, whining, angry.

Fucking let me in, ya cunt!

With things so strained at home, I decided to go visit the folks on the farm in Werribee. I could talk to Mum. I didn't think she'd understand, but I needed to tell someone I was losing it. As I drove down the driveway with the window down, soaking up that clean, country air, I passed the new yearling grazing in the paddock. It looked up at me with those brown, docile eyes as it chewed lazily on its cud.

I haven't seen you before.

It released a steaming stream of urine and wandered off to annoy a couple of sheep that had arrived to investigate proceedings. The scragglier of the two shook its head and spoke in a slow monotone.

Hey. Can you fix this?

A strand of barbed-wire had wound around its leg, cutting into the flesh.

Well, can you?

I turned slowly back to gaze out the windscreen as my car lurched onto the flowerbeds lining the driveway. Something fluttered in front of the car and I slammed on the brakes. Two chickens scarpered up and over the fence and off into the paddock.

The crazy bastard almost hit me! Who the hell does he think he is?

It's the son.

Oh.

They glared back accusingly and stormed off to the barn.

Mum's horse Casper wandered over to the fence to survey the damage.

'Hey Casper, do you know what is happening to me?'

Casper whinnied and turned away.

As I pulled up to the house I realised I hadn't heard Casper's thoughts. But the cow and the sheep and the chickens . . .

That night I drove home confident and calm. I would've picked the pattern sooner if I'd lived in the country. There were no bloody farmyard animals in the city. Thank God for dodgy Asian food.

❧

Mr Wong presents a steaming platter of pale meat on a bed of Asian greens accompanied with several dipping sauces.

'Enjoy, sir,' he says smiling. *May her herpes infect your tongue.*

'I think cooking her should've fixed that,' I reply, popping one of the anti-smoking pills from its foil.

'Of course.' Mr Wong nervously backs away. *I didn't say that aloud, did I?*

I swallow the pill with a forkful of the delicate flesh and shake my head. 'No, Mr Wong, you didn't.'

By tonight, I'll be able to understand my wife's thoughts perfectly. My marriage problems will be over.

APPENDIX 1: STORY NOTES

Jealousy

It's an *NFG* 69er. Hard to do. Fun to write. I've also adapted this into a five-minute play. Anyone want to do it?

The Last Days Of Kali Yuga

I witnessed *dukankali* in the foothills of the Kathmandu Valley—a very surreal moment in my life. I also unwittingly stood on the carved stone head of a Hindu god while watching the slaughter. I got shouted at a fair bit at this point. This merged with a story a friend of mine told me about a guy he shared a room with on his travels through Europe. This guy proceeded to creep my friend out with hints of what he enjoyed doing while travelling. This story won an Aurealis Award for Best Horror Short and a Ditmar for Best Novella.

The Feastive Season

A typical Christmas coming-of-age fable. No-one in Australia wanted to touch this due to the explicit nature of the story, which surprised me as I hadn't realised how conservative publishing was Down Under. I was even more surprised when it got sold in North America. Ain't that part of the world even more conservative? Not the good folks at *NFG*.

The Garden Of Jahal'Adin

Inspired by a visit to the Crac De Chevalier, a now-ruined castle in Syria. I took the historical events and inserted a corrupted Garden of Eden. And though we all love the Lionheart, he lost. Saladin was the man! Sarah Endacott took my writer's cherry—this was my first published story. I'd been writing for two years at this point.

The Punjab's Gift

Travelling in the Third World is mind-blowing, but you soon realise you're seen as money, as a mark, and that everyone has an ulterior motive for talking to you. After a while, you become very jaded and suspicious. And then someone opens your eyes again . . .

The Gift Of Hindsight

I didn't want the science aspect of time travel to get in the way, so rather than use science-fiction, I thought fantasy would be a better vehicle for what I was trying to say. I was gutted when Cat Sparks knocked this back from her second *Agog!* anthology; I thought it was a sure-fire winner. (Lesson 27: there is a *never* a sure-fire winner. *Ever*). *Aurealis* picked it up as their cover story and it was later nominated for Best Fantasy Short Story in Australia. In hindsight, it all worked out.

Shot In Loralai

My grandparents don't like what I write, and they especially dislike speculative fiction. As this story wasn't speculative and it had been nominated for The Pushcart Prize, I thought I'd try it on them. Grandad's response? 'It's too far fetched.' It's not though, it's all true. This was me trying to be a travel writer.

Hamlyn

Born from the SuperNova writing group discussions. Adam Browne was throwing around ideas about the Pied Piper myth and Brendan Duffy suggested that the Haines touch would be perfect for it. The editors of that issue of *ASIM* got a lot of flak for publishing that story, so a big thanks to Lyn Triffit and Lee Battersby for sticking to their guns.

They Say It's Other People

After reading Stephen King's excellent short 'That feeling, the one you can only say in French', I felt compelled to attempt something similar. Needless to say, my story bears no resemblance to the King's. Hell *is* other people.

Burning From The Inside

I spent a lot of time one summer working in Adelaide, knowing no one and with nothing to do. It gets hot in Adelaide. Real hot. And despite all the churches there, people just keep getting murdered, and murdered, and murdered. Apologies to Adelaidian Sean Williams who might want to do the same to me for writing this.

This Is The End, Harry, Goodnight!

When John Edwards appeared onscreen in Australia, *everyone* I knew was talking about it. It has to be, it's got to be, it must be REAL! Yeah, right. Harry Houdini, the world's greatest magician, was also the world's greatest spiritual debunker—something he didn't set out to do, he just wanted to contact his dead mother. The title comes from Houdini's wife, when she finally gave up trying to contact Harry after he died.

Slice Of Life

Me being nasty and lashing out at the world, while trying to express my love of cooking. I got too many American Psycho comparisons from my writer's group—though I haven't read the book or seen the movie, yet—which put me off trying to novelise this. James Cain from *Dark Animus* thought it had a great sense of humour. I hadn't realised that. Neither had Vogon.

The Skin Polis

A friend of mine, Duane, likes to study maps, and was fascinated with the shrinking water table in Australia over the last century. And we're still not doing enough about it—the Lucky Country indeed. The title comes from Iranian slang for the religious police, who are quite liberal with their batons when enforcing laws pertaining to showing too much skin in public.

Doof Doof Doof

One of my first well paid stories. I wrote it for my mate Giles who needed a 'myths' story for an elective paper he was doing at university. He got a B+. I got a slab of beer.

Mnemophonic

A piece about social control that Ben Payne accepted for *Potato Monkey*, but he got sidetracked on *ASIM*, and then *Aurealis*, so the issue it was supposed to be in never saw the light of day.

Slice Of Life II: Cooking For The Heart

Vogon told me to write this one too. He's also told me a whole lot more yet to see the page.

The Light In Autumn's Leaves

A ghost story where the dead are only dead within the confines of the house the elderly woman has trapped herself in. My grandmother, who is in her eighties, liked this one. She thought I got it right.

The Sky Is Turning Black

Nasty and paranoid. Comes from smoking too much pot late at night and sitting in the dark listening to other people talk.

Warchalking

Jack Dann, my Week 5 Clarion South tutor, suggested collaborating on stories to keep the spark going, and this hard-sf vision of hell from the mad mind of Claire McKenna resulted. Anything approaching soft and tender in this story was actually me (which surprised everyone workshopping this piece at Clarion South).

Doorways For The Dispossessed

While in Spain, I met a girl called Monica, who told me how she was practising a form of dream travelling she had been taught by a *sadhu* from India. Monica said it was very important that you close the doors before you wake up. When I questioned why, she didn't know. This is my why. As far as I know, the real Monica never had any success in forming a door.

Yum Cha

Three ideas rolling around in my head finally collided and exploded. This story burst forth fully formed despite my involvement. I wrote it as a puzzle for the reader to solve. This is an expanded, less cryptic version of the original five-hundred word story which really made the reader work.

PUBLICATION HISTORY

"Jealousy" (*NFG* 4, 2004)

"The Last Days of Kali Yuga" (*NFG* 4, 2004)

"The Feastive Season" (*NFG* 2, 2003)

"The Garden of Jahal'Adin" (*Orb* 2, 2001)

"The Punjab's Gift" (*StoryHouse*, 2004)

"The Gift of Hindsight" (*Aurealis* 32, 2004)

"Shot in Loralai" (*NFG* 1, 2003)

"Hamlyn" (*Andromeda Spaceways Inflight Magazine* 11, 2004)

"They Say It's Other People" (*Agog! Smashing Stories,* 2004)

"Burning from the Inside" (previously unpublished)

"This Is The End, Harry, Goodnight!" (*NFG* 5, 2004)

"Slice of Life" (*Dark Animus* 2, 2002)

"The Skin Polis" (*Fables & Reflections* 3, 2002)

"Doof Doof Doof" (*Dark Animus* 7, 2005)

"Mnemophonic" (previously unpublished)

"Cooking for the Heart" (*Lullaby Hearse* 4, 2003)

"The Light in Autumn's Leaves" (*Borderlands* 5, 2005)

"The Sky is Turning Black" (*Heist!,* 2002)

"Warchalking" (with Claire McKenna) (*Agog! Smashing Stories,* 2004)

"Doorways for the Dispossessed" (*Agog! Fantastic Fiction,* 2002)

"Yum Cha" (original version in *Antipodean* SF 48, 2002)

LaVergne, TN USA
28 January 2010
171421LV00004B/10/A